THE
COMPANY'S MAN

THE
COMPANY'S MAN

THOMAS M. BATTISTA

MILL CITY PRESS | MINNEAPOLIS

Mill City Press, Inc.
212 3rd Avenue North, Suite 290
Minneapolis, MN 55401
612.455.2294
www.millcitypublishing.com

ISBN-13: 978-1-936400-86-7
LCCN: 2010941049

Cover designed by David Scheuber
Typeset by Kristeen Wegner

Printed in the United States of America

I dedicate this book to:

My wife, Elaine, who has stuck by me through the most difficult
of times, even as I whined and whittled away on this tome.

My children: son Jamie, daughters Lisa, Dana, and Gina,
who have, through a family crisis, continued to show their
love and loyalty to us both.

My sister, Janice, who taught me how to dress, dance
and be the best baby brother I could be.

My agent, Emma Penick, who read the book, believed in it,
encouraged and guided me, and placed it.

Gerry Abrams, who said after we turned down a TV network
offer, "Write a book and they'll kiss your ass
on the corner of Hollywood & Vine!"

Maureen Lasher, who said after the first sixty-five pages,
"You're not writing about what you know. Write what you
know." So I threw out the old and started anew.

1

I WAS NEARLY TWENTY and 4F. Like so many before me, I fell in love with and married my high school sweetheart, Connie Mero. Little did either of us know that the groom standing beside her in St. Rocco's Church would ultimately serve two masters: good and evil. But I'm getting ahead of myself.

It was 1945; World War II was over. The mix of elation and confusion permeated America, including my home town of Providence, Rhode Island. No sooner was victory announced than the wealth harvested from woven woolen blankets and cotton underwear that supported the war effort was gone. An eerie silence fell over Providence. The continuous three-shift day ceased. The weaving mills stopped whirring. Finally, the chimneys coughed up their last gasp of smoke. There was a relentless turnover of people returning from battlefields to jobs, employed to unemployed.

We were first-generation Italians. Not being satisfied with the status quo of graduating high school and getting a job, I wanted and expected more of myself. My family wasn't supportive, financially or emotionally, of my notions on attending college. They were from the old country and only knew of hard work, take-home pay, Church on Sundays, and family. "Tony," my father would preach, "college is only for doctas 'n lawyas 'n dose rich kids who got nuttin' to do for four or five years. Ya gotta go out 'n get a job so you kin live 'n take care of Connie and ya family." My mother would grab me by the shoulders and literally place me in front of a mirror and boast, "Look Anthony you can get a job anywhere. You a tall, dark and handsome, like a Tyrone Powers."

Not taking their advice, I attended Providence College. It was very exciting, fulfilling...at first. Night school five times a week, two part-time jobs to support my wife and myself, but it was all about to change.

It got tougher. At practically the same time, my wife informed me she was pregnant, and I informed her how I proudly lost one of my jobs to a returning vet.

We were thrilled with the pregnancy and petrified over the loss of the job. I was outwardly optimistic but internally a wreck. My instinct clicked in. Who knows where it comes from but thankfully it comes. I reached out for the one person I loved and trusted.

2

MY FATHER'S OLDEST BROTHER, Uncle Joe.
As the elder of the Manfredi clan, he has this wisdom, this ability
to listen, and a natural, street sense of humor. He never let me
down. Because of his disposition, and because he was the best
Italian pastry baker in the neighborhood, he was nicknamed Joe
"Dolce"--Sweets.

I phoned him and asked if I could come over to visit.
"Tony, come ova wheneva ya want, I ain't goin' no place." Like
so many of my friends and family, Uncle Joe had many letters
missing from his vocal alphabet. The er's became long a's. Like remember became "remembah." The g, of ing was lost forever. And
forget about the th's. They became d's. He was indeed a "dees,
dems, and dose" kind of guy.

I went over to his bakery that very day and told him of
my dilemma and my dreams. As we sat in the back of the shop, I
couldn't help notice how particularly blue his eyes were that day.
Maybe it was because we were in a room painted antiseptic white,
or maybe it was because his spotless, starched apron was reflect-
ing the light a certain way, but they were blue, bright blue, bluer

than ever before. I would never forget them.

We enjoyed some "coffee an'." It was a neighborhood expression. "Do you want some coffee, and would you like some pastry to go with it?" After pouring my heart and guts out, his wiry, five-foot-six frame rose off the chair. Simultaneously, he reached into his pant pocket, retrieved a twenty-dollar bill and placed it in my hand. He stroked my black hair. "Tony, I used to have hair like yours. Now look. I'm the gray ghost." I faked a smile. He continued, "Let's see what we k'n do."

***

That was Thursday. Friday, Uncle Joe phoned.
"Tony, why don't you 'n Connie come over for dinner on Sunday. We eat 'round tree o'clock, and don't take nothin' we got everythin'."

As soon as I thanked him he hung up. Jesus he knows I'm hanging by my fingernails. Why didn't he say something about a job?

The dinner was great. My mother, father and sister Janice were there. My Aunt Ella, Uncle Joe's wife, and their four children, all older than me, and all still living at home, joined us. Connie melded into my family with ease.

She would catch me eyeing her hour glass figure as she glided from table to kitchen and back. She knew what I was thinking and responded with flashing dark eyes as she entered, then tossing her long black hair back she would spin and exit knowing full well she was teasing me. She could have been cloned directly from Ava Gardner.

With that many people we ate in the "front room". I was

always amazed how my Aunt Ella was able to serve up such large meals out of a small Pullman pantry. I loved all that family stuff, but I was not there for that. I needed some help and no one in that parlor could help me except my Uncle Joe and I wasn't too sure about that.

He hadn't called me aside. He hadn't given me some kind of sign. Nothing! Here we were saying our good-byes and nothing!

As we walked toward the door I made a point of being the last to leave so my uncle would have every opportunity to say something. I started down the stairs and just as I stepped on the second stair he put his arm around my neck and pulled the side of my face close to him, so his mouth lined up with my ear. He whispered. "Tony, give this guy a call." He stuck a small piece of paper in front of my face. On it was scribbled: DOM TRIANO— M.R.TEDES COMPANY ST 4-3703.

I should have known Uncle Joe would come through. "Uncle, is this the same Dom Triano from the neighborhood?" Uncle Joe nodded and kissed the top of my head insisting I let him know the result. "And, Tony, don't you 'n your wife be strangers. Come by tomorrow for leftovas."

I leaped down the tenement stairs singing one of my uncle's favorite songs, "I'll be down to get you in a taxi honey; ya better be ready by half past eight . . ."

3

I CALLED DOM, Monday morning, met with him Monday afternoon. It's amazing how you can live in a city all your life, ride buses, walk or drive by buildings that you know you've seen, but somehow, they never register. I must have passed these warehouses thousands of times. Unlike the dead weaving mills these were very much alive. Trucks, trailers, forklifts, conveyer belts: everything moving at once.

Dom spoke the language of the neighborhood. The same letters were missing from his vocal alphabet. There is this indescribable connection with childhood friends. We were the same age. Dom was chubby as a kid and over weight as an adult. Since then I put on a few pounds, but it went unnoticed in my six-two frame. His hair was thinning but his round face and smiling eyes still had that mischievous look. We reminisced about our growing up together from grammar school through high school. How our paths took different directions. But here we were, strangely, honestly reconnected.

"So, Tony, ya start next Monday night as a loader. Welcome to the M. R. Tedes Company."

While eating his meatball sandwich Dom told me how things had slowed down since the end of the war.

"So, Dom, how come I get to work if things are so slow?"

Without missing a beat, Dom stopped chewing and slid, what remained of the meatball, to the side of his mouth, puffing out his left cheek. "Tony, it's simple. I owed your uncle a favor. One good turn deserves another."

***

Connie and I had our first child, a daughter. We named her Anne after Connie's mother. My job was surprisingly flexible so I was able to continue my education.

While on the night shift, I went to classes during the day. When I was promoted from night loader to day-foreman, I switched to night classes. I worked hard at both and did very well. Dom and I were now foremen together and we often talked about where we were going with the company.

"Oh Tony, I'm happy doin' this stuff. I come in, do my shift, get paid, get vacation, get some benefits, den I'll retire."

Sounds of my father I thought. That is not what I want. Or expect. I told him how I read the annual report and concluded that the company was involved in all kinds of businesses.

Dom looked at me somewhat puzzled. "What annual report? I didn't get anything in my box."

I smiled, "I went to the personnel office and asked to know more about the company and I picked up these brochures."

"Tony, I've seen those things before. The sales guys carry them around. Now there's a bunch! Those sales guys are really something. They eat, drink, sell 'n make dough."

Dom unknowingly did me a good turn. I went back to the personnel office and this time it was to inquire about the sales department.

"Very unusual that someone from the loading docks gets a sales job. Brawn and brains you know what I mean." I should have expected that kind of response from a do-it-by-the-book personnel director. I was charming but tenacious.

Finally, after several visits, and a cursory sales manager's interview, I was given a chance to leave the docks for a trainee position as a production coordinator. From that low level job my career path was like the LeMans auto race. Very fast and lots of curves. From the starting flag to the checkered flag, four and a half years had flown by.

Dom was right. When I was promoted into sales I "made a lot of dough". I'd meet with Dom at least once a week to share a meatball or eggplant parmesan sandwich. He was delighted when I told him of my latest promotion. Dom "I just got the Director of Strategic Planning job". He smiled and said "Great Tony great! But what the fuck is it? I hope your take home is better!"

But as it came in, so it went out. We were on our way to another child. I was secretly hoping number two would be a son, but when Roberta came into the world that August 18, 1949, she stole my heart away. Although my schedule was already full, I managed to attend more night classes, striving for a college degree, with a secret goal of becoming a lawyer.

While in that position for only a few months, and traveling all over the eastern seaboard, I received a call from my Uncle Joe.

"Hey, Tony, I never get to see ya now that you're a big deal over there."

Feeling the old, Italian family guilt I mumbled, "Uncle, I know, but it's been nuts. With the kids, the job, night school, the traveling, it seems like I'm never around anymore."

I could always count on my uncle to understand. He never stood on ceremony. He immediately responded with "Hey, Tony, ya got a big job 'n ya got to do what ya got to do. You travel a lot, right?"

"Yeah, Uncle, a lot."

"Hey, Tony, where ya travelin' next? I mean not to Califoonya, but like 'round us."

His suggestion struck me as curious. Treating him like just another business associate on the phone, I reached for my calendar and with a tight ass corporate tone I responded, "Let me check my itinerary. I'm going to New Haven Connecticut, on Tuesday. I have to check out a costume jewelry factory the company owns there."

"Jesus, Tony, that's great! I haven't been there in years. When will ya be free? Can we get a bite to eat?"

My corporate mannerisms were dismantled by the surprise of his inviting himself. "Uncle, what about an early dinner, say around five?"

"Perfect! There's this terrific Italian joint on Worcester Street called the Snow White Cafe. I use to go there durin' the war. They serve homemade pasta that's almost as good as your aunt's. Don't ever tell her I said that."

As always his telephone conversation ended abruptly with "It's a date, Tuesday, five o'clock, Snow White Cafe."

***

The Snow White Cafe was not exactly out of the Walt Disney Studios. It was tucked away on a side street, but you couldn't miss it, because the neon sign was the worst reproduction of Snow White known to man. As soon as you turned the corner the blinking caught your eye. It was supposed to animate her in such a way that her arm waved you in, while her gown flowed in the breeze. However some of the neon tubes were missing or burned out. So her arm jumped from the lower position to the two top positions. I thought, if she could cross that jester with her other arm it would be the Italian sign language for "Up yours!" Her gown jumped from the back position all the way to the front one, so it looked like sweet Snow White was giving us her best bump and grind. Covered in dirt and pigeon shit, bumping and grinding, she looked anything but pure. Inside, if there was dirt and pigeon shit, you might never see it. The one dining room was a dingy beige. There were dark wooden booths perpendicular to the walls. About three or four feet from the back wall was a gigantic bar, flanked by spotless chrome National Cash registers.

I guess the key to the joint was the food; but for me, it was the artwork that covered the two side walls. As bad as the neon Snow White was on the outside, that's how detailed and colorful the Snow White and the Seven Dwarfs' scenes were on the inside. Snow White seemed to float through layers of cigarette smoke, while the brilliant colored Dwarfs glowed in the dinginess. At this early hour the place was practically full. I spotted Uncle Joe sitting in the last booth. He saw me and with both arms waved for me to come over.

During dinner Uncle Joe began telling me of an unusual situation in Pittsburgh. He'd overheard a conversation that connected a union rumbling with my Company. There seemed to be some discontent with the local teamsters, and if it got out of control, it could directly affect the Company.

"I immediately thought of you, Tony, 'n how maybe this information would be helpful to ya."

"Uncle, but why this mysterious meeting? Why in New Haven at a little neighborhood restaurant?"

"'Cause I was with some union guys, 'n it would be uncomfortable for me to talk about this inside info 'round our neighborhood. I only wanna help."

Uncle Joe proceeded to tell me how this Pittsburgh sheet metal mill was about to be hit with a wildcat strike.

"I remembered a few Sunday's ago when we was havin' dinner at your house, ya told me you was worried about this Pittsburgh mill, which was losin' money that was, I think you said . . . ," he paused, straightened up and continued, mimicking my company jargon, "being properly positioned for sale."

I was offended by his impression of me. I could feel myself stiffen, and right in front of Snow White I turned into a snotty, Waspy corpie.

"Well, Uncle, I am sure such a strike situation would raise havoc with the liquidation process."

Why was I being such a prick to this kind man? He's the only real father figure I could relate to.

He looked at me across the table and stuck a piece of veal in his mouth.

"Havoc!"

He chewed rapidly, and then blowing short bursts of air through his nostrils, he put another piece of veal in his mouth and chewed that one even faster. More nostril bursts. "Liquidation process! Tony, dey'll blow that fuckin' joint right off da map!"

I had heard uncle swear in Italian, and use minor English curse words and it seemed very natural, but I never heard him say the F word. He was pissed off at me, and he had every right to be. I came down from my high horse real fast.

"Sorry Uncle, I had a couple assholes to deal with today and I'm a little touchy."

Using the word asshole made me feel better. One for one. My "asshole," to his "fuck." Equals . . . well almost.

"Tony, the world's full of em."

We both continued to silently eat. My mind wandered and I began doing some quick analysis . . . If I could avoid a strike, sell the mill, we could incorporate language in the sale agreement wherein the unions and the new owners could sit down and work things out. Perhaps the union had heard of our plans to unload the mill, and a strike would stall, if not kill the sale. Then they would have some leverage to discuss all the company's past broken promises.

As Director of Strategic Planning, I was equal in rank to the director of Labor Relations, who had caused some of the union discontent. Knowing my boss, the Group VP, if I went to him with the news, I could hear him say, "This should be properly assigned to the responsible department head and . . ."

"So, Tony, what do ya think?"

I snapped out of my deep thoughts and explained the internal politics to Uncle. I indicated it was valuable inside information and I was going to take the chance and solve the problem on my own, be a hero, hope for a promotion.

"But, Uncle, if it doesn't work out, I'll be asking you for a job at the bakery!"

Uncle Joe encouraged me to "give it a shot," while warning me that union officials, although businesslike, were "tough cookies."

Uncle began to philosophize on how he believed all the unions throughout the country and maybe the world were somehow tied together. He told me of a situation in Providence, many years ago, where some teamsters were trying to break away from the national, and didn't care about the other support unions.

I always loved the old stories, so I encouraged him to go on.

"It was a mess. Picket lines, management against union, teamster against teamster, teamster against longshoremen, against steel handlers, a mess! It was like a plague spreading up and down the east coast. Finally, an all-union leader meetin' was held. I was there 'cause of my affiliation." The last part of the sentence was almost lost in his coffee slurping. "It was all settled in five minutes with two words . . . Mister Ted."

What?

"Mister Ted?" I laughed.

"Yeah," Uncle laughed back, "no one knows who he is. Even if there is a Mr. Ted, he was supposed to be this guy back then runnin' all the unions everywhere." Uncle Joe leaned over the table and in a softer voice continued, "And when the union leaders were told Mr. Ted wants it to end..." Uncle slammed his hand on the table and yelled "boom!--(startling us both) it ended."

He was outwardly pleased with his storytelling.

"Hey, Tony, that was a long time ago." His manner changed to one of longing as he returned to the present. He balled up his red napkin and lightly tossed it on the table, "Some people say Mr. Ted's still 'round, but no one knows for sure."

***

The following morning, from the time I lifted my head off my pillow, until I got my hands on the mills documents at the office, my mind darted from possibility to possibility. It was such a financial drain, the company was right in wanting to sell off the Pittsburgh mill. Someone in the company must have tipped off someone in the union that we were desperate to get rid of this loser. I guess the union felt they have nothing to lose. They could hold up the sale with the strike, then sit down and negotiate. Uncle Joe's encouraging words "give it a shot" kept ringing in my ears. I finished my cup of coffee and walked into the Senior VP's office and asked him if I could go to Pittsburgh to check out a few unresolved issues. He knew I was good, and didn't even ask what the issues were. He agreed I should go, but warned me not to make any unnecessary waves.

***

On the train to Pittsburgh I again reviewed all the paperwork. I concluded I had to meet with the union leaders and convince them somehow not to strike.

There was a ten-minute stop in Philly. A herd of people rushed into the car. A woman in her mid-twenties took the last seat. Her tall, lean body seemed to flow into a sitting position opposite me. She was blonde. Not floozy blond, but with a perfect blunt haircut a few inches above her shoulder. Blue eyes. Perfect white teeth. So different looking from all the Italian women in my life. Grandmothers, mother, aunts, cousins, my wife.

During the ride, I struck up a conversation with her.

More like a Q & A. I was interested enough to ask. She was very willing to share. She was in Philly visiting her mainline family, but lived in Pittsburgh. Her husband is a successful doctor. Both of them went to the best of schools. They met at the University of Pennsylvania. She was a student. He taught biology and did research. Though ten years her senior, she married him. They have two children, a dog, and summer at the Jersey Shore. We were both surprised to find how close our birthdays were. Hers on the eighteenth of December and mine on the seventeenth. She travels to Philly often to see her parents. Mostly her father, who isn't well. She seldom goes to New York City.

"Why?" I asked, slowing down the staccato repartee, "I think it's the most exciting city in the world!"

Her response was so animated. "The last time I was there it was with a group of friends. We went just before Christmas to do some shopping and to Radio City Music Hall" although she was seated she struck a comical ballet pose, "For The Nutcracker Suite."

With her open palms facing me, she began rapidly crossing both hands in front of her face, fanning the air. She whispered, "Too many people." Then wrapping both of her arms around her waist, in fake anger, she whispered louder, "Too crowded!" This last gesture tightened her pullover sweater around her upper body revealing her beautifully shaped breasts. Slightly bent over, she again whispered. "Too expensive."

Her eyes caught me stealing a glance at her bosom. She calmly straightened up, trying to nonchalantly reposition her sweater, but not before her two nipples nearly pierced the soft angora. In an attempt to compose herself she dead-panned, "And the weather's lousy."

Just then the train jerked just enough to help me gather my own composure. I looked out the window and we were pulling into the station. There was a moment, a presence, that I didn't want to lose.

"I know your first name is Chris. What is your last name?" She extended her hand. "McKay. Chris McKay." Our handshake was gentle. "And yours, Tony?"

I reached for my wallet. "Manfredi. Here's my card. I'm in New York City quite often, though the way you feel about it, I doubt we'll ever see each other there. But, just in case!"

She took my card and placed it in her handbag. We smiled and silently said our good-byes. We left the train for our separate Pittsburgh destinations, but somehow I felt we would be together again.

4

AS THE TAXI DROVE through the chain-link gates, there was a strange quiet for an operational plant. When I asked the driver to wait, he agreed, but only if he could leave to gas up and get a cup of coffee.

Life's full of negotiations! I agreed.

No sooner than I stepped out of the cab, the plant manager yelled some kind of greeting through an opened door. In his office, I listened to his quick, boring update, and then we began to discuss the sale. He brought out files, reports, accounting books, all the ammunition he needed to handle the barrage of questions from a headquarters ball breaker.

I fingered and toyed with a few items, made some unimportant notes on them and eased into the subject of the union commitments. The plant manager assured me everything was under control. I asked if I could meet the local union leader, and before I could finish the question, the plant manager in a half angry, half panicky tone said, "Nobody meets with the leaders during non-negotiating periods. That's once every three years."

"Well who do you talk to," I snapped.

He answered, "The shop steward!"

"Get him!" I snapped again.

The plant manager, clearly disturbed, reached for the phone, dialed and with a phony smile on his face, talked into the mouthpiece.

"How's it going Hank? Did your wife have the baby yet? Great! Look Hank, can you come up to the office, there's a guy from Headquarters who wants to meet you. What?" He looked at me while he listened. "No, not labor relations, he's in Planning." Starring at me he continued, "Okay, I'll tell him."

The plant manager's phony smile disappeared as soon as he hung up the receiver. Emotionlessly he told me that if I wanted a meeting, I should have called for an appointment. After delivering that message, a real smile crossed his face. I reached for the phone, and dialed 603; the plant manager was stunned that I knew the extension. It was easy. I watched him dial!

"Hank, this is Tony Manfredi. I have no appointment, but you and I had better meet now or I go over your head, and arrange to have your ass fired!"

The wait for him to arrive was longer than the meeting. He entered wearing his Ides of March black-and-red-checkered shirt with matching hat. No salutations. No handshakes. I told him I wanted to meet the union leader today. I had some important information for him.

Obviously annoyed, he made a phone call. The meeting was set. Nine p.m. in Hank's office. Room 603, directly across the alley. I sarcastically thanked him for his cooperation and left.

My taxi was waiting for me. Filled up, and the driver was kind enough to bring an extra cup of coffee for me. Too bad it was black! I asked him if he wanted to make another round-trip around nine. He was off duty, but it was his cab so why not. I returned to the hotel, ordered some food, threw the black coffee in the toilet and called Connie. Waiting for the nine o'clock meeting seemed like an eternity. Eternity? The meeting itself was almost eternity for me.

When I walked into Hank's office, I told myself to be calm but strong. As soon as I saw the three of them standing there in that nicotine-colored light, I became nervous and weak. The ceiling light, held by one yellow and black twisted strand of electrical wire, started to sway side to side from the breeze created by my opening the door. This eerie movement threw a dull spotlight on each character.

Hank, thinner than I remembered him from this afternoon, was standing straight ahead next to a metal filing cabinet. He was smiling. Diagonally across the small room, and leaning against the wall, was a dark-faced man, all dressed in black.

The spotlight swung, revealing a maroon mole on his left cheek. I thought, Great! That mole is the size of a nickel, and he's the size of a bison.

Straight ahead, but sitting in the chair next to the desk with his back to me was, I guessed, the union leader. He looked smallish from the back. As I entered he waved me in without turning around and gestured for me to sit behind the desk. I did. There was a long pause. I looked at his shadowy face. It was thin, and in need of a shave. He wheezed and spoke softly, "We always deal over the desk." He pointed to me, "Management behind"--pointing to himself--"me Dominic Gemma and the union on the side." It was the second iciest statement that would come from Dominic that night.

I started reaching into my briefcase for folders that I

knew were meaningless, but I needed time to get control of the situation and myself. While I was in the middle of nonsensical greetings and company positions, Dominic interrupted and asked, "Why the meetin'?"

"Well, Mr. Gemma, I'm here representing the company, and it has been brought to our attention that the local is planning a wildcat strike."

"What's it to ya?" replied Gemma.

Nervously I continued, "As you may know, Mr. Gemma, we are in the process of selling the plant, and a wildcat strike would slow down, if not nullify the sale. That, Mr. Gemma, would make our lives more difficult, and, Mr. Gemma . . ."

Before I could complete my next sentence Mr. Gemma reached over the desk and grabbed my wrist.

"Listen Mister Company Man, Mr. Gemma's life will go on, yours is in serious question. Your company screwed us around and around. We know how important the sale of this turd plant is to you, and we're gonna fuck it up and then maybe we'll talk about tryin' to even the score."

His grip was cold and strong. I didn't try to pull away, I was trying not to be scared, but I was. I wanted to remain cool and calm, and in that manner I responded with, "That's foolish."

Before the ish sound left my lips, Gemma was on his feet, the huge hulk moved across the office as if he were in a strobe light. His forearm, which was the size of a normal man's thigh, wrapped around my throat. Bent over me, I could smell the mixture of cigars and garlic on his breath, laced with armpit body odor.

I couldn't move. Now I was really scared! A quick tingle ran through my groin. It was the same tingle that occurred when, as a little boy, I was about to be punched out by the neighborhood bully. I flashed back on those days and remembered my anger after those confrontations. "I should have punched him in the gut, kicked him in the balls, I should have told him . . ." That little recall helped me to muster up enough anger, to cut through my fear, and enabled me to rasp out a company position void of punctuation.

"No wonder everyone's unhappy if this is the way you negotiate I will report this to the authorities and through proper channels do everything in my power to get to your superiors and have you thrown out of the union."

Gemma inhaled with a wheeze. As if echoing my unpunctuated sentence he exhaled, "Listen, Mister Company Man, I had you checked out and you're nothin', so no one's gonna miss a nothin', and because you know somethin' about the strike, somethin' has to be done."

Inhale. Wheeze. Exhale.

"So Mister Company Man, the somethin that's gonna be done, is to get rid of the nothin', and that's you." That was singularly the iciest statement Dominic made that night.

The wheeze continued. "I don't know how you got the inside info on the strike, but it's too bad you got that news. That's bad news." He glanced over to the shop steward, who moved in.

Hank reached across the desk and dragged a batch of papers, all sizes, and all colors, toward him. They were skewered together by a long spindle. The steward making a V for victory sign with his fingers slowly placed the V, palm down, under the papers and began to lift them.

With little effort, they were individually, and in bunches released from the spindle. As the last receipt fell free, the V slowly folded joining the other fingers in a claw-like grip over the ornate green base. The nickel-plated spindle stood tall, flashing in the swaying light. He lifted it and moved it toward my head, then over to the side just out of my vision. Trying to find the spindle, realizing it was now his weapon, my eyeball sockets nearly cracked as my eyes darted from side to side. Where would he do it? In my back, my neck, or will he arch his hand over my head and go directly into my heart. And then I knew for sure. My eye-darting stopped. They locked, staring straight ahead. I felt the end of the spindle scratch my earlobe. I jerked my head away. Hank snickered as he lightly tickled the cartilage. My God, he's going to punch that thing into my ear. I could feel the point entering my outer ear.

As his snickering and my fearful, loud breathing intertwined, I gasped for what I knew would be my last words. "Mr. Ted is not going to like this."

Followed by a mishmash of room noises, there was silence. Is this how death is? I had read where people leave their bodies, and before they go wherever they go, they can look back and review the scene as if frozen in time. But I wasn't moving anywhere and I didn't feel anything. Is death that painless? Even if you've been stabbed in the ear!

Suddenly Gemma's bony face appeared in front of me, blocking out the rest of the room. His eyes stared into mine and then he looked upward. The bison eased his grip and Gemma spoke, "Mister Company Man, what did you say?"

My God, it worked! I'm not dead. I'm alive. Mr. Ted worked!

I repeated my last gasp slower and calmer. "Mr. Ted is not going to like this."

"Tell me about it, Mister Company Man," Gemma demanded. "By who?"

I didn't think it would be possible for Gemma to get his face closer to mine, but he did. In controlled anger he repeated, "By who?"

"None of your business."

I couldn't believe that was my answer.

"All you should know is one of Mr. Ted's couriers told me to come down here and convince you guys that he doesn't want this strike to happen."

"Why?"

"I wasn't told, so if it's none of my business, it's surely none of yours."

Gemma backed away and ordered, "Choo-Choo, let him go. Hank can you believe this?" Gemma questioned. "First, it's all this company bullshit and now it's none of my business."

Finally, I found out who the Bison was . . . Choo-Choo. Fits . . . He's nearly the size of a boxcar!

I took advantage of the pause and embellished my lie. "Listen Gemma, maybe I'm over stepping my bounds here, but reading between the lines, Mr. Ted wants no strikes on the East Coast because it might affect the entire flow."

He countered, "What flow?"

I answered back, "Trucks, ships, cargo planes. Mr. Ted is going into a new business. Drugs."

"What drugs!" Gemma angrily exclaimed as he brought each of his hands closer to my face with all the fingertips on each hand touching one another and shaking them wildly. "What drugs!"

"Dope Mr. Gemma, dope. Some of it will stay, some of it

will move on. Mr. Ted doesn't want the flow to stop. One wildcat strike in Pittsburgh could give some other unions ideas. Normally, there would be no problem, but not for the next six weeks."

Jesus, I couldn't believe how well that went down. Thank God I read Confidential magazine.

In unison, they all kind of gave me an affirmative grunt.

Finally with more air in my lungs, and a normal heartbeat I stood up and said coldly, "No strike!"

They nodded. I won. What a feeling of excitement! These three thugs, me about to die and they bought the Mr. Ted bullshit. I loved it. Never have I been that close to the edge. I loved it so much I wanted the game to continue. Totally victorious I asked, "Where can a guy get a good dish of pasta?"

"Are you shittin' me," answered Gemma. "My joint and it's on me!"

All through dinner Gemma kept pumping me about Mr. Ted. I stayed with my fib taking care not to slip up. Gemma told me of some "businesses" he was in with Mr. Ted's blessing. "Gemma," I asked not wanting my edge to dull out, "if you're in business with Mr. Ted then you must know who he is." He stopped slurping his soup and looked me in the eye and said coldly, "I only got his blessing, that's it. Nobody I know knows who he is. Like you I'm just a workin' stiff." Gemma felt like we were from the same bolt of cloth. With a half smile I thought, If Gemma only knew!

5

WHEN I CAME TO WORK the next day, I was still high from my Pittsburgh experience. The offices looked different. I had never really noticed the rows of desks, rows of florescent lights and those rows of ten by ten cubicles, laughingly called offices.

"Tony," a faceless voice belonging to my boss beckoned from the largest office. I had already passed its open door, but I quickly backed up a few steps to greet him with my best company "Good morning."

He rose up his mug of coffee as if to toast me and asked, "So how was the Pittsburgh mill?"

My first inclination was to blurt everything out, but instead I said simply, "Everything seems to be in order."

Toasting me a second time and with a dirty old man's laugh said, "Okay enough to sell that turkey!" He put his coffee mug down and continued, "Tony, I still don't know why you went down there." By now I was amazed that here, my big deal boss, didn't even have a notion that they were about to lose the sale because of the unions, or, maybe, because of the way the company screwed around the unions.

"Well I just wanted to recheck the square footage of usable factory space." "Square footage," where did that come from?

This time there was no toast, just a puzzled stare and a distant, "Fine."

I knew instantly there would be no way I could take advantage of the save, and it was company business as usual. As I walked into my cubical my Pittsburgh high turned into a Providence low.

***

The entire day was a bust. I couldn't wait to get home and tell Connie. I knew she would be interested and besides I had to tell someone or I'd explode.

Six thirty on the dot, supper was on the table, and as always I started to review my day. For the first time I realized how boring my daily reports were, and how patient, understanding, and loving Connie was to listen to them. She would absorb what I was saying and at the right time asked questions. She deserved a medal. One for every tedious daily report. Little Anne spilled some milk all over the table and I blew.

"Shit!" I yelled with a mouth half full of food. "Every Goddamn night the same crap."

Connie sprung back in her chair. She was stunned. I had never blown my stack that way before. Little Anne jumped at my outburst. Her eyes opened wide, her chin began to quiver, and fighting back the tears she let go with a little girl's hurtful wail. The remainder of her food poured out of her open mouth, dribbled down her chin, onto her Howdy Doody bib, and settled in her lap. Connie quickly reached for Anne and, while looking at me, calmly called my name. "Tony." Then softer, "Tony, honey, what's the matter?"

As only Connie could, in a few seconds she was making everything all right. She was cleaning Anne's face with one hand while holding my forearm, calming me with the other.

Now in control of myself I said to Connie, "Honey I'm sorry, but something happened yesterday that I can't forget." Squeezing my forearm she asked, "What happened? You didn't say anything at breakfast or when you called me today. What happened? Was it that Pittsburgh trip?"

I reached over and patted her hand just as she was about to release me. "I'll tell you after supper."

***

Connie was the silent strength of the family. She had the gift of wisdom, an awareness that did not match her age. Eighteen months younger than me, we were married on her seventeenth birthday. June 16, 1944. For seventeen years she was taught to believe a woman should get married, be obedient to her husband, and although the sex act wasn't that great, it was what you did to have children. Be available for it, grin and bear it, get through it.

Funny how certain seemingly unimportant things stand out. During our dating and to this day I never remembered her having the slightest blemish on her skin. Even during that time of the month her skin remained pure. I kidded her about why her skin is so beautiful. You have that extra-pure virgin Italian olive oil running through your veins. Now, after having two children, her self-determination returned her well-proportioned hourglass figure to her. To us. She was the calm before, during, and after the storm.

The few hours that followed supper always seemed like the best part of the day. The kids were off to bed, the dishes were done, and Connie and I could relax. Sitting in our parlor we would talk, read, listen to the radio. Occasionally I would do some work, but I tried to keep this part of the day ours. Her, on the sofa, and me, in my comfortable armchair. My feet, resting on an old leather hassock taken from my parents' house. Even after years of use, it was still in great shape. Looking like a drum, its sides still firm, but its top nice and soft, cushioning my heels. I remember as a kid, not resting my feet on it, but turning it on its side, doing belly rolls all over my parent's parlor. It survived and I had already taught Anne the art of hassock riding.

***

"Tony, so what got you so upset at the supper table?"

I put down the newspaper and began to tell the story. From Uncle Joe's meeting in New Haven, to reviewing the situation at the office, to going to Pittsburgh, to almost getting killed, to no company recognition for it all. I told the entire tale looking down and gesturing to the floor. When I finished, I raised my eyes to Connie, who was frozen in her chair. One of her hands was locked on the front of her throat, while the other clutched her dress at her bosom. Her shoulders caved in around her. My story had frightened her very being. The first time telling the story out loud re-ignited my Pittsburgh excitement.

"Can you believe that Connie, I nearly get killed for the friggin' company and nothing, nothing happens."

She managed to speak. "My God, Tony." She swallowed a sob. "You did a good deed for the company. What you did was good. That's why you're where you are." She let go of her dress in attempted composure. "I know it must be maddening not to be able to tell them what happened. They probably wouldn't believe you anyway, and that could be a black mark against you. Tony, it's hard for me to believe it, and I love and trust you with all my heart. Tony, you always say how things work out for the best. It did, you're alive."

I fell to my knees and buried my head in her lap. She gently stroked my hair, and whispered, "The company knows how good you are and it'll take care of you. Of us."

As we walked toward our bedroom she was still trembling.

Why didn't I tell her everything? Why didn't I tell her about my high, my excitement of being on the edge, and my longing to be there again? Why didn't I tell her about Chris? What was there to tell? That I was smitten by her? Smitten is safe, acting on it is dangerous. Shit—there is that edge again. From our parlor to our bedroom, those few steps, those few thoughts excited me so when the door closed behind us, our mixed emotions collided into passionate sex.

We were not adventurous lovers, but caring sex partners. Like Connie, I had my own premarital brainwashing. I was led to believe that wives cooked, cleaned the house, had kids, and I shouldn't expect "a great piece of ass." I was unable to bring that philosophy into our marriage, let alone into our bedroom. Connie was a virgin when we married. So was I. We were led to believe, through such birds-and-bees teachings, to expect the worst sexually. But we received and gave each other the best, or so I thought.

***

Nearly three weeks have gone by since Pittsburgh, but still, in little flashes, and at the strangest times, it would come back. Just as I was about to get spiked in the ear for the hundredth time, my office intercom rang. I pushed the receiver button.

"Tony," a static ridden voice came screaming through the box, "get your ass in here as soon as you can, like within two minutes." As I entered his office my boss, Bob Flanagan, rose from his chair, half-circled around me, and shut the door.

"Tony, you're about six foot, right?"

"Six one," I responded as he stood along side of me.

"Well I'm only five eight."

With his arm around my shoulder, he guided me toward his desk, moving me around to his side of the desk. "That office of yours is far too small for you, so you can have mine." He stood there with his arms spread wide open gesturing about the office. His face lit up as he smiled broadly. I stood there, leaning slightly forward, waiting for the next line.

The smile was replaced by a look of surprise. Now his eyebrows lifted and he said, "It's yours, Tony, I've been promoted to New York and you've been promoted to my job. Tony, my job and this big office is all yours. Congratulations, Mr. VP!" He reached out and we shook hands.

"Bob, I'm dumbfounded," I babbled.

"Well, Tony"--now the smiles had reappeared and the eyebrows were back in place--"it will be the first time in your career you're dumbfounded. You deserve it, you earned it. From the tiniest task to the biggest chore you have always come through.

Your involvement in the Pittsburgh mill sale was outstanding. From the very beginning you put together the pieces that helped it go through, and then the trip to Pittsburgh in the final days . . ."

Here it comes, I thought. He found out. That's why the promotion. Here it comes . . ."

"The executive committee couldn't believe . . ."

Here it comes.

"That you would go down there and spend a day figuring out the usable square footage of the mill versus the entire amount. No one really cared but you. It didn't mean a thing to the sale we thought. But it did. There was a major miscalculation by the financial wizards, after you suggested they check it over. You almost gave the entire financial department a massive heart attack." He clutched his shirt around his heart area and started laughing loudly. "You should have seen their faces when I presented the results of your inquiry."

Suddenly remembering the "I presented," he returned to the company tone. "That kind of caring, that kind of follow-through, is what the company needs in senior management. That's why, Tony: with all your company accomplishments, being a good family-man, night courses until you graduated Providence College, it was easy for me to recommend you upstairs."

I couldn't believe my ears. I threw that inquiry into the financial department's hopper to cover my Pittsburgh trip, thinking it would get buried. It was as though I was trying to erase all the bullshit of what he had just said when I asked, "Anything else about Pittsburgh?"

"Pittsburgh?" He questioned. "Well, as you know the deal closed, we got out from under that dog, wrote down the loss, got the major tax write-off, and when all is said and done we did okay."

I lowered my head shaking it in disbelief when he said, "One other thing." I perked up knowing for sure this is it, it's that old company humor again. Holding the good stuff for last, "It's rumored the mill will be shut down before the year is out and leveled for a shopping mall of all things. Well, Tony, I have to get my bones off to NYC and you have to get in here, so let's get going. One other thing, your executive level will be increased, so you're in for a raise. Look through the personnel policy book for the appropriate level and that's where you'll be with next month's paycheck. Congratulations, we'll still be working together but long distance."

As I left his office I began to feel great. Somehow the office didn't seem so bland. The rows of fluorescent lights, not so bright. I was moving into a bigger office, with a raise. The company does take care of its own. So forget Pittsburgh.

***

"Mr. Manfredi," my secretary whispered through the intercom, "your Uncle Joe is returning your phone call."

I reached for the phone and with a smile on my face said, "Thanks for the tip."

With a question mark in his voice he responded, "What tip?"

"Remember a couple of months ago you told me about that possible situation in Pittsburgh? Well, it was on the money. Here's what's so strange about what happened. No one here at the company knows what I went through."

"Tony," Uncle interrupted, "you're talkin in circles. I don't know whatcha went through." He had placed a loud emphasis on "I."

"Jesus, Uncle Joe, I can't believe we haven't talked about it. I guess I just assumed I told you and that you knew. Tell you what, Uncle, let's get together this Sunday and I'll fill you in."

"Tony, can't. Your aunt's got me goin' to some christenin', you know, baptizin'. One of her commades' kids had a kid and I'm stuck. What 'bout coffee an' tomorrow afternoon?"

I responded positively without hesitation. "Great!"

He responded equally quick. "Member Lilla's coffee shop on Barton Street? How stupid, of course ya know, that's your ole neighborhood. I'll meetcha at t'ree o'clock."

Sticking my tongue between my teeth to place emphasis on the *th*, I said, "Three o'clock, Uncle, three."

"Hey college kid, at Lilla's we say *t'ree!*" We laughed and he hung up.

* * *

God! Lilla's coffee shop hadn't changed since I was a kid. The delicate tinkle of the bell attached to the door was drowned out by a Tallulah Bankhead-like voice. "Tony, your Uncle Joe's in boot' numba five." Mrs. Lilla hadn't changed that much either. Still small, still blackish-gray hair tightly pulled back in a bun, still wearing a hearing aid, and still that voice.

"Hi, Mrs. Lilla, how you doing?" I said with a sincere smile and extended hand.

"Tony, you look kinda the same, but what's "hi" and this handshake shit? I used to like it better when you'd say, hey Mrs.

Lilla, what's shaken and den try to steal a Devil Dog!"

We both laughed, she reached up and put the cheeks of my face between her hands and quietly said, "You look good, Tony. Your uncle said you was doin' great. I'm glad." There was a quick change from happiness to sadness as she let go of my face and glanced over her shoulder to an eight by ten piece of silk. Its white field and red border contained one blue star.

I remembered during the war seeing those little flags hanging in the windows of the tenements, or on the glass doors of the shops, telling the world that some member of the family was in the Armed Forces. Her sadness was, I'm sure, a quick flashback to her son Billy and me playing our war games. Always war games. As soon as he was old enough, he joined the navy so he could become a Frogman. The tragedy of it all was he joined young, was rushed through training camp, came home proud as could be in his navy uniform with the Frogman insignia on his arm, said a quick good-bye to family and friends, and was shipped off to the Pacific. Before we knew it, the war was over, but no Billy. He was reported missing in action off one of those Jap islands that John Wayne took single-handed. With Billy gone those movies seem like such bullshit. But Billy and I loved them. After the Saturday matinees we recreated the battles all the way home. Mrs. Lilla never put the little band of black silk over the flag acknowledging the death of a loved one. "Missin' in action ain't dead," she said.

Billy's death was the first time I used my special mental boxes. I could not believe my childhood friend was gone. So I stowed away the good times and locked up the not so good ones.

Mrs. Lilla lovingly patted my cheek, and with a distant smile directed me. "Boot' five."

Uncle Joe was already into his Boston cream pie and coffee. I ordered the same. "So tell me what happened in Pittsburgh?" He asked as he poured more half-and-half into his coffee. I began to tell him the story piece by piece, reliving every exciting, scary detail. It was like someone had pulled a string on my neck. Like those talking dolls, I talked nonstop. The only interruption was an occasional slurp as Uncle Joe drank his coffee. I wrapped up the story by saying, "I never told anyone at the company what really happened."

Cleaning the corners of his mouth with his thumb and index finger, he said, "Ya know, Tony, it's such an unbelievable story, maybe ya did the best thing by not sayin' anything. They might of thought ya was bullshittin' em. Hey, what the hell do you care, ya got a promotion anyways!"

"Well, Uncle, I got to tell you I was scared but excited. Do me a favor though; don't tell me about any other conversations you might have overheard."

We both laughed clicking our coffee cups together.

"Tony, speakin' of favors, one good turn deserves another, right?"

"Right, Uncle." Just for a second Dom Triano came to mind. *"Your uncle did me a favor and . . ."*

"Tony, in your job you get to travel 'round a lot right?"

I nodded.

"Will you be goin' to Bost'n in the next coupla weeks?"

"Not that I know of, but if it's important to you I can certainly arrange a trip. Why?"

"Well your ole Uncle Joe owes some guy some money and I wanna pay him off. I thought if you was goin' to Bost'n I'd give you the cash 'n you could pay him for me."

"Uncle, this is the fifties. You can write him a check, mail order it, or arrange for a--"

He put his hand up like a traffic cop stopping me in my tracks. "I know, I know that, but it's money I owe a bookie 'n you don't go doin' paperwork stuff like that. Besides your aunt would kill me if she ever knew I was still bettin'."

Cupping his two hands together and placing them at one end of the table, he continued. "I won some money here." He then moved his cupped hands to the other end of the table and finished his sentence. "And I wanna pay off some there."

"Uncle, excuse me for being so dumb, but why can't you pay your local bookie and he'll get it to Boston? And why the hell Boston anyway?"

"Tony, it's simple. The Bost'n bookie used to be here." He moved his cupped hands back to the original side of the table, "I bet wit' him here, I lost here."

The cupped hands moved again to the other side of the table to finish the sentence. "He moved there, I owe there. Just cause he moved to Bost'n! I still owe him!" He uncupped his hands and as if he had a pen in one hand and a pad in the other, pretended to write. "We're pen pals." Chuckling at what he just said Uncle Joe continued, "He stays in touch."

"Okay, Uncle, I'll arrange for a Boston trip, next week and bring him your money."

Trying to attract Mrs. Lilla, by pretending to sign my name in the air, I asked my smiling uncle, "How much loot will I be carrying big spender?"

Without missing a beat he said, "Forty-five grand."

With my hand still waving for the check I twisted my head back toward him and gulped "four--?"

He waved his finger in a no manner and said calmly, "For-tee-five thousand dollars." Seeing my amazement he continued, "I owed a lot, huh, but I won big."

I took a deep breath; I had no idea he bet that heavily. All I had heard of was an occasional horse race for a few bucks or a daily number they used to call the "nigger pool"—a title given by the bookies because a quarter could get you a bet that even the disadvantaged could afford. But in fact the original racket was run by blacks taking bets from their own.

"Cash, Uncle?"

"Cash, Tony. In small bills."

A waitress appeared and stood between us at the end of the table, "Mrs. Lilla's buyin' . . . but not the tip." I pulled out a dollar and gave it to her. As she stepped back to let my uncle pass, I saw out of the corner of my eye, Uncle Joe slip another bill into her apron pocket.

***

The following week he showed up at my house with two beat-up black cloth athletic bags. Printed on each bag, in faded gold capital letters, was GUIDO'S GYM with a tiny scripted one liner under it, *THE HOME OF THE GOLDEN GLOVES.* He handed them to me like he was giving me two bags full of shorts, jocks, and boxing gloves instead of forty-five thousand dollars in cash!

"Tony, what train you takin'? 'Cause I kin give you lift to the station if you want. But I got to go right now."

"Uncle," I said almost in a whisper looking left and right, thinking someone might over hear me, "I'm not taking a train. I'm going to drive up to Boston. I just don't feel safe on a train with all your money."

"Tony, whatcha ya whisperin' for? He peered over my shoulder looking into the house. "Is the kid sleepin'?"

I smiled shook my head no and asked in a normal voice for the directions to his bookie's place, what was his name, and what did he look like.

He gave me all that information in one breath. "Go to the North End neighborhood, Saint Francis Men's Club, ask for Pearlie. He's short, thin, 'n wears a lotta pearls. Call me when you get back, we'll eat." He turned and headed out the door. There I stood, flat-footed, with two bags full of cash, about to drive to Boston, to meet a bookie named Pearlie.

***

I called my secretary and told her I was off to the Boston area to check the Needham office and that I could be reached there at Bill Carpenter's office sometime after lunch. If any of my superiors asked I was reviewing their quarterly report.

Heading up the highway I continually checked the two bags. First I would glance at the one on the front seat and then the one on the floor. I locked all the doors and double-checked to make sure the front passenger door was firmly locked. The thought of me, stopped at a light, with some thief opening the front door and taking off with a bag, gave me sweaty palms. I really wished this whole thing were over. Frankie Lane was singing on the radio. "I'm gonna live till I die." Carrying the same tune I answered him, "I hope not Frankie boy!" The word *die* segued me from Frankie's song to Pittsburgh. Could this little errand bring me to that same live or die edge? Maybe I could play a little game with Pearlie the bookie. Maybe I could set something up to get me to that edge. But some two-bit bookie certainly would not be anything like Gemma and Choo-Choo.

The daydreaming put me at the Needham exit in no time flat. Automatically I started to exit, and then remembering my mission, I swerved off the exit shoulder back into the slow lane of the highway. There was a Chevy right beside me. I had not looked in my rear view mirror and cut it off. Simultaneously, I heard his horn blowing with the same anger that matched his face. I waved my hand in a gesture of apology and in return got the finger.

"You asshole," he mouthed.

"You jerk!" I yelled into my closed window.

Trying to be more cautious I looked in to my rear view mirror, and there filling the entire mirror and practically on my rear bumper, was the biggest, blackest car I had ever seen. I was startled that it was so close.

I accelerated and looked again. As it fell away I knew it was a Buick. Only a Buick has a grill that looked like buck teeth resting on the front bumper. I remember as a kid, thinking that the fronts and rears of cars looked like faces with grotesque expressions. This Buick had one missing tooth, which made it appear more menacing.

Off the highway and into the city I didn't know exactly where I was going. I spotted a cop and lowered my window. It was near lunchtime in the North End. I could tell, not by my watch, but by the delicious smells of garlic and olive oil wafting out of the tenement windows into my car. I asked the officer where I might find the Saint Francis Men's Club. He bent over and gave me a strange look. I was sitting on forty-five thousand dollars in cash, and I guess my nervousness was showing.

"Ah you a membah?"

No, I gestured.

He then pointed up the street. "Go to the stop sign and take a left, two blocks up the street there's a drugstore on the right. Right after that there's an alley, take a left."

He paused and scratched his chin, then continued. "Wait. Is that drugstore on the right or the left?" The Boston flat *a*'s got flatter. "If it's on the left, take a right down the alley, but if it's on the right, take a left."

He looked back into the car and said, "Right!"

I sat there pretending I understood what he had just said and remembered a story about a guy, who nearly got fired for being late on his first day of work, because he followed the directions from a Bostonian about Boston.

"Officer, for sure I go left at the stop sign?"

He nodded yes.

"Thanks I'll keep my eyes open for the drugstore and the alley."

As the cop started to straighten up he said "Ya kaunt miss it, and don't forget tah stop at the stop sign!" He laughed as I drove away.

I found the Men's Club without any problems. The cop's first directions were correct. Drugstore on the right, alley on the left. Or was it . . .?

Directly across the alley from the Men's Club was a tiny park. It was wonderful. Snuggled between two brick tenements was this oasis of green. Healthy grass, tree lined, and surrounding three manicured bocce courts were seven inviting park benches. Tucked far away in the corner was a beautiful grotto with a statue of Saint Francis of Assisi. Perfect. Saint Francis, fresh air, trees, grass, birds and bocce. When one is raised a Catholic, and an Italian Catholic to boot, you always said a quick prayer in front of saintly statues or at the very least, make a cross with your thumb on your forehead. I didn't want to let my upbringing down, so I said a quick prayer to Saint Francis to assist me if I needed it.

***

As soon as I stepped into the club, the smell of stale beer plugged my nostrils. The transition from sunshine to darkness caused my eyes and head to fill with black and white polka dots. Once in focus, the dots dissolved into black and white octagon shaped floor tiles. Christmas-tree lights all ablaze was the primary lighting. Swaggered around the mirrored bar, in and around the two blackened bay windows, crisscrossing the tin ceiling. What's it like during Christmas! Three old guys were playing cards at one of the tables, each nursing a glass of wine. The glasses were small, mismatched, water glasses, and the wine inside was a deep red. When wine was made at home it always came out that dark. It was called Dago Red and strong!

I will never forget my first taste of Dago Red. Though my grandfather had watered it down, it warmed my tummy, heated up my nostrils and caused me to cough like a two pack a day smoker. But after all my little boy antics, my grandfather stood there smiling proudly and I returned his with the manliest smile I could muster.

Carrying my two bags, I walked up to the bar and asked the bartender, who had his back to the room and was deeply engrossed in the *Police Gazette*.

"Is Pearlie around?"

He didn't move, he didn't respond.

"Excuse me, I'm looking for Pearlie. Is he around?"

He inhaled deeply, doubling the size of his shoulders and back. He lowered the *Gazette*. He never turned around to face me, but looked into the mirror at me. Obviously annoyed, he mumbled, "I'm a bartender not a sekkatary."

Before he lifted the *Gazette* back to its original reading position I placed the two bags on the bar and said, "It's payday for Pearlie so can you tell me where I might find him?"

The bartender turned slowly and looked me right in the eye, looked down at both bags and smiled. "I used to be a golden gloves champ. Middleweight. Twenty-six 'n oh. Then I went pro."

He left me hanging so I asked, "So what happened?"

Shrugging his shoulders he answered, "Oh 'n twenty-six!"

"Oh," I said in obvious disappointment.

"Oh's right," he quickly responded. I laughed, he didn't.

"Pearlie will be here in a little while, he knows it's payday." He turned his back to me, and returned to his *Gazette*.

Again I was left hanging. "Do you know when Pearlie will show up?"

Dropping his *Gazette* a little more angrily than before, he glared into the mirror and said, "Look, don't be a pain in the ass. Pearlie will be here when he gets here. So have a glass of wine and a piece of spinach pie and relax." He gestured with his head toward the booths.

I felt like a dog that had just been told to "SIT!" Obeying I walked over to a booth and sat. The silence was broken by the shuffling of playing cards and Italian chatter from the old guys across the room.

Over my shoulder a door swung open and closed. The door acted as a baffle, for each time it swung open, I could hear the faint sounds of classical music coming from the kitchen beyond. It was an opera. Puccini's *La Bohème*.

Through the swinging doors came a small thin man. Wearing what used to be a white T-shirt, and an apron that was stained with green and red blotches; I thought he was the dishwasher. He was so skinny, the apron string wrapped around his waist twice. He stopped at my booth and asked, "Ya want rosé or red?"

Remembering the Dago Red effect, I ordered the rosé. Wiping his hands on his apron he turned and walked through the swinging doors releasing my favorite section of the opera where Rodolfo and Mimi first meet. Rodolfo sings, "*Che gelida manina, se la lasci riscaldar.*" A few minutes passed, the swinging doors swung open again this time it's Mimi telling Rodolfo who she is. "*Son tranquilla e lieto ed è mio svago far gigli e rose.*" My dishwasher, turned headwaiter, brought me a small water glass full of rosé.

With the glass came a paper napkin, stainless fork and knife. A few minutes later he returned with the spinach pie, Rodolfo's tenor note in pursuit. The pie looked like an oversized turnover. A little bit of smoke was coming from it, warning me that it was hot out of the oven. It smelled great. I looked up at the waiter and said, "Hey if you keep coming through those doors I'll get to hear the whole opera." He stared at me as if I were nuts then turned and left. Under his breath I heard him mumble "*Stupido.*" Within seconds after he entered the kitchen, I could hear the opera coming through the doors loud and clear. He cranked up the volume allowing me to enjoy it while I devoured the best spinach pie I ever tasted.

Engrossed in the opera's dramatic closing, where Mimi is dying and Rodolfo is crying, and picking up the last spinach pie crumbs from the white paper plate, I hadn't realized how much time had passed. I had been in this joint for over an hour and no Pearlie. I started to get up when a falsetto voice from behind me squealed, "Looks like you liked my spinach pie." There was no mistaking it, there in all his splendor stood Pearlie.

"Pearlie it was delicious," I said.

"So you know my name."

Uncle Joe had been perfect in his description. Pearlie had more pearls on him than the Duchess of Windsor. On his left jacket lapel was a scrolled *P* in pearls, just below the knot on his tie was a stickpin that looked like a tiny bull's eye in pearls. When he sat down and shot some cuff, two gigantic pearl cuff links appeared, and if that wasn't enough, at close range I noticed his shirt was the kind you would wear to a black tie affair. No buttons, but studs. You guessed it, they were pearls.

A mental chuckle was forming as I said his name, "Pearlie, I have something for you from Providence." I turned in my seat and reached down for the two bags. I guess the move was too fast for Pearlie, because he yelled, "Don't!"

I turned to him. My eyes dropped to the top of table and there, staring back at me was the barrel of a gun with Pearlie's highly polished, manicured finger on the trigger. Surrendering, I brought both hands up shoulder high. Pointing the gun toward my seat and then the table, he asked, "What else is in the bag? Just leave it closed and put them on the table, one at a time." I was more than happy to comply. I reached down and picked up the first bag and slid it over to him. He opened the zipper and looked in. He smiled.

"Next."

I reached down and put the second bag on the table. He started to reach for it when I slammed my hand down on the top of the bag. Pearlie recoiled in surprise.

"Pearlie before I hand over the second half I think proper business dictates that you give me a receipt stating you were paid, I presume in full." Here I go again!

"A what?" Pearlie asked in disbelief.

"A receipt, you know a little piece of paper that says you were paid. And don't write it on flash paper."

He bowed his head and shook it left and right in utter amazement, half laughing he said, "Joe Sweets said you was a bright guy, but I thought he was talking about your job at that big company. 'A receipt and not on flash paper,' that's funny. Crazy, but funny! Do you know I never deal in receipts or any kind of paperwork?"

"Not true Pearlie, you know who bet what, when, and who paid you what, when, and who owes you what. I know you're smart, but no one can remember all those numbers, dates and names. You have to keep records. Right?"

He paused and pulled out a small pad in acknowledgment. I was amused how casually he laid his gun down on the bag and how it was all chrome with of course a pearl handle. As he fanned the pages of the pad I said, "See Pearlie, paperwork. Look, if you want to count it and then give me the receipt, that's perfectly acceptable. But no receipt, no bag."

He reached for his gun and I thought, *Trouble*. But instead he placed it inside his jacket and asked for me to open the second bag. I did. He smiled at the sight, shook his head again and wrote into his little pad. *Paid to Pearlie $45,000.00 from Joe Sweets!* He ripped it out of the pad and gave it to me. I glanced down at the tiny piece of paper and said, "Pearlie would you sign and date it?"

Our somewhat humorous exchange turned a little cold as he grabbed the paper out of my hand and scribbled at the bottom, *PEARLIE MAY 7, 1950.* He handed me the note. I took it and asked for my luncheon bill.

"Whenever you bring me this kind of dough, lunch is on me." He reached into the bag and pulled out a hundred dollar bill, folded it in half, and tossed it on my empty paper plate. "Buy yourself your own pad and pencil." Within seconds he was up and out of the club.

The kitchen's swinging doors opened and there stood my skinny waiter.

"Anythin' else?"

"Nope," I responded.

He started to leave. I grabbed his skinny wrist and with the other hand took Pearlie's hundred dollar bill, folded it in half again and stuck it in his apron string, demanding, "Buy yourself a front row center at the Met." And like Pearlie within seconds I was up and out of the Saint Francis Men's Club.

***

Exiting the club, the afternoon sun was on the wane, casting shadows all over the alley and the park. Pearlie had just left, but he was nowhere in sight and I was just as glad. This encounter did not have the same intensity as Pittsburgh; in fact, I found it to be rather humorous. Pearlie was such a character and

I didn't really believe he could or would use that gun. As I strolled down the alley I thought of Uncle Joe, and how a baker could get in so deep. But then again, he won big and he is obviously paying his bills, so who am I to judge.

I came around the corner just in time to see the policeman place a ticket on my windshield. He saw me coming and said, "I see yah found the place, but you stayed too long."

I didn't feel like trying to talk him out of the two-buck ticket and beside I was running late. I took it off the windshield and said, "Well now you know how to get here too!"

Ticked off, I opened the door and jumped in only to bang my head slightly on the rear view mirror. While starting up the car and adjusting the mirror at the same time, my heart began to pound. In the mirror was that ugly Buick with the missing tooth. In the front seat were two uglier guys. Darkly dressed, they just sat there like two giant lumps.

My hand trembled as I reached for the stick shift and put it in first. Could this be a coincidence, or are these guys following me? Where had I seen them? They appeared at the Needham turnoff when I cut off the Chevy. How long have they been following me? They're cops. That's it. They knew of the payoff and now I'm going to be arrested. They're cops!

Trying not to look directly into the mirror, but unable to resist, I peeked. As I slowly pulled out of the parking space I could see both guys simultaneously salute me. They pinched the rim of their soft hats and saluted me! I waited a bit longer at the intersection and concluded that they would not be following me, but as I pulled away I still wondered who they were.

I arrived at the Needham office very close to closing time. Two out of the three people still there had already gathered their things.

"We really didn't think you were going to make it," said Bill Carpenter, the office manager, as he was reaching for his raincoat. I told him I had to go into Boston on a personal matter. It took longer than I expected. I apologized for being late. I hate being late. My apology was barely accepted. It certainly didn't stop his secretary and another woman from filing out the door.

The office manager, now with his raincoat completely on, looked down at a hard covered report and said, "Here's the quarterly you wanted to review. I would stay but my daughter's in a school play and my wife would kill me if I were late." The word *late* was coated with poison.

"Well, Bill, I understand. I have kids of my own. Do you mind if I take the report home with me?" He shook his head no and headed for the door.

"Just shut the door on your way out, it's locked and all set." My *thanks* was obliterated by the slamming of the door.

I was as anxious for him to leave as he was. I immediately reached for the telephone and dialed Uncle Joe. "Uncle, it's Tony."

"Tony, how did it go?"

"Fine, Uncle, except there was one strange thing."

"Wha?"

"I was followed."

"You was what?"

"Followed, Uncle. You know tailed like in the movies. I saw these two guys waiting for me when I came out of the club."

"Are ya sure?"

"Of course I'm sure. How many Buick's do you know with missing teeth?"

"Wha?"

I knew I wasn't making any sense. "Uncle, when I was on the highway I saw this black Buick behind me with a missing chrome strip out of its grill, and when I came out of the club, the same Buick with the missing chrome strip was there waiting for me. The missing chrome strip looks like the grill's mouth is missing a tooth! The Buick was missing a tooth!"

I was getting very hyper. "So, Uncle, how many Buick's do you know with missing teeth? I'm telling you I was followed."

"I know a Buick like that. It's the Vespia brothers' car—"

I interrupted. "So who the hell are the Vespia brothers?"

"Tony, ya done good. You made the delivery, ya done good, 'n I thank ya—"

Again I interrupted, "so who are the Vespia brothers?"

"Tony, maybe we shouldn't talk 'bout this on the phone; come by the bakery tomorrow and I'll tell ya."

"No Uncle, I want to know now!"

"Okay. Forty-five grand is a lotta dough. I wanted to make sure it got to Pearlie all right. So I asked the Vespia brothers to watch over you. You know like those Brinks trucks. A bodyguard. No--a money guard. It's not that I don't trust ya, Tony, I would never ask ya to do it if I didn't trust ya, but funny things sometimes happen and I couldin' lose that dough to a funny thing. They did me a good turn 'n went along for the ride."

There was an obvious pause. He had finished talking and I was thinking of good turns. A lot of people do a lot of good turns for my uncle.

"Tony, ya there?"

"Yeah Uncle, I'm here. Well thanks for the guards; I wish I knew about it earlier, it would have made the trip easier. I delivered the dough to Pearlie and got you a receipt."

"A what?"

"A receipt! A simple signed statement saying he received the money from you on this date. It's good business to do it that way."

"Tony, you're bu-tee-full. See ya tomorrow?"

"Yeah, Uncle, I'll see you tomorrow. Coffee an'?"

"Coffee an'" As usual he hung up first.

***

Uncle placed a clean white *mopeen* holding two *shfooly-adell'* on the table. That's a dishtowel with Italian pastry. He was pouring the coffee and began to giggle. "I called Pearlie right after you 'n me talked yesterday. He couldn't believe you asked for a receipt. He was laughin', said you was great. He was a little pissed off that you gave the cook the hundred bucks." I smiled because I thought I was great too.

"I wanted the cook to go to an opera and I figured he didn't have the wherewithal to do so, so I gave him my tip from Pearlie.

"Uncle, you don't have to answer if you don't want to, but I have to ask the question. What's going on with you?"

Sipping his coffee he asked, "Whatcha mean?"

"Well," I continued, "first you send me to Pittsburgh where I'm almost killed. Then you send me to Boston to pay off a bookie and have me followed. No--I mean protected! What's going on?"

Uncle stopped sipping. "Tony, first of all, the Pittsburgh thing was a fluke. I got some inside info 'n I passed it on to you hopin' it would help you out at the company. And it did, maybe not directly, but it did. Do you think for one minute I would have told ya if I thought there would be trouble?"

I sighed and looked down at my coffee. "I don't get it, Uncle."

"What's to get?" he shot back. "Pittsburgh had nothin' to do wit' Bost'n. Bost'n was a good turn for me."

There was silence in between coffee sips and slurps.

Good turn hung in the air.

"Tony, I don't wanna bullshit you anymore. You see this bakery. It's been in the Manfredi family for a long, long time. My father, your grandfather, started it. He worked his ass off to get it goin'. My mother and father, goes back to the old country to visit, and--*boom*--she finds out she's pregnant. She stays, has a kid, your father. Two years later my father has enough money and sends it to his wife and she and your father sail to the States. All that time I helped 'n worked the bakery. My father died a baker. I'm the oldest kid 'n I feel responsible for this bakery business.

Your father didn't want anythin' to do with it. So it was up to me to keep it goin'. Like my father, it always gave us a livin'. But I wanted more. Durin' Prohibitin', through some good turns 'n connections I began bookin'. I ran numbers, 'n sold booze. Ya know odds 'n ends, to make a few extra bucks. The bakery is fine 'n so are the sidelines. I'm givin' ya this history less'n 'cause I'm not gettin' any younger 'n it's tough for me to get around. So if you're willin' once in a while I would like to ask ya to do a good turn. Just now 'n then. Ya travel a lot and that's good. Tony, I'm not talkin' crazy stuff here. Simple stuff. Good turns!"

I knew the bakery story because I heard it so often, but the sideline part was a five-star bulletin.

"Uncle, I'm happy to help you out, because good turns are what it's all about. Just do me a good turn, when I go on other mission, let me know everything!" We agreed and ritualistically clicked our coffee cups together. I walked out understanding a little bit more, and deep down in my gut, excited about my next errand.

**

That weekend I did brain and brawn chores. Saturday, I rebuilt a closet to accommodate my company single-breasted blue suits. *Boring!*

I unplugged the drain in the kid's bathroom, retrieving a Colgate toothpaste cap, an assortment of bobby pins, and a fingernail file! All grotesquely woven with blonde hair.

"Connie, no wonder this drain didn't work!" I yelled through an empty house.

Sunday, it was the eight o'clock Mass, followed by a breakfast of pizza *frette*. Small, flat pan fried pizza-dough pancakes, piled high, covered with sugar, and washed down with strong coffee. Even at nine thirty in the morning there was an aromatic competition between the freshly ground morning coffee and the simmering tomato gravy, which would be served up later that afternoon over macaroni. I loved Sundays. In the morning we fulfilled our religious obligation, ate well, read the Sunday papers, and I listened to the radio.

The radio was special to me. It was given to me by my father, and according to folklore, he won it in a crap game. As a kid, I listened to all the serials. The adventurous ones, the scary ones, and the ones I liked best, the cops 'n robbers. We listened to all the news on that radio. The nightly war reports, and the ending of the war, would stay with me for the rest of my life. It was particularly exciting to listen to the shortwave. On clear nights you could hear everything. I imagined the Nazis, deep in the Atlantic, talking from their U-boats, to spies right in our own neighborhood. The best part of that old Zenith was it had five buttons below the dial that you could preset to any radio station. I would sit at the kitchen table and just reach back push a button and change the station. It drove Connie nuts.

Sunday morning radio was the best! A little classical music got changed when the pipe-organ sonatas came on. The Italian hour helped me maintain the language, but was changed when they went into half-Italian, half-English commercials. Big band with pop vocalists got changed when Vaughn Monroe came on. R & B, rhythm and blues, a colored-sounding station that played some exciting, primitive music, changed when it became too gospel-like.

Both Saturday and Sunday nights would be taken over by the brain. It was Saturday evening right after supper that I first looked at the report. I reviewed the quarterly report from the Needham office. It was the financial hub of the New England territory. Most of its billing and collections came from the immediate Boston area.

"What am I doing looking at this thing," I mumbled. I'd only used it as an excuse to get up to Boston for my Uncle Joe's errand. But I stayed with it, just in case I was questioned Monday. Lots of numbers and little footnotes tied to asterisks, roman numerals, lowercased letters, and caps.

It seemed normal but there was something that didn't fit. It bothered me all day Sunday. That night I took another look and still, I couldn't put my finger on it. Then almost peripherally, I spotted it. The aging collection section. Sixty percent of our collections were coming in after a hundred and twenty days, ten percent after ninety days, five percent after sixty days, and twenty-five percent within thirty days. It was out of line with our policy and I wondered how long it had been that way. I was scribbling a note to myself when Connie wrapped her arms around my neck. I could feel her breasts softly cup the back of my head and her silky nightgown rustled in my ear. That was another thing I loved about Sundays.

***

Most Mondays, in most companies, are slow getting started. This Monday I was full of piss and vinegar. The aging report was burning a hole in my brain and I couldn't wait to get into it. The company policy was very clear on collections. Under the Collections section, page 1, section A, paragraph I: "Eighty percent of all outstanding receipts are to be collected within a sixty day period." Blah, blah, blah . . . "With no more than three percent of the receipts outstanding beyond one hundred and twenty days. These receipts are to be classified as bad debt reserve and will be reviewed quarterly." One line all by itself in bold caps read, ONLY AFTER A WRITTEN REQUEST HAS BEEN REVIEWED BY SENIOR MANAGEMENT, CAN A VARIANCE BE APPROVED BY THAT SENIOR MANAGER.

"Francine, check the files for any written requests from anyone in the Needham office regarding a variance on either aging accounts or receipts. Get me the last two years of quarterlies from that office. Find out how long what's his name, the manager, has been there and in his present job. Francine, keep this quiet."

"Yes Mr. Manfredi." She stopped writing in her short-hand pad and asked, "Now do you have time for a cup of coffee?"

"Sure Francine sure and see if you can steal a cookie."

A couple of minutes passed and Francine walked in with my coffee, but no cookie. She immediately saw the disappointment on my face and said, "Marie, from the steno pool, is on her way to the locker room to get you homemade wine biscuits her mother made."

I nodded, Francine left, but as if going through a revolving door, she reentered with some wine biscuits wrapped in a paper napkin that exclaimed HAPPY ANNIVERSARY.

"Marie was going to have them with her lunch but she wanted you to have them."

"Thanks Francine, and thank Maria."

"Marie," corrected Francine. "She hates *Maria*; it sounds too holy."

"Thank Marie, and her mother, for the cookies.

"The information ?"

Francine was staring at me and then glanced down at the wine biscuits.

I immediately picked up on her priorities. So I took a bite of the biscuit and it was delicious. "Fabulous, Francine, fabulous. Tell Marie fabulous.

"Francine, the information please?"

She broke into a smile and did an about-face heading for the door, responding, "Right away, Mr. Manfredi, right away."

I could hear faint exclamatory chatter of "He liked the biscuits" . . . "Did he?" . . . "Yeah" . . . Their voices trailed off as they headed, I hoped, for the files on the Needham office.

I had a feeling I was in for a long wait, so I started doing make work stuff. I was pleasantly surprised when Francine returned with her arms full of reports. As if dealing a deck of cards she laid one folder at a time on my desk.

"Mr. William Carpenter's personnel file, last year's quarterlies, the previous year's quarterlies, and as you have this year's first quarterly report, here is April of this year, with year-to-date figures."

Strange with all that efficiency I somehow preferred the wine-biscuit, coffee-doting Francine.

"Thanks, Francine, stay close I may need you to take some dictation."

"Right, sir. Do you wish more coffee to go with what's left?"

I looked down at the remnant of what were the wine biscuits and realized I had gone through them like shit through a goose. "Maybe just a half a cup."

I started reading Carpenter's file. He's been with the company for several years. He was a financial clerk, assistant accountant, accountant, got his CPA along the way with some financial assistance from the company, became the number-two guy at the Needham office four-and-a-half years ago, and headed it up for the last three-and-a-half years. A native of the area, he worked exclusively out of the Needham office for the M. R. Tedes Company. Married, kid, Kiwanis Club. Nothing jumped off the page, pretty standard, okay team player.

I next checked the most recent report. April of this year with year-to-date figures. The same over weighted collection report. I was moving the reports around when in walked Francine with my half a cup of coffee.

"Francine I can't find the file that would indicate requests from Mr. Carpenter to senior management for policy variances."

"If it had to do with policy, it would have to be part of his personnel file," Francine answered.

"Then is there another file on him, or that office, that might give me some insight on the aging report or receipts or--"

"Mr. Manfredi, there is the master file that incorporates all outlining office communiqués with headquarters in New York by sender. They are kept for two calendar years and stored somewhere in New Jersey for seven. After that--"

"Thanks, Francine, who do we talk to get the last two years?"

This stumped her but before she could answer I said,

"I got it! Get me Bob Flanagan in New York."

***

"Hello, Bob, Tony Manfredi calling. How are you doing?" I so dislike the bullshit repartee, mine and his.

"No, I haven't outgrown my or your old office yet." Bullshit.

"Connie and the kids are great. And your family?"

More bullshit!

"Great I'm happy to hear that.

"Bob I need some help.

"Yeah, that's right as always." God will the BS ever stop!

"I need to get into the general file of a William Carpenter who runs the Needham office."

Out of frustration I cut him off. "Yeah, yeah, that's him.

I'm looking for a particular piece of information. Has he ever requested from any senior manager a variance for aging receivable? If so, to whom and what was the response?"

"Can do? I don't want to put you out, but you know how I am, it's burning a hole in my desk."

I got the feeling he was not so happy.

"Thanks Bob I'll wait to hear from you. My love to your family." Ugh!

***

The day was coming to a close and no call from Bob Flanagan. Just as I was about to write him off for the day, the phone rang. He told me he went back two years. Double-checked personnel, and no requests either way. He wasn't interested in hearing my appreciation and hung up. It was decision time. *Should I stay and dig into the report, or head home?* All my decisions should be so easy. *I'll stay.*

It was just as easy to find where Mr. Carpenter started reporting late collections. Maybe they were legitimately late. Maybe he wasn't aware of the policy or the section indicating the request. Maybe, maybe . . . maybe he's a crook!

The entire year of 1948 was nearly perfect. In order, except for in the third quarter when there was a fifteen percent slippage in the ninety-day section. No big deal. I started taking notes. On to 1949. There was some quarterly slippage here and there. However, there was a substantial amount of increase in the billing.

It's too strange to let go. If Bill was taking money out of the receipts, it was mostly in small amounts, with occasional bigger ones, and then he funneled the dollars back in at various later dates. If Bill was tapping the collections he was doing it brilliantly.

I now had all the necessary information. I thought it was time to take a run up to Needham.

I was waiting for the elevator when I spotted a pay phone. I went over dropped in my coin and called Uncle Joe. One-and-a half rings.

"Bakery."

"Uncle Joe?"

"Yeah. Tony?"

"I have to drive to Needham tomorrow on company business, are there any errands you need to have taken care of?"

"Tony, where ya callin' from? Ya sound funny." I realized I was practically whispering into the phone, cupping the mouthpiece in my hand, totally suspicious, totally guilty . . . of what!

"Uncle, I'm sorry," I said in a normal voice straight into the mouthpiece. "I'm at a pay phone on my way home and I thought I would give you a call."

"Hey, Tony, ya sound better. Nah, there's no errands to do, but thanks for thinkin' of me. You're a good guy, Tony. My love to ya family." He was gone.

I stood there for a moment with the receiver still in my hand, feeling discouraged that all I had to do in Needham was talk to Bill about his aging report.

***

"Daddy did you bring me a surprise?" yelled Anne as I entered the house.

"Not today" I answered. "How about a hello and hug instead?"

"Hello, Dad," she said with a little disappointment, but her hug was for real.

"Where's Mom?" I asked, knowing exactly where she would be. In the kitchen putting the last touches on tonight's supper. I walked into her domain and placed a firm kiss on the back of her neck as she stood over the sink washing some vegetables.

"I'm starved."

She half turned and smiling asked, "For what?"

I whispered, "Dinner first, dessert later."

While I was fingering through the mail, Connie mentioned Dom had called a few minutes before I came home and asked if I would call him at his house. Connie wrote the number down on the back of a coupon advertising 5 CENTS OFF ON DUZ. I hadn't heard from Dom in some time and I was curious why he would be calling me at home. I asked Connie if I had time to call Dom before supper, but before she responded, I was already dialing.

"Hello, Dom, this is Tony Manfredi returning your call. What's up?"

Like at our house it was suppertime. He had a mouth full of food but managed a "Hey, Tony." I chuckled to myself, remembering all those days we sat having lunch at the loading dock, talking with our mouths full.

He swallowed and continued "I'm wonderin' if you can help me out. I've been tryin' to get on the night shift at the warehouse for a few months now and their givin' me the run around, sayin' I'm too import'n' to move from days to nights, 'cause most of the shippin' is done durin' the day. Tony, that's really nice, but

I really want to get on nights. I thought you bein' at the office, maybe you could talk to someone and see what you can do. What do ya think?"

It was so refreshing to have someone on the phone talking business and getting right to the point without all the chit and chatter/fancy patter.

"Dom, who did you talk to about your request?"

"Applegate in personnel."

When I asked Dom for more information, he cut me off.

"Tony, I really don't want to talk about it over the phone. Can we get together and talk?"

"Of course, Dom. Let's see. Today's Thursday; I have to drive up to Needham tomorrow. Saturday, I promised the kids we would do something; what about Sunday after Mass? Or do you want to meet next Monday?"

"Tony, would you like some company on your trip to Needham tomorrow?"

I was a little surprised that he would want to move so quickly, but I was happy to have the company and I owed Dom the time.

"Hey, Dom, that's great! Can you get off the dock okay?"

"No problem. I feel the grip comin' on as we speak! What time?"

"I'd like to be on the road by eight thirty."

"Easy. I'll have Peggy make a coupla eggplant sandwiches, I'm eating sausage 'n peppers now and they make great sandwiches, but tomorrow's Friday. No meat! So is eggplant okay?"

"I'd love Peggy's eggplant. See you around eight thirty; I'll pick you up."

***

Eight thirty on the dot I pulled into Dom's driveway. Some things don't change. It was like we were kids again. Only instead of a bike, it was my car; instead of a whistle, it was a car horn. One toot and Dom came crashing out of that door the same way he did years ago. Even his body movements were the same. He was a little thinner then, and had a lot more hair, but it was the same old Dom. Whenever we went on an "outing" Dom's mother always supplied the lunch. Now it was his wife Peggy. Even the brown bag looked the same: big and already slightly soiled from the olive oil dripping through it. I could tell there was enough food to feed an army, and fruit to boot.

"Hey, Tony, you're like a fuckin' alarm clock, right on time!"

I laughed, he got in and we were off to another outing.

We no sooner were out of the driveway when Dom turned on the radio. He fiddled with the dial until he found the station he was looking for. The car filled up with "Sixty Minute Man," and I was amazed at how Dom knew the lyrics, and even now, a little bit older, he still had that natural singing voice. He sounded great as he sang along with Billy Ward and the Dominos in a falsetto's harmony. He must have known I was enjoying it because he lowered the radio and said, "Tony, not bad, eh. I sound just like those 'mooh-len-yoms.'" That was neighborhood slang for Negroes. *Melanzana* was Italian for eggplant. Eggplant has dark skin. Eggplants . . . melanzana . . . Negroes!

"Dom, once you got it, you got it!"

"Tony, speakin' of mooh-len-yom, do you want a sandwich?"

I looked at him, he looked at me. "Dom, it's only eight thirty. Of course!"

We both laughed as he turned up the volume on the radio. "Sixty Minute Man" blared out, muffling the unwrapping of the wax paper as we took our first crack at Peggy's eggplant sandwiches.

The bonding of our friendship began for real. While we chewed through our sandwiches, we reminisced about the old days. We laughed at some of the nicknames and the stories behind them.

Like Mickey Cruise, aka Ronald DeFilice. Called Mickey because he was very small, slight, and quick like Mickey Mouse. At eighteen he became an Arthur Murray dance instructor. To work there, you had to take a code name. His was Mr. Cruise. Now he's Mickey Cruise.

We laughed like kids and segued into Dewey Plant, alias Bob Rocco. He used to take care of his bedridden mother's plants. The big, lush green kind that never flowered. Her voice would ring out, yelling, "Come do the plants!" Within seconds he would appear at her bedroom window, watering the plants ever so carefully with a big lemonade pitcher. He was doing the plants. Doing . . . dewy . . . plants . . . plant. Dewey Plant! When Dewey Plant's old lady died he went crazy. There she was dead. Him screamin' at the top of his lungs "Ma! Ma!" and tossing those plants out the window all over the sidewalk. It took three or four guys to calm him down!

"Tony, whatever happened to that crazy bastard?"

"As I hear it, when he joined the service he legally changed his name to Dewey Plant and is doing time in the brig for beating up, or maybe even killing, some *mooh-len-yom* for calling Dewey a motherfucker."

We were silent, deep in our own growing up flashbacks,

when I broached the subject of his shift change.

"Tony, only because it's you can I tell you why. I told you how good I was doin' durin' the war with the overtime and everythin'. Well, I liked the extra dough and missed it when it was gone. At first I let it go. Ya know--what was, was, and now it ain't. Except I really missed the fuckin' dough. So I started doin' a little bookin' with all the right blessings of course. A horse race here, a 'nigger pool' there."

"Dom, where did you do this booking?" I asked.

"That's the point, Tony. I was just doin' it around the warehouse. You know, I know everyone at the joint and they could trust me and I was always available. Well the more bookin' I did, the better it got. But here's the rub. I was on the day shift. That's where most of the guys are. Ya know, Tony, tonnage. But I also had to do my job! So I thought, if I could change shifts, I could work nights, with less to do, have a whole new group of guys to book with, which I was unable to do while workin' days, and free up my days to concentrate on the day crew, which there are more of, but not have to work it. Get it?"

I closed my eyes for a second, and shaking my head in a disbelieving fashion answered, "I got it. Dom, all this moving around for some extra dough from booking? I got it, but it--"

Like last night on the phone he interrupted, "Tony, there's a few other things goin' on that makes it worthwhile."

I put my right hand up, stopping him like a cop would stop traffic. "Dom, I don't need to know any more. I'll handle it for you. In fact I'll call that Applegate guy when we arrive in Needham."

***

Before we knew it we were turning off the expressway onto the Needham exit ramp. I pulled into the parking lot and asked Dom to come upstairs. I wanted him there to answer any personnel questions that might come up regarding his request.

I opened the office door and we both walked in. The receptionist looked surprised. Her eyes jumped back and forth between Dom and me. Finally, with a long yellow pencil, she pointed to Dom, and with a disapproving air ordered, "Sir, deliveries are in the rear of the building."

It was an honest mistake: me in my navy blue suit and Dom in his khaki pants and plaid shirt. But none the less I was disturbed. Equally disapproving, I responded, "He's with me."

Her pencil dropped, as did her attitude.

"Oh Mr. Manfredi, I thought . . . he . . . well, I . . ."

"Forget it Miss . . . ?"

"Gertz, Miss Gertz," she responded, nervously fondling her brooch, which tightly cinched together the collars of her blouse.

I toyed with her discomfort.

"Miss Gertz, Mr. Triano is an associate of mine, who travels with me on meetings of this type. Before you announce me to Mr. Carpenter, is there a telephone I can use in private?"

"Certainly, Mr. Manfredi, right this way." She led us into a small office with a long table, four chairs, and no windows. All four walls were lined floor to ceiling with accounting ledger books. The only opening was the door, which begrudgingly allowed entrance to this tomb.

"Thank you Miss Gertz, we'll only be a moment. Is this a direct trunk line to Providence, or do I have to dial the number?"

"No, sir."

"No, sir, what?" I continued to pay her back.

"Ah, no, sir, you can dial any Providence extension direct by using *seven* in front of the extension number."

She suffered enough. "Thank you Miss Gertz. You have been most gracious and efficient. I appreciate your help."

She was relieved. She half-smiled and left. Dom leaned across the table and whispered, "Tony, you're like a fuckin' iceman. Thanks." I smiled a sincere warm smile back into his appreciative face and dialed 7-4111.

"M. R. Tedes Company information."

"Operator can you connect me to Mr. Applegate in personnel."

Two rings and . . . "Mr. Applegate's office."

"Good afternoon, this is Mr. Manfredi from strategic planning calling for Mr. Applegate. Is he there, please?"

His secretary told me that he was in a meeting and would be available in about a half hour.

"Could you ask him to call me at the Needham office at extension two seventy."

Following quick, courteous good-byes, I hung up and turned to Dom. "I have to go in and see the man who runs this office on some company matters. I'm sure my friend Miss Gertz will let me know as soon as Applegate calls. So however you want to kill time is your call."

As we started for the door Dom said, "I think I'll go down to the car, take a little ride and have some fruit." I patted him on the back and told him to come back when he got lonely, and gave him the car keys.

We shook hands and as he left, I turned to Miss Gertz, "I'm ready to see Mr. Carpenter now."

***

"Tony, it's nice seeing you again. This time we'll have more time to spend together." Carpenter's welcome seemed sincere enough but I didn't like the inference.

"Thanks, Bill. Again, I have to apologize for being late the last time, but it was unavoidable, and here I am"--looking down at my wrist watch--"a few minutes early."

For the next several minutes, which felt like hours, we exchanged company gossip: who got promoted, who got fired, who's good and deserving, and who's not good and doesn't deserve that big job. It was typical company small talk. How could I participate and tolerate it! Inside I screamed out for the directness of the Doms of this world.

"Bill, I took your quarterly report home and studied it. Following up with more input from New York, I was able to get most of the answers, but I couldn't get a few and that's why I'm here, hoping you can help me out."

My briefcase was full of backup material, but I chose to show Bill a one-page memo that clearly outlined the situation. It was the simplest of reading and it took Bill the smallest amount of time to figure out where I was going.

"Well, Tony, this is quite an accusation."

Just by the way he delivered the line, if I were a jury I would have found him guilty as charged. "Bill, I am not, nor is anyone in the company, accusing you of anything. You can see how the aging of collection jumps off the page, and all we want is some reasonable explanation."

He took the memo in both hands and leaned back, not gently but slamming his back into the back of his chair. He studied the memo for a while. He leaned forward putting both of his elbows on the desk. Again he slammed his back into the chair.

"Bill?" I gently questioned, "any thoughts?"

He took the memo and as if pitching a baseball card and threw it toward his desk. "Sure I have thoughts," he said through clinched teeth. "I thought you Providence strategic planning boys, who only care about getting to New York, could be on time for an appointment."

I was stunned by his answer.

He went on. "I thought if a guy worked his ass off he would be rewarded. I thought the company would watch out for its people, I thought the company cared." Each time he said *thought*, he would move, in cadence, from the back of his chair to his desk. Bill's face got redder; the corners of his mouth began to load up with spit. His average build seemed to swell. He was not in control.

"Bill" I said as calmly as I could, "take it easy. The company does care about you. That's why I'm here to help."

From left and right, Bill swept his hands to the center of his desk gathering up whatever was in their path. He flung the contents toward me. By now he was yelling hysterically.

"Care? Care?"

Papers fluttered and floated down, a pencil bounced off my shoulder. An ashtray flew past me hitting his office door. Bill was now out of his chair and moving around his desk toward me, his mouth now foaming with saliva, his face nearly purple. From out of nowhere, Dom Triano appeared. He grabbed Bill from behind. His bear hug trapped Bill's arms so they hung helplessly along his side. Dom stopped him cold; Bill could not move. My first instinct, as I came out of my chair, was to slap the shit out of him. Instead I controlled myself and placed my hands, one on each of his shoulders. I could feel his collarbones under my thumbs.

Looking past Bill into Dom's face I saw his head gesture toward the door. I turned around, and standing there in utter disbelief was Miss Gertz. "Miss Gertz" I ordered, "get Mr. Carpenter a glass of water. He's not feeling very well." She turned quickly to get the drink.

Surprised I asked,"Dom, I thought you took off?"

"I was going to, then I thought I'd wait 'til ya talked to Applegate. I heard some yellin so....."

We carried on this brief exchange oblivious of Carpenter's sobbing as his body began to slump in Dom's arms.

"Dom, let's get him into his chair."

Just as Dom dropped him into it, Miss Gertz reappeared at the door with a glass of water.

I whispered, "Here Bill take a mouthful of water and try and pull yourself together. It'll be okay. There must be an explanation, and I'll help you out in any way I can. Here, take some water."

His sobbing was under control. All he did was gulp, swallowing his own phlegm and pride. When he finally reached for the glass his hand was shaking as if he had some kind of nervous disease. I helped him lift the glass to his mouth. He took a mouthful and swallowed. I looked up at Miss Gertz who was still standing in the office, practically on tiptoes, watching the goings on.

Dom, getting his revenge, growled, "Get the fuck out!"

She couldn't get out fast enough.

He turned and asked, "Tony, should I hang around just in case?" I nodded yes. Dom shut the door and stood in front of it.

I paused, took a deep breath, and facing Bill, I sat on the edge of his desk.

"Bill do you feel like talking about it?"

He nodded yes.

"Then let's take it from the beginning."

Bill took another mouthful of water, and as soon as it cleared his throat he began to tell us how he got caught up in this scheme. He told of how he was a faithful employee for years, and how proud he was to be a part of the company. Then, in detail, he unraveled this tale of jealousy and greed. It's the old keeping up with the Joneses routine. Except it wasn't the Joneses, it was the sister-in-law!

Both sisters are blue collar "Southies" from Boston. Bill's wife's younger sister married well and took on the air of a New England snob. From the same blue collar existence, Bill's wife moved into a white collar lifestyle that eventually took the Carpenters into white collar crime. In person, or constantly on the phone, the sisters would compare notes. What's in, what's not. Who bought what, when, and for how much. *This* private school, *those* dance lessons, *the* Country Club, that dinner party, their vacation: on and on it went. Bill's wife Sally, full of envy and jealousy, hounded this poor guy until he felt he could do nothing else but steal. He told her he got the extra money from bonuses and stock transactions, when in fact he didn't have to tell her anything because she really didn't care. She was a taker and didn't give a damn where it came from. After over an hour of nonstop talking, Bill took a break.

"Bill I can't believe you allowed yourself to get into this mess. I can understand how it happened and because of your love for your wife—"

"Love for my wife!" he interrupted. I hate that bitch. All she ever did was complain! I never measured up. Socially, financially, sexually, I always fell short."

"Then why did you go along with it?"

He shook his head in disbelief, like it was the first time the question was asked, or at least the first time he faced up to it. "I don't know. I guess I liked the notion of extra money myself. I . . . maybe it was the challenge of fixing the books and going through all the steps of setting it up so the money would come to me as I needed it for as much as I needed. I felt in control. I . . . uh . . . I . . ."

He was stuck on a point. I wanted to hear it. I was angry at his weakness--and her greed.

"You *what*, Bill?" I pushed unsympathetically. "You *what*, Bill?"

He looked up at me. His eyes filled up with tears. "I felt strong; I felt like a man. I loved the thrill; I knew I was doing wrong, but I loved it."

For the first time I felt sorry for this guy. I knew of his excitement, for I longed for mine to return. Different, but very much the same. I put my hand on his shoulder and in a hushed tone said, "I understand now Bill. I understand."

He put his face in his hands and cried. Not the hysterical sobbing that preceded his confession, but deep down hurting that poured out in tears.

I looked over to Dom. He was motionless. Standing there, guarding the door, he was totally mesmerized by Bill's tale.

"Dom"--the calling of his name seemed to snap him out of his trance--"let's give Bill some private time and go call Applegate again." I reached over and patted Bill's back as we left.

Miss Gertz was like a statue behind her desk trying her best to pretend nothing had happened, or better yet trying to prove to Dom and me that she never left her desk to eavesdrop. We silently walked by her into the ledger-lined office. With all those accounting books all over the place, I thought of the old saying "If these walls could talk." In Bill's case they did.

I dialed Applegate and got his secretary. She very efficiently put me through.

"Mr. Manfredi, this is Mr. Applegate, how may I help you?"

"Mr. Applegate thanks for taking my call. I normally would not get involved in personnel matters, but this is one of particular importance to me. There is a loading dock foreman by the name of Dominic Triano. He has been with the company for some time and recently has requested a change in shift. There has been no response to his request and he has come to me for advice and possible assistance."

"Mr. Manfredi let me get his file and take a look. Can you hold on for a moment or shall I call you back?"

"I'll wait if that's okay."

"Sure one moment please."

I looked up at Dom and put my hand over the mouthpiece of the phone and whispered, "He's getting your file."

"Mr. Manfredi, I have Mr. Triano's file. Employee number 037245358." I could hear papers being shuffled and I remained patiently quiet.

He told me how his request was being evaluated and he couldn't say how it would turn out.

"Mr. Applegate, again I don't want to interfere in your department but I need him to move to the night shift immediately." There was this deadly silence. For the first time our Mr. Applegate was showing some signs of not being so courteous. He accused me of demanding not requesting the move.

"Mr. Applegate, part of the strategic planning department is to stay on top of things—present--but with heavy emphasis on the future. Mr. Triano is more than a trusted employee. I will tell you this in the strictest of confidence, knowing you'll respect it. Mr. Triano is an old, loyal friend, who for some time has kept me informed as to the goings on at the warehouse. There is serious trouble brewing there, and it's apparently coming out of the night crew."

"What trouble, Mr. Manfredi?"

"Big trouble" I half whispered, "and I can't get into it over the phone.

"Look Mr. Applegate I don't want to be pushy, but this thing is smoldering as we speak, and the company needs to get Mr. Triano on the night shift so we can get a hold of this situation. If you need further verification, then call Bob Flanagan in the New York office." I knew that if Mr. Applegate did call Bob, Bob would yell through the phone, "Give Manfredi what he wants." Bob was a Manfredi fan. "Look Mr. Applegate, perhaps I should call Mr. Flanagan and have him call you directly. This is too important to the company for us to have this departmental ping-pong game."

Then I said the magic word.

"I cannot take the *responsibility* for what might happen. The record will have to show personnel did not respond quickly to the situation; therefore the *responsibility* lies with personnel, and Mr. Applegate, as far as this situation is concerned, you are personnel, you are *responsible*."

There was a pause then he responded, "Mr. Manfredi, I don't understand why instead of Mr. Triano trying to change his shift, himself, you didn't call in the first place."

"Good thinking, Mr. Applegate"--giving him a courtesy stroke. "Because of the sensitive nature of this situation, it was thought we best send Mr. Triano through the normal procedure. But when he didn't get results, I became involved. George --may I call you George?"

"Of course, Mr. Manfredi; may I call you Anthony?"

"Sure, George," I nauseatingly pounded home his first name.

"George, this is big stuff and, George, the company and I appreciate your cooperation. When can the change take place?"

"Well, today is Friday, and as much as I would like to move quickly, I can't honestly effect the change until midweek next week, and that would be pushing the paper mill to the maximum."

"Perfect. If there is anything I need to sign off on, please forward the paperwork on to me, but please use the confidential routing system."

"No, Anthony, because of the nature of this situation let it appear as though Mr. Triano's original request was granted. Just a little slow in getting to him."

"Smart thinking, George, I like that. Let's get together one day in Providence."

"I'd like that, Anthony." We hung up.

"Dom, you're on nights starting next week ."

"Tony, you're bu-tee-ful."

I grabbed him in a playful headlock and reminded him, "One good turn deserves another, right?"

"Right," he chuckled. Releasing him and straightening up my suit I said, "Let's check on our patient."

We walked back into Bill's office. His eyes were red and swollen.

"Bill this has been hard on all of us. Let's take the weekend and figure out what we can do to straighten things out. The problem really is, how can you repay the money. We really don't want this thing to get messy with all sorts of criminal charges, so let's think about it. It's a tricky one, but maybe there is a solution. Okay Bill?"

It was as if he didn't hear a thing I said. He was vacant.

"Bill, did you hear me." He nodded yes. I thought about picking up all the papers that were thrown at me, but instead I called for Miss Gertz.

Her eagerness to finally get invited into the office was dampened when I ordered her to "clean things up and see to it that Mr. Carpenter leaves soon." I picked up my briefcase and on my way out couldn't resist a last shot.

"Bill I know this has been tough, but I still can't figure out how you went through all that money. It looks like seventy or eighty thousand dollars. Let's get creative, so we can save this whole mess." Miss Gertz finally got what she wanted, the punch line. She stood there with her mouth opened as I bid her farewell.

Dom and I flew down the stairs. I was anxious to leave that heartache behind. Standing next to the car I started fishing for my keys.

"Tony, is this whatcha lookin' for?" Dom was dangling the keys next to his earlobe as if they were some oversized jeweled earring.

"Come on Carmen Miranda, give me the keys; I want to

get the hell away from here."

Dom brought the keys away from his ear and walked over to me and stood by the passenger's side of the car. He opened the door and with a wave of his hand invited me to get in. "Tony, you had a big day. First that poor bastard upstairs, then that azzhole Georgie, the least I can do is drive."

I got in and he shut the door behind me. I immediately rolled down the window to let in some air. Dom put both arms on the opened window and face-to-face said, "Tony, if I forgot to say it, thanks for the shift change. If I said thanks, then thanks again anyhow."

"Dom, even if you didn't thank me, I know you are thankful. Let's go home."

The drive was uneventful except one brief exchange in which Dom suggested he give me a little taste of his action because I helped him out. I tried to discourage him but he wouldn't hear of it. Three separate thoughts jammed together. I liked how he broke in and grabbed Carpenter. I liked being driven. I liked the idea of getting a piece of Dom's action.

***

The two weeks that followed my Needham/Bill Carpenter visit were consumed with company stuff! Reports here, returning phone calls there, justifying decisions, answering questions while creating new ones. Throughout this meaningless make-work nonsense I would place calls to Bill in an attempt to find a solution to the problem, but mostly to see how he was holding up. He wasn't helpful and he was not doing well. On occasion he would break down, whimpering rather than crying or sobbing. Never was he lucid, unless I brought up how much money was missing. Then he always corrected me. I would say "Bill somehow we have to find a method to replace the seventy-thousand --," and as clear as a bell he would interrupt, "It's eighty-seven thousand, three hundred and fifty-two dollars . . . exactly!" After pounding home the word *exactly*, he would slip right back into nothingness.

The last time I talked to him was Thursday of the second week. After that telephone call, I decided I should take the issue up with Bob Flanagan. Because I found the embezzlement by accident, and I was trying to work it out with only Carpenter, I had not really shared it with anyone except Dom. The "protect your ass" company mentality slipped into my psyche, and I thought it wise to bring someone else in on it. Friday, I worked most of the day on preparing the documents again. After writing a carefully worded cover letter, I put it in the confidential pouch to Bob Flanagan, New York City.

Friday night as I placed my head on my pillow ready for sleep, I felt a wave of relief come over me. I had finally brought someone else in on the situation. The phone rang, shattering my contentment.

"Tony, this is your favorite night shift foreman wishing you a good night."

"Dom?"

"You got it, Tony! It's been a bu-tee-ful week thanks to you. Have a nice weekend."

Before I could say anything the line went dead. Connie half asleep, rolled over and putting her arm around my chest mumbled, "Tony, who was that at this hour?" I kissed her forehead and answered, "My driver."

***

When I walked into the office Monday, that light-hearted feeling of relief was still with me. It was boosted by a wonderfully balanced weekend. Good time spent with the kids, completed chores, an exceptionally sexual Saturday night, a short sermon at Sunday's Mass, followed by one of Connie's breakfasts, newspaper reading, radio scanning, and a Sunday night sexual encore.

I was enjoying my second cup of coffee, shuffling paper, and wondering if Bob Flanagan had read the Bill Carpenter dossier, when Francine announced through the intercom, "Mr. Flanagan is on the line and he doesn't sound good." I knew he read it!

"Bob?"

"Tony, this is bad. Get that thief out of the office today."

"Bob?"

"What the hell got into him anyway?"

"Bob?"

"I've already got a call into legal. That bastard."

"Bob?"

"Tony, sometimes I wish you weren't so good."

"Bob, I'll take that as a compliment, but more importantly Carpenter is on the edge. I have talked and visited with him since I uncovered the problem and the poor guy is on the edge."

"Edge my ass! Tony, you get him the hell out of there now! Get up to Needham and throw his ass out of the office. Legal and I will take it from here." *Slam!*

That second cup of coffee suddenly looked gray and uninviting. I shoved it aside and dialed the Needham office direct.

"Mr. Carpenter's line, may I help you?" What an understatement.

"Miss Gertz, this is Mr. Manfredi; may I speak to Mr. Carpenter."

Dead silence. "Miss Gertz?"

She responded first by clearing her throat, then she said, "He has not arrived yet."

I instinctively looked down at my watch. The Bulova told me it was nearly ten fifteen. He was always there by eight thirty.

After grilling Gertz, I was told he left on Thursday and she hadn't heard or seen him since.

"Miss Gertz. I'm going to put my secretary on the line. Do you know where he lives?"

She replied affirmatively.

"Good, give her Mr. Carpenter's address, phone number, and directions to his house."

I punched the intercom button, "Francine, Mr. Carpenter's secretary Miss Gertz is on the line. She will give you some information I'll need for my trip."

"Right, Mr. Manfredi . . . Sir?"

"What is it Francine?"

"Sir, I have some homemade *wandies*. Do you want some for your coffee?"

I couldn't believe this domesticated nut! I wanted to tell her to shove them, but instead I hurriedly said, "Put some in a bag for my drive." I hung up and called Dom at home. I was glad he agreed to go with me. I had an uneasy feeling. So much for Monday-morning relief.

***

I drove while Dom ate Francine's wandies. Most of the flaky, powdered sugar cookies ended up in Dom's lap! Francine's typed directions were perfect. We pulled up in front of a picture-book Cape Cod cottage. It reminded me of the movie *The Enchanted Cottage*, but something told me this cottage was not enchanted.

As we got out of the car and moved toward the white picket gate, a man appeared from behind a shrub. His soft hat made him look like one of those Hollywood gangsters.

Dom must have gotten the same feeling. He decisively moved to his right, creating a triangle between the three of us. His eyes never left the soft-hatted stranger who finally spoke.

"Who are you guys? And what are you doing here?"

Dom looked at me and I responded with a hand sign that read WAIT A MINUTE. I looked directly at the stranger and coldly said, "We are associates of Mr. Carpenter. Who's asking?"

The stranger rolled the palm of his left hand over to reveal a badge. "Lieutenant Walsh, Needham Police."

These dangerous confrontations still excited me. The feeling never really leaves you once you've tasted it. I was disappointed when he turned out to be a cop. What I really wanted was to have the guy turn out to be some punk that Dom and I had to deal with. Brawn and brains. I told him how we worked for the same company as Bill and were here to review some operational matters. This cop cared very little about what I had to say.

"Yeah, we're doing some reviewing ourselves."

For a split second I thought Flanagan and legal had already contacted the police, pressed charges and the arrest was taking place.

The Lieutenant continued. "Before I let you guys in

there can I see an I.D., and I hope you got strong stomachs because it ain't pretty." Dom and I showed him our driver licenses and company employee cards. He barely looked at them, accepted them as fact, and opened the picket fence gate to let us pass.

The front door opened into a little hall, and from it you could see the dining room on the left and the living room on the right. Directly ahead of us was a staircase. The inside of the house was immaculate. Unlike my house after a weekend, this place was spotless. Then I remembered Bill telling me of his wife's compulsive cleaning habits. Dom and I looked at each other. Dom broke the silence with "Neat house ain na."

Lieutenant Walsh responded, "The mess is upstairs."

It was my turn. "What mess?"

As if he didn't hear my question he continued. "We took the bodies out yesterday and the lab boys just finished up, but there's still blood and brains scattered here and there." Walsh's comment was so matter of fact he could have been a real estate broker showing us the house.

As soon as I got to the second floor it was as though I had walked into another house. An overturned table in the hallway. The lamp it held was broken in pieces on the floor. On the opposite wall, to out of the three pictures of the Carpenters were damaged. The glass on his photo was cracked. The third I assumed was Mrs. Carpenter, smashed in the middle of the hallway. Strangely, a young girl's photo was untouched. As I passed one bedroom I looked in and it was obviously their daughter's room. Things were still frilly and neat.

I next passed the only bathroom on the floor. The white sink, practically pulled off the wall, was covered with blood. There were blotches of blood on the wall to the right of the medicine cabinet and as if sprayed with red Windex, the mirror was spotted with blood.

Directly across the hall from the bathroom was the master bedroom. Everything, literally everything, was turned over, broken, cracked, smashed, destroyed. The bed was covered with dried blood. The scene took my breath away. As I lowered my head and looked down at my feet I saw reddish stains on the carpet. I moved my feet tracing them back toward the bathroom. I had not reached any conclusion but Walsh thought I had.

"You got it! The way we figure it, they, the Mister and Missus got into a fight. He kicked the shit out of her first. Then he drags her into the bathroom, once to cut her wrists, and once to cut her throat. When we found him he had a lot of her hair in his hand, so the lab boys think he dragged her around by her hair. The lab boys haven't verified it yet, but somewhere along the line he fucked her. We think she cashed in when he cut her throat. He throws her on the bed, grabs his shotgun, sits in this chair and--*bang*--both barrels in the mouth. You can see part of his head on the back of the chair and some more over there near the window seat."

Again, the good lieutenant rattled through the description like a real estate broker.

"Tony," Dom intervened, "this Carpenter was a real 'coo-gootz.'"

Walsh, always the cop, asked, "What was he?"

Dom, without dropping a beat said, "A coo-gootz. Crazy!"

This time I intervened, "Lieutenant, *coo-gootz* comes from *cucuzza*, Italian for squash, which is slang for someone who's crazy." Walsh laughed and said, "You got that right."

Walsh's three-minute explanation wiped me out. We walked down the stairs and wandered into the squeaky clean kitchen.

Standing by the counter, Walsh told us it was a clear case of murder-suicide, but he would have to take some information down from us for the record. I gave him an abbreviated version of our Carpenter involvement while Dom opened and scouted the refrigerator.

"Officer, who found the bodies?"

"Their kid found them."

"Oh shit," I said.

"Yeah the kid was spending the weekend at her aunt's and was dropped off Sunday night. She found them. Went screaming to the neighbors who called us."

"Oh shit," I repeated thinking of my daughters, "that poor kid. Where is she?"

"She was in rough shape and was taken to her aunt's."

Was it parental responsibility or guilt for unraveling this whole thing that overwhelmed me?

"Officer, do you have the address of the aunt's house? I think as a company representative I should go there and offer some condolences. Try to help."

Walsh flipped through his pad and gave us the address. As we were leaving, he reminded us to be available for further questioning, but he doubted if we would be needed. He concluded, "Clean case. Murder-suicide."

***

It took less than ten minutes to drive there. They might

have lived close to each other, but they were eons apart in status. The Carpenters neighborhood, although nice, was modest compared to the aunt's. The grandeur of the houses was overwhelming. The architecture ranged from turn of the century Victorians, to stately Georgians, to sprawling Mediterraneans.

We pulled up in front of the aunt's house. It was a Southern colonial. The vertical white, square pillars ran the entire length of the building holding up a massive roof that covered the front porch. The lawn gently rolled down to the sidewalk, and was perfectly split by one straight single path leading to the front door. When I rang the doorbell, it took forever for the chimes to stop. An older colored woman, dressed in a gray and white uniform, opened the door.

"Good afternoon I'm Mr. Manfredi from the M. R. Tedes Company and I was an associate of Mr. Carpenters." It suddenly dawned on me I didn't know the name of the aunt. I ad-libbed, "Is the lady of the house available?"

The housekeeper looked at me then Dom, and in a Southern accent that reflected the house answered, "Won minute, suh." A few minutes passed when we were reluctantly invited in and ushered through an echo-filled foyer into a huge living room. There, sitting on a dusty rose chintz love seat, petite, dressed to the nines, hair recently coifed, was the aunt.

"I'm Lilly Wilkens," she sniffled, "Sally Carpenter's younger sister." Patting the end of her nose with a delicately embroidered hanky, this original taker's demeanor reeked with self-centeredness.

"Mrs. Wilkens, nice to meet you," I lied and continued, "I only wish the circumstances were different." I reached out to shake her hand, she extended hers but made sure I could only hold her fingertips.

"This is my associate Mr. Triano." She knew better than to extend any part of her hand. Dom nodded. affirmatively.

"My maid Betsy said you are an associate of my late brother-in-law, correct?"

I didn't get a chance to answer. She continued, "Yes, Mr. Manfredi, this is the most tragic thing that could happen to a loved one. It's already caused so much anguish and embarrassment." Anguish I could understand. Embarrassment I couldn't and wouldn't deal with.

"Embarrassment, Mrs. Wilkens?"

"Why, yes, Mr. Manfredi. By tomorrow the entire community will have read about the tragedy. Everyone knows she's my sister. By Wednesday's bridge I'll be the laughing stock."

I didn't let her finish. "Where is their daughter?"

She got up from the love seat, freshened up her ruffled collar and started toward the two huge doors glancing upward to a grand stairway. She turned and said, "She's upstairs in the guest room, sitting on the bed, staring at the wall. She hasn't uttered a syllable since last night. I think she is not well and may have to have special care to get her through this ordeal. She may have to be placed in an institution where she will get the attention she needs. In fact my husband Lawrence thinks we should do it right away. We can't have her here in the state she's in. Lord only knows what she might do. My children are already frightened of her."

I couldn't believe my ears. "Your children are frightened?"

She patted her nose. "Yes. They think she's gone crazy and might attack them. We have to put her away."

This phony bitch scared the shit out of her entire family.

She patted her nose again and in a suspicious tone continued. "What are you doing here anyway? This is really none of your business."

I took a beat. "Mrs. Wilkens, Mr. Carpenter and I worked for the same company. I visited him regarding some confidential business matters."

I could see her mind going a mile a minute. Pointing a manicured finger at me, and with a clenched jaw said, "You're the man who caught him. My late, darling sister confided in me. Bill, that louse, told her what he was doing and how he thought he had been caught. You're the man who brought this plague on us."

She started to walk past me toward the love seat. I reached out and grabbed her arm. She looked at me with disdain. I moved my hand up from her arm to her throat, pushing her backwards until her body slammed against the fireplace. Her head became wedged between the mantel and my hand. Dom bolted across the room. Quickly but quietly he closed the huge doors and stood in front of them. I knew no one would get by him.

"Listen, you phony Southie," I said giving each word equal importance, "yeah, I found him out! But from where I stand, thanks to you, your baby sister put them into the shitter. Their blood is all over your fancy-schmansy dress. I am here to do one thing and that is to try and help their child. You will not, I repeat *not*, put her anywhere until you hear from me. If you do something rash, Mr. Triano, who is much more of a North End kind of guy, will pay you a house call, and he is not the gentleman that I am. Understand Mrs. Wilkens?"

She had a difficult time nodding yes because my large hand was still around her tiny throat. I released her and gently fixed the ruffle around her shoulders.

"Now may I see your niece?"

As viciously as it started that's how calmly it ended. Lilly and I walked toward the huge doors and Dom in his best gentlemanly manner opened them.

Ascending that grand staircase, I realized, clearly for the first time, what I needed in my life. I wanted to be continually placed on the edge. I was addicted and I wanted everything that comes with it. The power, the danger, the results, the excitement. Now all I had to do was find out how I could continue to feed my addiction. It was thrilling just thinking of the possibilities.

6

"AMY, DARLING, this is Mr. Manfredi he's a very close friend of your"--she swallowed hard--"of your family. He would like to talk to you darling."

There, sitting in front of me, with her hands folded in her lap, was a beautiful little girl. Her dark hair emphasized her green eyes, which in return brought out the near transparent whiteness of her skin. She stared straight ahead, right through her aunt and me. As I bent over to greet Amy, Aunt Lilly backed away and began to leave the room. A slight head gesture to Dom was correctly interpreted and he followed her out the door.

I was overcome with sorrow and pity for this poor child. In a near whisper I said, "Amy, my name is Mr. Manfredi. Tony Manfredi."

My bending over her wasn't working. She never moved. I slowly squatted, Chinese style, in front of her so that we were face-to-face.

"Amy, I'm Tony. A friend. I'm sorry about what happened to your folks, and I'm here to help if I can. If you'll let me. I was a friend of your dad's." I felt like a hypocrite. I continued,

"He was a special man, who loved you very much." There was no verbal response, but her tiny hands moved across her lap pinching the material of her skirt as they passed. "Amy, I have two little girls. They are not as old as you. In fact, one of them is not even a year old. Her name is Roberta, and I was thinking, she could sure use a babysitter this summer."

She looked down at her fingers. I took that slight nod as a breakthrough sign.

My brain and heart where in mortal combat. Disbelief in what I was saying but overcome with compassion. I continued. "Yeah, little Roberta could sure use someone to take care of her this summer. By the way, Amy, how old are you?"

Very slowly, but decisively, she raised two clenched fists from her lap to either side of her face. Once positioned she popped open her hands, separating all the fingers on each hand. There, framing that beautiful little face, were ten tiny outstretched fingers. Crazy, but the only thing that came to mind was one of my Uncle Joe's songs. In the same careful whisper, I began to sing it. "Ten baby fingers, ten baby toes, waiting down in Tennessee for me. Kiss every finger, kiss every toe, home sweet home I'll linger for they need me there I know." She smiled, my eyes filled up and I knew what I had to do.

In the next hour I called Connie. With equally great compassion she immediately agreed to have Amy live with us until something was resolved. Aunt Lilly was relieved.

"Why I think it's the most generous idea that anyone could imagine," she said as she headed for, and posed in front of, the same fireplace where earlier I had nearly choked her.

"Why thank you for thinking so, Mrs. Wilkens," I responded in my best satirical Katharine Hepburn accent. She couldn't wait to get rid of the burden and not be embarrassed at her Wednesday bridge game.

I left the room and this time as I ascended the stairs I didn't have those same fantasies as before, but a feeling of righteousness, goodness, purity.

When I entered the room she was looking out of the window.

"Amy, I just got through talking to everyone and they all think you'd be great as Roberta's babysitter." She turned around and looked right at me. The glassy stare had disappeared and some depth had entered her eyes. "Now here's the best part. Because school will be over in a few weeks, I have arranged for your schoolwork to be sent to our house so you can study there."

Her eyes dropped to the floor. I was losing her. "That is, you can study while little Roberta is sleeping." She looked up again.

"Thank you Mr. Man--Mr. Mank--Mr. . . ." She spoke for the first time and was embarrassed that she couldn't get my name right.

"Amy, how did you know? Everyone who I care about calls me Mr. Man!"

She smiled a full little girl's smile. "I knew it all along Mr. Man."

A strange conflicting braid began to form in the deepest corner of my soul. Was the need for excitement and power obtainable only from the other side wrong? My job, family, and now, Amy seemed right. It wasn't even a matter of right and wrong or good versus evil. Certainly work and family was right, yet the desire to cross over and do wrong never approached being evil.

***

Amy entered the Manfredi family in grand style. She totally stole our hearts, and became one of us. She babysat Roberta and did a fine job. We were determined to remove all the scars of her past. She was not committed to attend dance lessons, riding lessons, elocution lessons. Our intention was to rid her of those pressures, hoping what she had experienced would fade from her memory. Unfortunately, some nights were awful. Her bloodcurdling screams would awaken us. Dashing into her bedroom, we would find her in the same spot, staring at her bed screaming, "Mommy! Mommy!" Poor little Roberta. Stunned out of a sound sleep, holding on to her crib for dear life, cried in horror. It took hours to calm Amy down from her recurring nightmare.

The holiday season, that wonderful time between Thanksgiving and Christmas, is a cure-all. Like the story of the three Magi, three gifts were presented to the Manfredi family.

The first two were shared by all of us. With some help from Uncle Joe, we were successful in our adoption of Amy. Our entire family helped to dissolve the horror she had experienced. Her nightmares were vanishing. She had rediscovered that home and family was safe. Then Mr. Applegate and Bob Flanagan came through and arranged to have Bill's investment plan, pension, and insurance placed in a high-interest account to be paid to Amy on her twenty-fifth birthday. Carpenter's deeds were virtually expunged from the company files.

The last gift was for me alone. I received an out-of-the-blue phone call from Chris McKay, the woman with the *Ipana* smile that I met on the train to Pittsburgh. "Just called to wish you a Merry Christmas," she said. "I'm in New York City doing our Christmas routine. Shopping, *Nutcracker*--"

I interrupted. "I'm glad you didn't throw out my card. How long will you be in the city? I'd love to see you again." My heart was pounding; I couldn't believe I had said that.

"We're heading back tomorrow morning."

I pursued. "When will you return?"

"Ah." Very slowly she answered measuring each word, "Probably not until next Christmas."

I backed off. "I know you don't like New York. Too crowded, too expensive. How's the weather?"

"Lousy!" she quickly answered. We both laughed, just as we did several months ago on the train.

Hoping, I asked, "May I have your phone number so I can call you if I'm in the area?"

Shattering my hopes she answered in a whisper, "Let's try for next Christmas. I'll call you." We wished each other a happy holiday and hung up.

As she gently placed the ear piece back on the hook she wedged herself in the corner of the phone booth and tried to reason why. Why the phone call? Why him? She reflected back on her father and tried to touch the comfort and safety he brought her. As crazy as it was, she attached that same comfort and safety to Tony...a stranger. A stranger she meet on a train. Enclosed in that tiny phone booth she felt safe, away from the hurt that longing brings.

***

Several months had passed since the last holiday season, and although much of my efforts were spent on the job and our expanded family, I never lost that low-level desire for living on the edge. On occasion I would left-handedly hint to my Uncle Joe, that if he needed anything done in one town or another, I was heading that way and . . . blah, blah, blah. Nothing! He never even nibbled, let alone bit. Then one Sunday after an early dinner, he invited the kids and me to take a walk.

"Tony, after ya aunt's feast, we need some exercise, right! Let's go to the playground, take the kids; they could use the exercise too." En masse we left the tenement. As if let out of a cage, the kids yelled all the way down the stairs. Outside they ran comfortably ahead of us, stopping and waiting for us to okay each street crossing.

The playground was about three blocks away. Sundays were always quiet in the neighborhood. It was early spring and it felt good knowing another winter was behind you. We approached the deserted playground. As soon as we entered the gravel grounds, the children scattered around the empty pool in all directions.

In a short time, that big, empty swimming pool would be filled to the brim with water. Screaming kids splashing away the gray clouds and bringing on the sun. At one end of the pool, a bronze lion's mouth, now only formed a silent OH, but come summer it would roar, gushing out cool water where kids pushed and shoved to get under the huge faucet.

"Tony, I never understood why they don't keep the playground house open durin' the winter. It would be nice to go there 'n hang out, play a little cards, ya know, bullshit with the guys."

I looked at the boarded up windows and bolted shut door. I remembered as a kid playing ping-pong in that house, finger pool on screwed-to-the-floor tables. The arguing. The fun.

"Uncle, it's pretty run-down besides you have the neighborhood bars and clubs to go to: Venice Hall, the Almy Street Bar, Joe Newport's." I paused and thought of Joe Newport.

"Uncle, can you believe, all the years growing up and knowing of Joe Newport's, I've never been in there, and I still don't know his real last name. Why *Newport?*"

We began circling the empty swimming pool. The cadence of our steps was perfect for storytelling. Uncle told of how Joe Newport, back in the twenties, conned these "Ah-med-egons" into letting Joe check out the seaworthiness of their sailboat. I loved how my uncle would use words he grew up with, like *Ah-med-egons*. That's an Italian insult directed at the pure-blood Americans. Instead Joe Newport used the yacht to hall liquor from Canada to Newport, Rhode Island. He made lots of money, and that's how Joe Rocchio became Joe Newport. To this day the name stuck.

We both laughed at the story and I could tell Uncle Joe loved reliving it. We circled the pool. Each in our own way enjoyed revisiting the story.

"Uncle, two questions. Why is he never called just plain Joe, but always Joe Newport? And wasn't there a lot of money made during those days? Why isn't Joe Newport financially set? Instead he runs a neighborhood club."

Those blue eyes lit up and he responded, "First, that's more than two questions. Lots of money was made in those days. He made a lot of dough 'n lived a lot too! He has no regrets. He loves that club and is able to stay in touch with the guys while makin' a livin'. As for his name? His name is Joe Newport. Like one word. Just like I'm known as Joe Sweets, not Joe, not Sweets, Joe Sweets."

The afternoon was heading for dusk. It was getting late and time to go. The telltale sign was when Uncle Joe buttoned the top button of his white-on-white dress shirt, and then pulled his home made, shawl collar sweater closed.

"Little chilly ain't it, Tony."

I put my arm around his shoulder and brought him closer to my body in an attempt to keep him warm. "Hey kids," I yelled over my shoulder, "let's head home it's getting late." Naturally, various disapproving responses came from all corners of the playground, but they knew it was time to go, and started moving slowly toward the exit.

"Tony, ya got some family. Ya done good. And what you did for that Amy is above 'n beyond. 'N your job! Jesus I love to talk about my big-shot nephew. Tony, this is very hard for me to do, but I feel like I got to do it."

I could feel his body quiver. At first I thought he was just cold, but my Uncle Joe was nervous. I couldn't believe it!

"Uncle, what is it? Is there something wrong?"

He looked up at me and squeezed his sweater, closing it a little more. "It's gettin' chilly, Tony. I'm a little chilled."

"Tony, through the years you've picked up little odds 'n ends about me 'n my friends. What we did, what we're doin' and you know what kinda guys we are. We all grew up together 'n went through a lot together. They're like another family to me. The same loyalties, loves, carin', protection. The same providin' I do for my own family goes into that other family. Even though we ain't related, you know like blood relatives, there's this other kinda relationship, other kind of blood that keeps us . . . together . . . in touch."

I was in a trance. I was speechless and I could feel my

heart picking up its pace as he spoke. I was hearing everything he said as I simultaneously, mentally flipped through our lives. I recounted the stories and put them together. I knew where he was going and I was beyond excited.

"Tony, since the war things changed. It's a crazier world even though it's at peace. Things seem to be under control, but they're not. What seems to be okay . . . ain't. Some different thinkin' is needed durin' these changin' times. Some different approaches. Tony, I am about to tell ya somethin' that nobody knows, 'n once you hear it, it must remain locked in your brain 'n guarded by your heart. Whether you accept it or not, it must remain with you 'n the secret taken to your grave." He looked down to the ground on the word *grave*. As he raised his head, he transformed from a chilled little man, to a rigid cold steel I beam. His blue eyes were riveted to mine. "From when I was a kid, off the boat, I had to work to make a go of it. I was helped by my friends, that other family. I was good to them 'n they was good to me. We helped each other 'n we do fine. You read in the papers or hear on the radio stories about gangsters, racketeers, hoods, the Mafia. They even make movies about these tough guys."

I couldn't help but notice how he threw away the word Mafia and followed it by the light movie comment.

"Tony, this business is like a family-owned 'n -run business. It's got bosses, rules, like your policy stuff, costs 'n profits. It's well organized 'n we're always lookin' to the future. Tony, I would like to know if you'd be interested in joinin' the organization. I have already put in a good word, 'n they like what I have to say, 'n what you have done 'n stand for." I remained silent. "It's nothin' you can discuss with Connie or your friends--"

I interrupted him. "Uncle, I think I know what you're

asking and I got to tell you I am interested but confused. How does all this happen? I mean, how do I leave my job and go to work for your other family and . . ."

Uncle Joe let go of his sweater and reached up putting both of his hands on my shoulders and said, "Who's askin' you to change anything? Your life goes on. You keep workin' at the company. You keep gettin' promoted every other minute." We both smiled. "Keep raisin' your bu-tee-ful family, nothin' changes except you also work for us. That is, work for us on a part-time basis to see how everythin' goes."

He glanced over my shoulder at the kids and continued. "Tony, that's the beauty of this whole thing. Nothin' changes. You can move round the country freely as this company man, while doin' stuff for us. Once we see how you do, you become more involved. Tony, we see what you accomplished. Ya got brains 'n style. We need that. We know you."

I reached up and grabbed his two wrists firmly, pressing down so his hands were now locked on my shoulders. "How do you know?"

Again those steel blue eyes welded on mine. "We tested you."

I let go of his wrists and started to turn away, but his frail hands were holding me tightly in place. I was flabbergasted and angry all at the same time.

"You tested? You tested me? When?"

He didn't let go. "It started in Pittsburgh at that plant. I gave you that info legit. I got it from the organization with no other reason than to help you out. I almost gotcha killed. Who would have guessed that, that stupid union goon would take ya on. It wasn't till you told me what happened that I began to think of you in a different way. The Pearlie visit was a test, but all that's bullshit. In my heart I know you're one of us. That's the only test, 'n you pass with flyin' colors. We need you and that's what counts.

Again those Pittsburgh images returned, and how ironic that Uncle Joe's hands were skinny but strong like Gemma's. The Pearlie receipt, the toothless Buick, the excitement was back and this time I wanted it to stay. I knew I needed it. My answer came out naturally, "I need you too."

7

I SO WANTED last spring's playground meeting to remain a milestone, a direction. But summer was almost over and Uncle Joe asked for nothing of me. I longed for some sign but nothing. I calmed myself with the notion that if the playground meeting meant anything it would eventually surface.

My position and responsibilities at the company and as husband/father drew all my attention. I threw myself into both.

It was like a refresher course at the company. I re-reviewed things I had totally forgotten about. I felt secure knowing how diversified the company really was. It was a conglomerate made up of many companies, some large, some small, but all reporting to the President and his executive committee.

Richard Q. Armstrong, President and Chief Operating Officer, was perfectly cast as the C.O.O. Very tall, about six five, athletic, well schooled, and as Waspy as they come. He was brilliant in the area of acquisition. He would buy companies in dire straits. With his executive committee he would get them back on their feet by selling off pieces, condensing them, and when advantageous, sell them, while turning a profit every step of the way. Richard Q., as he was respectfully called, was the ultimate corporate gorilla. Charming, smart and deadly.

His executive committee consisted of five handpicked men. Outspoken but loyal to the core, they fought amongst themselves, but pulled together when Richard Q. called. The one woman that was ever present was Karen Hunt, Richard Q's executive assistant. She knew everyone and everything. She chain-smoked, took tons of notes, and spoke in a deep graveled voice that most men would envy. Her main, self-appointed mission was to protect Richard Q. at every turn. Lower-level management gossiped about how she ran the company and Richard Q. was only a figurehead. Close, but not true. Make no mistake, he does run the company, but she could too! Richard Q. and his committee have an equity position in the company. It is privately owned and funded by NYNEB, New York/New England Bank, which holds the majority of shares.

As V.P. of Strategic Planning, I reported to Bob Flanagan, Senior Vice-President, who reported to Edward Gormley, Executive Vice-President, Finance. I was, up to this point, far removed from that group, but I would become and remain part of it.

The company owned Bedford Woolens, a sizable textile mill in New Bedford, Massachusetts. Purchased for practically nothing just prior to World War II, it specialized in heavy woolen weaving. As luck would have it, the war broke out. Richard Q. went to Washington and through his lobbying secured a huge contract to produce most of the woolen blankets for the Armed Forces. It was a bonanza. But now the war was over and the profitability of the mill had fallen dramatically. Bob Flanagan instructed me to put together a presentation with "alternatives to the downward spiral of the mill."

"And, Tony," he warned, "this is your first time in the barrel with Richard Q. and his gang, don't screw up." I knew if the plan was accepted, Bob would take the credit, and if it bombed he'd lay it right in my lap.

My plan was an aggressive one. My presentation pointed out how, during this high-profit period, we gave into the exorbitant demands of the various unions. Now the high-profit period was over, but the unions and the cost of operating it remained. With the proper research behind me, I recommended we not sell the mills, but stay in the weaving business. However, we should close down the Bedford Mills, move the equipment to the Deep South where the non-union help is cheap, and get into cottons and the new synthetics. We could convert the existing mills to low and middle income housing complete with its own shops, Laundromat, movie theater, and recreational center. The investment for the switch was sizable, but as I pointed out, the return on the investment would be substantial and we would eliminate the mill's continuous losses.

Many hard questions were thrown at me and had to be answered:

Questions of finance. The move was inexpensive. Our trucking company made the haul and what couldn't be trucked down was sent by railroad. The building of the mill was done by our construction company, on land purchased dirt cheap from a farmer who thought, because of the sale, he had died and gone to heaven. The conversion of the mills to housing and the various support facilities was also done by our construction company, and it spawned TMT the Tedes Movie Theater chain.

Product. It was determined that synthetics were the fabrics of the future and the combination of cotton and synthetic material was the way to go.

Perception was the most difficult. Richard Q. did not want the company to come off as a union buster or taking advantage of the "poor colored and white trash of the South." We created two separate community campaigns to deal with his concerns. It wasn't the North against the South, but a coming together of the two.

My aggressive plan was accepted. Now it was time to take another aggressive move with my other job.

***

"Uncle Joe, how about some coffee an' with your favorite nephew? I can be there within the hour." There was silence.

"Uncle?"

Finally he said something. "Tony, of course you can come over. As soon as I heard your voice I remembered somethin'. But I'll tell you when you get here." *Hang up!*

I arrived at the bakery and Emilio, the skinniest baker in the world, pointed his dough encrusted hand to the back of the shop. "Tony," his toothless mouth clapped, "your uncle's in the back; he's waitin' for ya, he's got coffee an'. I'll put some dough aside for ya to take home. It's good for pizza, but don't make it to t'ick." Ah those missing *th*'s! I nodded gratefully as I passed him. He continued clamoring about thick pizza and how he doesn't like anchovies, but eats them anyway.

Uncle and I greeted each other with a kiss on the cheek and an embrace. The espresso-coffee smell filled the little office and wetted my appetite for it and the "an'." "Uncle, the company is going to implement a plan I designed and I think there is room for your company to participate."

He poured our second cup and corrected me. "*Our* company."

"Yeah, right!" I said sarcastically. "I want to be a part of your world or I would have told you at the playground to go and find yourself another boy. I don't have all the pieces yet, but I know it's right for me. You even said it. You knew. And what do you do? Nothing!"

Uncle Joe reached across the table and grabbed my two wrists. As if my tirade fell on deaf ears, unruffled he said, "Tony, remember on the phone earlier I said I forgot somethin' and you reminded me of it when you called?" He didn't give me a chance to answer. He reached down on the floor next to his chair and brought up a small package wrapped in white butcher paper. The kind he used to wrap the dough in for his customers. He placed the small package in front of me.

"Go 'head--open it. I can't believe I forgot to give ya this. See Tony, your uncle is gettin' a little..." he never finished the sentence but took his right hand and formed a gun pointing the barrel to his temple. Translated from Italian sign language, he's losing his mind.

I looked down at the package and, using the knife we used to cut the pastry, I slit the one piece of tape holding it closed. Released, the package's petals almost automatically opened revealing a stack of dollar bills, or so I thought. Not dollar bills, but twenties mixed in with hundreds, with a few tens thrown in for good luck. I had no idea how much was there, and I wasn't about to count it. I looked up in amazement.

Uncle Joe was smiling. "It's ten grand, give or take a few.

T'anks!" My first instinct was to rewrap it, kiss Uncle Joe, and run out of the shop screaming with joy. Instead I rewrapped it, and slid it across the table to Uncle Joe.

"I appreciate it, and I'm thankful for the thought." My anger, sarcasm, directness gave way to disappointment and hurt. "Uncle, I don't want to be a two-bit or"--pointing down to the package with two fingers--"a ten-gee errand boy."

He reached across the table taking my two fingers and gently bringing them down on the package of money. "You ain't 'n won't be an errand boy anymore. I was right." His blue eyes mellowed and filled up slightly. "Tony, they're things you must learn. And you will. You are of us, you belong." His eyes became clearer. "Tony, from that afternoon at the playground, till you're in the ground, you're one of us. You cannot quit, or retire like in your company. You are in forever." He was so precise in his speech. An eternity passed and nothing was said.

Uncle Joe broke the silence. "What's this thing you say we can be part of?"

"Uncle, all I'm going on is what I hear, or read in the papers about the Mafia."

He put his hand up to stop me. "Tony, does this hand look black?" Kidding he lifted his other one. "Tony, does this hand look black? Of course not. Here's one of the things you got to learn. There's no such thing as the Black Hand, the Mafia. Maybe years ago, but not today. We are an organized organization. The Mafia is a title that's kept alive by the cops 'n the newspapers. It's good readin'. People like to hear about it. What pisses me off is every Italian is Mafia, and every Mafia is Italian. It's bullshit! Look at it this way. Our family, our organization, is like a distant cousin' of the Mafia. I just gave ya ten grand. Have I taken you down to some dark cellar 'n asked ya to cut ya finger 'n mine to mix our blood? Have I asked ya to go kill somebody before we can talk some more? Of course not! It's folklore! It's bullshit!"

He took a sip of his coffee and said, "Go 'head."

A little bewildered, I said, "Well, Uncle, based on all the folklore"--we both smiled--"I understand that the vending machine business is one of our ongoing enterprises and there may be a place for us to participate. We own the Bedford Mills, and we're moving that operation to the South. The buildings will be converted to housing, with shops, a movie theater, and laundromats. All of which can use machines. If there is interest from the organization, let them make a competitive bid. I'll feed the necessary information to you to make sure it's competitive, resulting in us getting the contract. It's done nice and clean. Simple and legit. No Mafia muscle."

"Tony, I like it. I'll tell the organization the plan and if everyone okays it, we'll do it. In one case the folklore's right. That is one of our businesses. In the other case we don't muscle unless we're asked, or have to. When do ya need a yes or no?"

"I'm going to New York City sometime next week to button up the plan. I should know by the time I leave."

Uncle Joe drank the last of his espresso. When the cup hit his saucer he was up, on his feet, and simultaneously said, "You'll have the answer by Tuesday."

The meeting was over. I got up and as I entered the main part of the bakery there was Emilio waiting with the wrapped dough. Remembrance and panic spun me around heading for the coffee table. Stopped in my tracks by Uncle Joe, he was holding the slightly opened package. Calmly he said, "Tony, this is the real dough."

He handed me the package full of bills. I turned and Emilio handed me another package. Unlike my Uncle's package, the pizza dough was soft to the touch. Emilio filled his toothless mouth with a half-smoked black Italian cigar called a stogy, and reminded me, "Tony, remember: not to t'ick or ya lose da flava."

Uncle Joe chimed in, "Don't spend it all in one place."

Awkwardly juggling both packages I left.

***

"Francine, try to find a phone number for a Dr. McKay in Pittsburgh. I want his home number not the office number. I don't know his first name, but he spells it capital *m*, small *c*, capital *k*, small *a, y*." Yelling back through the office door at me she asked, "Mr. Manfredi there probably will be a dozen McKay doctors in Pittsburgh. Can you give me any more information?" I really didn't want to. I was already feeling guilty about something that hadn't even happened. *How stupid*, I thought. "Yes Francine," I yelled back with great abandonment, "his wife's name is *Chris*." Now that's stupid!

***

The rest of the morning was business as usual. Just before lunch, Francine came into my office. She reported finding one Dr. McKay with a wife named Chris but they would not give out their home number. She handed me a small piece of paper with a phone number on it and added, "The doctor's first name is John."

Francine is a very accepting secretary. By now she would have either asked me if I wanted something to eat, or she would have done an about-face and headed out the door. Why was she hanging around? I tried to hide my guilt.

"Yeah, this uh, uh . . . Chris McKay was a friend of Sally Carpenter's and I'm trying to contact her to verify and ask her a few questions about Sally. I just don't want any more surprises in Amy's life."

I was lying through my teeth and I didn't know why, and using Amy made me feel all the more guilty. I could tell Francine bought it all.

"How about something for lunch?" That's the Francine I know and love.

"No thanks, Francine, I'm having an early dinner."

Her smile held as she did an about face and marched through the door, shutting it as she exited. Privacy at last!

I picked up the phone and called the number. I was told that under no conditions would I be given the doctor's home phone number. That if I wished to talk to Dr. McKay directly, he would return to the office at two o'clock.

Sure I'll talk to him after two o'clock, and say what? "I met your wife on the train. She's fabulous. Her perfect smile with beautiful breasts gets me. Or . . . she called and I'm returning her call. Or . . . I would like to take her to *The Nutcracker Suite*. Or . . . I would love to fuck her!" I thanked her and hung up.

I immediately picked up the phone and dialed a number. The phone rang once.

"Bakery."

"Uncle, I need some information. I need to get an unlisted home phone number of someone in Pittsburgh. Any ideas?"

"Tony, tell me the name."

"It's a Dr. John McKay; his office number is M.O. one,

five, zero, seven, five. I need it because--"

Uncle Joe interrupted. "I'll call you back as soon as --" He hung up.

The rest of the afternoon dragged by. I was putting my desk in order when the phone rang. On the third ring I looked at my watch. It was five thirty. Francine had left. I had to answer it.

"Hello, this is Tony Manfredi."

"And this is ya Uncle Joe. M.O. one, five, oh, seven, five's home number is M.A. one, five, t'ree, seven, four. Say hello to Connie and the family."

He hung up. His last words echoed in my head. *"Connie and the family! Connie and the family!" Does he already know? Dumb, Tony, dumb.*

I pressed down on the headset lever, released it and dialed the operator asking her to connect me person-to-person to Chris McKay at MA 1-5374 in Pittsburgh. I hung the phone up thinking how smart of me to just say *Chris McKay.* Chris could be a guy. There's no way this Chris could be a guy. I thought back on our train ride and, although her breasts seemed ever present, I remembered how spirited she was, and even when talking of the awfulness of New York City, there was this pleasantness in her manner. Her voice was so energized, so full of expression.

My thoughts were interrupted by the ringing phone.

"Mr. Manfredi, I have Mrs. Chris McKay on the wire."

Was it my imagination or did that operator punch the word *Mrs.* a little hard. The operator went off the line, there was a click, and I heard, "Hello."

I didn't answer because I wanted to hear her talk more in an attempt to make sure it was the same Chris from the train.

"Hello, who's calling please?" That still wasn't enough.

I jumped in.

"Can you speak a little louder this is long distance calling and I . . . we don't have a very good connection." Another lie.

"Hello, this is Chris McKay." She was speaking louder and slower.

I took a breath and asked, "Is this the same Chris McKay who has a sick father in Philly?" *Oh my God*, I thought, *why did I use that as a test line?*

"Is my father all right? I mean, yes, this is the same Chris McKay who has a sick father in Philadelphia. Please, who is this? Is my father okay? Hello!"

It was a cruel test but it worked. In a calm voice I asked, "Is this the same Chris McKay who hates New York City--too crowded, too expensive? If it is, you have just won an all expense paid trip to deserted New York."

"Tony, Tony Manfredi?"

Jackpot!

"Yes, Chris, it's me. Sorry about the father business. It was cruel. But I wanted to make sure I was reaching the right Chris, and that was the only thing that came to mind. I couldn't wait for you to call me; in fact, I was not sure you would have. It's nearly been a year."

"I would have. I planned on it. Tony, how did you get this number? John prides himself in keeping his residential number a big secret."

"Chris, how I got it is unimportant. Now we can talk. I know there are several weeks before Christmas, but I am going to New York next week, and if you were going to do some early shopping or catch the rehearsals of *The Nutcracker*, perhaps we could meet and have lunch, or a cup of coffee, or something." I could hear my voice trailing off at each request.

"Tony, when will you be going and for how long?"

I was encouraged. "I'll arrive next Wednesday and stay until Friday. Chris, I would really love to see you."

"Me, too." She was as nervous as I. "I'll go to Philly and see my dad, and train in from there on Wednesday. It will be late in the afternoon, so we can't have lunch. Perhaps that cup of coffee? I'll have to almost turn around and head for Pittsburgh."

"Chris, can't you arrange to do some shopping Thursday so you won't have to rush back?" I wanted her to stay, spend the night . . . with me.

"John would think I've gone crazy after all the nasty things I've said about the City. I can't and I shouldn't."

"Then coffee it is. Call me at the New York office and let me know what train you'll be taking and I'll meet you at the train station. My number is--"

She interrupted. "Tony, I kept your card, I'll call you Wednesday." Now her voice began to trail off. "I can't believe this."

"I can. See you Wednesday."

As soon as I hung up I picked up the phone and again dialed the operator. This time it was for the Statler Hotel. It was not where I usually stayed, it was further to the office, but it was directly across from Penn Station. I was very excited about seeing her, and driving home I imagined us together in the hotel. *Ease up, Tony, it's only a cup of coffee.*

***

Everything that happened in the next forty-eight hours

happened at the eleventh hour. Tuesday, I was literally walking out of my office when the phone rang.

"Tony, Uncle Joe. Okay on housin' plan."

This time I was short. "Thanks, Uncle." I hung up.

Wednesday morning, I was in the New York office waiting for what I hoped would be the final meeting on the Bedford Plan. I was nervous as a cat. The phone rang. I snatched up the receiver. "Hello, this is Tony Manfredi."

"Do you know where I can get a cheap single seat for *The Nutcracker*?"

My nervousness disappeared. "Yeah lady there's this scalper who hangs around Penn Station. He'll help you out."

"If he's the tall, dark, and handsome one, tell him I'll be there on train number one oh nine at five twenty-seven.

"He'll be there." We both hung up.

I grabbed my presentation material and was off to see Richard Q. and the gang.

The morning flew by, and so did the presentation. Lots of questions with lots of right answers. We took one pee break at ten forty-five. While mingling in the hallway, a gravelly voice, accompanied by a cloud of cigarette smoke, came up from behind me.

"Tony, you're doing great." I turned and there about a foot away was Karen Hunt. A tall, thin woman, dressed in a masculine, herringbone suit complete with white shirt and rep tie. Cigarette smoke like a light gray, inch-wide ribbon ran from her mouth, over her thin top lip, up into her nostrils. It stood out against the backdrop of chiseled cheeks and chin, sharp nose, and a severe short haircut.

"Thanks Miss Hunt. It's an exciting project."

She took my arm and guided me a few steps away from the others. "Tony, the name's Karen. And it's exciting because you make it so. The numbers speak for themselves, but the descriptive, the sales pitch, is what will make it go." I was outwardly pleased, because I knew Karen would say the same thing to Richard Q. and it would register loud and clear.

"Thanks Karen, but I owe a lot to Bob Flanagan who is very supportive and has given me a lot of room to put it together."

She took a long drag on her Camel cigarette then forcefully blowing the smoke out of the left side of her mouth, said, "Flanagan's an asshole. He'd cut your balls off in one second if there was a problem." Another big drag, this time she held the smoke in, releasing it as she continued to speak, adding heat to an already hot conversation. "He'd cut your balls off 'cause he doesn't have any of his own. Richard Q. knows, and Richard Q. will deal with it when the time comes. Meanwhile keep your head down and your nose clean."

She noticed I was staring at her cigarette that had developed a long ash. She tipped the cigarette with her index finger dropping the ash to the floor and said, "Things can happen that quickly. It's time to go back in. Kick some ass."

We worked through lunch. Huge platters of cold cuts and cheeses were brought in complete with cherry tomatoes, pickles, black olives, and lots of garnish. The only drinks available were bottles of Coke and ginger ale. I reached for the sliced bread and realized just how white-bread the entire room was. My name was the only one that ended in a vowel. Even the lunch was Waspy. Not a slice of salami, or provolone cheese. The closest it came to being ethic were the black olives and I guess the cherry tomatoes could qualify.

Following another pee break I was heading back into the conference room and there standing by the cylinder of sand was Karen. She took her last drag and buried the cigarette butt in it. With her other hand she gave me a close to her vest thumbs up and whispered, "We'll be out of here in a few hours and you'll be a hero for a long time."

I smiled and looked down at my watch. A few hours would get us out by six, the bullshit good-byes . . . six thirty, a half hour to get to Penn Station . . . seven. *Shit, I'll miss Chris by an hour and a half! I don't even know what time she's leaving to go back. Shit!* Here I was involved in a major career move and I was pushing to get out by five fifteen to meet some lady I met once. It didn't make sense, unless you're determined to live on the edge.

At five twenty I was putting my papers away, the meeting was over, and it was a success. Thank God, Richard Q. had leapfrogged over some insignificant issues.

"Tony, nice work." A broad smile came over Richard Q.'s square face. It matched his size. "If you have time we're going up to Forty-Five and have a pop or two." *Shit!*

"Richard Q. I would love to but I'm running to the train." He looked puzzled. "Aren't you going to be here tomorrow morning for the final review?"

"The review, oh of course. I'm not taking the train home I'm going to meet my old Uncle Joe, who's training in from Providence. When he heard I was coming to New York City he wanted to know if I would meet him and take him to see his older sister in the Bronx and have dinner with them on Arthur Avenue. He doesn't get around much and his sister isn't well." *What bullshit!*

"What time is his train coming in?" I didn't know if he

was asking to see if we could squeeze in a drink or if he was really interested.

"Around five thirty. They usually run late but I . . ."

He reached over and with his huge hand closed my briefcase. "Get going. No uncle should be left waiting in that hellhole; Karen will see to your briefcase." He looked over to Karen. With a lit cigarette wedged between her index and middle fingers she saluted us both. "Karen, call my driver and tell him to take Tony to Penn Station on the double. Tony, see you in the morning and say hello to your uncle." He laughed heartily and left the conference room followed by all the attendees, like ducklings waddling after their mother.

***

Thanks to the waiting limo I arrived at the station's track 28 at five forty. The 109 had just pulled in. Discreetly I glanced into the glass case housing a poster advertising a Broadway musical. It was THE KING AND I. There was Yul Brynner, bald and in bloomers, and me, a full crop of black wavy hair. I checked my tie, hair, general appearance. Not bad. I felt eminent success within the company, as well as my other career. I unconsciously began to hum, "Getting to know you, getting to know all about you." I thought of those wonderful thirties and forties movies that ended with scenes at railroad stations. Love affairs, heart-wrenching good-byes, long runs down platforms, him or her jumping off the train into the embrace of their lover, sealed forever in the steam of the engine and the closing credits. Why did all those things happen at the end? My love affair, I hoped, was only beginning. Was I nervous or excited? I really didn't know the difference. Should I stand at the doorway, or go onto the platform to meet her?

I started to move through the doorway, when I got my answer. A huge arm crossed my chest.

"Detraining passengers only, bub."

Well he wasn't exactly another Choo-Choo but I got the message. I took a few steps backward. Between the conductor stopping me, and the rush of people exiting, I saw petite Chris, being swept along with the crowd. She almost slipped by me. I forced my way through a cluster of passengers and came up behind her. Grabbing both of her upper arms I bent over. Yelling a whisper through her hair into her ear, "Anyone for *The Nutcracker?*" She turned to me and it was as if the entire station had suddenly emptied.

All I could see was her, all I could hear was my heart pounding, all I could feel were her arms firmly held in my hands, and at that very moment all I wanted was her. She turned in and answered, "Tony, you made it."

"Did you have any doubts?"

I could tell she was as nervous and as excited to see me as I was to see her. She didn't know where to place her glances. My brown eyes followed every move, until they captured hers willingly. "There's a quiet little restaurant across the street let's go and have that cup of coffee." As I turned her around the crowd and the noise returned. In a gentlemanly fashion I offered her my arm. She took it. I placed my hand on hers, and within three steps she placed her hand on mine. She was more beautiful than I had remembered. So refined, delicate, sensuous.

We came out of the station and the cold air forced us to bundle up, bringing our bodies closer together. Never leaving each other's side we darted across Seventh Avenue. Back on the side-walk, we laughed at our sprint to safety. She yelled, "You have to take smaller steps, or learn to carry me." I picked her up so her body cradled my arms, "There will be no small steps with us." Boldly, for the first time, we kissed each other on the lips. It was a kiss that would stay with me the rest of my life. In my darkest hour, I could conjure up that moment and feel the softness of that kiss. Its warmth on that cold night.

Nothing was said for the next few moments until we entered the restaurant. I helped her off with her coat, she unraveled her scarf, and when she removed the navy blue woolen tam from her head, her soft golden hair fell perfectly even with her shoulders. I took off my scarf, topcoat, and hat and in one heap gave it all to the hatcheck girl. Still not a word was said. I cupped her elbow and guided her into the dining area. Finally I broke the silence.

"A quiet booth for two."

A very dapper maitre d' acknowledged my request. I slipped him five bucks. He reacted like I gave him a hundred.

"Thank you sir! Madame, do you wish an aperitif?"

She looked at me, questioning.

"May I order for us both?"

She nodded approvingly.

"Your smoothest brandy at room temperature please." I took a deep breath and unnecessarily adjusted my necktie. "How was the train ride?"

She brought her hands up from her lap, spreading her fingers on the table. Her gold wedding band glowed in the candlelight causing a battle between my guilt and annoyance. She sensed my discomfort and gently returned her left hand to her lap, well out of sight, then calmly answered, "It was fine. The time goes by when you . . . when you . . ." She was having difficulty coming up with the right word.

I said what I felt. "Fantasize?" As if in slow motion she uncomfortably moved around in the booth. It excited me.

"Well women are not supposed to fantasize. That's reserved for men only, but I did fantasize about our meeting. So in answer to your question, the train ride was wonderful and very scary at the same time."

Our brandies were delivered on a tray, in two snifters, along with an unlighted candle. The maitre d' bowed slightly and offered to warm them further. I really didn't want him hanging around so I tasted mine and nodded acceptingly. He placed Chris's snifter in front of her and left, leaving his paraphernalia on our table.

She picked up her glass with both hands. I, in proper masculine manner, held the snifter in the palm of one hand. I reached across the table and as the two glasses clicked I toasted, "To fantasies, scary though they may be, they are wonderful." We both sipped the brandy and as it warmed my body, I knew it was doing the same to hers.

"Chris, I don't know what this is all about, or why the telephone calls, or why we are even here, but all I do know is I'm glad. I do have fantasies, and I didn't know if I wanted them to go beyond that stage, until I saw you. You are more beautiful than I remembered. If all we have now are minutes, then I'll accept that. I want us to meet again and again, but not for minutes."

She took a sip and I could see a calm coming over her. "Tony, I want to and will see you again. It's so strange for me to be doing this. It's out of character. When I think about it, it's almost laughable. I meet you on a train, we have this carefree, innocent conversation, we say good-bye and I can't forget you. I was almost wishing you wouldn't show up so I could put these feelings to rest. And when you did and I felt the strength of your hands on me, I knew I was in for an emotional roller-coaster ride. I don't know anything about you, but like you, I feel this incredible closeness that makes our being together special."

She reached across the table with her left hand and touched mine. Her wedding band seemed to all but vanish. I didn't care about anything except us. Her marriage, mine, our kids, our other lives. I cupped her hand in both of mine. She watched as a part of her disappeared.

"Chris, I know where I want this to go, but I know I don't want it to be this way. Like you, this is out of character for me. I'm not a player. I don't travel the railways of the nation trying to pick up women." We both appreciated my trying some humor. "I haven't felt this way about a woman in a long time. It's not that old cliché' stuff I feel like a kid again. This is very adult. I don't want to have sex with you. I want to make love to you. Jesus, I can't believe I'm saying all this. This is not what I had thought about."

She stopped me cold. "What were you thinking of?"

I looked down at her tiny hand being held captive in mine and slowly, deliberately answered, "Sex. I thought we would meet, run up to my hotel room, which conveniently is in this building, have sex, and go our separate ways."

I raised my eyes from our hands and looked directly at her. "That is until I saw you, touched you, kissed you." Our eyes were locked together, and in the silence that followed, I saw her bosom heave. Through her beige, silk blouse the tip of her breasts protruded so strongly, that the entire outline of her nipples appeared. This time she made no attempt to hide her signal. I squeezed her hand tightly, and with my eyes riveted to her breasts, felt my own stiffness coming on. I was barely able to whisper, for fear of exploding in my trousers, "When?"

She too was breathless. Was she also about to explode? "I'll . . . I'll be in New York the week before Christmas. Same old routine. We could meet then. I don't know how or where, but that's when I'll be in the City next."

A little more relaxed now, I said, "Our birthdays." She looked at me in a puzzled way. I picked up her expression and ran with it. "Our birthdays, Chris. They're only a day apart. Let's celebrate our birthdays together. Will you be in town for them?"

She looked defeated.

"Yes, Tony, but part of the routine is dinner with our friends on the--" She looked at me with an animated question-mark face. The game was on! I picked up the challenge.

"Eighteenth! But what year, the lady hasn't said."

She laughed, "Right. And the year will be announced later. Much later!

"Tony, we have dinner on the eighteenth and it would be impossible."

I let her off the hook. "Chris, birthdays are a big deal in the Manfredi family as well, so the seventeenth and eighteenth belong to our families. Let the nineteenth be our day of celebration. Yours and mine."

We lifted our snifters and together we sealed our fate with a click and a sip. That click chiseled the nineteenth in stone.

With our emotions under control I asked her about herself. In a shorthand version she gave me her life story. Her drone delivery saddened me. She was an only child. Her mother was very strong--domineering to be exact. Her father was an educated man. A man of culture who appreciated the art of life: the beauty of a rose, the sound of a symphony, the love of his daughter. Both parents came to the marriage individually wealthy, which enabled them to live their lives individually. Her mother was very generous with her time--for all acceptable charitable causes that is. He, twelve years older than his wife, dabbled at employment as a writer/editor of the cultural column in the Sunday *Philadelphia Inquirer* and consultant to the State of Pennsylvania for the Department of Arts and Education. Chris's nanny, Rose, died when Chris was seventeen. Even now, she loved and missed her surrogate mother. From K through the twelfth grade, Chris attended the same all girl's Catholic school, and at age seventeen had her debutante's coming out party catered on the lawn of their home.

She didn't date much, and when she did it was usually sons of people who her mother thought were "correct." Her father understood the stifling that was taking place. He was living it, and sadly had surrendered to the convenience of his lifestyle. He tried unsuccessfully to convince his wife that their only daughter should go abroad to college. Instead, like other members of her family, she attended the University of Pennsylvania, where toward the end of her freshman year she met her husband to be, John.

When she mentioned he was ten years her senior, and her father's name was also John, it was clear to me she was unconsciously bringing her father into her marriage. It was also clear that husband John was not a man of the arts, but a driven doctor, totally immersed in his practice. There, his ego was stroked daily. As for that private time with his family, all that business about keeping his home phone number a big secret, was so that he could spend time with his two sons to the exclusion of Chris, or lock himself in his study, working on his latest paper that would save the human race from one plague or another. His desire to be immortalized in the annals of medical history was obsessive.

Chris on her own decided to have a second child. She knew too well that the life of an only child was not the best. Her first son, approved by husband John, was, of course, named John. Her second son came nearly two years later. She was reprimanded by her husband for "not watching it!" He was named Albert by his father after, you guessed it, Schweitzer. They lived comfortably, not as grandly as her parents, but very comfortable. Their summers on the Jersey Shore started precisely the day after school was dismissed, arriving back at home precisely the Thursday before Labor Day, because Dr. John did not want to deal with "all that Labor Day madness." During the entire summer he would appear just in time for Friday's dinner, and stay until exactly six thirty Sunday, immediately following dinner. He would call every Tuesday and Thursday at exactly six p.m. His vacation consisted of two weeks. The first week commenced July second, because he could take a few extra days wrapped around the Fourth. The second week started on the second Friday in August. The latter was dedicated entirely to fishing with his fellow doctors and their sons. No wives, no daughters.

During this entire autobiographical spew, she only brightened when she talked of her father. It was painfully obvious that this beautiful woman was living her life wrapped up in gauze. Never clearly seeing out and certainly no one seeing in.

Her story was over. I reached across the table and had to pry open her tightly clinched hands. The story interesting for me was painful for her. I pulled them to my side of table extending her arms as far as they could go. I bent over slightly and kissed each opened palm. They were moist from her emotional tale. I closed them and whispered, "Hold them until the nineteenth." It was time to go.

I pulled out enough cash to pay for the drinks plus tip. Her dark brown pleated skirt seemed to stay in place as she swung her legs around the edge of the booth. She had the most shapely legs. Small ankles. Perfect calves with just enough muscle tone. Like she had on the train, she caught me looking, and like on the train she was embarrassed. She attempted to straighten her skirt and get up at the same time.

I crouched down Chinese style and held both of her hands in her lap. "You don't have to be embarrassed with me."

She squeezed my hands tightly bringing them deeper into her skirt so I could feel the warmth of her swallowing them. Her mouth was totally parched so her lips nearly stuck together, she managed to whisper, "I'll never be embarrassed whenever I'm with you--only wanted."

The walk back to Penn Station was silent. We held each other's hand tightly. Through that union, messages of warmth, desire, love were transmitted. There was no reason to talk. We both knew we would be together, and the next time, we would be closer.

The platform was dimly lit and crowded with commuters.

"The seven-oh-five must be a popular train. Look at these people." I was making small talk. I did not want her to leave. I wanted her to stay . . . with me . . . in my hotel.

"Chris, don't go. Stay." Her tiny hands clutched both of mine, and although she was unable to wrap hers around mine, I felt totally, tenderly engulfed.

"You know I can't, but you know I will. The nineteenth is ours. I hope it will always be ours. I am stepping out into something that is so unexplainable, so frightening, so alluring . . ."

I brought her hands closer to my chest and as her body pressed mine I could feel her breasts, soft but firm, surround our hands. We kissed gently on the lips. I didn't want anything to move or change. Our kiss grew deeper. Beneath our coats, jackets, sweaters, skirts, trousers, a sexual battle broke out. Her breasts, bursting toward me, attacked first. My penis, now firm with lust, countered. What started as a tender kiss exploded into oral passion. Our tongues leapt into each other's mouths, darting, searching, feeling, swelling out of control. Her mouth was no longer parched as in the restaurant, but wet with our exchange. On cue the whistle blew, the steam shot out from below the train, "All aboard" was yelled, and she left my arms for the Pullman. No tears, no good-byes, but little gasps of frustration, minor attempts at composure, and the unmistakable knowledge that we wanted each other desperately.

The train slowly rolled past me. She had just left my arms and already I missed her. I stood there as the swirl of steam all but vanished and the train was no longer in sight. I was the last person remaining on the platform. Leaning forward, to do what I don't know, I looked down and saw the tips of my shoes overlapping the platform edge. She had brought me to the edge. Do I step back or remain?

8

THE THURSDAY MORNING review went per-
fectly. Everything was approved, including the responsibilities
list. Richard Q. joked, "It's only right that the Italian amongst
us handle vending machines." If only he knew.

The remainder of the day was dedicated to company
headquarters' office politics. Meaningless visits behind closed
doors, ear straining in the men's room, an out of the way luncheon with my boss Flanagan, where he told me he was pitching me for his assistant's job in New York. There was no position
there, but he was trying to create one. I was fulfilled with my
company accomplishments, but impatient waiting for the other
life. Whatever it was.

Fortunately, no one invited me out for drinks or dinner so
I was in my hotel room early, right around dinner time. I ordered
some room service, worked a little, but really found myself fak-
ing it all. I thought how maybe I should just check out and head
home. I had to leave early in the morning anyway. But when I
checked the train schedule, it wasn't worth the dash to the next
train and the one after that got in too late. I thought about call-

ing Uncle Joe and telling him I had control of the vending machine situation, but decided calling him from my hotel was not a wise thing to do. Already I was being careful.

Nothing seemed to hold my attention. I lay on the bed, flat on my back, fully clothed in trousers, shoes and socks, shirt and necktie. I loosened my tie and stretched my arms up toward the ceiling. Looking at my hands I slowly brought them down to my nose. I had hoped, twenty-four hours later, that I could still smell her. I would be satisfied with the slightest scent. Nothing. I clasped my hands together placing them behind my head. The warmth of the pillow against the back of my hands relaxed me. I was forcing myself to think company thoughts. Usually during moments like this a phone ringing in your ear is disturbing. This time it was a welcomed sound, for it gave me something to do. I reached over and picked up the receiver. "Hello."

As if speaking in a tin can, the operator asked, "Mr. Manfredi, will you accept a collect call from Dr. Chris McKay?" I couldn't say yes fast enough.

"Tony, this is Dr. Chris McKay. I called to report you passed yesterday's physical with flying colors." I smiled.

"Doctor I appreciate your call and thank you very much for fitting me in. But for the fees you charge why are you calling collect?"

The playing doctor game was over. "Tony, I'm at home and John's at a hospital meeting. The boys just went to bed and I was thinking of you. I had to call collect because John checks the telephone bill very carefully. He's convinced the cleaning woman calls long distance to every member of her Southern family."

"I'm glad you called. Call collect anytime. I've been thinking of you too. Today was a quiet company day, and I just couldn't get you out of my mind. In fact I was just lying on the bed trying to think company thoughts but couldn't because they were erased by thoughts of you."

She took a deep breath. "They must have been strong thoughts, because I felt them all the way down here."

"Chris, they were beautiful, loving, sensual thoughts. God, I wish you were here."

Another breath. "I will be, I don't want to stay on too long, so I'll say good night and think of you lying there. See you on the nineteenth."

Before I could say anything else I heard her softly click off the line.

Chris looked through the window into the darkness and realized how alone she was. Married yes, mother yes, but so alone. Except for her father she was so isolated from the males in her life. But then there was Tony. The stranger on the train.

9

IT WAS THREE O'CLOCK on the dot when we sat down for dinner at Uncle Joe's. With twenty people gathered around the Thanksgiving Day table, it was shoulder to shoulder, but no one cared. Everyone welcomed the thought that we would not be moving from that table for the next four or five hours. It was holiday time and Aunt Ella, as always, did it up.

Antipasto. Fresh roasted peppers with anchovies, home-made pickled eggplant that was "put up last year," thinly sliced prosciutto ham, spicy salami, imported provolone cheese that had such a bite it itched the roof of your mouth. Big green olives and bitter, black, wrinkled ones. Everything doused in virgin olive oil and dark wine vinegar.

That was the cold antipasto! The hot one, called *mista fritta*, was served at the same time. Dipped in egg batter and deep fried, these pieces of celery, artichoke hearts, cauliflower, and huge mushrooms were piled high on a platter and set in the middle of the table. With this came the tomatoes, mushrooms, bell peppers, artichokes all stuffed with breadcrumbs and herbs.

That morning, Uncle Joe had Emilio bake and deliver, huge round loaves of bread. He came upstairs carrying his offering. With his half-smoked but unlit stogy, firmly stuck in his toothless mouth he reminded me of an Italian Popeye cartoon. One glass of wine, a "Happy Thanksgiving" toast, and he was off to his own celebration. The loaves, still warm, where sliced and placed at strategic points on the table.

Some ziti macaroni was next, along with meatballs, sweet and hot sausage, braciole, rolled beef stuffed with bread crumbs, olives, and other "secret ingredients."

And finally the turkey! Big, browned to perfection, and juicy. It was stuffed and surrounded by sweet potatoes, and white potatoes, and whole onions and carrots and . . . and . . . and . . . cranberry sauce, both whole and jellied, freshly made applesauce, and boats of thick mushroom-based brown gravy.

As always Uncle Joe did the carving. And as always he made the first toast, then anyone at the table could follow. To my Cousin Letty, any day now the man of her dreams will come into her life. To Cousin Lou thanking God he returned from the war safe and sound and with a good job. It was my turn. "Thank God for my family, my job." And pointing my glass directly at Uncle Joe I continued, "And to the future." He put down his carving utensils and lifted his wineglass in a returning gesture.

"*Saluté*, Tony; *saluté tutto famiglia.*" Our eyes locked. The softer blue of his eyes confirmed our toast--to both families. Indeed I had a lot to be thankful for. The Bedford plan was a major feather in my cap, my family was healthy and caring, the vending machine deal was placed with the proper company, and in a few weeks I would be with Chris.

***

The three weeks went by quickly. Chris and I had one brief telephone conversation. She sounded nervous or frightened. We wished each other happy birthday and confirmed our afternoon meeting at our little restaurant on the nineteenth. Nothing else was said.

I walked down Seventh Avenue toward the Statler in the first snowstorm of the season. The air was crisp, clean, and the falling snow, like Chris's kiss, was pure. I hoped the snow would stick and that more would fall guaranteeing a white Christmas. A white Christmas. How perfect. I entered the restaurant and immediately began disrobing. First my soft hat. I unraveled my scarf. Finally, in one simultaneous motion, I tucked a glove in each of my coat pockets, and wrestled my way out of my double-breasted, tan polo monstrosity. Each removed article shook loose some snow. I watched a beautiful flake dissolve into a tiny droplet.

The same maitre d' greeted me as if I were a regular. I hadn't noticed how elegant a man he was. A Cary Grant type. He introduced himself as Ralph. Ralph! Not Rafael, Ralphino, but Ralph!

"Your party is waiting. I sat her in the same booth."

"Ralph I'm impressed and I am . . ." I hesitated for one guilty second. Then with abandoned bravado I extended my hand and answered, "Tony, Tony Manfredi."

As soon as I saw her sitting there, it happened again just like our first meeting at the train station. The entire room emptied. No sounds, no people, only her. As I approached the booth she looked up and smiled. It was a timid, nervous smile, but it washed over me melting away my lingering chill.

Ralph was doing his job. "Madame, Monsieur Manfredi." He bowed and left.

Caught up in his elegant introduction I reached across the table and in a gallant gesture picked up her hand, bent down and kissed it, and whispered, "Madame McKay." I sat down next to her. We were already closer than the last time. It was as if we were together for years. So easy to talk to. So relaxed. So genuinely interested in each other's conversation.

***

It was less intrusive just to follow Ralph's luncheon suggestions. When the shared dessert and coffee was served, we both knew the time was near. Our conversational tones changed. The phrasing became softer. There was a breathlessness in our delivery. I could feel the cadence of my heartbeat and my pulse pick up. There was a low burning excitement building up throughout my body.

She was talking and for the first time during our luncheon I was not listening. I had wandered into the land of lust. I wanted her, needed to have her.

She paused in her conversation. It was my moment. I slowly reached for her hand. I imagined the veins on my wrist pulsating to the same rhythm as the pulse growing in my groin.

As soon as our hands touched, Chris, through a deep swallow whispered, "Tony, ask for the check."

As if he had the booth bugged, Ralph appeared with check and coats in hand. I reached into my wallet and left a stock of bills covering our luncheon and a very Merry Christmas tip. Ralph did not reach for the money but knew he was in for a special holiday treat. He merely smiled and swung the table out enabling Chris to exit ladylike.

She passed between Ralph and myself and began heading for the exit. Cupping her elbow I gently turned her in the opposite direction. She seemed a little confused as she looked to me, then Ralph, and the exit. Ralph, who was not at all confused, draped the coats over my arm, bowed and disappeared.

Leading Chris, I began to walk toward another door. We exited the restaurant and entered the lobby of the hotel. We took a few steps and stopped to look at each other. In those few seconds of hesitation we knew. This was what we both wanted. An arriving elevator chimed, and as if inviting us to enter our love affair, its doors opened and closed around us.

***

I never woke up before to such a montage. A snow-filled street, a quiet restaurant scene, a silent elevator ride, carefully edited lovemaking images that seem to have accelerated the act. Everything was woven together. I didn't know if I was dreaming or if I was awake. I couldn't get my bearings.

Lying there in bed, Johnnie Ray began singing "Cry" out of the bedside table radio. I was awake. I dropped my arm down toward the floor and positioned it so my watch picked up the light slipping from under the bottom of the closed bathroom door. Seven fifteen. I had to think a.m. or p.m.

Of course p.m. or else why would the bathroom light be on.

At exactly that instant I threw the covers back, and with a completely awakened and excited body ran to the bathroom door. I swung open the door and the entire bathroom hit me like one big flashbulb popping in my face. The whiteness of the walls and tile, together with the brightness of the chrome fixtures screamed, "Empty!"

For another split second, while the spots dissolved from my eyes, I thought, *Maybe it was a dream. A fantasy.* But I knew it was real. I could still feel the presence of her body. I wrapped my arms around my bare shoulders, protecting them from the winter night air slipping through a slightly opened window next to the bathroom door. I entered the bathroom and placed my head down into the V created by my arms. The scent of her filled my every pore. *When did she leave? Is she coming back?*

God I missed her and we were only together a few hours ago. I smiled inwardly as I remembered kidding her about her scent. "Baby powder! Johnson's Baby Powder!" But in that innocent scent she was alive. I lifted my head and now completely in focus saw some writing on the mirror above the sink. I walked over. The radiator warmed the tiled floor making my slow barefoot steps comfortable.

In small print, right in the middle of the medicine cabinet mirror was *12-19 ALWAYS* and under that line an imprint of her lips. As if calling out to me I bent over the sink and gently kissed the lips on the mirror. I was hopelessly lost in the memory of our lovemaking, when I was quickly brought back to reality as my semi-erection touched the cold porcelain of the sink. I jumped back feeling very foolish.

My foolishness turned into anger. "Always!" I yelled and bolted out of the bathroom. What the hell was the name of her hotel? Maybe she just went downstairs for something. Why didn't she wake me up? I began pacing. It's a very funny sight. Me naked, pacing back and forth, covering my private parts from the cold air at one end of the room, while waving my hands frantically the rest of the time. All this to the accompaniment of Johnnie Ray's "If your Sa-wheat-heart, sends a let-ter of good-bye . . ."

I didn't care about being discreet. I picked up the phone and clicked the bar. Plopping down on the bed I asked the operator for the Waldorf.

The phone began to ring, just as my friend Johnnie was heading for his big finish, "Soo let your hair down . . . and go on baby and . . ." The Waldorf answered, and I faded out Johnnie's last big note.

"Dr. John McKay's room please." It began to ring and ring!

"I'm sorry sir there doesn't seem to be anyone in the room. May I leave a message for Dr. McKay?"

I turned on a bitchy, faggy intonation, "Well, operator this message is really for Mrs. McKay, not the doctor. Would you please ask her to call Mr. Mann her hairdresser before she leaves the city? Thank you and Merry Christmas to you, too!"

I hung up the phone rather pleased with myself. Where did that come from? It was a fun piece of business. I jumped out of bed and headed for the bathroom to take a leak. As I passed the mirror I looked at the writing and the now slightly smudged lip print. *She'll call.*

***

I walked back to the bed; sitting there for a moment, calming myself I called Connie. I was too guilty to stay on the telephone with her, so I told her I was up to my ass in the proposal, I was going to have a quick drink with some of the corpies and probably order room service. The kids were fine. She was fine.

Her "I love you," stung my ears. I couldn't respond. I hung up feeling pretty low. The hell of it is I do love her very much.

I tried to justify my actions as one of those casual businessman-out-of-town affairs, but deep down I knew that was not so. I had never experienced such an incredible sexual encounter. I knew my feelings for Chris went deeper than sex, or did they?

The phone rang. I instinctively looked down at my watch. Nine ten. "Hello . . . hello?"

Someone was there, but all I could hear were background sounds. People talking, laughing, room noises.

"Hello," I said a little louder.

A delicate whisper-like voice came through the other end. "Mr. Manfredi? This is the afternoon maid, Chris. You sure made a mess of your room."

My heart started pounding. "Madame, why did you leave my chamber with nary a fare-thee-well?"

She giggled.

"Chris, where are you? I woke up and you were gone. Jesus, I miss you. Come back."

"Tony, I can't. I'm at dinner with John and our friends. I couldn't concentrate on anything except you." She was leaving the first thing in the morning.

Her voice grew quieter; I had to strain to hear her.

"Know this, it was the best I ever had; it was the best I ever gave." She sighed.

I closed my eyes and I could see the dryness of her mouth breathing into the telephone. I was instantly aroused. "Chris--"

She interrupted, stronger this time, "I have to go, call me next week."

10

"SPRING HAS SPRUNG" and so did a lot of other things. The Georgia-based South Bedford Mills plant was on schedule and well on its way to being completed. During the entire process, I was able to get as close as anyone gets to Richard Q. Indirectly, through Karen Hunt, I was told he liked my style and thought one day I could be important to the company. Directly, he promised me the first set of sweaters that came out of the mill.

"Hey, Tony, he means it," said Karen in a swirling cloud of cigarette smoke. Coughing uncontrollably she spit, "He usually takes firsts on everything. You're real special."

I came up with a North-South plan that made sense to the company and the organization. The blending of my two lives began to take shape and I loved it. It gave me the prestige I expected with the company and the edge I longed for with the organization.

The company was trucking down, practically nonstop, all the equipment for the moving of the mills. Often the trucks returned to the North empty.

The South is where most of the cigarettes for the world

are made, and it presented an opportunity to get the organization involved. If we could get our hands on tons of cigarettes, before the tax stamp, I could arrange to have them delivered by the company-owned trucking company, M. R. Trucking. They could be distributed for a profit everywhere.

"Tony, who's gonna drive em?" Uncle Joe asked me as we discussed it over coffee an' at Lilla's before Easter.

"Uncle, I can handle that, more important, who's going to get them?"

"Tony, I know some people in Atlanta. The Ciancolas. They've helped out before. They can get the cigarettes. We've had screwups in the shippin'. It's amazin' how many hijacks take place. Some we don't even know about!"

There was one little tooth ache!

From the very beginning a Georgia based newspaper, *The Georgian Journal*, started a campaign against the company and the move. We were known as the "same post war carpetbaggers that invaded the South after the great Civil War." It was annoying and had to be dealt with, but first things first.

I called Dom Triano. I explained the plan and told him to make it sound like his caper. He got a few of his buddies to drive the trucks. Through the company's transportation department I arranged for the legitimate drivers to drive the mill equipment South. One rig was left behind and after securing a hauling contract the other was driven back to the North with two drivers. It was reported as an efficient usage of M. R. Trucking manpower. The Ciancolas gave us the cigarettes on an as needed basis.

Dom would make the call. "Mr. Ciancola, do ya think we can get 'lucky' next Wednesday?" Wednesday he went to the Ciancola warehouse and picked up a truckload of Lucky Strikes.

Or, he would call and say, "That 'old gold' bracelet I need, can it be ready by Thursday? I wanna give it to my wife Friday for our anniversary." Like clockwork, Thursday, M. R. Trucking would show up at the warehouse and pick up a load of Old Golds. No hijacking, no problems. Everyone shared in the profits. Like my old days as a sales coordinator I arranged everything and made sure everyone got what they needed when they needed it. And I had a place to put my profits.

Back when my uncle gave me the money in the bakery he suggested I get a safety deposit box at the Haven Vault Company. I did. It was a large, three-story, cut-stone building, with a heavy slate roof. Located in the middle of the downtown industrial area, if you didn't know where you were going, you would never find it. It had no name or street number.

After going with him a few times to make a "deposit," I stupidly asked him, "What bank is it associated with? Is there insurance on what you put into the boxes?"

"Tony, it ain't associated with no one, 'cause most of the people who deposit there don't wanna be associated with no one. As for the insurance, no one's lost a thing there yet."

I was intrigued by how they only allowed one person per floor. But that's the way they did it. One depositor, one time, one floor. No guests!

I only kept cash in my safe with a simple hand written note to Connie. It said:

MY CONNIE,

WHATEVER IS HERE IS YOURS TO DO WITH AS YOU LIKE. BUT KEEP IT IN CASH. I LOVE YOU. YOUR TONY.

It was a wonderful, secret little game. I had placed several thousand dollars in my safe. There was a great comfort in knowing it was there waiting for me.

***

The Southern deal offered more than just cigarettes at a profit. I decided to make a Northern run with Dom. I wanted to experience it all. The notion of running a stolen load of cigarettes excited me, and besides Dom and I would have screams talking about the old days and our plans for the new ones. I also liked the idea of Boss and Underling.

Standing on the corner in Macon, Georgia, I saw Dom pull out of the Ciancola warehouse. It was obvious by his gear shifting that he had a full load. He slowed the rig down just enough for me to run alongside for a few feet and jump up onto the running board and into the cab. As soon as I slammed the door shut I was overwhelmed by the loudness of the radio.

"Have Mercy, Mercy Baby" was blaring away. Just as the backup singers sang, "Have mercy, mercy Baby," Dom in rhythm yelled, "You're a careful mothafucka, and I gotta hand it to ya." In perfect sync with the beat, Dom pulled a chain releasing two blasts from the roof-mounted air horns. He was having a ball. Still singing along with Billy Ward, he continued, "Let's go home, Tony Manfredi!"

We pulled onto the highway and traveled maybe ten miles when Dom reached over and turned down the radio. "Fuck!" He yelled looking into his outside rear view mirror. "A fuckin' cop. I wasn't even speedin'. Fuck!" He down shifted and started to pull over to the shoulder.

"Hey, Dom, so much for me being a careful mother."

"Tony," still looking in the mirror he said, "pretend you're sleepin'. I'll keep you out of it."

The huge Mack truck came to an abrupt stop in a swirl of dust and hissing air brakes. Dom left the engine running. He pulled up the emergency brake and jumped out of the cab onto the pavement.

I closed my eyes and slouched down in the corner of the cab. I positioned myself so with just the opening of one eye I could see, through Dom's rear view mirror, the cop and Dom at the rear of the truck.

The next time I peeked, they had walked behind the trailer out of sight. Thinking they were coming around to my side of the truck I started to reposition my body so I could see out of my mirror.

I heard some creaking, metal-on-metal sounds, some muffled voices and a huge slam. A few seconds of quiet passed and Dom's door opened. He jumped in. Just as he reached down to release the brake the police car pulled alongside of us and entered the highway at full speed.

"Can I wake up now Dom?"

Dom started complaining, "That fuckin' cop, pulls us over for nothing." He gestures to the speedometer, "He doesn't say I'm speedin'"--he gestures to the light switch on the dash--"or my lights ain't right." Then, with both hands gestures wildly around the cab, "Nothing.

"He wants to know what I'm haulin'. I told him cartons. He wants to see. So I open the trailer door, and like a fuckin' neon sign blinkin'"--his two hands are opening and closing--"is Lucky Strike! . . . Lucky Strike!"

Dom placed both hands on his chest and continued his

tirade. "He asks for my driver's license and company card. I show him and he says okay take it easy. Can you believe that shit?"

"Dom, that's it?"

"Yeah, do you believe that shit. I got a hot load screamin' Lucky Strike and that's it!

"Hey, Tony, maybe the reason he let us go, he thought you was Snooky Lansing from Your Hit Parade." He started to laugh loudly. "Can you imagine Snooky Lansin' singin' "Have Mercy, Mercy, Baby" like the Dominos do it? What a fuckin' joke."

He started to imitate Snooky Lansing doing the song. If I hadn't been so puzzled about that cop stopping us I would have appreciated the humor of it more.

"Dom, I couldn't tell. Was that a local cop?"

"Nah, Tony, he was a state cop. He told me he's been patrolling this stretch of highway for years and seen some bad stuff. He wanted me to drive safe and enjoy"--Dom went into a full southern drawl--"wondaful Southern hospitality, and ya all come back, ya heah."

I couldn't put it together. Why did this state cop pull us over?

Except for the radio playing some great blues, we drove for the next hour or so in silence. The warm air flowing through the open windows of the cab added to the peacefulness. The quiet was disrupted by Dom's double-clutching and downshifting. He slowed down and started edging off the road and headed into a huge parking lot loaded with trucks of all descriptions. A red, white and blue neon sign two stories high blinked ANZIO TRUCK STOP.

"This is the joint the cop told me about. It's supposed

to be the best food on the highway. He said the guy who owns it survived the Anzio beach landing. He swore he'd never let it be forgott'n."

We had a bowl of navy bean soap and a BLT. Served up with pride by Master Sergeant Jasnowski. To prove his rank, on one of his large arms was a tattoo of master sergeant stripes. They were clearly visible because he neatly shaved the hair away. He was the best short-order cook I have ever seen work and he saluted us as we left.

We weren't on the road fifteen minutes when a car pulled alongside us. The passenger was yelling to Dom and pointing toward our trailer wheels. His pointing and yelling became so animated it convinced us to pull over.

As soon as the truck came to a complete stop, Dom jumped out of the cab. I looked in his rearview mirror and saw the car fade behind the trailer. Within seconds a man appeared at my window. At first, all I could focus on were his teeth. Those that remained were rotten or covered with chewing tobacco.

He pointed a long barreled six-gun at me and said, "Now y'all be real nice and we k'n get this thang over with, real quick like."

I was totally taken by surprise. I looked through Dom's cab window expecting him to appear with his hands in the air. He didn't and I began to worry about him. He can be such a smart ass, and I felt these hillbillies would just as soon shoot him then put up with his shit.

The door opened and there was Dom in one piece, but I could tell by the look on his face he was pissed. He looked past me, toward my new running board friend, and said sarcastically, "These hicks said they'd blow your head off if I didn't drive them to where they wanna go. Do you fuckin' believe it? We are fuck*ing* hijacked!"

The unwanted passenger waved his gun. "Now that ain't friendly. But hell you Northern boys don't got much upbringin' anyhow. So just start up this rig and drive on down the road till ah tell ya to turn. 'N der-rive slow cause ah don't want tah fall and hurt mahself."

Dom did as he was told. We drove about a quarter of a mile and our guide yelled, "Ya turn at the next road. Ya kannit miss it. It's got a big ole pile of stones painted white 'longside."

This tobacco-chewing rebel was getting under my skin. I could see the pile of stones ahead. I flashed back on Pittsburgh and Choo-Choo, on what Uncle Joe would think, on the money I would lose, on how pissed off this whole thing was making me.

As calmly as I could, I said to our pirate, "Well, Mr. Ted is not going to like this one bit. This cargo is a hands-off shipment."

I waited for some response. Nothing. I tried again. "Buddy, did you hear me? I said, emphasizing *Mr. Ted*, "Mr. Ted is not going to like this."

He looked at me in the strangest way. "Ah don't know no Mistuh Ted and ah ain't yaw buddy, so you best be quiet 'n drive afore ah lose mah tempah." I guess you have to be an Italian goon to know Mr. Ted.

As we approached the pile of stones, Dom downshifted to slow us up, and started his wide turn onto a little dirt road. The cab of the truck bumped up and down, and swayed from side to side as we went from pavement to dirt. My rebel was having a tough time negotiating the turn. His hand that held the gun was well inside the cab, and it bobbed up and down with every bump.

His other hand, totally encrusted with black grease and dirt, was locked onto the outside rearview mirror.

There was another huge bump and the gunman's arm sunk low into the cab, nearly touching my leg. Instinctively, I grabbed his arm, bent it back at the elbow and yanked the gun loose. He tried to bolt, but I held the back of his coat and neck pulling him closer. I had never held a real gun before, but like a pro I stuck it in his face, and calmly, angrily said, "Relax you shit kicker or I'll blow that fucking chewing tobacco through the back of your head."

His eyes bugged out as I brought the gun closer to his mouth.

"Dom, how many are there?"

Dom, whose hand was welded to the stick shift, answered, "Two others, but there might be more at the end of the road."

I looked at my frozen prisoner and asked, "Well now what do you all think? How many and where?" He couldn't get his eyes off the barrel of the gun. With a shaky voice he answered, "Jest me 'n mah two brothas, tain't no one else."

"Shit kicker you'd better not be lyin' or you're dyin'," snapped Dom from across the cab.

"Ah tain't lyin', 'tis just the three-un us."

"Well, Dom, do you believe him?"

Dom looked at him and then looked at me and answered, "I'd be tellin' you the truth." Then he sniffed the air in the cab. "I think he shit his pants and he's not about to meet his maker with that load."

I appreciated his humor. "Dom, I got to tell you, I feel like a jerk. Here we are hijacked, I got this asshole by the short hairs, and I don't know our next move."

Dom laughed. "Tony, from here on it's routine. I'll stop
the truck, where Mr. Shitass here tells us to. One of them will get
out of the car and come to my side, the other will stay in the car;
when we're both out, they'll ask us to unhitch the trailer, and if
they don't get nervous or crazy let us drive off into the sunset.
That's the hijacker's routine."

Dom's facial expression changed from monotonous to
mischievous. "But we gonna fuck 'em up. Right? Right! You just
hold on to that cocksucker 'n leave the rest to me. By the way, if
I need help, please feel free to jump in."

I touched the hick's lip with the barrel of the gun. "Now
you will tell us where we're supposed to stop, won't you?"

He nodded. We headed down the dirt road for about a
hundred yards. There was a gradual hill. As soon as we reached
the top, my captive told us to pull up under a big tree on the
downside of the slope. We did. Dom looked over and whispered,
"It's time to rock 'n roll!"

Dom's eyes were riveted to his rearview mirror. "Just as
I figured. This yo-yo is walkin' up to us like it's Easter Sunday.

"Tony"--Dom continued without taking his eyes off the
mirror--"just hold on to your guy."

My grip grew tighter, and I parted his lips with the barrel of the gun. I could feel the pistol's metal scratch against his
rotten teeth.

From Dom's side of the cab came a bodiless voice. "Now
y'all come on down here or mah brotha will surely blow yaw part-
nas head clean off."

Dom opened his door and for a split-second, between
Dom's body and the steering wheel, I saw the hijacker standing

there all alone. Dom's huge frame blocked my view as he lunged out of the cab, completely covering the unsuspecting thief, knocking him to the ground. In quick moves Dom was on him then off him. Now standing behind the bandit, Dom's left arm was firmly wrapped around his catch's throat while his right hand held the pistol, pressing the barrel against the back of its former owner's dirty neck.

"Hey, Tony, look what I caught. Now I got one too!"

"Dom, for a guy who eats so much you're pretty quick. So far the routine is right. What about the car in back?"

Dom and his prisoner took a few steps to his right and looked back to the car.

"Tony, one more hick with a shotgun."

Dom spoke to his captive. "Is he your brother too?" He nodded. "Good, then tell him to throw his gun out the window or he's gonna be two brothers shy. *Tell him!*"

"Red," yelled Dom's captive, "we'd betta not mess with these boys, y'all throw yaw shot gun out the windah and come on ova here quiet like."

Red complied.

Dom told both of them to lie face down on the ground. They did. I instructed my guy to back up onto the truck fender as I opened the door. I walked him around to the other side and now there were three.

Dom gave them a quick frisk and found no other weapons.

"Tony, I hate touchin' these 'ski-vos-es'"--*schifosa* is Italian slang for unclean people--"I feel like I should hose down right away."

"Dom, I want to find out how they knew about the load."

Dom pushed my guy on top of the two brothers so he was back to back with the other two. Dom asked me to see if there was any rope in the truck. There was and I handed it to him. He made a loop at one end and placed it around the left wrist of brother Red. For the next several minutes Dom pushed, rolled and shoved our captives around on the ground. In a maze of dust and flying rope he cinched their wrists together. Somehow I had the feeling Dom had done this before.

He told them to stand up. After some slipping and stumbling they finally made it to their feet. It was a comical sight. Our hillbillies could not believe what had just happened to them.

Proudly, Dom pointed to his catch and boasted, "Tony, they look like the Three Stooges tryin' to be hillbilly hijackers." He pulled at the rope, walked them over to the big tree and wrapped them around it. The outer two faced us while my captive, the poor bastard in the middle, was getting his face crushed against the bark of that old magnolia. Dom tied the wrists of the outer two together. They were secure.

"Dom, check out the car while I talk to our friends."

Dom handed me his gun. There I stood facing the three men with a pistol in each hand. I wanted to relish the moment. I loved it!

I started my inquisition. "I'd like to know who I'm dealing with. Now I know his name is Red"--pointing the gun to Red--"now who might you two be?"

"Will," said my rotten tooth man.

"Rusty" mumbled Dom's catch.

"Red, Will, and Rusty. Good wholesome names. What is this hijacking business all about?" Silence.

"Boys, I asked a simple question. I'm curious. Anyone?"

Will spoke up. His face, tight against the tree trunk, caused bits of bark to fall with each word. "Is y'all the law?" Dom came out of nowhere and answered the question. "Kinda. We make sure none of the rules get brok'n . . . and you fuckas broke the rules real bad. So answer my man's question or . . ." Dom walked over and put the shotgun under Red's chin.

"Red this twelve-gauge is yours, and you know what a mess it can make. So?"

Red was more than happy to talk. "We doin' some robbin' heah 'n theyah. But we ain't hurt nobody nohow."

I asked, "This robbing you're doing is it always hijacking?"

"No sir" Red continued, "We jest taken to hijackin' 'cause it's been so easy."

I became curious. "Easy? How come so easy?"

Will interrupted, "Red you hush up!" Dom was on Will in a flash. He pushed the shotgun against Will's jaw, wedging Will's face between the magnolia trunk and the twelve-gage's double barrel.

"Will, if Red hushes up, you get opened up."

Red spoke up, "Will should ah?"

Will squeezed out two words, "Damn sure."

"We git some inside information, from a brotha."

It was my turn. "Brother? How many brothers are there?"

Red answered, "We three 'n Ray Don."

"He's the inside information guy? Ray Don?"

"Yessuh."

"Where is he and where does he get his information?"

Red suddenly sounded frightened. "Will, ah don't know what ta say. Will?" There was silence. A slight breeze came up making the air smell sweet.

Dom released the shotgun pressure from Will's jaw.

"Tony, I know that name. I seen it somewheres.

Ray Don . . . Ray Don. Shit! Where did I see that name?"

Dom and I started retracing our steps.

"Dom, I got it. The cop! Why did he pull us over? Even you said you weren't doing anything wrong. And why did he want to see the load?"

Dom was straining to put the visuals back together. He did. "Tony, he was wearin' a fuckin' nametag.

Whenever a cop stops me I always go to the badge number. I can't remember his, but I remember the nametag, Ray Don Schaffer." Dom spun around to the three captives, "Hey Curly, Moe, Larry, you're last name wouldn't be Schaffer by any chance?"

Finally, Rusty, the only one of the Three Stooges who hadn't spoken up lamented in the deepest bass voice, "Ah swayah, Ray Don is gonna be rightly angry at us."

"Rusty, boys, you pay no never mind to old Ray Don. Just tell him things didn't go your way.

"Dom, let's hit the road. Leave these guys here, they'll find their way out, but let's at least make it interesting for them."

Dom checked all the knots. They were tight. He exchanged my two pistols for the shotgun and headed back toward their car.

It was an old beat-up dark green, four-door DeSoto. He put a bullet in each tire and then opened the trunk and put one in the spare. He put the sixth bullet right through the middle of the windshield making a clean hole right under the rearview mirror. He tossed the pistol as far as he could into the open field.

He jumped into the truck and started it up. "Tony, I'm gonna make a U-ee; hope Ray Don's not gonna give me a ticket!" He started laughing and drove the truck up the dirt road about twenty yards and in one move made the U-turn.

I backed away from the threesome, knowing Dom would cover me with the remaining pistol.

I was in the cab and just as we were about to take off, Dom fired one shot into the tree trunk right above Will's head. Dom yelled, "Make no mistake about it, boys, don't fuck with us or the next one will be between your eyes. Y'all come North and visit, ya heah!"

11

THE TRUCK ROARED back onto the highway. We
were on course heading North toward the Carolinas. The excitement from the caper was dying down and I wasn't happy about
it. I wanted it to go on, just like the others. In fact I wanted more
of the gunplay edge. I liked holding two pistols. I liked Dom's
shotgun antics.

Our awkward silence was broken when simultaneously,
but using different words, we talked about and agreed on, how
those hillbilly hijackers can't get away with that bullshit. We
have more loads heading North, and the other guys might not
handle it as well as we did, and besides, they're fuckin' with the
wrong guys! "Dom, the map shows there's a town coming up
called Mathison. If it's big enough I got a plan."

It was big enough for us to store the rig behind a motel,
rent a car, and head back on down the same highway.

"Dom, old Ray Don said he patrolled the same stretch of
highway, so it should be relatively easy to find him."

Find him we did. Dom spotted him just as he was pulling
into Anzio's. The late afternoon haze gave the big neon sign an

eerie glow of importance. We pulled our rent-a-car directly across the highway from the diner's one-way exit.

I got out and lifted the hood. Dom sneaked out of the front passenger's side into the backseat and lay down alongside the twelve-gauge. Our officer must have only had a cup of coffee, because he was out of the diner in about ten minutes. As soon as he approached the exit driveway I started waving my arms moving over to the highway side of the car. He saw me and like a Good Samaritan threw his red lights on and shot across the highway pulling in front of our car. He climbed out of his car and walked toward me adjusting his black gun belt. My eyes immediately went for the nametag. It was our boy all right.

"Officer, thanks for stopping. My car just crapped out and I can't figure it out."

He looked at me. I was sure he recognized me. It only added to the excitement.

"Well, boy, the way ya was wavin' I sure thought you was in bigger trouble than a stall. I ain't no mechanic, but ah k'n call ya a tow trucker who is." He started to turn away and head for his car.

"Officer, maybe that's too big a deal. I think I know the problem. Do you know anything about battery cables?"

He looked at me in disdain. "Hell yes, ah do."

Putting on my best pleading face I asked, "Then, Officer, could you just look and see if I'm right about the battery cable being disconnected?" I gestured to the passenger side of the car. I led. He followed.

Ray Don placed both his forearms on the fender of the car. As soon as he looked under the hood he had two surprises. Both of the battery cables were firmly attached, and before he could rise to chew me out, the second surprise was my sticking a six-gun in his ribs.

"Now Ray Don," I said softly, "Red, Rusty and Will send their best, but if you don't do exactly as I say I'm going to deliver you my worse."

He immediately began to sweat.

I reached behind him and unbuttoned his revolver holster and eased the weapon out making sure it was below the car's fender level so no one passing by could see. I put it behind me slipping it into my belt. I could feel the barrel rest on my butt.

"Now Ray Don just ease over to the back window and put your head and shoulders inside. I'll talk to you from the front window. We can kinda visit."

His sweating continued, a mixture of two parts fear, one part anger. He positioned himself as instructed. Dom, still lying flat, produced the double-barrel pointing it directly at the cop. "Well, Officer Schaeffer, how about a Lucky? No. How about an *un*-Lucky?"

I put my head through the front window and in "company-ese" said, "Gentlemen, the reason I called this meeting was to clarify the company policy on transportation. It can be a very quick constructive meeting, or it can last an eternity."

Dom jumped in, "Like dead Ray Don, you know, ee-turn-na-tee."

I picked up from where Dom left off. "Officer Schaeffer, if you understand, all that is needed is a nod of approval." He reluctantly nodded. "Now, Officer, I can tell by the way you responded that perhaps this is not your favorite moment and you would like it to pass, but perhaps, with some explanation. So simply put, there will be on occasion some M. R. Trucking rigs coming through this area. Under no conditions should they be stopped and certainly under no conditions should they be relieved of their cargo. Officer, nod if you understand." He did.

"Now, Officer, there will be repercussions if this policy is violated." Dom couldn't hold back, "Yeah, like percussionin' your whole fuckin' house." I looked at Dom, and it was obvious we were both enjoying the game.

"Thank you. Well put. My associate does have a way with coming to the point. Officer the agenda is complete. This meeting must conclude. So just to review, we know who you are and where you live, and we expect you to follow policy. Although your brothers are temporarily out of commission they are in good health. We also expect to remain in good health. But just in case, we have arranged for some associates to stop by and visit your brothers, that is, if we're not at a certain place by a certain time. So we must run.

"Oh, there is some good news. If the policies are adhered to, you and your brothers can expect a bonus for your cooperation. Please go to your car and speed off into the sunset. You can return later and pick up your gun, which will be waiting for you by the roadside."

I followed him to the front of our car. He got in his car and sped off. I slammed our hood shut and jumped in. I remembered the pistols. I emptied both of them and tossed them out the passenger's side window.

"Tony, I'm kinda use to havin' this twelve-gauge next to me, so if it's okay with policy I'd like to keep it for awhile."

"Fuckin' A, Dom, fuckin' A."

***

Several weeks and many uninterrupted hauls later, Dom was traveling the same highway. He saw Ray Don's squad car in the Anzio lot. He pulled off the road and ran back. He placed a Scotch-taped brown paper bag on the front seat. The bag was addressed to Red, Rusty, Will, and Ray Don. In it was five thousand dollars.

12

ONE WEEKEND WITH THAT kind of excite-
ment kept me going for all those weeks that were normal . . . regular. The North-South plan still had that tooth ache: *The Georgian
Journal*. The newspaper was published in Atlanta, but its circulation included the entire state.

For generations it was owned and operated by the Wyatt family. Just under *The Georgian Journal* masthead were two
bloodhound dogs. The one on the left, perfectly placed under the
t of the *The*, held a tiny American flag in his mouth. The one
on the right, under the *l* of *Journal*, held the Confederate flag.
Stretched between them, mouth to mouth, was a banner that
read *THE WATCHDOG OF THE STATE*.

They believed in their motto, and for whatever the reason, were trying to put the Bedford Mills in the doghouse! The
campaign first appeared in their editorial section, which was
meaningless as no one reads the editorials anyway. But then it
began to appear in all sections of the newspaper. Virtually every
day they carried negative stories on the project. Always linking
it back to "that Northern owned M. R. Tedes Company," they

stuck to their carpetbaggers theme. With statements like "The only reason they are here is to take advantage of our poor working class . . . deplete our crops . . . break the Northern unions . . . impregnate our women . . . disrupt the harmony of our coloreds . . . destroy the South!"

We still weren't concerned until they pasted a series of pictures all over the front page of Richard Q. and his entourage stepping out of the company plane. The headlines screamed, NORTHERN COMPANY HEAD BRINGS GEORGIA TO ITS KNEES! The picture showed Richard Q. stepping out of the DC-3 onto a small square platform, held in place by a colored man on his knees. That picture should have driven Richard Q. crazy, but it was another one that got him nuts. This one showed the entourage, all identifiable, except for a beautifully dressed, long-legged woman.

"Jesus H. Christ!" He threw the newspaper across the conference table. "Karen, get Alan Morris down here right away. No bullshit excuses why he can't come South." Karen was on her feet and headed for the door. She stopped, spun around, returned to the table, retrieved her newly lit Camel, and left.

As soon as the door closed he turned to me.

"Tony, this Southern plan is your baby. Morris is coming down to help. Help *you* out!" He leaned forward on his elbow, and pointed his Waspy, long, manicured index finger at me. He had positioned it in such a way so his eyes peeked over the knuckles of his hand. He was taking aim and I knew it!

I had a few choices. Should I jump up, break his Waspy finger and tell him, "If you want to flaunt your snatch, then take the heat" . . . or calmly pacify him with "I'll do whatever you suggest."

I chose the middle ground.

"Richard Q, with all due respect, the plan is working perfectly. I was not asked to be a part of the P.R. campaign, but as you may recall, you voiced your concerns from the very beginning, and I included a two-part plan as a single vital strategy in the overall scheme. The first was to deal with our leaving New Bedford and the establishment of the New Bedford Housing Projects for low-income households."

Richard Q. started to interrupt with what I knew was going to be a boardroom tirade. I cut him off.

"Excuse me sir. The second part, was to deal with the Southern notions of the North. To my knowledge, the North has been handled; however, it is obvious the South has not. Be that as it may, I will, with your blessing, get involved and get the matter settled . . . and soon."

He backed off. "Tony, you have a direct approach to everything. I like that. Not only do you have my blessing, but I'll tell Morris you're the point man on this one." He smiled, "I like you, Tony. You have brains and balls." With that, he was on his feet, heading for the door. I called after him, "Have a nice evening. Enjoy their Southern comforts."

I knew he was going to sashay over to the hotel and enjoy some of his own Southern comfort. Namely, that long-legged, mysterious passenger.

Alan Morris arrived late the next morning. He went directly to the Bedford Mill's offices. He was a slight man, with short, dark, curly hair that perfectly matched his perfect, tightly cropped, beard. He was built in such a way, that whatever he put on his back, which was always expensive, looked . . . perfect! Even in the near noonday warmth, he dressed, looked, and acted cool. Light tan three-piece suit, white batiste cotton shirt, beige and pale yellow stripe tie, topped off with a natty white Panama hat.

I was impressed with his low-profile control. When he arrived he knew he was in trouble with Richard Q. I was impressed with his efficiency. Out of courtesy, he shook my hand, opened his alligator briefcase and pulled out a manila file. Labeled in red print was COL. WYATT. He had somehow, in a short period of time, put together a dossier on Colonel Andrew J. Wyatt III.

His oral salutation was a question. "Why are all these Southern boys called Colonel?" In my mind I smiled, thinking, not all of them, accompanied by the vision of the Three Stooges tied to the magnolia tree.

I didn't want to verbally fence with him so I simply accepted his thesis. Picking up the file I asked, "What do you have to go on?"

In a most gentlemanly fashion he took it out of my hands and placed it on the conference room table. It remained closed.

"He's a good old boy, a native son." Out of character, Alan began playing at being a Southern preacher. "Parents, grandparents, great grandparents: all Georgians. Both sides! Pillars of the community, God fearin', profit lovin' folk! Own lots of things: property, businesses." He took a deep breath and continued. "I suppose people. Had to own people way back then when coloreds were slaves and whites were . . . colonels."

Morris smiled and liked his little impersonation. So did I. He walked around the table and took off his jacket. Fastidiously placing it over the back of one chair, the preacher routine was replaced by the cool PR man.

"Can a person get a cold drink around here?" I thought, *He's like an iceman. The last thing he needed was a cold drink. What he really needed was something hot!*

"Absolutely, Alan, what would you like? A soft drink, ice tea or lemonade?"

Without hesitating he asked for lemonade. I opened the conference room door a crack. My two-lemonade order interrupted the secretary's *Life Magazine* reading. When she got up to fetch the drinks, I couldn't help notice *The Georgian Journal* on the seat of her chair. The little Southern belle was reading the dirt and ditching it under her butt!

I thought of Chris's fabulous derriere, then how I got her phone number from Uncle Joe, then how I should call Uncle Joe to try and get a lead on the good Colonel, and finally how the information probably would come from the Ciancola family.

I looked back into the conference room and Alan was picking what appeared to be lint off his shirt. "Alan, I have to get something and use the men's room, I'll be right back." He ignored my statement and kept on picking.

Alone with the secretary in the outer office, I instructed her to give him the lemonade and make sure the glass was spotless. She was young, and in a plain Jane sort of way, attractive. The rear of her full cotton skirt was partially caught in the crease of her ass. She indeed did have a nice one that gently flowed from her tiny waist. *Lucky newspaper!*

I headed down the hall into a small office. I called Uncle Joe at the bakery, asked him to check out the Colonel. He said he would contact the Ciancolas and either he or Mr. Ciancola would call me. I gave him my hotel room and phone number.

When I entered the conference room Alan was holding the glass of lemonade up to the light.

"Alan it's a good year. *Vintage la Georgiere, dix-neuf, fifty-two.*" He barely acknowledged my attempt at humor.

"Tony, one can't be too safe these days. Especially down here, where their hygiene is years behind ours."

I reached for my glass, lifted it up and in a toasting gesture asked, "What's the plan?"

As if ignoring my question he first answered, "This is good lemonade." But then he took a big swig and continued, "You and I go see the Colonel." It was the first time I felt included in his thoughts, but the inclusion was empty, as I knew it had only come about because Richard Q. had spoken.

As Alan finally began to open the manila file for us to review, the coldness of this legitimate business, versus the warmth of the illegitimate one, came home to roost. There was such a difference in the purpose and personnel. The company was so colorless, so void of emotion, cold. While the organization was full of color, in its people, its purpose. It overflowed with passion, danger, and results. The company was the perfect front for the organization. I had the best of both worlds.

***

It took Alan nearly three days of constant phone calling and message sending to set a meeting with the Colonel. At least he got a response. I hadn't heard a thing from either Uncle Joe or the Ciancolas. The confirmation to Alan's tenaciousness came to the Macon plant in a telegram.

MR. MORRIS:

COLONEL WILL MEET WITH YOU. STOP.

ONE HOUR WED 2PM. STOP.

HIS OFFICE ATLANTA. STOP.

REGARDS

RJ, SECT.

Alan slid the telegram across the conference room table. "Well, Tony, we have a date with the good Colonel. He gave us the privilege of driving all the way to Atlanta to meet with him for one hour. What a generous man." Alan was not the least bit happy. I on the other hand, had a gut feeling that the end result of this entire episode would be profitable.

"Alan the good news is his newspaper hasn't been paying much attention to us for the last few days. Maybe the attack is over. Maybe he's willing to back off."

Alan wasn't buying any of it. "Tell me Tony, what's the bad news?"

I took his jab on the chin and countered with a knockout punch. "He's waiting until Thursday's edition."

***

I don't know why I expected to see people running around yelling *Copy boy!* Or huge rolls of white paper going into a maze of machinery only to come out the other end as completely printed, neatly stacked, packages of newspapers. I guess I went to see too many movies. Instead we entered a huge, three-story, Carrera marble rotunda. Directly ahead was a stairway that resembled a graceful bridal train. Ascending the milk white marble staircase, my hand cooled on the matching white banister. We landed on a wide balcony that continued for a 360-degree circle around the entire second floor.

Looking up to the top of the dome, painted on the ceiling was an enormous man, whose white hair almost looked silver. He stared down on us. Dressed in a white three-piece suit, he held a Panama hat over his heart. His other hand was raised above his head in a Statue of Liberty pose, clutching a rolled up newspaper. He held it tight, like a club. From either side of the mural came the bloodhounds. Larger than life, they looked vicious holding the flags and banner in their mouths. I turned 360 degrees to read the banner; it was the same as on the newspaper masthead . . . THE WATCHDOG OF THE STATE. It was a strong visual.

I was still staring at it when I heard a voice echoing throughout the rotunda, "Mr. Morris, the Colonel is expecting you." Both Morris and I looked in different directions until I spotted a tiny man peering over the third floor balcony. "Go to the third door on the right. It will be open for you. Once you are in the stairwell, you can't get lost, there is only one exit."

He disappeared and as we followed our instructions, the only audible sounds were our heels clicking against the marble floor. Just before we reached the third door, I looked up over the banister at the ceiling. I whispered, "Alan I think they changed their Sistine Chapel. Probably after the Civil War." He joined me in my upward gaze. I pointed to the left, "See, looks like the American flag was painted in and look to the right at the word *State*. I think *State* use to be *South*." He was unimpressed. He reached for the slightly ajar door and we were on our way to meet the Colonel.

We entered a tiny, darkly paneled office. We were immediately greeted by the small man from the balcony. He looked down at his gold pocket-watch. Prissier than on the balcony, he continued. "The Colonel appreciates punctuality. You are right on time. Please sign the guest book and I'll announce you." He pointed to a black leather bound book that was placed at the corner of his tidy desk.

"RJ do you have a pen?"

He quickly turned. His squinted eyes and tightly sealed lips dared one of us to repeat the question. I did.

"RJ . . . pen?" He reached into his inside jacket pocket and pulled out a beautiful Waterman fountain pen. Unscrewing the top off, he couldn't help himself: "The Colonel also appreciates efficiency." I couldn't help myself, "RJ that's why he's got you." We both signed and waited for our official introduction.

RJ opened two mahogany doors. With Morris on one side of him and me on the other, in unison we stepped into the Colonel's office. RJ reached down into his testicles and came up with the necessary vibrato, "Colonel Wyatt, Misters Morris and Manfredi." He backed out between us, pulling the doors closed as he exited.

"Gentlemen, this is yaw meetin', but mah clock's tickin'." He sat behind a huge mahogany desk. On it was an ornate brass ink well, flanked by two opened mouthed, pen-holding bloodhounds. A black leather-bound desk blotter; a magnificent Tiffany lamp; a crystal ashtray, unusually mounted on a two-inch high brass ring.

All this glitter made the inactivity of the desk more obvious. The entire office was void of any wall decoration. The four walls were paneled with dark wooden three-foot squares and windowless. The two doors we just came through disappeared perfectly into the woodwork. The floor was covered in the plushest cream-colored carpeting. Two inviting black leather chairs were symmetrically placed in front of his desk. His chair, his desk, our two chairs. That was it. No other furniture.

The Colonel could have been the man in the big painting out in the rotunda. They dressed alike, looked alike, but their eyes reflected a different look. The rotunda Colonel had a twinkle. Our host's eyes were vacant.

Alan started, "Colonel I'm glad we were finally able to get together. I flew south just so we could have this talk."

The Colonel locked and loaded and took his first shot. "Well lots of *foul* fly south when the temperature changes."

Alan undaunted proceeded. "Colonel, Bedford Mills has come South, to Georgia, for one purpose, and that is to continue to operate the company, profitably of course, but to offer the consumer, quality at a reasonable price. We were unable to do that up North. We are not here to quote *The Georgian Journal* 'as Carpetbaggers,' unquote. We think, and we would like you to believe, we can become an asset to your state."

Alan was pleased with his opening remarks and sat back in his chair. The Colonel was not buying it. "Mistuh Morris, suh, that's pure unadulterated poppycock. Y'all don't believe for one minute that ah am dumb enough to buy that bull-shit."

Alan leaned forward and tried to say something. The Colonel leaned forward on his desk and shut Alan down. "You just wait boy. Your Northern company's heah to take advantage of our po' folk, both white 'n colored. Steal theh land, pay them both 'nigger' wages and put the, to quote you, 'profits,' in your pockets." The Colonel was grandstanding and proud of it.

I knew these two guys would continue to verbally beat each other up and that would lead nowhere, so I interjected, "Colonel, differences can make for positive as well as negative results. What can we do to at least try and change your mind? We're here to let you know we're not the bad guys from the North. Like your newspaper, we have morals and responsibilities. Also, like your newspaper, we are a profit-oriented company."

He looked over to me. It was my turn. "Y'all must be Man-whatever. Ah didn't thiank you Eyetalian boys spoke so nice." I wanted to jump up and give him an Eyetalian whack that would knock him all the way back to the plantation. Instead I did the company thing and took the shot. Hating myself I half-smiled and answered, "Colonel I guess it's the schooling. You know, take us off the streets and into universities, you never know what might happen." He smiled and leaned back in his chair.

"Ah hate to thiank what might happ'n if some of our folks got schoolin'."

As he spoke I focused on the ashtray and the two-inch-high brass ring supporting it. It was a shackle! A slave's shackle that was brass plated and used to hold a crystal ashtray!

I knew this meeting was about to be over so I locked and loaded. I leaned forward and lifted the crystal ashtray off the shackle. I unclipped the lock and with both hands started opening and closing it.

"Yes Colonel, I wonder what would happen if some of your folk got schoolin', got smart, got work?"

He was furious. He jumped up out of his chair, and reached into his top middle draw pulling out a newspaper. "Ah was goin' tah wait till this meetin' was ova to give y'all my latest suhprise. Well the meetin' is ova soona than expected so heah 'tis. An ad-vance copy of tomorrah's *Georgian Journal*. We're gonna be all over you like a kudzu."

I had to ask. "A what?"

"A kudzu, boy, is a vine of the South. It grows so fast it k'n smothah almost anythin' it has a mind to latch on to."

He tossed the newspaper onto his blotter so the front page faced us. Three huge pictures side by side of Richard Q. and our long-legged mystery woman jumped off the page. Him holding her elbow going into a restaurant, them holding hands across a candlelight table, them holding each other's waist going into his hotel.

The headline told it all: "Can the Future of the South be Left in the Hands of the North?" We didn't have to read the text. Alan lifted the newspaper, folded it and said, "Colonel I'm sorry that's the way you feel. You just cost my family and me our position with the company."

I almost gagged. Alan wasn't even married! The Colonel didn't budge. He'd won the battle to save the South. I reached into my pocket and threw a nickel on his desk. "Thanks for the paper."

As soon as we were safely on the sidewalk, I took over. "Alan, let's face it, Richard Q. is going to go crazy when he sees the paper. But who cares about the South! We have to keep the story out of the Northern papers, and off the A.P. . . . U.P.I. . . . or whatever those news wire services are called. That's your job. I'll pick up the pieces down here."

Alan looked at me and for the first time I saw a hint of compassion. "Tony, you got the tough assignment dealing with that Southern putz. I can handle the North and the wire services."

I didn't stop instructing. "And we have to team up and handle Richard Q. together, or both our families will be without breadwinners." He knew I was giving him a little ribbing and we both smiled.

"By the way, Alan, who is that woman anyway?"

He just looked at me without a thought of answering.

"Come on Alan, not that it really matters, but I'm curious, and I think she's great looking."

Alan gave in, "Tony, I have a good feeling about you, so I'm telling you and then you can forget it. Richard Q. is one of the great players of our time. He would screw anything that looked female and was still moving. His favorite? Prostitutes. Screw, pay, leave. No commitments, works into his schedule, nice and clean. This prostitute is different. He thinks he loves her. Whenever he travels he takes her along. Only the immediate staff knows. He has never said anything, but she must be a great lay. He's nuts over her. I think he would be more pissed off if he lost her than losing his job or his family. He's nuts over her." He shook his head; he had a tough time digesting his last statement.

"Jesus, Alan, Richard Q. in love with a hooker? How do you figure it? Well let's go and save the happy couple!"

***

I dreaded going to the mill the next morning because by then Richard Q. would have read the *Journal* over breakfast, and I was sure before Alan and I had a chance to discuss our plan, we would be out of our jobs. But I wasn't about to go down without fighting.

I instructed Alan to get the latest financials on the *Journal*. One might think that would be difficult to come by in less than twenty-four hours, but the company had the resources to do it.

I, on the other hand, called on Uncle Joe to speed up the inquiry into the paper, and in particular, into Colonel Wyatt III. Uncle came through with flying colors. I knew I couldn't share it with Richard Q. and Alan, but I would use it, if I had to.

Richard Q. surprised us all. He came in with the newspaper tucked under his arm. Alan, Karen and her Camels, Richard Q., and I sat around the conference room table. Richard Q. calmly addressed us, "Alan, Tony, the *Journal* is getting on my nerves. I want that Southern gentleman's balls. It's become a personal matter with me now. Tony, there would be no reason for you to know this, because it's been kept a secret. Until now. The woman in these pictures is my mistress, but one day she'll be my wife."

Karen coughed the silence away.

Alan jumped in. "Richard Q. the story will not appear anywhere in the North. It's a Southern piece of garbage and it will rot down here. I have taken the necessary steps to guarantee that."

Richard Q., who was slumping on the conference table, hovering over the *Journal* so it was surrounded by his arms, turned to Alan. The word *guarantee* was taken from Alan's speech and jammed back down his throat by Richard Q.

"Alan, then you should get up North now, so I'm *guaranteed* it doesn't get past the Mason-Dixon Line. I can't *guarantee* any other opportunities for you Alan, if you drop the ball." Alan didn't need anything further. He was on his feet and out the door. Karen showed her nervousness by putting out a freshly lit cigarette, only to put another one in her mouth and light up.

Most of the company's management team would have followed Alan out the door as fast as their wingtip shoes could carry them. I choose to stay. I had some business to attend to.

Richard Q. slowly turned toward me.

"Richard Q. before you give me marching orders, I want to know how serious you are about the Colonel's balls." I was as blunt as he was pissed.

"I can bring them to you on a silver platter, but I have to have your approval."

He liked it. He straightened up in his chair, and Karen, not wanting to miss a word about castration, leaned forward toward the table.

"I'm listening, Tony, I'm listening."

"Richard Q., the Colonel is not going to back off. I think he's enjoying this new 'Civil War.' The only way we can get him to stop is to buy him out."

Richard Q. was obviously confused and surprised. He looked over to Karen and nodded his head toward me as if to say, "Is this guy kidding!" He turned to me. "Buy him out! This guy is Mr. Southern Righteousness. We can't buy him!"

I picked up on his misdirection. "Richard Q., I don't mean buy him off . . . I mean buy him and his newspaper out!"

I reached for Alan's financials on the Colonel's precious *Georgian Journal*. Knowing that Richard Q. was a quick study on such matters, I pointed out only those areas I had circled in red during breakfast.

"Richard Q. the newspaper is obviously a good one. And based on our Southern growth projections, it's going to get better. Look at the pretax profits. The costs are incredibly low for such a statewide operation. I think the Colonel has been doing exactly what we are starting to do with the mills. That is, do it economically. Low overhead, non-union, huge income, great profits."

I flipped through some other pages and continued my pitch. "The *Journal* has lots of assets. Real estate, producing farmland, banking partnerships, utilities. Look here, they own a piece of the local gas and electric company. But that should not be our focus. All we want is the core. The newspaper and those elements that support it."

Richard Q. really got into it. He devoured the pages and indeed he was a quick study.

"Tony, if we go in, strip out all the junk, come up with a newspaper net figure, and offer him twelve times his pretax profit earnings against that figure, I could make the financing fly."

Almost as if disappointed he put the documents down and said, "Tony, this is all well and good, and very exciting, but what makes you think the Colonel will sell? That rag has been in the family for generations. It's the power base for his entire operation."

I began gathering up the financials. "Richard Q. if I get the Colonel to sell on a twelve-times earning basis, which I feel is very generous of you, will you clear it?"

He looked over to Karen who was feverishly taking notes on a cigarette ash covered yellow legal tablet.

The pause in our conversation caused her to look up at Richard Q. Their eyes locked for a second and she answered for him with a question, "Does Richard Q. get the Colonel's balls in the deal?"

I answered, "Figuratively speaking . . . yes!"

***

Back at the hotel that evening I mentally put together my plan. I was going solo, but that was okay. I needed a totally convincing piece of information before I could launch a full assault on the Colonel. I was told by Uncle Joe that it was big, it was coming through Ciancola, but I had to wait.

I made two phone calls that touched what were becoming the two halves of my life. I called Connie and we reviewed the goings on of the Manfredi clan. The kids, the house, Connie, were all in working order and fine. I then called Chris, and for approximately the same amount of time, we talked of our passion for each other. Sexually aroused, our conversation climaxed with whispered yearnings and longing to be with one another.

Moments after I hung up, the phone rang. I was expecting either Connie or Chris to be calling back and was caught off guard by the gruffness of the caller. "Mr. Manfredi?"

"Yes, who's this?"

"Mr. Manfredi I'm a friend of Joe Sweets."

I wasn't taking any unnecessary chances. "You didn't answer my question. Who is this?"

The gruffness became a little impatient. "This is Chink . . . from Atlanta . . . cigarette wholesaler . . . real good friend of Joe Sweets."

I was a little embarrassed.

"Oh, Chink. I'm sorry, but we never spoke before and you can't be too careful." Trying to lighten up the conversation I continued, "Joe Sweets has told me of your relationship, so I know your last name. But he never mentioned your nickname, Chink. You're certainly not that!"

The gruff impatience turned into a chuckle. "Nah, I ain't a Jap."

His tone quickly returned to gruff directness. He delivered his message without a pause, without punctuation. "Joe Sweets asked me to do some inside work on your newspapah friend it's all sappose to happen this Friday night and you should get a package delivered to ya ova da weekend, wit' any kinda luck it'll be Sad-ah-day but Sunday for sure. Good luck." Chink was gone. How come they all talk and hang up the phone the same way?

I had planned on hitching a ride to New York on the company plane, then training to Providence for the weekend. But after Chink's call I decided to wait for the piece needed to close *The Georgian Journal* deal. As I thought about my change of plans, the uncomfortable evening temperature was cooled by a revolving ceiling fan. The slight hum from it lulled me to sleep.

***

I was surprised that I had slept until ten. I took a quick shower, didn't shave, and dressed casually. Sick of the hotel menu, I ventured out into the already warm day in search of a hardy Southern breakfast. I stopped by a smoke shop and bought *The Georgian Journal*. Like most Saturday newspapers, it was thin. I wanted to rip into it to see if we made it again, but I teased myself by waiting to read it over breakfast.

I found a coffee shop that was perfect. Sitting just outside the door, on a fruit box, was an old colored man. He was playing the blues on a small harmonica. It was the most soulful sound, and I wanted to invite him in, but even in my short Southern stay, I knew that was a no-no. So I could continue to hear him, I decided to sit close to the door.

I entered unnoticed. The medium size room only had a few lingering customers, who were only interested in the scraps from their breakfast. Sprinkled around the room were about twenty wooden square tables each with four matching bentwood chairs. The green walls above the dark wainscoting served as background to many cardboard and tin advertising billboards.

All of them selling one product: cigarettes! They appeared everywhere. The Old Gold dancing pack, "Lucky Strike means fine tobacco," Camels, Chesterfield with its ornate old English lettering, and of course the bellhop--"Call for Philip Morris"--and the extra-long Pall Mall . . . "and they are mild."

The three ceiling fans were slowly turning, just enough to make my menu flutter and gently sway the cobwebs against the tin ceiling. I ordered ham 'n eggs and coffee. I got ham 'n eggs, three biscuits drowning in brown gravy, a huge portion of grits and coffee so strong it made Italian espresso taste like a milk shake! It was delicious. I ate and read through the *Journal*, checking each page for the latest on the Carpetbaggers. My blues player was still there wailing away. There was not one word about us. We made it.

I was the last customer in the shop to leave. As I exited my blues man for the first time took the harmonica away from his mouth. He smiled and he didn't have a tooth in his head! He had to be playing for nearly two hours. I pulled out three singles, folded them, and slipped them into his worn plaid flannel shirt.

"You're a fine player. I love the blues."

He just nodded his appreciation in return. I walked toward the hotel, and with each step, his own version of "St. Louis Blues" got fainter.

It was nearly two o'clock when I entered the hotel. I went directly to the message desk. "Mistuh Manfredi, there's a gentleman who insisted on waitin' for y'all. He wanted to be escorted to your room 'cause he had somethang to give ya personally. Felt it was all right 'cause he said he was a friend of yours."

He smiled hoping I would match the folded ten-dollar bill he was putting in his vest pocket.

It must be my package.

"He is a friend," I said, handing him a twenty. "Thank you very much."

There were only two elevators in the hotel, both of them slow. My room was on the second floor so I dashed up the stairs. When I got there, I instinctively put my ear to the door and listened. It was quiet. I unlocked it and entered. Sitting in a chair, which he had moved so he would be directly under the ceiling fan, was a slight man dressed in a blue and white striped seersucker suit. His white shirt was already wrinkled from the day's heat. His tie was too big for his body, and it forced his shirt collar to twist and turn in all the wrong directions. Casually lying on his lap, but tightly clutched in his hands, was an eight by eleven tan envelope.

He stood up as I approached him. "Mr. Manfredi. I was told to deliver this to you personally. I've been here since noon." He nervously handed the envelope over to me. He was glad to get rid of it. I reached into my pocket in an attempt to retrieve a tip. He knew what I was trying to do. "Don't bother Mr. Manfredi, Chink pays me very well." He left.

I hung the DO NOT DISTURB sign on the outside doorknob, closed and locked the door. As a back up, I hooked the chain lock. I didn't know what to expect, but I knew I didn't want to be interrupted.

The package was a lot heavier than it looked. I tore one end open, but had difficulty getting its contents out of the envelope. I walked over to the bed held it upside down and shook it. A rain shower of black and white, four-by-four-inch photographs came pouring out. They hit the bed, scattered, and at first glance the photos, some turned right side up, while others showed only their white side, created a puzzle within a puzzle. There were small images of several people in each photograph, while others contained only two or three images. I didn't really know what I was looking at. In the mess of photos, was a folded piece of paper. I opened it. Scribbled in pencil it read:

TONY - MY #1 PIMP GOT THESE FOR YOU.

THE COL. IS A REGULAR. WHAT A FREAK.

I BURNED THE NEGATIVES. HOPE IT HELPS. CHINK.

I began to arrange the pictures, turning over the ones that fell white side up, and attempting to establish a sequence. I was completely dumbfounded at the pornographic mosaic I had created.

The first picture established the location. It was an entrance to a plantation. Each of the two closed gates held a sign: THE RASCOE PLANTATION on one, and NO VISITORS on the other.

The rest of the photos were all shot in the same room that looked like a huge bedroom with a sitting area off to the side. Scattered about the room, on the floor, the love seat, the bed, the chairs, even a coffee table, were males and females. Very young males and females. Some, I was sure, were barely teenagers. They were involved in all sorts of sexual situations. From the traditional mission, him on top of her copulation; to oral sex; to anal intercourse; to threesomes, in a variety of sexual combinations.

There were some obvious ground rules. All the activity was heterosexual, it always involved a colored with a white, and it wasn't until I examined the photos closely did I see, that the couples were shackled together. Either ankle to ankle, wrist to wrist, or ankle to wrist. In only one case was there a different shackled arrangement.

There in the middle of this black and white sexual maze was our Colonel. Like a plantation lord that would make his ancestors proud he sat there presiding over the event. He held a whip in one hand and a chain attached to a brass shackle in the other. This one of a kind brass shackle was around the neck of, in one picture, a colored boy, and in another, a colored girl. In both cases they were jerking the Colonel off! I'd swear it was the same brass shackle that held up his crystal ashtray in his office. It must act as a constant reminder that he is the master and everyone else is the slave.

The Atlanta Register is the afternoon newspaper and the archrival of the *Journal*. The next day I bought the Sunday edition of the *Register*. On its front page I scotch-taped six photos, carefully chosen and arranged to visually tell this complicated story in the simplest manner. Then using the *Journal*'s headline from a few days ago, "Can the Future of the South be Left in the Hands of the North," I crossed out the word *North* and with a black pen inked in *South* with a question mark.

My plan was in place. Between the figures I received from the company and the pictures I received from the organization, the Colonel would be lucky to get eight percent pretax earnings! There was no question that two Tony Manfredi's were evolving, with one common goal.

* * *

Unlike Alan Morris' attempts to set up a meeting, I got the Colonel's attention right away with a telegram:

RJ

MUST MEET WITH THE COLONEL THIS TUESDAY. STOP.
REVIEW OF RASCOE PLANTATION IS NECESSARY. STOP.
2 PM. THANKING YOU IN ADVANCE. STOP.
TONY MANFREDI.

RJ called and left a message with our secretary, "Two p.m. on Tuesday is fine. Would you like a late lunch?" Talk about Southern hospitality. What an attitude change!

***

I arrived on time and went through the same entry process as before. This time though I felt in control, I was on the offensive.

When I entered the Colonel's office there was an unmistakable mix of apprehension and disdain in the air. He wanted to shake my hand and cut off my arm at the same time. "Well Mistuh Man what brings y'all back to the *Journal?*" *Here we go again.*

I was in no mood to mess with this guy so I set the stage, "Colonel the name is Manfredi. You know Eyetalian? Keep it simple, just call me *Tony.*"

He stroked his white goatee, "Why of course, Tony, let's keep it simple. Now what k'n ah do for ya?" I reached into my briefcase to retrieve the financials. Bent over, I heard the Colonel take a deep breath. I placed the folder on his desk and began my presentation.

"Colonel the M. R. Tedes Company, who owns the Bedford Mills, has become very interested in the newspaper business. I might add, we probably would not have even thought of this opportunity if it had not been for your journalistic efforts. We did some financials on your organization, and quite frankly were astounded at the returns you enjoy. It occurred to us then, that your business is a good one. In fact, I'll give you a little inside information. As a result of the study, we believe publishing, newspapers, magazines on into radio and now television is a business for the future.

"We have determined mass media is where we would like to place a substantial amount of our future investments." I was out and out lying about the latter, but it was playing well, and as if in another thought pattern, I was very intrigued with the idea of mass media. I continued. "With that brief preamble, the M. R. Tedes Company is prepared to buy your organization for eight times its pretax earnings."

He started to rise out of his chair. His body swelled and his face reddened with anger. He was about to blow. I wasn't about to let him spoil my moment. "Relax, Colonel, we'll talk about the Rascoe Plantation in a minute, but first hear me out."

He stopped his upward movement, but I knew it was only temporary. I stared straight into his red face and ordered, "Colonel, sit down and listen to how my company is going to make you a wealthier man and preserve your integrity."

As if everything were amiable, I continued while he listened. "Colonel we are not interested in your entire organization. There are certain holdings that do fit my company's profile; however, we would still pay eight times earnings inclusive. Understanding that nearly eighty percent of those earnings are from the *Journal*. You can look at our offer as a twenty-percent bonus."

I was flipping through various papers backing up my

statements. I came across a section that was headed BROADCAST; it revealed that the *Journal* owned two television stations. A network affiliate in Atlanta and the rights, called a building permit, to one in Miami. The notion of mass media crossed my consciousness again.

"Colonel the only variance on the plan would be to include the two television stations. One currently on the air in Atlanta, and the other to be built in Miami at a later date. This inclusion would vary the figures slightly of course."

I was even amazed at my matter-of-fact approach. But he wasn't. He blew. "Listen you Yankee hotshot wop, there ain't no way Colonel Andrew J. Wyatt the Third is goin' to sell any part of mah organ-eye-zation! Why if it were another time I'd have your guinea ass taken to a field and shot. Y'all go back up North and tell your bosses Colonel Wyatt ain't interested in sellin' nothin' from mah organ-eye-zation."

I reached down into a close zippered section in my briefcase. I pulled out a newspaper. "Colonel you sure like to use the word organ-eye-zation. Maybe it's just the word *organ* that you like."

I tossed the pasted up *The Atlanta Register* in front of him. "A picture's worth a thousand words, hey Colonel?"

He couldn't believe his eyes. There, staring back at him was the visual six-picture storyboard I had pasted beneath his old headline.

"Colonel obviously this is a joke. The *Register* doesn't have these pictures, but that can be easily arranged. You know the first amendment, freedom of the press. By the way, the *Register* could have a series of articles, day after day, week after week, all with exclusive pictures."

He slumped back into his chair holding the newspaper. Barely audible he said, "This is blackmail." He looked across the desk to me, he was defeated and for just one split-second I felt sorry for him.

"Colonel you will find in time, this Yankee wop will be of great assistance to you. In fact, I will start now by upping the company's offer to ten percent pretax earnings, keeping the television stations in the purchase and placing you in a consultancy role, at full pay until retirement age, sixty-five. Everything else you still own, including the Rascoe Plantation. Of course once the transaction is completed, the Rascoe Plantation visual presentation will be yours as well."

The Colonel continued to look at the pictures. I wasn't sure if he heard me or not. In a gentle tone I asked, "Colonel did you hear what I said?"

He looked up at me. "Ah heard every word. Suh, can there be no kindness in your heart? Can y'all not bring this shame on mah family's name? I'm beggin' ya, I'll be forevah beholdin' to you."

The volcano had cooled. There would be no more eruptions.

"Colonel you have passed beyond the point of no return. We cannot retreat to another position. This entire unfortunate situation has brought us to this desk this day. The company very much wishes to enter the mass media business and we intend to do so. We would like very much for you to be a part of this new venture. I don't believe there are other options."

He knew there was no way out. If he said no to the deal I might just give the photos to the *Register* and that would destroy him and the *Journal*. Because every Georgian knew the Colonel and the *Journal* were one, neither would recover from the scandal.

"Colonel I will arrange for our legal department to contact whomever you designate to initially put together a simple deal memorandum outlining the particulars as discussed. Soon after, formal papers can be drawn, followed by the necessary financial transactions. Colonel you will find the company to be very efficient, and this process will be over quickly."

He folded the *Register* in half, burying the porno strip. "Ah will have RJ in ready to receive your people."

I reached across and slid the folded newspaper from under his grasp. "Colonel this is safer with me. I will be very involved in this transaction, and I guarantee you these photos, and the others I have, will never see the light of day." I was totally sincere.

He looked up at me, and I knew that although he hated my guts, he could do nothing about it. "Tony, how do ah know?"

The two Tonys answered in unison, "Because I said so."

***

Back at the hotel I called Richard Q. He couldn't believe his ears. "Ten over? Tony, you're a goddamn genius. Look I'm going to send the plane down to pick you up tonight. I want you here to head up this buy. And if it goes through, and the way you're talking it will, I want you to run this whole new area. Hell, we'll even set up a new division and you're it! See you tomorrow. Great job."

13

THERE IS A WONDERFUL CALM that comes
over you after a victory. There is also a tremendous loneliness,
when no one is near to share it. "I'll go from rags to riches, if
you'll just say you care, although my pockets may be empty, I'll
be a millionaire." Tony Bennett's tenor was coming through the
radio and his musical message was perfect.

Pacing about the hotel room I felt all the optimism and
love he was crooning about. The Christmas holiday season was
over, but because of all the activity, I was not suffering from my
usual first-quarter blues. I was becoming more involved in my
Uncle Joe's operation. I had closed *The Georgian Journal* deal last
spring. I was given Senior VP stripes and was heading the Media
Division just as Richard Q. had promised.

The promotion meant a move to New York City. We
wanted to live in the suburbs, with a good school system, in a
home that we could afford. The company allowed me time to find
just the place. So Monday through Thursday I lived at the Statler,
and in Providence on the weekends. The two living arrangements
complemented my two lifestyles.

We just signed the closing papers on a lovely home in Byram, Connecticut. Byram is a community on the New York-Connecticut border. Sandwiched between the New York State line and Greenwich, Connecticut, the latter being the most expensive community on the East Coast. Byram had the same lush acreage, views of Long Island Sound, beautiful homes, at a third of the Greenwich prices! Plus a terrific grammar school for Anne, and a highly regarded public junior high school for Amy. It was known, along with all the tiny towns just over the border, as a "bedroom community." We could move in around March fifteenth.

But here it was mid-January 1953, and I'm in another bedroom community, the Statler, waiting for Chris. We had been together on our day, December nineteenth, now she was on her way to be with me again. Not that our love making was restricted to only December nineteenth, we would get together as often as possible, and each time we couldn't wait until the next.

I stopped pacing long enough to look out of the same bedroom window I had looked out of the first time Chris and I were together. I drifted back to one of our incredible afternoon lovemaking sessions. Still in bed, I had kidded her about our meetings.

"Chris, if I sent the particulars of our meetings to the company analysts, and asked them to do a feasibility study, they would look at the data and the analysts would give us thumbs-down."

She was lying on her back and with a confused look blurted, "What do you mean"--raising both her arms straight upward, she pointed both thumbs down and mimicked me--"thumbs down?"

I reached up and gently took a thumb in each of my

hands. I lowered them to either side of her body pulling the bed sheet tighter across her breasts. Nearly whispering I began to explain. "I mean if the analysts took the amount of time we spend together, say six to eight times over a period of a year"--I bent over and kissed her left breast through the sheet--"versus the amount of time we spend talking about it, at least once a week, more like two or three"--I moved over to her right breast and repeated my kiss--"overlay the risk versus the reward, they would have to turn their analytical thumbs down on us."

Simultaneously, as I concluded my statement, I pressed a thumb on each of her risen nipples. Her eyes closed in perfect pace with my gently applied pressure.

Barely audible she murmured, "What do those analysts know about this. They could never analyze these sensations. Analyze . . ." She paused and licked her lips. She was lying absolutely still. I felt the slight beating of her heart under my thumbs.

With her eyes completely closed she continued to whisper exciting herself with the word *analyze*. "Analyze"--lick--"analysts"--lick--"ana . . ." She inhaled so deeply her breasts pushed my thumbs upward, and as she exhaled she breathed, "Anal . . . let's do something anal."

Her daring always excited me. From that first afternoon of lovemaking, we became uninhibited lovers. We had both elevated ourselves to the most sensual acts. We got there easily by revealing our desires. We were addicted to each other. Hopelessly in love or lust it didn't matter.

Chris, a virgin when married, only performed oral sex on her husband once. It was after our first sexless meeting in New York. When she returned home, she was so aroused that during that evening's lovemaking, which was usually over in minutes, she slipped under the covers. She laughed recalling the incident. She wanted so much to perform oral sex that she was almost out of her mind. When she went under the covers, John's whole body stiffened in horror. She only thought of me. She felt the heat of his penis on her lips. Not knowing exactly what to do, she sucked maybe three times and he exploded. "I was dumbfounded," she exclaimed to me. That was the only time, until me. She never was the recipient of oral sex, until me.

These sexual flashbacks, like those of my illegal exploits, simultaneously created an excitement and a longing for their return. On that first afternoon, the beginning of our lifetime affair, we were willing, but inexperienced. She, as well as I, matured into experienced lovers, but only with each other.

Sex with Connie is tame, and Chris's sex with John is almost nonexistent. My job with the Tedes Company, although challenging and rewarding, appears humdrum, compared to my involvement with Uncle Joe's company. In both cases the levels are miles apart.

***

Chris arrived at the room. As soon as the door closed, a gentle kiss was to be the bellwether for the rest of the afternoon. We enjoyed our room service food. The conversation was light and humorous. We touched each other everywhere, but never made love. It was easy for us to relax with one another.

14

WITH RICHARD Q.'S Washington influence, the
company was able to quickly clear the license through the Federal
Communications Commission for the Miami television station.

The whole operation was new to the broadcast industry.
The station, known as an independent, was not affiliated with
any of the three networks, and had to supply its own programming by purchasing it or producing it locally. We were the first
independent and for a long time the only "Indie," as they were
called in the broadcast business, in Miami. Its call letters were
WMRT-TV Channel 11.

There were other independents in the United States. All
in major cities like New York, LA, Chicago, Boston. Miami was
considered a lesser city or "market" and perhaps that's why the
Colonel sat on the building permit so long, not putting the station
on the air. The Colonel obviously didn't have the research we had.
Miami was a comer! The population moving from the Northeast
to the South, in particular Miami, was enormous. In addition to
the great weather, there was a strong possibility that gambling
would be legalized. In fact, some of the newer beach hotels were

designed to include casinos. Gambling alone would create a new industry, employing hundreds of thousands of people. Tourism would become the number four Miami commodity behind black-jack, craps, and the slots!

With the help of Mr. Ciancola who I now comfortably called Chink, we had no union problems. Our deliveries of ma-terials were on time and intact. Our deals on building and land purchases were below market. We were able to buy, build and be on the air July 4, 1953.

In Atlanta, the television situation was entirely differ-ent. The station in that market had the highest ratings because it was a CBS affiliate, WCOL-TV Channel 2. When the ownership changed from the Atlanta Broadcasting Company to the Tedes Broadcasting Company, in an attempt to pacify a very hurt Colo-nel Wyatt, I requested and received the WCOL-TV call letters in his honor. In a special, private presentation I gave him a brass rectangular box with the call letters on the top. "Colonel sealed inside this box are all the Roscoe Plantation pictures."

He looked at me disbelieving what he had just heard.

"If you want to, you can break it open and see for your-self."

He covered the box with his hands and smiled. "Tony, I believe you." He was right to believe me. They were all there and sealed with a lifetime guarantee from Chink that the pimp and delivery boy who got them would remain silent.

For several months after the deal closed, the Colonel re-mained despondent. All his piss and vinegar was gone. We both knew he could do nothing. Even though he was a bastard, and a sick bastard at that, I felt sorry for him.

One afternoon we met at the station. I wanted to cheer

him up, include him in somehow. I showed him the new opening to the local news. It boasted, "Channel 2 . . . The Big News
. . . The Watchdog of the Community." It was a flashy opening,
bloodhounds and all.

He viewed it with mild amusement. I was not comfortable with the situation.

Miraculously, when we walked into the studio, with its
lights, mikes, cameras, and personnel running around, he lit up!
Showbiz! This could keep him happy, content, silent.

"Colonel," I began to pitch him, "I wanted to show you
the new Channel 2 Big News set. We're going with a whole new
look this February in time for the rating period."

"That's nice, Tony, real nice." *Don't lose him Tony.*

"Well Colonel, I want to ask you something."

He stopped.

"I was wondering; you're a well respected, powerful man
in this area. People, the same people who read *The Georgia Journal* and watch WCOL-TV news, believe in you. You can sway
their thinking, you can bring new viewers to Channel 2, you can
make the South, and in particular Atlanta, a better place to live
and raise a family."

I couldn't believe what I was saying to this degenerate!

"I talked to the news director and recommended you do
the editorials following each of the six o'clock news programs
during the week."

The Colonel was flabbergasted!

"Colonel, you pick the issues"--and at a successful attempt to be humorous, I continued--"except for the Northern
Carpetbaggers routine." His smile was broad and genuine.

"Now, Colonel, the news department will do all the re-

search. They'll write it for you, but of course you can change it
here and there to meet your standards and style. All anyone is
concerned about is, can you deliver it live on camera five nights
a week?"

"Tony, ah'll whip through the week like shit through a
goose. Piece a cake boy, piece a cake!"

The Colonel was in his glory. He was there every day.
Reading, rehearsing, telephoning, enjoying. Poor RJ. He had to
apply the Colonel's makeup before each editorial and was stuck
with dealing with the crank calls after. The Colonel was a hit.
He became a celebrity, was given award after award, and savored
every moment.

I only got nervous once. I asked the news director to nix
the Colonel's editorial series on orphanages and homes for delin-
quent teenagers where he personally wanted to research the subject matter.

***

I must admit that while the Colonel was becoming a
media star, I too was falling in love with the business of show.
My primary responsibility to the company was to make this new
media/entertainment division profitable. That I would do, but I
would also have fun doing it.

The two television stations were entirely different from
one another. The station in Atlanta was straight laced. It carried all the CBS Network shows and was concerned with its news
broadcasts and public affairs programming. Community image
was most important. It was indeed the most respected TV station
in Atlanta, and one of the most copied throughout the country.

It was a huge profit center.

The Miami station on the other hand, was a freewheeling creative beehive. It had to come up with its own programming seven days a week, twenty-four hours a day. It was at the Miami station that I became totally involved. Movies made up the bulk of the programming. *Morning Movietime . . . Movie Matinee . . . Evening Cinema . . . The Late Movie . . . The All Night Movie . . .* and on the weekends it was *The Drive-in Movie* and *The Weekend Flicks.* You get the picture!

They also produced kid shows. A host, a bunch of kids from the area, and cartoons. Big money was made on religious programming on the weekends. In the large studio the station would put up a series of religious sets. The preachers, one after another, would show up each Sunday morning with cash in hand. They paid the program coordinator, got into their "customized" set, and went on the air preaching their version of God. No cash, no God!

15

IT WAS A BRIGHT AUTUMN MORNING

when Dom picked me up at the Providence train station. I wanted to make a deposit at the vault. When I opened the door to the car we were both stunned. He, by my sudden appearance, and me, by nearly being blown off my feet by the car radio! As usual he had the volume all the way up. The parking lot was filled with a hard-driving tenor sax.

Dom, even after the slight fright, could hardly sit still. "Tony, this fuckin' music can't help but get ya goin'."

I watched him as I got into the car. In rhythm, his hands were tapping the steering wheel, his left foot was pounding the floor, and his mid section was weaving and bobbing.

"Dom, if old farts like us get a kick out of this music, imagine the kids, the teenagers. They must love it."

He reached over and lowered the volume on the radio. "Tony, ya' know what? You got something here with this music. The kids do love it, but there's this somethin' stoppin' them from goin' all out."

"Dom, I don't get it."

Dom continued with excitement. "Well, I go past some kids in the neighborhood and they have the music playin', ya know, like a radio on the stoop or a Victrola in the front room turned way up. They're dancin' around and fake singin' with the mooh-len-yams singin' on the record. But when you get close they stop, or turn down the music. Somethin's botherin' them."

Without a pause I answered, "Dom, it's racial."

Dom looked at me puzzled. "Wha?"

"Dom, I'm telling you it's racial, colored, mooh-len-yam. The kids love the music, but feel uncomfortable about it being sung by colored people. They want to let go and enjoy it but can't."

"Tony, with all due respect, Sinatra, Tony Bennett, Doris Day, 'n so on can't do this stuff. It's colored because the coloreds are doin' it."

"Right Dom, so why don't we do it? Colored music, done up white. We just cover over the colored stuff."

Dom was obviously confused, but his faith and loyalty took hold. "Okay Mr. Music Fuckin' Genius, what next?"

I stroked my five o'clock shadow. "I don't know, Dom, but if you're right, there is something there. All we have to do is find the answer."

Big ideas often start with a small notion. This one would turn into a moneymaking monster.

***

What was left of 1953 blitzed by. It was early spring 1954. The colored cover-music idea stayed with me, and whenever I forgot about it, Dom would kiddingly remind me of it.

"Hey, Tony, did you sign Frank Sinatra to do some doo-wop tunes yet? Get it, Tony, Sinatra . . . doo-*wop*."

"Very Italian, Dom. Just drive."

Dom was about ready to deliver his comeback line when I grabbed his forearm. He froze. I looked at the radio speaker.

"Hey kids, it's five p.m., do you know where your parents are?" The voice was deep, clear, clean, with just enough contempt.

"This is Bobbie Jay, on W . . . OH . . . OH . . . KAY. Don't be a snob, turn up the knob, 'cause it's time to rock 'n roll!" The intro was followed by what I found later to be his theme song. A big band, playing bluesy stripper music that, even coming through the small car-speaker, made the hair on your arms stand up. It was exciting!

"Dom, I heard this guy the last time I was in town. He's got something. Maybe he's the way into the music business."

"Tony, he's been in Providence for about a year doin' his bit. He's great, but he plays all that colored stuff we was talkin' about."

"Have you ever seen him, Dom?"

"Nah, why?"

"Say a novena tonight that he's white. I'll call him tomorrow for a meeting."

Why do showbiz people feel the need to play hard to get. Before leaving town I called from the Providence train station. Bobbie Jay was not interested in taking my call. I said I would call back. I did, the next day from New York. When Bobbie Jay heard Mr. Manfredi from New York City was on the phone he came running. He didn't know me from Adam, but *New York, maybe it's the big time!*

Using his best radio voice he announced, "This is Bobbie Jay. Whatcha got to say?"

I wanted to respond "Nothing asshole" and hang up, but I didn't.

"Mr. Jay, I--"

He interrupted with a pat line, "Hey, what's with Mr. Jay, just call me Bobbie or Bobbie Jay."

Now I really wanted to hang up before I threw up.

"Thanks Bobbie. I'm Tony Manfredi and I head up a division of the M. R. Tedes Company that's involved in mass media."

"Hey Mr. M, mass media sounds religious." He laughed in baritone.

I ignored his attempt at humor.

"Bobbie, that's Tony, or Mr. Manfredi."

There was an uncomfortable pause. *Fuck him,* I thought, *if it's not him I will find someone else.* I swear vibes do travel the phone lines, because he certainly picked up mine. In a slightly lower register he said, "Sorry, Tony, what can I do for you?"

"Bobbie we are in the television business and have plans to expand in all areas of mass media . . . I mean entertainment." I didn't want to give him another shot and maybe lose the control I achieved. "I have an idea that I would like to present to you, get your thoughts, and perhaps we can do business. I get up to Providence often for business."

"Well, Tony, I work Monday through Friday five to ten. I need about an hour before airtime so anytime before, let's say three, or after ten."

"Let's say three tomorrow, and if all goes well, we'll pick it up at ten-oh-five."

"Hey, Tony, I like your style. Done."

I needed to know. "Bobbie before you hang up I know most deejays use stage names, I'm assuming Bobbie Jay is not your real name."

"Tony, mah man"--just the way he said *mah man* I had a bad feeling--"*Bobbie* is for real, *J* is my middle initial"--I actually crossed my fingers--"and *Russo* is the last. My confirmation name is Joseph. Anything else, Anthony?"

Oops, a little sarcasm. I uncrossed my fingers.

"Bobbie with your style and showmanship you had to be Italian. I just wanted to make sure. I hope I didn't insult you."

He relaxed. "No problem, Tony, you take so much shit in this business I get defensive, particularly about my background. See you tomorrow?"

"Tomorrow Bobbie Jay, tomorrow."

***

I love train rides. Pittsburgh, the plant, Chris McKay. Some of my best opportunities started with a train ride. Could this be another?

Dom was there waiting for me. I hesitated before opening the car door. He waved me in. I opened the door and was surprised by the silence.

"Dom, where's the music?" He waved his hand toward the roof of the car. "Broke. Da fuckin' speaker broke."

I couldn't resist. "I wonder why?"

He gave me the finger and laughed.

As we pulled out of the lot he began his report. "Tony, this Bobbie Jay guy is from New Haven. He didn't grow up in the neighborhood, but on the west side of town." He shrugged his shoulders as if to say "Not my fault."

"So, Dom, that's where he got his taste for colored music. That whole area is a colored slum."

"You got it, Tony, but he's clean. His old man is a shoe-maker in that neighborhood. His mother is dead. He's the only kid. His father thinks his son's job as a deejay is a joke. He wants him to take over the shoe store.

"You drive through that neighborhood and all you hear is that station. It's like they have the dial welded in place."

Now I was confused.

Dom continued, "They listen to that station hour after fuckin' hour. But what's so nuts is Bobbie Jay is the only one playin' that mooh-len-yam music."

"Is he married?"

Dom shook his head no.

"Girlfriend?"

"Don't know, Tony."

"Dom, you're slipping."

"If ya would have given me more than twenty minutes to get this info, maybe I'd know more."

"Dom, you're the best."

"Tony, quit jerking me off! Can I come into the station; I never seen how they do it. When I was a kid my grandfather told me, there was a midget band in the radio playin' all that music. I believed him up until I was, oh, sixteen or seventeen when I started drivin'.

"No fuckin' midget band could be in every car. Right?"

In unison we yelled, "Right!"

We slowly drove by what looked like a storefront business

gone broke. A single metal door separated two large, blackened, plate-glass windows. It was obvious that the black paint was applied with a brush. In spite of the seediness of the place, it was, without a doubt, the correct address. On one of the blackened windows, in uneven script, were the call letters WOOK, and on the other, in straighter block letters, 1150AM.

We parked and walked up to the metal door and, following the written directions thumb tacked above a rusty button, we rang the bell. The door squeaked open, and a gum-chewing female dressed in navy blue pedal pushers and a red sweatshirt asked us to come in. She looked like a teenager--ponytail, crooked teeth, pimples--but I'm sure she was in her twenties.

With blandness in her voice she greeted us. "You must be Mista Manfredi. Bobbie's expectin' ya. Who's he?"

I looked back at Dom who was already straining his neck to see the inside of the station. "That's Mr. Triano. He's with me."

She looked past me at Dom, unimpressed. "Well Bobbie wasn't expectin' two guys."

"You're right. I brought Dom along for you!"

She didn't get it. She looked confused. Then she looked Dom up and down and answered, "Yeah, well I'm engaged anyways."

"Lucky guy, ah . . ."

She did get it. "Sue, my name's Sue, but everybody calls me Suzie with a z." "Well, 'Suzie with a z' . . ."

"No just Suzie, you don't have to say with a Z; that's just how I spell it, with a z." Am I not getting it?

"Well Suzie, while I'm with Bobbie, maybe you could show Dom how the station works. You know a little tour."

"Oh sure, but it won't take long." She gestured to a door with a hand printed sign, on legal tablet paper warning KEEP OUT LIBRARY! I approached the door and gently knocked.

Being in a radio studio, and knocking on a library door, one would tend to be quiet. Well, obviously that is not the case. When the door swung open, the legal paper became airborne as it tore away from the tape. Snatched in mid-flight by a smiling Bobbie Jay he boomed, "Mah man, Mr. Manfredi."

He looked down at the former sign, crumbled it into a ball and tried to hook-shot it into a wastepaper basket. He missed.

"Good hands, lousy hook shot."

He enjoyed my play-by-play commentary. With both hands free he extended them to me. An unexplainable phenomenon occurred. They're called a variety of things. Vibes, miracles, gut, happenings. Call it what you will, it happened as soon as our hands clasped each other. I knew this union was right.

He was completely different than I had expected. The Russo name conjures up a darker-skinned Italian. He was very fair, almost freckled. Light brown hair, blue eyes, five feet eight, well built, but most important, beyond his awful taste in clothes, he looked clean-cut . . . American!

But he dressed in Dago dreck. Pale green pegged-pants with dark green saddle-stitching down the outside of each leg. His pale yellow rayon shirt's breast pockets were weighted down with a pack of Old Gold cigarettes in one and a heavy Zippo lighter in the other. It was tightly cinched at his waist by a thin, Speidel-watchband-looking silver belt. The buckle was perfectly placed on his left side.

His voice and attitude were his boldest features. The voice was acceptable, but if he were to become the music imprimatur of this generation, I knew I had to tone down his attitude.

We sat opposite each other at a table covered with few record albums and hundreds of 45 rpms. I spread a few aside to make room for my forearms.

I reminded him how I head up a newly created entertainment division of a large company. A movie chain (slight exaggeration) one newspaper, two television stations, with future plans in the music business. "That is for those who have vision and wish to take a chance."

"Go man, go," he said. See what I mean about attitude.

"The music that you play, rhythm 'n blues, could be the new wave of popular music--"

He interrupted, his personality changed, and he matched my businesslike tone. "Tony, you call it rhythm 'n blues, others call it R 'n B; I call it, and I only want to call it, rock 'n roll. It's my phrase, I created it and I'm going to make it part of the American lexicon." *"Lexicon"? Where did that come from?*

"Bobbie, and I want to help you make that happen. Tell me a little about yourself."

Arrogantly he shot back, "What's with the third degree?"

"Bobbie, I'm not looking to hire you, I'm looking for partnership. If I'm going to be that closely involved with someone, I want to know them. I'll tell you anything you want to know about me, or the company. Just ask."

He mellowed.

"Bobbie it's that show business bullshit you were talking about on the phone. Don't be defensive with me. I understand."

That got to him.

"Well, Tony, I'm from the colored part of Providence. There were only four other white families in the neighborhood.

My closest buddies are colored." *Well, so much for getting him to play white music.* "My old man is still there, putting heels and soles on shoes. I wanted to get out. Not that it was bad, but I wanted more." I held back from blurting out white music could get you more. "I started listening to these old 78 records on obscure labels, and I fell madly in love with their music. Their, the colored music, excites me. Coming from that neighborhood I have a special feeling for it. I appreciate it. I graduated high school and went to night school to try and get some kind of education. But all I wanted to do was to be involved with the music business, particularly the colored music business, but . . ."

An opening. "But what Bobbie?"

"I love it, but not every white person does. It's very narrow. I don't want to be spinning colored records, talking rock 'n roll, while the rest of the world is listening to something else. It's so hard. I believe in the music, my notion of rock 'n roll, but I'm also a realist." He had totally opened up. His honesty was welcomed.

"Bobbie, you practically did my pitch. I'm here trying to bring two forces together that I believe will be around for a long, long time. And you're the glue that will keep them together. I'm talking about your rock 'n roll, slightly scrubbed down, and television."

I leaned forward on my forearms into his totally confused face. "Bobbie I have a plan. We own an independent television station in Miami. We program that baby, twenty-four hours a day, seven days a week. I want to put on a show, let's say an hour a day, Monday through Friday, around four o'clock for the teenagers to watch. You'll host it. We'll play your rock 'n roll. We'll have an audience of teenagers who will dance to the music.

We'll have guest stars appearing; you'll interview them."

He put up both his hands in an attempt to slow me down. "Woah, woah, wait a minute! If the colored music is only marginally accepted up North, what makes you think"--he made a quotation mark sign with both his hands--"'my rock 'n roll' will be even close to being accepted down South, where coloreds drink from different bubblers and piss in different bathrooms?"

Here comes the deal-maker or -breaker.

"Bobbie Russo, because a big part of the plan is to make the music more acceptable to the masses by finding artists, white artists, to record them." He started to interrupt but I wouldn't let him. "We'll find them. You'll produce them on our label. We'll market them and if I'm right, sell the hell out of them to everyone regardless of race. Bobbie Russo, that's the way rock 'n roll, your rock 'n roll, will become part of the American lexicon. And along the way make you a very famous and rich person." His passion for the colored music wanted me out the door. His ego, his desire for fame and fortune, kept me there.

***

I stayed for the first hour of his show. There was no doubt he was performing for me. His energy was higher than usual. One minute he was yelling into the mike and then, introducing a ballad, he practically whispered into it.

"Hey, I know it's early afternoon, but let's put our bodies close together and enjoy the Harptones, on the Paradise label . . . 'Life Is But a Dream-*m-m-m*.'" He segued from his *m-m-m*'s to the mellow harmonies of "Life is but a dream, and I dream of you . . ." He cut his mike. His smile remained. It was deep and genuine.

"Bobbie Jay, why do you always smile when you're announcing?"

"That's how you make it sound happier. I'm happiest when I'm announcing."

That moment was captured by both of us. The Harptones singing a love song, the honesty of what he was doing, the future partnership.

"Bobbie I want to make a deal. I guess we pick this up at ten-oh-five tonight. Are you up for dinner?"

"Mah man, let's do both dinner and deal."

I reached over the audio console and shook his hand. "I'll pick you up at ten-oh-five." He gave me a thumbs up and I left.

***

It seems like the deals that take forever to put together, end quickly, while the ones that come together quickly, last. Bobbie Jay and I put it together over dinner that night. He was past the black versus white music. He agreed with me that the music had to "cross over."

We decided on setting up a separate company, which would concentrate on finding, signing and recording talent. It would distribute and publish the music. I would arrange for all the legal paperwork, and financing through the M. R. Tedes Company. He would retain a fifteen per cent equity position. The company would own eighty-five percent. For hosting *Dancetime* on WMRT-TV, Miami, and functioning as a record producer he was paid twice his old WOOK deejay salary. MusicTides, Inc. was off and running.

16

IN A MATTER A MONTHS the *Dancetime* TV show
was a smash. It captured the teenage audience and kept them
glued to the set for one hour. We quickly expanded it to a two-
hour show. Our success came from playing the colored music,
while all the dancers on the show were white. Bobbie Jay's hosting was lily white. No pegged pants. No colored speech pattern or
mannerisms. I picked out his wardrobe. Conservative suits, sports
jackets, and slacks, always with shirt and tie, was the dress of
the day. This large group of dancing whites in the studio, and a
huge at home audience watching them, led by one of their own,
became comfortable with the colored music.

Every personal appearance made by Bobbie Jay was sold
out. He called them *Dancetime* Hops, and all he did every Friday
and Saturday night in and around Miami was play the music.
First, at local high schools, then larger halls, and finally at the
various civic centers.

The television business is a small one. Everyone knows
what works and what doesn't. Programming is the key to success.
We received calls from other Eastern independent TV stations,

asking if they could buy the *Dancetime* show. Using the telephone company's Telco lines, we were able to tie together an Eastern *Dancetime* network.

The first to sign on was Philadelphia. I went there personally to do the deal. After a brief visit with her father, Chris met me at the train station. She was pleasantly surprised when I showed up with a rented car.

"Hey lady, need a lift?"

She smiled her perfect smile. "Only if you're going to Pittsburgh, and only if you promise not to keep your hands off me."

I reached across the front seat and opened the passenger door. "Yes and yes!" She jumped in and we were off to a private drive to Pittsburgh.

I planned to spend the night at a local hotel alone. We planned to have each other for lunch the next day. I planned to get the Pittsburgh Independent signed on to the *Dancetime* network. All the plans worked out perfectly. If I had to, I would have given *Dancetime* to the station for nothing, just to come to Chris's town to see and make love to her. I enjoyed being on her turf. It raised the level of excitement for me. The station was so eager to sign on it almost took the fun out of it.

Washington, D.C., was next. Then came Boston and Cleveland. Finally the biggest television market in the country joined the lineup. New York City! Which convinced our stuffy Atlanta station WCOL to carry the show. The fees paid by the stations more than covered the Telco lines and production costs of the show. *Bobbie Jay* was becoming a household name up and down the Eastern seaboard. His public appearances expanded into all the hooked up cities. Even some of the smaller towns in between, which only heard of him, but never had seen him, wanted him. I had created a marketable personality, which could now be used as the launching pad for my expanded music plan.

The first crossover song and group was a smash. The song, "Glory of Love," was originally recorded by an all-colored group The Five Keys. When first released, nearly eighteen months before, it was a mild hit. Then Jay put together four white guys in their early twenties from the New Haven area. Because it was the white hairstyle of the day, he called them The Brush Cuts. I argued and won the point that the name was too obvious . . . too white! The group's lead singer and their harmonies had a cleaned-up colored sound, and I thought the group's name should also sound colored. The impact of the group being white would be tremendous. It could create a word-of-mouth campaign that would put the group--more importantly--the concept over the top.

While in New Haven, I rented a car to drive to a studio to meet with Bobbie. It was a Chrysler. I called the group *The Imperials*. It stuck. They sounded colored, but were as white as one Irishman and three Italian guys could be. As unofficial wardrobe master, I dressed them in black three-button Ivy League suits; blue button-down shirts; thin, black knit ties; and black tassel loafers. Topped off with short hair and white attitudes. Bobbie Jay plugged them on *Dancetime*. After a carefully planned tease campaign they appeared on the show. You could almost hear the gasp up and down the eastern seaboard as the colored sounding, but very white Imperials made their debut.

The Imperials where an instant hit. At last, there was a group that every white teenager could openly identify with. They could buy the 45, take it home, and not worry about what their parents would say. Every radio station in the country was playing

"The Glory of Love" and feeling safe. After only two weeks of release, *Billboard* magazine, the bible of the record/music business, ranked it the #3 best seller. In its third week it became the #1 single and remained there for nearly three months. During that time, The Imperials released two other crossover songs, The Chords "Sh-Boom" and Joe Turner's "Shake, Rattle and Roll." Both hit the Top 10. In fact The Imperials had the #1, #2,and #4 hits in the country. The #3 spot was held by Archie Bleyer's "Hernando's Hideaway." Go figure!

Uncle Joe was amused by my plan to set up a talent management business for the organization.

"Tony, we manage things 'n people every day."

I suggested we call it Sweet Management. He thought it was cute, his ego was stroked, but he refused saying, "Tony, too close. You put two 'n two together, and you get me! No thanks!" He did want the potential income from the acts, and demanded fifteen percent of the gross, plus expenses. I agreed.

Outside the M. R. Tedes Company, using bogus names and minimum financing from Uncle, I established a company to manage talent.

It was easy for me to convince The Imperials to sign with the management company. The hottest vocal group of 1954 was the first act on the Mann Management roster. It was also easy to maintain the management company with only one act. A secretary/bookkeeper, cheap office space, and a two-line telephone. Most of the revenue was in cash from personal appearances. I "deducted" thirty percent for commissions and expenses and sent the skim to Uncle Joe.

I created an accounting system that worked better than Bill Carpenter's. The tenth of every month brought a printed report for my approval. It reflected the income from all sources including the seventy percent cash balance. Mann Management deducted its fifteen percent, actual out-of-pocket expenses, and withheld monies for taxes. Mann Management was legitimate and profitable. The balance went to MusicTides, Inc. After all expenses were recouped, Bobbie Jay received his fifteen percent, The Imperials split the balance fifty-fifty with MusicTides, Inc.

***

The year 1955 was only a month old when this simple moneymaking operation exploded. Bobbie Jay had discovered a young, handsome kid in Philly. His name Mike "Snooky" Traficante. Like Bobbie Jay the name didn't fit the face. Snooky looked like a college student with a DA haircut. At nineteen, he admitted to only shaving once. His skin was the male version of peaches and cream. With sandy blonde hair, blue eyes, a well-proportioned six footer, he was an Adonis. His soft speaking voice and his crooners singing voice rounded out the package.

We changed his name to Johnny Diamond. We cut his DA. We dressed him in khaki pants, varsity-letter sweaters, button-down, open collar shirts, white sweat socks, and what ultimately became his signature, white bucks. He was going to be our Sinatra, our Crosby, our Como. But behind that manufactured Joe College exterior was a wild man!

To kick off the whole Johnny Diamond phenomenon, we decided to broadcast the *Dancetime* program from Philadelphia. For three days, the director of the program was instructed to watch that kid. Take shots of him dancing, talking to the girls, use him on bumper shots going to commercials. Subliminally,

Johnny was being exposed to the viewing audience.

Away from the broadcast studio we had rehearsed his "impromptu" appearance. All the questions. All the answers. Just enough of his hometown Philly background would be revealed to prove he was from this fine city, and explain how he "just happened to be on the show and just happened to be discovered." It was Lana Turner at Schwab's Drugstore all over again. How, on the spot, he made up the name Johnny to maintain his anonymity. His revelations would be filled with vulnerability. He would talk of his desire to become a rock 'n roll singer.

He practiced his singing. His guitar playing was uneducated, but full of honesty. He was ready.

Halfway through Thursday's program, Bobbie Jay pulled Johnny out of the audience. The interview went off perfectly. It looked like it was indeed happening before your very eyes. You were witnessing something special. "The making of a star."

He was asked to sing. The studio audience applauded encouragement. He had to get his guitar in his car.

"Okay, Johnny," smiled Bobbie Jay, "you get your guitar and we'll get some money from these advertisers. Hey guys up there in the booth, I know we're winging it, so go to commercial." He laughed his genuine laugh, the audience went wild. Johnny was picked up on camera running through the studio doors. Running for his guitar and stardom.

After a two-minute commercial break, the camera opened up with Bobbie Jay and Johnny standing side by side. The entire studio audience was moved from their bleacher seats and placed on the floor in a circle around them. There was no entry music, no usual wild applause. Bobbie Jay in a low, sincere, choked up voice introduced Johnny.

"Kids, while we were off the air, Johnny told me he was dedicating, this, his first song, to the late and great Johnny Ace." Then Bobbie Jay looked up toward the studio ceiling, and raising both of his hands upward continued, "And Johnny we know you're up there, reach down and help him out." He then looked right into camera, and with watery eyes said, "And you out there, open up your hearts and let Johnny from Philly in. Here's both Johnnys' 'Pledging My Love.'"

Johnny strummed the first chord on his guitar and sang, "Forever, my darling, my heart will be true . . ." Taking it instantly from colored to white, he sang the shit out of that song. He held a close up like Garbo. It was television magic.

The only thing we couldn't control or rehearse was the reaction of the audience. That was the gamble. When he finished the audience, which was silently sitting around him, jumped up screaming, whistling, applauding. The girls were crying; it was overwhelming.

The next day's show brought more surprises. Bobbie Jay opened the show by announcing, "Kids, yesterday we introduced a member of our studio audience. He called himself Johnny. He wanted to be a rock n' roll singer and he sang the late and great Johnny Ace's 'Pledging My Love.' The phone rang off the hook. More telegrams from fans than ever before. You loved him and so do we. Now kids one of those phone calls came from none other than the lead singer of The Imperials, Tommy Bee."

The studio audience went wild with cheers and screams just by saying The Imperials.

"Hold it kids. That ain't all. The news was so incredible I asked my good buddy Tommy to call us live on the show today, and right after this two minute message we'll talk to Tommy Bee of The Imperials from Hollywood, California."

The audience's crazed response and music from The Imperials blended into a perfect segue to the commercial break. When the show came back, Bobbie Jay was sitting on a stool with a telephone. He talked into the phone allowing the hundreds of thousands of viewers to eavesdrop.

"Tommy, how's ma' buddy?"

"Great," crackled an obvious long distance voice.

"Tommy, tell the kids what you told me yesterday about Johnny from Philly."

"Well Bobbie, I was in Cleveland watching your show. I was almost out the door going to the airport heading for the West Coast, when I saw Johnny from Philly perform. I was stopped in my tracks. I called in the rest of The Imperials."

The studio audience roared. Bobbie Jay gestured for them to be quiet.

"The Imperials were knocked out by him. So I called our record company. I told the execs at Tides Records we have to sign this guy. I said I would put my reputation and next year's royalties on the line for Johnny." Tommy was laying it on a little thick, but it was working.

"They agreed to a two-record deal right on the phone."

There was a slight pause and with a minimal hand gesture Bobbie Jay triggered an audience frenzy.

"Tommy, mah buddy how can we thank you?"

"Get Johnny in the studio right away, and let's see if he can open for us on our next East Coast tour. See ya, Bobbie Jay, and kids keep on rock 'n rolling with The Imperials."

The audio man must have had a fit, because the frenzy

grew louder and louder until it all became distorted. Bobbie Jay tried his best to quite things down but he couldn't, so he did the only thing a good emcee can do under those conditions, he went to commercial.

Two minutes later things had quieted down and Bobbie Jay had regained control of the audience. He purposely stayed away from any mention of The Imperials.

"Kids here's proof that wonderful things can happen. Here he is, Johnny from Philly."

The audience went wild again. As I lay there on the hotel bed next to Chris I smiled at Bobbie Jay's abilities. He wanted to save any further frenzy for Johnny and not have any Imperial spill over. He indeed was a *master* of ceremony.

Johnny smiling his wholesome smile, holding his guitar by its neck, as if dragging it, strolled to center stage. Bobbie Jay and Johnny shook hands.

"Well Johnny dreams do come true don't they?"

Johnny stuck to the script. He didn't answer, but mustered his best choked up gulp and nodded affirmatively.

"Got another song for us?"

Humbly he answered, "Yes Bobbie Jay. I sang Johnny Ace's 'Pledging My Love' yesterday. He's no longer here, but his music is. It was his biggest hit. So while they're still so much a part of our lives, and especially mine, I would like to sing The Imperials biggest hit 'Glory of Love.'"

The audience responded as if The Imperials were actually there. Johnny hit his first chord and he sang a slow haunting version of their rock 'n roll hit. It was spellbinding. He finished, the audience went wild, and Bobbie Jay forced his way through the mayhem, to make a rock 'n roll proclamation.

"Johnny we can't continue to call you Johnny from Philly, so I have an idea. It all started here on *Dancetime*, with you singing the late and great Johnny Ace's 'Pledging My Love.' Ace is a winning card. You're a winner and a shining star! So I want the world to know you as"--he paused dramatically--"Johnny Diamond!"

The audience went nuts. There must have been one hundred camera shots taken of Johnny, Bobbie Jay, the audience. Yesterday's version of Johnny's 'Pledging My Love' played over the shots. The deed was done. Hokey and contrived, the star was created and launched.

Immediately following the show, a car rushed Johnny Diamond from the studio to the train station. Bobbie Jay arranged for some newspaper and magazine reporters to be at both ends of the limo ride. They took pictures and asked questions in the staged crush. Bobbie Jay, like a politician, spread his answers over the group.

"Johnny Diamond is making his dreams come true. He was discovered on *Dancetime* and we're off to New York City to record his first 45."

Bobbie Jay and Johnny waved and thanked the press, then entered the train heading for the first-class section. To get there, they had to pass through one coach-class car. As they plowed down the aisle, people turned in their seats, wondering what the commotion was all about. Soon these coach passengers could boast to their families and friends, that they rode the train from Philly to New York with superstar Johnny Diamond.

Dom and I were already on board waiting for them. We had swung the back of a seat from one side of its bench to the other, creating a comfortable face-to-face settee. The energy level was high. We all shook hands, Bobbie Jay and I embraced, the train whistle blew, and we were off to the big city.

It was nearly six thirty when Jay made his hunger known. I acknowledged his request. I told them to go to the dining car and charge the meal to my seat. Dom stayed.

I gestured for him to come closer. "Dom, make sure they don't rush." Dom never needed a lot of direction. He nodded acceptingly. He stepped into the aisle and followed them out.

As soon as they left the car, I stood up and headed in the opposite direction. One car away, toward the engine, was the sleeping car and Chris. Crossing between cars, a January gust of cold air filled my open suit. It wasn't until I was well inside, moving sideways down the narrow aisle, did the chill really touch my bones. I reached compartment D and just before knocking, shook the chill lose.

"Who is it?" Her voice was close to the door.

"It's your personal porter."

There was a metal-to-metal sound as she unlocked the door. It opened, and there with the dimming lights of Philadelphia streaking by behind her, stood the love of that part of my life. As if we were dancing partners, when I stepped in, she stepped back the same distance. I reached for her with one arm and closed the door behind me with the other. She moved into my embrace and we kissed. The train whistle blew, steam blurred the passing lights. *Credits.*

After making love most of the way, our post-sexual peace was interrupted by the distant yelling of the porter, "New York City . . . fifteen minutes."

We had fulfilled another wonderful, crazy notion. She would take the next train back to Philly where she would finish her visit with her father. The fact that she would not get back to his house until one in the morning was meaningless to us. We had to be with each other, for making love where we first met, on a train, was too exciting to pass up.

When I returned to my seat, Bobbie Jay and Johnny were sound asleep. When I sat down next to Dom he stirred, opened one eye, and whispered out of the side of his mouth, "You okay?" This time I nodded affirmatively. "I got 'em shit faced. We only been here about a half hour."

I smiled at him. "Thanks, Dom."

"No problem." No questions, no gestures, no looks, just unconditional acceptance.

***

The two recording sessions went perfectly. Johnny was backed up by a stand up acoustical bass, grand piano, drums, and like all the fifties songs, a tenor saxophone. The first 45 featured 'Pledging My Love.' The second 45 was 'Glory of Love.' Each was recorded with about an hour or two of rehearsal and technical checks. I was amazed that not even a piece of sheet music was present.

Johnny tuned his guitar to the Steinway and sang the first verse to give the studio musicians the key. Like a Hollywood musical coming to life, the trio joined in effortlessly. First the bass, then the light but steady right hand of the piano player, the drummer, using his brushes on cymbals, supplied the rhythm, while the tenor sax ad-libbed in the background. The only correction made was by Bobbie Jay, who wanted the tempo of "Glory of Love" slowed down. Two sessions, a couple of hours, delivered two megahits for Tides Records and Mann Management.

***

After the second session, the walk from the Madison Avenue and 57th Street recording studio to the Plaza Hotel was straight into the wind. It was freezing cold. The long shadows of the skyscrapers were turning the gray afternoon into charcoal. As I did when I was a kid, I scurried a few steps ahead of Johnny, Bobbie Jay, and Dom, and then turned to face them walking backwards. I could feel the wind bouncing of my back, as we engaged in happy, optimistic conversation about the future success of Johnny Diamond and his recording career.

There was a pause in the gaiety, and I was about to turn around, when Johnny said, "I'm freezing. I bet a good piece of ass would warm me up."

It was not uncommon among guys in a feisty mood to talk about getting laid. This was different. His tone wasn't in keeping with the fun of the moment. I looked up at the tall buildings and as I passed them in my backward direction, they appeared like upside down icicles. That visual and Johnny's tone sent shivers through my entire body.

I tried to melt things down. "Johnny I'm sure a handsome future superstar like yourself can easily go out and find some interested lady. If not in New York tonight, certainly in Philly tomorrow."

His response was quick. "Tony, I don't want to go out and hustle some chick. I want you guys to get me laid." His emphasis on the *you* stopped me in my tracks. Our fast-pace walk came to a screeching halt. Johnny and I were nose to nose. Dom immediately took the temperature and was by my left side in a flash.

Hoping he was kidding I half-smiled and asked, "You want me to get you laid?"

He wasn't kidding. "Fuckin' right, Tony."

I took a quarter of a step toward him, leaving no room between us. I tapped the left side of his chest with my index finger. Winter steam pouring out of my mouth was the outward sign of my inner anger.

"Listen, Snooky Traficante, I'm only interested in your voice not your cock. We're promoters not pimps."

Johnny took a half-step back and started to raise his right arm. Dom grabbed his forearm and stopped its flight waist high. The pressure Dom was asserting crushed Johnny's topcoat from the cuff to the elbow.

Johnny winced. Dom's head motioned no. Bobbie Jay stood there in amazed silence.

Johnny, trying to be his bravest said, "You're my manager, you're suppose to take care of me."

Feeling things were back under control, I answered, "Just as I have already demonstrated, I will take care of you. I will make you the rock n' roll superstar you dreamed about. But I won't get you laid. When you become rich and famous, if you need someone to get you a piece of ass, you'll be able to hire him yourself. In the meantime, Snooky, just sing."

My eyes told Dom to turn him lose. He did.

Johnny shook his sleeve and rubbed his forearm trying his best to ignore the pain. I took a side step and gestured to Johnny to start walking. He did, with Dom by his side. I moved next to Bobbie Jay who was still dumbfounded. I let Dom and

Johnny move down the sidewalk several feet before I put my arm in Bobbie Jay's encouraging him to walk on.

"Bobbie we may have a superstar nut on our hands. But we'll handle it." His look was a mixture of confidence in my statement and confusion about his role.

"Bobbie you continue to produce talent and hits, we'll take care of everything else. Like any other business deal, if our friend Snooky gets to be a bad investment, we will sell it, trade it, liquidate it. We'll handle it."

***

Bobbie Jay executed a perfectly planned promotional campaign culminating in Johnny's first 45 release. Johnny was in every record trade magazine, followed by stories of his "discovery" in *Life*, with two pages of pictures. He appeared on the *Dancetime* show several times. Behind those scenes the newly appointed Vice-President of Marketing for Mann Management, Dom Triano, schoomzed with the leading East Coast rock 'n roll disc-jockeys. Dom's love and understanding of the music endeared him to the deejays, and they responded. Through them he was introduced to their bosses, the unknown power behind the music, the radio station program directors, PDs. They in fact, not the deejays, created the playlist. The list consisted of records chosen by them and then played by the deejays. I concluded that from a marketing point of view neither the DJs nor the PDs were ever attended to.

Dom was great! His mixture of street smarts, good time Charlieism, open-ended expense account, and music savvy made him the perfect host. They were "entertained" like never before and never again. Dom bought them drinks, food, gifts, trips, women, and we got the airplay necessary to generate hit after hit. For the wine, for the women, we got the song! By the summer of 1955, when Johnny's 'Pledging My Love' was released, the public and the record industry were welded together waiting for the pop phenomenon known as Johnny Diamond.

17

THERE WAS ANOTHER COMING together on July 4, 1955. The Manfredis decided to celebrate our daughter Amy's Sweet Sixteen birthday in grand style.

Well on her way to becoming a beautiful adult, she had moved through the trauma associated with the death of her parents. She completely sidestepped those awkward stages reserved for teenagers. No braces, no knobby knees, not too fat, not too skinny, no sibling rivalry, no parental displeasures. Connie, who had learned from her own lack of motherly guidance, educated Amy on the natural order of things. Barely twelve, she had accepted her first period with cool expectancy. Now at sixteen Amy's top priority was to get her driver's license.

The birthday party took place on a newly added screen porch that invaded the already small back lawn.

During the preceding workweek, at a Richard Q. meeting, under the heading of corporate chit and chatter, I had mentioned the upcoming Saturday birthday party.

"Hell, Tony," Richard Q. said, "Sweet Sixteen is real special." He went on to say how he had a weekend house off the

Merritt Parkway and it would be easy for him to swing by. I didn't know if he was sincere or he just wanted to use the birthday as an excuse to visit his weekend house with his long-legged hooker.

Karen, in her affixed cloud of cigarette smoke, entered the appointment in a black leather book. The gold letters branded on the cover, unequivocally trumpeted its owner:

RICHARD Q. ARMSTRONG

PRESIDENT & CHIEF OPERATING OFFICER

M. R. TEDES COMPANY 1955

It struck me that whenever Karen entered something in that book it was chiseled in stone.

She coughed, "What time, Tony?" I moved my eyes from Richard Q. and directed my answer to the top of the opened diary. "Two o'clock would be fine."

With a scroll-like move, Karen wrote *2P*. As she closed the book, Richard Q. reached for his private phone and waved us both out of his office. The door no sooner shut behind us when Karen said, "He's coming to the party. He wants to show you he cares about you. He's well aware of the success you're having with the Media Division. He wants to keep you happy."

Every *He* was punctuated by two pointing fingers squeezing a cigarette. I was waiting for another "He" statement and was caught off guard when she asked, "What's the kid's name?"

For the first time since knowing Karen, I got angry at her callousness. My response showed it. "The kid, my oldest daughter's name, is Amy." As if I had said nothing, she took out her pen and entered the name next to the *2P*.

My anger grew, "That's *Amy* with a *y*." She finished her

entry, took a drag of her butt, dropped it on the floor, and while rubbing it out with her foot, blew the smoke out the left side of her mouth. "Y."

"Why 'you getting pissed off?" she asked. You saved her life. You should be proud, not pissed. See you Saturday." Before I could respond, she turned and walked down the hall fishing her suit jacket pocket for another smoke.

***

The weather for Amy's party was perfect. Eastern Julys can be filled with humidity. This Saturday was filled with sunlight and dry warm breezes. About ten or twelve of Amy's nearest and dearest were there. Three girls to one boy. Dads with teenage daughters like those odds. Anne and Roberta were in their finest party dresses, desperately longing to be teenagers.

Having lived in the area for just over two years Connie was able, with little effort, to assume and execute the role of hostess. The mix of our ethnic upbringing and this newly quasi Wasp lifestyle was perfectly balanced. The menu consisted of a variety of finger sandwiches and potato chips with dip. The centerpiece was a square dish filled with a three-inch-high lasagna. While the finger sandwiches were picked at, the lasagna was devoured.

Connie was passing through the living room heading for the kitchen, to prepare the birthday cake for presentation, when she spotted a black Cadillac limousine pull up in front. She didn't recognize the car, but it was obvious to her they were coming to the house. She called for me. By the time I reached the living room window, two passengers were standing on the sidewalk. Although he said he was coming, I was still surprised.

There standing on my front lawn was Richard Q. Just behind him was Karen. I expected a pair of long legs to exit from the backseat, but Karen dashed that illusion when she slammed the door shut. I ran through the front door of the house, and we greeted each other with handshakes and smiles. I guided them to the side gate where we entered the backyard just as Connie came through the door carrying Amy's cake.

Everyone broke into "Happy Birthday." Amy glowed brighter than the one centered sparkler, surrounded by fifteen burning candles. Connie proudly placed the cake in the middle of the table and invited Amy to make a wish before blowing out the candles.

"Amy, don't worry about blowin' out the sparkler," Uncle Joe yelled from behind the all female choir. "Like you, it'll burn bright a long, long time."

She smiled a full smile, blew Uncle Joe a kiss, took a deep breath and with a swirling head gesture got them all. She was officially sixteen. As the applause, laughter, and singing gave way to excited chatter, I introduced Richard Q. and Karen around. First to Connie, who had only been in Richard Q's presence during company functions; they greeted each other like old friends. Karen on the other hand, had never meet Connie. She nodded with a reluctant acceptance of this Connecticut housewife. Connie read it beautifully.

Karen had placed a cigarette in her mouth and as she was lifting the lighter up, Connie clasped both her hands around Karen's and said, "Tony has told me so much about you and your support of him and his notions. He thinks you're the brightest and the best, and how there aren't too many men who can hold a candle to your abilities. It's truly a pleasure."

Karen was stunned. Most of the company wives ignored her, feared her, don't understand her, are jealous of her success, and most of all resent, her closeness with Richard Q. For the first time ever I saw Karen put away an unlighted cigarette.

"Well thank you, Mrs. Manfredi."

"*Connie*, Karen. *Connie* is fine. Let me introduce you to the birthday girl and her friends." Connie took her by the elbow and walked toward the bevy of teens. That show of affection and lack of pretense would endear Connie to Karen forever.

Introductions can conjure up different emotions in people. When I introduced Richard Q. to Uncle Joe and they shook hands I was electrified. Sure Uncle was aware of my two "careers", but he wasn't living them. It was my moment. My two bosses. Both pleased with their fair-haired boy. The electricity was short-circuited by Richard Q.

"Uncle Joe, Tony has spoken of you. Older sister in the Bronx, Arthur Avenue, as I recall. Tony's very fond of you."

In Richard Q's attempt at being social he put me into the crapper. My eyes darted to Uncle Joe. His remained welded on Richard Q. He never skipped a beat. Nodding his head affirmatively he responded.

"Yeah, my older sister. Good lady. Good cook."

"That's right! My driver took Tony to the train station. Our meeting went long and I didn't want him to be late for your arrival and dinner at your sister's." *How the hell, and why does he have to, remember all that mundane information?*

I started to say something. Anything!

Uncle Joe reached up and affectionately grabbed the back of my neck. He laughed. "Yeah, Tony ate like a *scuse de mod*."

Richard Q. put on his puzzled Wasp look.

"That's an Italian expression for someone that eats too much." I was trying to save my ass as a translator. We all laughed, but only Richard Q's laugh was sincere.

"So my nephew's doin' good at work."

"Uncle Joe, doing good is an understatement. He's doing great!" It was clear Richard Q. was relaxed and having a good time. He left his company face in the backseat of the black Caddy. I had never seen him in this light and I liked what I saw. I didn't like however what I saw in myself. My deception. My lying to Uncle Joe, the most generous, most important man in my life.

How do I handle it? What should I say? I'm sure over the years he has strayed into sexual situations and, Italian folklore being what it is, most Italian men, particularly those involved in illegal businesses, have *coo-mahds*, mistresses. He would understand. But how embarrassing for me to reveal the whole story. How we meet, his unknowingly helping me get her phone number, our continual meetings, how we're addicted to each other. I was getting very tense.

"Let's have some cake," exclaimed the birthday girl. Amy put her arm under Uncle Joe's.

"No, Amy, not this minute, I'd like to walk off your Mom's lasagna. Go. Enjoy."

Uncle Joe turned her lose. She looked at Richard Q. "Mr. Armstrong would you take Uncle Joe's place?"

He was smitten. "It would be my pleasure." He gracefully took her arm and they disappeared into the back yard.

"Tony, look at that Caddy," Uncle Joe said. "Must be a mile long. Do ya think I could sit in it?" I put my arm over his shoulder, and we started walking toward Richard Q's car.

"Why not, Uncle, you helped him buy it."

"Yeah, Tony, some car huh." He was looking into the car with no intention of getting in.

"Uncle, I have to explain about your sister, Arthur Avenue." He ignored me.

"Jesus ya could put ten people back there."

"Uncle, I'd feel better if I told you what all that bullshit was about."

He spun around. "What am I a fuckin' priest? So you confess to me. Wha. Wha do I do? Give ya t'ree Our Fathers 'n t'ree Hail Marys. Now say a good Act of Contrition, 'n all's forgiven! Tony, we ain't in a confession box, we're at your daughter's birthday." He was pissed.

"Uncle, I never want to keep anything from you but--"

He pressed his hand against my chest. "Stop. I know ya never keep anything that has to do with business from me. I got a feelin' this is personal. So it's none of my business."

I should have let it go, but I didn't, and I'm glad I didn't. I learned a rule that governed that half of my life that July afternoon. "Uncle, I just didn't want you to think...." He cut me off.

"Tony, there's somethin' ya got to always remember. Never *think* the next guy is gonna fuck ya. *Know* it! If ya know it, then you can do somethin' about it. If ya know it, you'll always be safe. You have to be so close to your people that you know what they're thinking all the time. If ya start gettin' nervous, lookin' over ya shoulder, ya history. There's a fancy word for what I'm tryin' to say, but I can't think of it."

I knew the word. "Paranoia."

"That's it, Tony. Paranoia. You get that disease 'n it's over. Paranoia will kill ya. If the bad guys don't get you, the good guys will. Ya just got to know."

It sounds so simple. I understood exactly what he meant. Dom. I know him. He would give his life before mine would be taken. Whereas my old boss, Bob Flanagan, would cut me and serve me up at any opportune time.

"Thanks, Uncle Joe. You never let me down." He looked down at the ground and with the grace of a ballet dancer, moved a lose stone with the point of his blue suede shoe. He toyed with the rock just long enough to gather his emotions. Looking back up through watery eyes, he looked directly into mine. A deep swallow, and with a quiver in his voice, "You, too, Tony. Ya never let me down.

"It's an important rule. Know ya people. Surround yourself with those you can trust. School's out. Let's join da party." He looked back at the Caddy limo.

"Hey, Uncle, want one?"

He smiled. "Too long. Besides I like my Olds."

18

THE SUMMER OF '55 came and went very quickly
if fact the rest of 1955 whizzed by, and took 1956 along with it.
But the time was well spent. The music business was getting so
big, that keeping Bobbie Jay in Miami during the week hosting
Dancetime, and traveling to the North for recordings and shows
became inefficient. So with a minor presentation to, and a major
approval from, Richard Q., the company purchased its third television station in Philadelphia.

The four million dollar price tag enabled us to move
Dancetime to a city nearer the action, nearer Chris. Without any
presentation I convinced Uncle Joe to take on the financing of
the purchase. The company always endorses the use of other
people's money. The interest is a minor cost of doing business and
keeps the company in a cash rich position.

Privately Uncle Joe met with some of his union people.
They agreed to take on the deal with only a quarter of a point
higher than the banks, but with a longer payout and less paperwork. The company bought the station for cash to satisfy the
sellers and the FCC. Once closed it was refinanced through CUF,

Consolidated Union Fund.

Teenagers are a universal breed. Like the Miami kids the Philly kids adopted *Dancetime* as their own. It's a different show when it's a hometown show. Although they were fans before the move, their attitude, dress code was all Eastern. With eighty percent of the viewing audience coming from the Northeast the program's ratings doubled! With Bobbie Jay, the music, *Dancetime* all in place it was indeed a bonanza.

We signed a chubby little girl from Albany, New York. Janice Marenelli. She had an untrained natural voice. We thinned her down slightly, changed her name to Tina Marie. Gave her heartbreaking ballads of love lost and loneliness. Her first six releases sold over a million 45s. She was the first female singer to have all of her singles go to the number one position on the top forty.

The Imperials continued to sell record after record. We moved Johnny Diamond into the movies, turning out a B movie every six months. Other single and group acts were signed, recorded, managed. Some of them only had one hit and were never heard from again. Whether it was the one-hit wonders or the megahit act, Tides Records became the hottest record company in the business, while Mann Management became the most powerful in the personal management field. Established stars from television, motion pictures, and records came to us for representation.

***

The year 1957 was only a few months old when I received two different private-line phone calls. One was from Uncle Joe requesting a coffee an' meeting. It wouldn't take long, could we meet at the bakery.

I was about to call Dom for company to Providence when he called me. Dom's call seemed more pressing, but I asked him if it could wait until tomorrow. He could tell me all about it on the drive up to Providence.

We hung up and I was just about to place the lock back on the phone dial when I impulsively picked up the receiver and dialed Chris. I always got nervous when I called her at home. From that first time, cruelly asking about her father to now. On her end of the line, there was a big difference. I still fought to maintain the secrecy, she on the other hand, like her lovemaking, was totally uninhibited. Not that she was indiscreet she just wasn't as concerned with who knew that I was on the other end of the line.

Most of the time when I called she was alone, but a couple of times her sons came into her room, and she shushed them away with, "Boys, Mommy is talking to a very dear friend, and I want to be left alone." Only once, that I know of, the good Doctor was there. She told him it was her old high school sweetheart. Just enough adulterous flirting to make it exciting. No question she caught my disease. Danger-itis. Only her symptoms were slightly different.

As soon as I said hello, she responded with, "I wish I could see you right now. I would make love to you fully clothed." My penis hardened, helping me answer, "I'll be in Philly Wednesday wearing a new navy blue suit." She responded, "Same place, same time, different sex."

We hung up.

***

Dom picked me up. We were no sooner out of the drive-way, when Dom took a deep breath and started his report. I knew it was going to be serious, because when I opened the car door I wasn't blown off my feet by rock 'n roll music.

"Okay, Dom, what's up?"

He tilted his head to the right in a "like you won't be-lieve this one" manner. "Tony, our favorite superstar is actin' up again. This time it's not 'I wanna get laid' or 'get me more shit to smoke'; it's, it's . . ." Dom was stuck.

"Dom, what is it? There's nothing that that jerk could do to surprise me."

"Tony," he slammed both hands down on the wheel, grabbing it so tightly his knuckles whitened through the black hair on his hands. "Get fuckin' ready for a major fuckin' surprise!"

I didn't know my next word would take on such special meaning. "Shoot."

"Tony, that coo-gootz wants to change management, along with his record label, movie deals, personal appearances, merchandising--every fuckin' thing. Johnny's got this hair cross his ass that he needs a change. The cocksucker wants to go to Wil-liam fuckin' Morris!"

I wanted to blurt out "Kill that mother-fucker!" Instead I calmly asked, "When did all this good news happen?"

Dom banged the steering wheel with the heel of his hand. "He's been droppin' hints for a few weeks. Then last night we was talkin' on the phone, he says, 'I need a change.' Me like a jerk, think he's talkin' about broads or dope, but he ain't. I try to con him with some bullshit, gettin' laid' talk, 'n he shuts me down with, 'listen you fuckin' dummy, I'm dumpin' you 'n your big-shot buddy, Tony. I wanna change so I can be me, not someone youse created.' Tony, do you believe this jerk-off? 'So I can be me!' Who the fuck is he anyways!"

"Dom, you do a great Johnny Diamond."

Dom wasn't laughing. "Tony, no fuckin' around. This is serious. I'm responsible for that azz-hole."

"Dom, you're right this is serious and we shouldn't be fucking around. I was waiting for this to happen. I had hoped it never would but he's a greedy, ungrateful guy and it's in his nature to do this. I know him. No matter what we would have done for him, he would do this. So don't feel the pressure of the responsibility, feel the pressure of the solution."

Dom stared straight ahead. His animated anger went silent. I continued, "I don't want to lose him to the Morris agency or any other agency. If he doesn't remain with us, he doesn't remain . . . period." Dom's stare grew deeper. "Dom, he's a volatile person. Everyone knows that. His friends. His fellow performers. His fans."

I knew I would have to make this speech one day.

"His friends are fair-weather friends. His fellow performers are jealous egomaniacs. Ah, but his fans?" I took a dramatic pause and shook my finger, "They are the true loyalists." My tempo picked up. "They must be protected. They must not be let down. They must feel their Johnny Diamond left the stage in grand style. They must tingle with memories every time they hear one of his songs, or see one of his movies. They must love him and miss him, even after he's gone. That's your responsibility, Dom. Your only responsibility. I know you and you'll handle it just fine."

The rest of the Providence trip was driven in silence. My thoughts were of how is he going to do it, and I knew he was thinking the same thing.

***

It was a relief when we arrived at the bakery. Emilio was standing on the sidewalk talking to a dark, overweight woman, who clutched a large white paper bundle next to her bosom. I overheard his closing line: "And *senora* don't make a da pizza too tick. It loses da flava. *Ciao bella.*" The woman nodded affectionately and waddled up the street.

I got out of the car. "Emilio she looks like she knows how to make a good pizza."

Emilio looked up the street at her battleship-size backside. Without taking his unlit stogy out of the side of his mouth he spit a brownish glob into the gutter. "Tony, maybe she should not eat so much pizza." He looked over my shoulder at Dom. "Way, Dominic, welcome home!" It was the first time Dom cracked a smile all morning. He waved back at Emilio.

"Tony, ya uncle's waitin'"

I walked through the empty front section of the bakery into the backroom. Uncle immediately rose to his feet and greeted me with a smile, a hug, and a kiss on each cheek. "Coffee an', Tony?" I nodded yes. "Emilio," Uncle yelled through the door.

"Uncle, he's outside talking to Dom."

"Hey, how's Dom?"

"Great!" If he only knew.

"He's a good boy. We miss him 'round here. But it's more important he's by your side." Like a delayed reaction from Uncle's earlier yell, Emilio walked in carrying a round metal pizza pan holding two espresso coffee cups and four, perfect-for-dunking biscotti.

"Dom's goin' to see if some ah da guys are 'round."

"Thanks Emilio," I said taking the tray from him. "If he comes back before we're through fix him up with some coffee an'."

I turned to Uncle toasting him with my cup: "So, Uncle, what's up?"

"Well, Tony, this is like one of those cowboy 'n Indian movies."

I dunked my first biscotti and looked up at him as if looking over the rim of eyeglasses. "Okay John Wayne tell me about it."

Uncle crunched *his* biscotti and told me how things are going great. Everybody's happy, everybody's making a few bucks, and now's the time to prepare. I held the biscotti between my teeth and through the side of my mouth questioned, "Prepare?" I crunched. "Cowboys and Indians?" *Crunch!*

"Yeah, Tony, prepare."

Leaning forward Uncle continued, "There's whisperin' goin' on that some other people like our show business 'n wanna get in. Course they don't know our connection. So I think we got to prepare for anything."

I put the remainder of the biscotti in the saucer. I was quickly losing my appetite.

"Ya remember those cowboy 'n Indian movies where the wagon train got into a circle when they saw the Indians gettin' ready to attack? Well, before they was surrounded by the Indians they kinda surrounded themselves, protectin' themselves. That's what we got to do. You started with Dom some time ago, that's good. Now ya need more."

As I swallowed, the mixture of bitter espresso and my own saliva, heightened my excitement of what might happen. I was going to be placed on the edge again and I welcomed it.

Uncle leaned back. "Dom's a rare combination of brains 'n muscle. Those guys are few 'n far between. I'd like to put a little more brains 'n a lot more muscle on the payroll."

"Uncle, that's your call, but the cut remains the same. It would be difficult for me to raise the ante this far into the game. I know the grosses will be bigger because of the business we're doing, so maybe that will offset some of the additional personnel costs." He's talking brains and muscle and I'm talking cost controls.

He never ceases to amaze me. As if he were in my brain, he said, "Tony, you're like a corporate pain in the ass. Who's talkin' personnel costs here. We're talkin' keepin' our business goin'. Who cares about the cuts if there ain't no business. Sure everything remains the same, but the people." I nodded acceptingly. Uncle continued, "First the brains.

The brains I'm talkin' about is legal brains. Johnny T'ree."

"Johnny Three?" I blurted out.

Uncle proceeded with his résumé. He's John Caprio's son. They're both from the neighborhood. Johnny's a sharp lawyer about my age. Went to Brown, then to a New York law school. He's been in New York City working for some big stiff law firm. He told his old man how he hates it and wants out.

"So, Tony, one thing led to another 'n here we are." I'm sure my silence prompted Uncle's next disclaimer. "Tony, we put him in the management company, 'n if ya don't think he's got what it takes, he's out."

Pissed that there were more directives coming I spoke up.

"Suppose I don't want him in, in the first place?"

"Tony, I got to give him a chance." Uncle went on to explain. His father and my uncle are partners. His son is no dummy. He'll do all that outside consul work.

"What does Johnny know about us?"

Uncle was quick to answer. "All he knows, is he's gonna be the inside lawyer for this showbiz management company. He knows Dom runs the office. All he knows about you, is you're my brilliant nephew from the neighborhood who's doin' great in the corporate world."

"Okay Uncle, but if he's nothing, he's out. Now what about the muscle?"

"Ah, yeah, muscle." Uncle took a sip.

"Remember when you went to Pearlie's to deliver the dough I owed him?"

"How could I forget? It was the best spinach pie I ever had."

"Yeah, spinach pie my ass. Pearlie almost shot ya in the balls when you asked for a receipt!"

I nearly choked on my last mouthful of espresso.

"Jesus, Tony, you crack me up with some of your stuff. Anyways, remember the two guys who followed you?"

"Yes, toothless Buick."

"Wha?"

"Never mind go ahead like if I don't already know."

"Yeah, well, the Vespia brothers are goin' on the payroll for awhile till we see what the other people have in mind. They'll take orders from Dom."

I raised both my hands in a surrendering gesture. "Hold it Uncle. The Vespia brothers will take orders from Dom? There's a new brainy lawyer being hired? What the fuck is going on? I was under the impression things were going along beautifully. I had organized, orchestrated, arranged this whole fuckin' operation so it was legitimate and profitable. And now this?" I wanted to get up and storm out, but my underlining faith in my uncle preempted my leaving.

"Tony, I know it looks funny. But no one's tryin' anything funny. Look we're tryin' to keep things like they are. We don't want the other people to know our connection. If the whispers get louder, the Vespia brothers tell Dom or me. Then either me or Dom tells the Vespias what to do. If the shit hits the fan we got Johnny T'ree in place."

As if ignoring what was just said, I countered, "One important caveat."

He countered, "What's that? That word. *Caveat.*"

It was an unkind thing to do. Perhaps I did it unconsciously, or perhaps I knew very well he would not understand that word, so I used it to slap him around a little.

"*Caveat. Caveat emptor.* It's legal mumbo jumbo for 'buyer beware.'"

He wasn't impressed. He wasn't hurt. He wasn't angry. "Yeah, Tony, what should I beware of?"

I folded my arms and began. "Before any orders are given, I want to be involved in the decision. When the whispering comes to you or to Dom, *I* want to know. We'll talk and *I'll* tell Dom what to tell the Vespias to do. If the shit hits the fan, *I'll* determine how and when we can best use Johnny Three."

There was a long pause while Uncle stared at his espresso cup, turning it around and around in its saucer. He finally looked up, "Tony, that's why you're here. That's why you'll do it all. Saluté my nephew, saluté." We clicked our tiny cups together and the wagon-train circle was closed.

***

The drive back to Byram was a little more traditional for Dom and me. He had the radio blasting, harmonizing to virtually every song with his tenor voice.

"Dom, I know a good record label that will sign you."

"Tony, no fuckin' way. I like bein' the man behind the scenes."

I reached over and lowered the volume. "Dom, do you know about the Vespia brothers or Johnny Three?" Dom was a little surprised at my question. It must have really bothered him because he turned the radio off. "Sure I know them. We grew up with Johnny Three. Since grammar school he was called Johnny Three. His old man was Johnny Junior and his son was baptized John the Third." He paused in reflection. "And the Vespias belong to Joe Sweets. What's that got to do with the price of tomatoes?"

He didn't know. Uncle Joe was leaving it up to me.

"Dom, they are joining Mann Management. Uncle Joe Sweets said we may need some brain and brawn. What do you think?"

It was obviously not that big a deal for Dom.

"Tony, as long as they don't slow us down. Anyways it's your call. Johnny Three is supposed to be a good lawyer. His old man and Joe Sweets are like this." He created a braid with his middle and index fingers. "I guess Johnny Junior needed a favor, and you know one good turn..." I answered. "Deserves another!"

We laughed. He thought the conversation was over and reached for the on knob of the radio. I stopped him with my next question. "What about the Vespia brothers?"

Dom withdrew his hand slowly and returned it to the steering wheel. "They're from the old school. Tough as nails and as loyal as a seein' eye dog. I think I'm tough but I won't wanna fuck with them. One's enough, but two of them is beyond the beyond." He shook his head in disbelief. "Joe Sweets must be expectin' some heavy stuff to put them on."

"Uncle Joe told me some people are interested in our show- business." There was an awkward silence. Dom put on the radio. Johnny Diamond's "Heaven and Paradise" shattered the quiet. We both starred at the radio.

"It's our fading star, Dom."

"Fallin', Tony, fuckin' fallin' star. Accordin' to my scientific calculations, it will fall 'n hit the earth sometime next week."

"Dom, it's not the Vespia meteor is it?"

"No, Tony, it's my responsibility. Remember?"

How could I forget.

***

There is such comfort in knowing things will be handled by people you trust. The thought of not having Dom by my side frightened me. I had to sell him hard on joining me in New York, and we both had to sell his wife even harder on the idea of moving out of the neighborhood.

She, like Dom and me, was a first generation Italian-American who held tight to the old world traditions. Family and friends were everything. It was tribal. Her leaving her neighborhood, where she knew all the shopkeepers, where her parents were only two blocks away, where her 'girlfriend from birth, for

Christ's sake' lived across the street, second floor in the back. These thoughts were completely unacceptable to her.

I had gone through it a couple of years earlier with Connie. Although Connie was reluctant, her wisdom, her desire for my success and a better life, won out. In fact it was Connie who finally convinced Peggy to move. The Triano's rented a small house in Stamford. Now Dom was close enough and like we handled those hillbillies together we were ready for what might come our way.

19

IT WAS THREE O'CLOCK in the morning when the phone rang. I struggled to free my arms from under the blankets. I clipped the third ring short by reaching for the phone, pulling the headset down close to my pillow.

"Hello."

It was Dom. "Tony, I'm sorry to call you so late but it's important."

I forced a few blinks, hoping the banging of my eyelids would wake me further, making me seem more alert.

"Dom, what's up?" "He's gone, Tony. Johnny Diamond just killed himself."

"Jesus." I didn't need to be awakened any further. "How?"

"He was drunk or doped up . . ."

"How, Dom?"

"Russian roulette."

"What?"

"Russian roulette, with me."

"Where are you?"

"The downtown Cleveland Hilton Hotel, Presidential Penthouse suite."

"Anybody know?"

"Yeah Johnny Three; he was here."

"Stay put. I'll call you back."

Hoping not to wake Connie, I gently lifted the covers and slipped out of bed flattening my covers and tucking part of them under Connie's back. She stirred from her fetal position. I whispered how there was an unexpected business development. I was going into the kitchen to make a few calls and have some coffee. Nothing I can't handle.

"Tony, be careful," she said.

I kneeled on my side of the bed and bent over. In the darkness, my kiss landed in her hair. It was a very sensuous feeling. I wanted to walk around to her side of the bed and without any inhibitions place myself in her mouth. I knew she would be warm from her night's sleep. I also knew it was impossible, for as sexually willing as Connie is, this type of lovemaking is beyond her. However, if it were Chris, she would welcome it.

While putting on my robe I realized the passion I was really feeling was not totally sexual, but perfectly mixed with what was just told to me on the phone. I had asked for a man's life and got it.

I entered the kitchen and put the light on over the stove. The glow was enough for me to find the coffee and get it perking. My briefcase was on the floor next the kitchen table ready for pickup and travel right after breakfast. I reached down and opened it slightly retrieving my black telephone book. I moved the telephone from the counter to the table. I called Alan Morris.

"Alan, this is Tony Manfredi. Sorry to wake you so early

but it's very important."

He answered with a grunt which is not part of Alan's personality.

"I want you on the next plane to Cleveland to handle what I know is going to be a press free-for-all."

"Tony, it's after three a.m."

I looked down at my wristwatch. "Right, three nineteen to be exact. Since when do we get paid by the hour? I would never call you like this if it weren't very important. And that's what it is, very important!"

"Jesus, Tony, nobody goes to Cleveland." I smiled at his response and I could hear the smile in his voice. "Cleveland it is. I'm awake. What's so important?"

"Our superstar Johnny Diamond just killed himself. He was playing Russian roulette with his manager and lost."

"Somehow I knew I was going to be needed with this guy. Only I thought it would be a rape charge, a dope thing, but not this. Where in Cleveland?"

"The downtown Hilton. Presidential Penthouse suite. Dom Triano is there as is John Caprio the management company's attorney."

"Why the attorney?"

"Coincidence. He's new to Mann Management and I guess Dom was showing him the operation."

"Some operation. What's with that Dom anyway?"

I ignored the inference and answered the question. "He manages a lot of the acts on our record label. Talk to him first. I've got to get to Richard Q. Keep me posted. Call me as soon as you arrive. Alan, if you can't get out right away, let me know and I'll try to get the company plane. But I need you there before

Cleveland wakes up."

"Cleveland will never wake up."

"It might after this. Call me."

I called Richard Q. at his apartment. His wife answered. She told me he was out of town. She sounded annoyed at my calling, but was more annoyed at my reminding her of what we both knew: he was not out of town. "Sorry to disturb you Mrs. Armstrong."

Click.

I checked my book under *H.* In pencil, next to *Hooker, A.* was a Manhattan number. I dialed it. A sultry voice, that I envisioned belonging to those long legs, answered, "Hello."

"Good morning." *"Good morning."* I couldn't believe I said that.

"I don't know if I have the right phone number, but I'm Tony Manfredi and I'm looking for a Mr. Armstrong."

There was a slight pause. "Mr. Manfredi"--she said my name particularly slow--"it's nearly three thirty."

I heard some breathing and rustling of material. A male throat cleared on the other end of the line. "Tony, what the hell's going on?"

"Richard Q. sorry to do this to you, but I thought it was important enough for you to know this before your day begins."

"Tony, I know you don't waste these kinds of bullets. What is it?"

"Richard Q., it's ironic you should mention bullets. Johnny Diamond just blew his brains out in Cleveland."

He couldn't resist. "That's easy to do in Cleveland."

We both enjoyed the moment.

"I just wanted you to know before you heard or read it.

I don't have all the particulars but Alan Morris is on his way to handle the press. It's going to be a big story and we want to control it."

There was a slight pause. "Tony, I think it would be better if Alan got there before anyone else. Send him on the plane. I'll call the Captain and get his ass in gear."

That's what I like, good executive thinking.

"Great idea Richard Q. I'll call Alan and get him headed for LaGuardia. In fact, I was going to go later, but I think I'll hitch a ride as well."

"That makes me feel better. Keep me posted." When he hung up I knew her long legs would wrap around him and the phone call to the Captain would be delayed by the length of time it took Richard Q. to cum. I guessed, oh, maybe two or three minutes!

I called Morris again.

"Hello Alan. The company plane's yours. I'll meet you at LaGuardia in . . ." I looked down at my watch. It was nearly three-thirty. "In an hour and a half. If the wheels are off the ground by five fifteen, we'll be in great shape. Okay?"

"Tony, I'm glad you're with me on this one. I have some bad feelings."

"Can't be any worse than our old Colonel."

"The Colonel, what a character. By the way, Tony, how did you pull that thing off anyway?"

As much as I liked Alan and respected his abilities, there was a low-level distrust that occasionally surfaced. It happened twice this morning. First with questions of Dom and now the Colonel.

"Alan, I know how to talk to people."

He wasn't going to let up. "Yeah, I've seen you in action, and you're the best, but what did you talk to him about?"

"Alan, the plane's waiting. I'll tell you over coffee."

"Right! See you at LaGuardia." He was excited about the coffee conversation. I had no intentions of bringing it up, let alone talk about it.

I started to get up to pour my first cup of coffee and was startled by Connie's appearance in the kitchen. "Connie you shouldn't have gotten up."

"Tony, is everything all right?"

"Well Connie, it will be. Johnny Diamond had an accident."

"Is he all right?"

"I'm afraid not. He's dead."

She placed a hand on each of her cheeks and shook her head left and right. It was an old world Italian gesture, used exclusively for death announcements.

"I have to go to Cleveland and deal with the situation."

She automatically reached for my cup filled it with piping hot coffee. "Do you want something to eat before you leave?"

I shook my head no and took a sip of coffee. It tasted great. Coffee usually does at this hour of the morning. As I headed for the shower I kissed her on the cheek.

"Tony, be careful. I love you."

Her *be careful* prompted me to make a quick call.

"Bakery!" The sound of dough-mixing machines nearly drowned out Emilio's voice, so I thought yelling was necessary.

"Emilio. This is Tony Manfredi."

"Hey, Tony, whatcha doin' up so early?"

I caught myself and lowered the volume. "Emilio, I

didn't want to call Joe Sweets at home so early, so would you give him a message for me. It's important so don't forget."

"Sure, Tony, what's da message?"

"I'm off to Cleveland. Johnny Diamond killed himself."

"That's it?"

"That's it."

"Okay, Tony, my love to da family." He hung up.

"*That's it!*" Emilio's been chewing on that stogy too long, but then again, for him it may be just another killing message to be delivered.

***

The wheels left the ground at five ten. It would take us about three-and-a-half hours door to door. I called Dom from the airport and he was sending a car with Johnny Three to pick us up.

Only a doctor, who Dom described as a "rock 'n roll doc," has seen Johnny Diamond. He signed an official death certificate, legally labeling Johnny's demise a death by suicide. Because he was this rock 'n roll doc, there was no reason to swear him to secrecy. He had a cup of coffee, was paid his fee, and left.

When we stepped out of the plane, we only had a few yards to walk to a waiting black Cadillac sedan. Johnny Three was standing by the opened rear door. We greeted each other like old buddies.

"Morning Johnny."

"Morning, Tony." A sincere handshake was included. Nice, even though we barely knew each other.

As I entered the sedan, with full company decorum, I introduced Alan to Johnny Three. "Alan Morris, John Caprio the

Third, the in-house counsel for Mann Management. Alan is vice-president of company relations."

They nodded acknowledgment of each other's position. Johnny encouraged Alan to get in the back with me, shut the rear door, and ran around to the front passenger's side. We were off and running.

Johnny was a little on the chipper side. "So, Tony, can you believe this!"

I knew where he was headed. I leaned over to the right. Hoping I was out of the rearview mirror's range, I put my index finger over my sealed lips then pointed to the driver.

Johnny caught on, calmed down, and continued. "So, Tony, can you believe this? Johnny Diamond broke all the attendance records at the Cleveland Arena."

"How nice" was Alan's response, which ended any further conversation from any of us.

As we entered the lobby of the hotel, Alan's eyes starting darting around looking for that obvious journalist, who would bust this story wide open without our input. But the lobby was just waking up. A couple of bellhops sipping either their last cup of coffee before retiring or their first cup upon rising, a black maid dusting some palm leaves, two freshly scrubbed businessmen scurrying off to their early morning appointments, the perennial night clerk, who couldn't wait to be relieved, and a huge hulk of a man. He was sitting fully clothed, I mean, suit, topcoat, soft hat, and all, in a passageway to the elevator.

The hulk's eyes met mine and with an insignificant nod, I approved the presence of one of the Vespia brothers. Alan and Johnny were well behind me as I headed for the elevator, so it was comfortable to give Vespia an Italian gesture consisting of an opened palm with a simultaneous upward head jerk.

Translated: *So where's your brother?*

He slowly moved his head to the left. My eyes followed. Down a long hallway, stood the other Vespia. His huge body nearly blocked out one of the two glass doors that sealed it. His back toward me, he guarded them and the street beyond. No one was going to get through that wasn't welcomed. If that failed, then for sure, no one was going to get on the special elevator marked PENTHOUSES.

I pressed the elevator button waiting for Alan and Johnny to catch up. As soon as we were side-by-side, the elevator doors opened and the operator asked us our names and what suite were we planning to visit. We passed muster and rode up. I was waiting with an answer to Alan or Johnny's question regarding that hulk sitting next to the elevator. It never came. They never put it together, why should they. What do they know about toothless Buicks, bookies named Pearlie, and brawn.

***

I think we all took the same deep breath as Johnny Three unlocked the Presidential Suite's door. He opened it and let me enter first. Dom started to get up, but had a tough time taking his eyes off the big Motorola TV. Dave Garroway raised his hand and with a calming voice signed off, "Peace." *Get ready Dave for tomorrow's tribute to the late and great Johnny Diamond.*

"Tony. Great seein' ya," Dom said. He spotted Alan and instead of our embracing he settled for a man-to-man handshake.

"Where is he, Dom?"

Dom made a head gesture toward two closed doors. I

opened one and took a step into the bedroom. The bed was not slept in. A room service table at the foot of it. An empty, straight-back chair to the right of the table. In the opposite chair, covered by a tablecloth, sat Johnny. You would expect to see blood oozing through the white linen, but there wasn't. There wasn't any sign of violence.

The food tray was on the floor. Only a little coffee was used up. I stepped over it and pulled down the tablecloth from Johnny's upright body. It got hung up around his knees so I dropped my end of it. The only thing that moved was a few whisks of hair on his slightly tilted head.

Alan, Dom, and Johnny Three stood silently behind me. I bent down a little to see what I could see. His eyes were open and reflected total disbelief. There was a moist trickle of blood coming down the side of his left cheek. I traced it up to what looked like a bad scrape on his temple. There was more blood matted to his hairline and sideburns.

His right arm was hanging straight down and below his hand, on the floor and partially hidden by the tablecloth, was a revolver. In amazement I stepped back and motioned to the three witnesses to come closer. "Can you believe this guy? Even dead he thinks with his cock." I pointed down to his crotch.

Just like he had done so many times, Johnny Diamond was crushing his tight Levis and clutching his balls.

"Johnny, throw that tablecloth back over him and don't touch a thing." The rest of us left the room.

"Do you guys want some breakfast?" Dom asked as he shut the door.

Alan and I looked at each other. Alan shocked by the request, me pretending to be.

"Sure, Dom. Some coffee would be fine. Alan?"

He gathered his composure. "Some very hot tea with fresh lemon slices. And Dom ask them to send an extra cup filled with very hot water."

Dom's look prompted Alan to continue. "I like my tea extra hot and the water heats up the cup. It also gives me a chance to make sure it's clean."

Dom shrugged and headed for the telephone. While he was ordering I started to prep Alan. "Dom is his manager. He called the doctor first in hopes of saving him. Other than us no one else knows. Let's let Dom fill in the rest."

Johnny Three returned to the living room.

Alan asked him, "Where were you when this happened."

Johnny didn't miss a beat. "Sitting right there on that sofa. We ordered him some coffee because he was loaded."

"A little tipsy," I interjected.

"He was also tired. So Dom took him into the bedroom where they said they were going to play one-for-one gin before bedtime."

Alan didn't understand. I gave the explanation. "It's a one hundred dollar, one hand game of gin, no knocking."

"Right, Tony. I was going to leave when Dom asked me to stay. He said something like 'The way Johnny plays gin it won't be long.' Or something to that effect. It couldn't have been five minutes. I must have gone into a half-sleep and like in the far distance I heard this pop. Still dosing, Dom shook me awake. I jumped up and said, 'That was fast!' Dom didn't laugh. He went over to the phone and called the doctor. 'Doc there's been an accident. Get over here right away.' When he hung up he told me Johnny had shot himself. Then he called you, Tony."

Alan like a detective continued his interrogation.

"Did you check out the bedroom?"

"I just went in and saw what you saw. Johnny was already covered with the tablecloth."

Dom was through ordering. Alan turned his questioning to him.

"What happened, Dom?"

"We went in to the bedroom to play some one-on-one gin. I'm lookin' for the cards 'n when I turn around Johnny's got this gun in his hand. He says, 'No one-on-one gin, one-on-one roulette.' I think he's kiddin' but he ain't. He says, 'Either we play my game or you're dead for sure.' I know now he ain't kiddin'. I try to con him out of the gun. He ain't buyin'. Next thing I know he spins the barrel 'n says, 'The star goes first.' He puts the gun to his head 'n pop! It's over. I couldn't believe my eyes. I check his wrist pulse. Nothin'. I go into the living room, call the doc 'n Tony."

Alan stroked his neatly trimmed beard.

"Alan," I picked up the conversation, "that's the story that goes out only with more flair. He complained about his loneliness as a star. He couldn't get close to anyone because most people wanted a piece of his image, not the human being. He couldn't trust anyone except of course Dom. He was obviously suicidal. The Russian roulette game was just a trick."

I stopped my spiel for a second and rethought my last sentence. "No forget that trick business. He challenged the only man he knew would play fair with him. Dom. Dom tried to talk him out of it, but he was too determined. It was his bad luck. The first round, the one and only bullet in the chamber, killed him. Anything else you come up with has to make him go out the superstar who was unhappy with his success. No business problems.

Alan we want martyrdom here. Make sure you get in the idea that Johnny loved Johnny Ace and how he was discovered in Philly and sang "Pledging My Love" on *Dancetime* and how he was named after Johnny Ace right there on TV and how Johnny Ace later killed himself playing Russian roulette."

I was pumped up. "The same bullet killed them both."

Alan was taking shorthand notes.

"Alan, let's call the cops. You take it from here."

Alan went to the phone just as there was a knock on the door.

"Room service!"

Dom and I headed for the door. We opened it. The waiter was more than willing to wheel the table into the room but we took it away from him. Dom signed the check. I turned back toward the door to make sure the waiter had left. He did. I gave Dom a head nod and he stepped outside pretending to look for the waiter. I looked down the outside hall with him and whispered, "Vespia brothers."

Dom needed no further direction and talking into an empty hall said, "Shit I forgot to give the guy a tip. I'll be right back!"

Dom got to the Vespia brothers who disappeared as the suite filled with police. Uniformed and in plain clothes, they scurried about the rooms. The rock 'n roll doctor was summoned and arrived with his medical credentials intact.

Crime scene pictures were taken of Johnny propped up and on the stretcher. A picture of Dom, sitting alone on the sofa in fake disbelief, was also taken.

Johnny Three was the surprise of surprises. He handled

himself and the authorities perfectly. We were saving Alan for the press, who after being held outside in the hallway, gushed into the room.

The journalist sea was parted as Johnny's stretcher rolled through them. He was covered with a blanket, but that didn't stop the cameras from flashing. One brazen newspaper reporter reached for the blanket and flipped it back. One light bulb flashed. He had obviously arranged the timing of his move with his cameraman.

Dom flew off the sofa and grabbed the reporter's arm. He was going to hurt him badly but stopped when our eyes met and I gave him a negative head move. Before the other cameras could shoot, Dom flipped the blanket back. The whole episode only took seconds. But that picture of Johnny Diamond, starring directly into the lens, lingered around the world in magazines, newspapers, and on TV for months.

The Cleveland Police Department signed off on the case as suicidal. Alan had executed the PR plan to a tee. Within weeks after his death, Tides Records put out a commemorative two-disc album, with pictures. The first pressing was for two-and-a-half million copies. Nothing like that ever hit the record business. His movies were re-released in theaters and sold out. We hired our tight-ass CBS television station in Atlanta to produce a documentary on Johnny's life. It was so well produced the CBS Television Network bought it for broadcast during the important rating period. It was hosted by none other than Bobbie Jay. Months had passed and Johnny Diamond, though gone, was not forgotten. He remained, even from the grave, a money machine, without royalties.

20

NEARLY TWO YEARS LATER, Dom and I were strolling the shaded streets of Byram.

"Dom, I can't believe in a couple of weeks, it will be Amy's birthday."

"Yeah, Tony."

"Johnny Diamond." Not even realizing it, I said his name out loud. "He was with us then."

"Tony. Wha? Do ya miss him?"

I shook my head no. "It's just strange not having that pain in the ass around."

Dom laughed. "He was a pain. Everywhere!"

"How did you do it, Dom?" He was surprised at my question.

We stopped in the middle of a deserted lane. He looked up at the trees. The birds were gently singing their summer songs.

"Do you really wanna know?"

I automatically looked up and down the street checking for eavesdroppers.

"Yes."

Dom put his arm in mine and we slowly walked the lane.

"Well, Tony, it was pretty easy. I played to that azzhole's ego 'n cockiness."

He went on to say how the show at the Cleveland Arena was great. More than ever he owned the audience. After the show they went to his dressing room.

"So, Tony, he's sweatin' like a pig, drinkin' champagne out of a bottle. In the room was me, Johnny Three and his valet, that faggot what's his name, 'n two girls. I mean girls. They were about fifteen, sixteen." In disgust, he continued. "He was offerin' them champagne, which was something he always did. He would eyeball some young pussy and after the show send that faggot to get them. Most of the time a twosome. Usually friends, a few times they was sisters.

"Anyways, that night, Johnny Three 'n I walk in, 'n he right away screams at me to 'get that fuckin' wop lawyer out of here.' Johnny Three's smart. He backs right out. He starts yellin' at me about our record deal, the lack of class in our representation of him, the script for his next movie was a piece of shit, how come he's not doin' primetime television, 'n last but not least, he's not wearin' any more Joe College crap.

"With that he, throws the bottle of champagne against the wall. He already had his shirt off, so he starts to drop his khaki pants. The faggot is gettin' excited over this shit. The two girls can't believe their eyes. They look down as he's undoin' his pants. I step in front of him, between the kids 'n tell him not now. Let's talk about it at the hotel.

"'Fuck you. You fat Dago.' That's what he says. I'm pissed but not showin' it. He pushes me aside 'n drops his pants 'n Jockey shorts.

"'Get out of the way. I want these young things to see Johnny's cock.'

"He reaches over 'n grabs one of the girls by the head 'n forces her face right into his cock. Tony, he didn't even have a hard-on. He couldn't get it up! I don't know if he ever could! The other girl started screamin'; the faggot yelled at her to be quiet. I couldn't take it. I grabbed both girls by the arms 'n almost threw them out the door.

"Johnny was crazed. Da faggot made a move toward me, 'n I gave him one of those Tony Manfredi stares." Dom struck a pose and made a funny face that was supposed to be scary.

"Da faggot stopped in his slippers. He was the next one out the door."

Dom went on to say that Johnny stopped yelling and told him we was through. He was going to sign with William Morris in New York. In the limo, from the arena to the hotel he busted Johnny's balls. By the time they arrived Johnny was so pissed off he couldn't talk. He went right to his bedroom. Dom's plan, like a script, was being followed perfectly.

Johnny always arranged for a big breakfast to be delivered right after each concert. When room service left, within two minutes Dom got him crazed and up for Russian roulette. Johnny went to his bedside table and took out this twenty-two pistol that he always carries around and threw it on the bed. He pours a cup of coffee and puts the tray on the floor.

"Tony, I pick the gun up and cup the chamber as if shakin' the bullets out. I show him six. I hold up one bullet 'n put it into the chamber. I spin it.

"'Who goes first azzhole,' I say. Of course his balls and ego's on the line he says, 'Me you fat fuck.' He grabs the gun 'n bingo end of story."

Dom wore me out with his blow by blow. It took a moment to digest it all. "Dom, what if you had to go first? How did you know the first trigger pull would be the loaded chamber?

"He was so worked up he would never let me go first. I palmed the bullets." I looked puzzled. "I never emptied the chambers. It looked like I did, but I palmed five extra bullets. I threw *them* on the table. I was holdin' one from the chamber, so he could see I put it in the gun 'n spun the barrel. After I asked him 'Who goes first azzhole,' he grabs the gun. Staring right at me he spins the chamber 'n oops! He's history. I empty the gun 'n called the doc."

"Dom, you are a piece of work." I would have really been pissed if you had to go first."

He smiled. "For you, Tony, I would go first anytime."

I put my arms around him and we hugged.

"Hey, Tony, these Ah-med-egons might think we're some queers or somethin'."

"What about the Vespia brothers?" I asked.

"I picked the day 'n asked them to come by just in case."

"Dom, you're a piece of work."

"You said that already."

"Did I?"

"Did I?" mocked Dom.

Dom's roulette story stuck with me. It bothered me that Johnny Three was so involved, and I wanted to make sure he was not too curious, so I called him.

"Hello, Johnny, this is Tony Manfredi; we haven't had a chance to talk one on one since Cleveland and I would very much like to do that." I asked him to come to our house for dinner and before he could object, I said it would be just him and whatever family members would be around. We agreed to meet about six in Greenwich at the train station.

I called Connie next and asked her, knowing full well she would say yes to my "Johnny" invitation.

"Of course, Tony. It's Friday so I'll make some nice fish. Maybe some linguine with fresh clams or with lobster sauce or some calamari or--"

"Connie whatever you decide, it'll be the best meal he's had in a long time."

Why, on occasion, is a phone call to Connie followed by a phone call to Chris. I understand fully the guilt-ridden calls to Connie following a love making session with Chris. I called her then.

"Chris, I just want to tell you how much I miss you."

"Tony, I can't believe you're calling. I was sitting here trying to write a letter to my father and all I kept thinking of was you. I knew if I told him, he would approve and in his own elegant way urge me to continue pursuing my happiness."

I was a little surprised at her statement. "Chris, I don't think anyone, no matter how close, should know of our love affair."

There was disappointment in her voice. "I know. But when I'm not with you all this guilt comes rushing toward me. It's like some huge wave and I can't get out of the way of it. It crashes over me." She paused. "When I was a little girl swimming off the Jersey Shore, sometimes I would get tossed and lost in a wave. It was terrifying for me then and it's so frightening for me now. My father would pull me out of that wave and hold me close. I knew I was safe. Maybe that's why I want to tell him so he can pull me out of this guilt and I will be okay." Her voice quivered.

Slowly I said, "I am the one who will make you safe. I am the one who will protect you."

She gathered her thoughts. "I'm not a person of deception, of lies, of sneaking around. It's eating me alive."

I too feel the guilt of our love affair. I once tried to explain it to Uncle Joe and that ended my sharing it with anyone. I wondered who really did know. Did Doctor John know? Did Connie know? The doctor was such an uncaring insensive person I doubted it. Connie on the other hand had this built in radar. This intuition that never failed her. Would she dare delve into that heartache? I doubted it, but I couldn't help thinking she knew. Somehow she knew.

"Chris, things are the way they are. I never want us not to be together. We both must accept the complications that go with our love. I have. You must." There was a pause and a deep inhaling from her side of the telephone. She unconvincingly sighed, "I will."

"If I were with you now Chris, I would kiss you wherever you wished to be kissed. Touch that place, think of my lips there, and tell me softly where."

Her inhaling became deeper and longer as was the pause that followed. "My inner thigh." Now I inhaled to control my own urges. "Mark the spot, so my first kiss will find it."

The train pulled in at six ten. Johnny was one of the first passengers to get off. After a quick look to the left and right, he spotted me. His appearance was lawyer-esque. Dark suit, A-shaped briefcase. His slight frame was topped off by short, neatly parted dark brown hair. Brown eyes. Not particularly good looking, but his athletic carriage exuded confidence and made the whole package attractive.

He slung a canvas bag over one shoulder. His nose, though not broken, had the spread of a seasoned boxer. I remembered his athletic accomplishments at LaSalle. He was a year behind me and in his junior and senior years he made All-State wrestling, track, and I think baseball. He received a full athletic scholarship to sprint at Brown University, and made the All-American team. He chose NYU law school. Brown was paid for, but he worked like a dog every summer on road construction to earn the rest of his tuition at NYU. Uncle Joe told me his father made up the difference by being lucky with the horses.

"Tony, this is so terrific. Thanks for asking me." His handshake was firm and genuine, just like when we met at the Cleveland airport.

"It's my pleasure Johnny. It's good to get to know the people who are going to keep us out of trouble. And Lord knows Dom needs all the help he can get." We both exchanged a courteous laugh and got into the car.

As we pulled into the driveway I invited him to leave his tie and jacket behind. He was more than willing to oblige. He also left his athletic bag, but took his briefcase. We entered through the backyard. Connie came out of the backdoor.

"Tony, you should have brought him through the front. Hi, Johnny, it's been a long time." Connie passed me by, extended her hand, and as they touched she kissed Johnny's cheek.

"Connie." Johnny, holding both her arms continued, "Connie Mero you look great! Yeah, it's been a long time."

A little annoyed I interceded.

"Connie obviously you remember Johnny from the neighborhood."

"Remember him? He lived right across the street from me. Johnny Three was the first boy I ever kissed." They both laughed. I didn't.

Connie was all smiles. Actually there was a glow around her that made me jealous of their friendship. She took Johnny by the arm and led him toward the patio table.

"So Johnny Three, tell me what's been going on in your life. The last time I heard, you were out of law school and going to work for a big law firm in New York. Your mother told me all about it. She was so proud of you, God rest her soul." There was that reflective pause that comes immediately following that statement. "Tony, can you believe his parents," then, re-acknowledging his mother's death by placing a compassionate hand on his chest, continued, "I mean his father, still lives in the same house he did when we were kids." It was a quick trip down memory lane.

I asked for drink orders. Cold beer for Johnny white wine for Connie. She reached over and held his hand. "So fill me in." She knew about the scholarship to Brown and the New York law school.

As I poured two ice-cold bottles of Narragansett Beer into frosted mugs, and cool white Suave Bolla into a wineglass, I assessed the Johnny-Connie relationship. It was my own guilt with Chris that triggered it. I put to rest my jealous notions. They were two childhood friends who had grown up together and were happy to see each other. But why didn't Connie tell me she knew him when we talked about the invitation I had extended?

I sat silently and listened to their stories. They laughed at their reminiscences and I couldn't help being an appreciative audience. There were things about Connie that I never knew. Cute little things, like how nervous she was when she made her First

Holy Communion. She pretended she was getting married and that was what enabled her to calmly walk down the aisle.

"Johnny I have to tell you this. It wasn't so much Holy Communion as it was penance. When I told Father Telli I had committed a sin by kissing you, he yelled at me saying 'Connie if you keep it up and you die you'll go straight to hell even before you make your Holy Communion.'" Connie toasted, "To Father Telli!" We all clicked our glasses. She looked straight into my eyes. She had drifted off somewhere for a moment. Was she wishing to return to Johnny's first kiss? Was she wishing for more kisses from me?

The linguine with calamari marinara sauce was delicious. We just were finishing our dessert when Amy came home. Her entry would brighten any room. She came over kissed me then her mother. I introduced Johnny as one of her mom's old sweethearts. She kidded Connie about being a loose adolescent. She shook Johnny's hand, and asked Connie if she needed help cleaning the dishes. Connie was not about to let that offer go by. She excused herself and with Amy, took a load of dishes into the kitchen.

"Johnny, are you comfortable? Need anything?" I asked. He shook his head no, then as if rethinking it, said, "Yes, Tony. A life like yours."

I was pleased with his wish. I walked over to my father's old radio, and tuned in Alan Freed on WINS. Little Richard's "Jenny, Jenny, Jenny won't you come along with me."

"Here I am nearly thirty-two and I love this music. It must be the lyrics!" I looked over my shoulder from the radio to Johnny. "What part?"

He looked puzzled. He must have thought I was still

talking about the music.

"What part of my life?" I asked.

"All of it. Family. The company. The excitement. The love. The respect."

I was taken by his response. "Thank you Johnny. I'm a very lucky man. It doesn't happen just by chance, and I know once you have it, you have to be appreciative, always be aware of it, and willing to do whatever you have to, to keep it. Besides my life what do you want for yourself?"

He took an obligatory sip of his coffee. "I love working for Mann Management. It's so different than that A-med-egon law firm. God what a mistake that was thinking I could make it in the Wasp world with a name that ends in a vowel."

"I'm doing it."

He tilted his head to the side and lightly closed his eyes. That's Italian for *So?*

So what? Does he know more than what I think he knows? I thought of Uncle Joe's rule: "Know your people, Tony." Thoughts of Uncle being a friend of Johnny's father lead to maybe he knows more than I would like him to know.

"Tony, you run things your way. I forget you have a boss."

"Yeah." I was relieved to get off those negative thoughts. "His name doesn't end in a vowel. It begins with one. *Armstrong.* I don't believe in that Wasp-Wop thing. Anyway they take care of their own, just like we do. The only leveler is your ability. If you're good, your name doesn't mean a thing."

"Well, Tony, from where I sit, you're an independent company within the company."

"That's true only up to a point. When I decide to buy

another television station, which by the way we're planning to do, and I'll be spending millions of company dollars, not only do I consult with Armstrong but I do a full presentation telling him why I think we should. It's not dissimilar to the record business. As long as a recording artist is selling records we'll go along with him. But if his sales fall off . . . well . . . And as long as I'm making money for the company, I'm fine. I screw up? I'll have to look for a new label."

He liked the record label comparison. It was time to get to the point.

"Johnny, I'm not one to beat around the bush. I asked you to dinner because I wanted to find out more about you. What your plans are."

"I'm flattered, Tony."

"So you should be. My success is not only due to my own abilities, but to the people I surround myself with. I don't believe in hiring down. I believe in hiring people who have talents and who can be trusted. I know you have the talent. I've seen you work in person, like that awful situation in Cleveland. I read all your memos. Review your negotiations. Dom speaks highly of you. I'm impressed. Now the question is one of trust."

He was thrown by my trust statement.

"How can I prove my trustworthiness?"

"You can't. It is either there or it isn't. I'll know if it's there, right after you do."

I patted his knee which seemed to ease his trustworthiness concern.

"Johnny, there are things I would like us to do together. I would like to hire you as a freelance consul for the company."

"Tony, like I said earlier I'm flattered."

I started standing. "Good be flattered, but first you're off to see your family in Providence."

He stood.

"If you see my Uncle Joe, send him my love. Then Monday, come over to the company, say around eleven. I would like to get you involved in the purchase of this television station in Los Angeles. It may involve a few trips out West. By the way, before we start to negotiate for the station, we should settle on a pay schedule. Present it Monday; if it makes sense we'll proceed, if not we'll have some coffee an', then I'll send you back to Dom. Which reminds me, I spoke to Dom about this possibility and he's in favor of it, provided he doesn't lose you entirely." I hadn't talked to Dom really, there was no reason too. His loyalty to me included total acceptance.

21

WHEN I RETURNED from taking Johnny to the train station, Amy and Connie were shoulder to shoulder in front of the kitchen sink. Their animated conversation became stilted when I entered. That's the sign of "Quiet, it's Dad." As I headed toward the patio Connie said, "Tony, I think you should stay and listen to our conversation."

"Boy this is a first!" Amy looked at her mother in disbelief. "Mom, are you kidding!" I couldn't imagine what was going on, but I knew it was going to be big.

"Amy, there is no way you can pursue this without your father's permission. As a matter of fact I don't even know if I can give you my approval."

I had had it.

"Okay, ladies, let's have it."

Amy turned around wiping her sudsy hands with a dishtowel. Connie continued to wash dishes. "Dad, about a week ago I was driving in Port Chester." "How bad was the accident?"

"Tony, no accident." Connie turned and waved a soapy hand at me. "Just listen."

"A couple of the girls and I went to a drive-in restaurant there. We were sitting in the car when this guy, about your age, came over to my side of the car. He said he had seen me around before and asked my name. I just told him *Amy*. He introduced himself and gave me his card. Phil Bolton."

Untrustingly, I asked, "So who's Phil Bolton?"

"He's a big deal with the Cosmo Modeling Agency."

I sat there in calculated silence. The quiet turned Connie around. Amy waited for some support from her, but it didn't come.

"So, Amy, what does that mean?"

"Well, Dad, Mr. Bolton wants me to go to the city and interview with him, take some pictures and maybe he'll sign me up to do some modeling."

Able to make decisions for the company on my own, I always looked to Connie's wisdom when it came to the kids. "Connie, what do you think?"

"Tony, I don't know. If she were older, then I would probably feel a little bit better. But only eighteen and just out of high school? I don't know."

I stiffened. "I do."

"First"--I extended my thumb--"she isn't eighteen yet. Another month. Second"--I kept my thumb in place and extended my index finger--"she graduates in two weeks. Third"--keeping the other two fingers rigid I extended my middle finger--"what about college? All the reviewing, exams, campus trips. You got accepted to Pembroke, which as I recall was 'the only College you would accept.' Four"--I extended my ring finger leaving my pinkie buried in my palm--"there is no question you are a beautiful girl. You have the height and the look, but are you photogenic."

I brought my two hands together as if in prayer. "Lastly, is this Bolton on the level?"

"Dad, he gave me his card."

I shook my head at her naiveté. "Amy, honey, I'm not saying he's anything other than what he is, but just maybe he's some hustler who uses this play to get whatever it is he wants."

Connie looked dismayed. "Tony, do you really think so?"

"Connie, think about it. He's working a Port Chester drive-in restaurant! This is either another Lana Turner drugstore discovery or some scam. Amy, give me a few days to check it out."

"But, Dad, I was to call him Monday and set up an appointment."

"Amy, your father is right. Let him check it out first. I'm sure he has the contacts to do it quickly."

"But, Mom, I'm supposed to call him Monday and--"

I cut her off. "And you tell him you can't get to the city until Thursday. By then I'll know."

"But, Dad, suppose he says no. Suppose he wants to see me right away?"

"The answer is easy. *No!* Amy, either you handle it, and give me until Thursday, or it's a dead issue." She looked to her mother for help. Connie shook her head no. "Your father is right. It's a couple of days."

Amy looked back at me hoping for a change.

"Amy, I know this is very flattering and exciting. I just don't want anyone taking advantage of you. If it's all legit, I'll get equally excited. Thursday."

"Okay, Dad." She always knew when to back off, but never entirely. "Do you think I could know by suppertime Wednesday night?" The tension was broken. "Amy, if I find out by breakfast Monday you'll know." She threw her arms around me. "Thanks, Dad. I love you."

As soon as I arrived at the office I called Dom. "Have you ever heard of the Cosmo Agency?"

"Are they bookers?"

"No, Dom, they're supposed to be a modeling agency."

"Nah, Tony, I don't know em. Do you want me to check around?"

"No that's okay. Dom, that reminds me. Johnny Three is coming over here for a meeting. I liked the way he handled himself in Cleveland. I would like to see if we could bring him along with us. What do you think?"

"Tony, he's from the neighborhood, 'n his old man and Joe Sweets go back a ways. I think he's good people, but you know better."

"I'll put him on this Cosmo Agency thing. Do you need him for anything?"

"Not before you need him, Tony."

"Thanks, Dom. How's Peggy?"

Dom opened up about lots of sex but no kids. How they talked about adopting using Amy as an example but Peggy wouldn't buy it.

"Dom, maybe I should talk to her about the adoption issue."

"Tony, she loves 'n respects you. Be my guest. If you pull it off, I guarantee you eggplant sandwiches the rest of ya life!"

"Deal!"

We hung up.

***

Eleven o'clock. My intercom buzzed.

"Mr. Manfredi. A Mr. Caprio is here for his appointment."

"Thanks, Francine. Send him in."

"Need some fresh coffee, sir?"

"Sure, and ask Mr. Caprio how he takes his?"

I thought her food and drink phobia would be left behind in Providence with her mother. It sometimes drives me nuts! But all in all I'm glad she's with me. You can't replace that kind of efficiency and loyalty. She was just born to serve. She must have some Irish blood in her somewhere.

The door opened and in walked Johnny Caprio followed by Francine with a plate. "I made some pepper biscuits last night and I thought you two Italian boys might enjoy them with your coffee."

Johnny was obviously pleased. I was passively pissed!

"Thanks, Francine." With a little more sarcasm, which I knew would go over her head, I jabbed, "Don't forget the coffee."

"Oh, no sir. I put some fresh on." Her swirling exit caused the layers of crinoline to crackle. Her gray flannel, poodle encrusted skirt, twirled with excitement. *To serve! Yes! To serve!*

Johnny Three and I talked about the old neighborhood and my Uncle Joe, whom he'd gone to see on his trip home. Turning to business, I asked if he'd considered his fee.

"I have," Johnny answered in readiness and continued. "I think the best way to do it is I work for nothing, but the company picks up all my miscellaneous expenses."

I responded with a surprised question. "Work for nothing?"

"Yes'" Johnny continued. "I would want to run it by Dom first, but the way I see it Mann Management's largest client is the company. All our recording talent is on the TIDES label. We have exclusive, personal representation contracts with other talent like Bobbie Jay. Mann already pays me very well. So unless your projects take me completely away from my Mann responsibilities, I think no money other than expenses is fair."

Acceptingly I said, "Provided Dom approves, it's done." We both knew he would.

We shook hands. Francine entered with the coffee and without any food-related commentary she left.

I brought up what this meeting is all about. The purchase of a TV station in Los Angeles. Having finished my presentation, I said, "There is one thing I would like you to check into."

He took a sip of coffee and by his stare I knew he was all ears.

"This is more personal than business, but seeing how you and Connie were childhood sweethearts I didn't think you would mind."

He smiled.

"My oldest daughter has been approached by a Phil Bolton from the Cosmo Agency." I handed him Bolton's business card. I asked if he could find out what it was all about without telling them who he represented. He agreed.

Johnny contacted Phil that same day and set up an afternoon meeting. Cosmo was the third largest modeling agency stateside. It had no international representation. Phil was the number three person in charge. Position one was held by Mrs. Cosby and a distant number two by Mr. Cosby.

She was the former Maureen "Moe" Philips of the Park Avenue, New York City; Belleview Avenue, Newport; and "my daddy's very rich" Philip's fame. She married Lewis Cosby of the "unknown." The agency received its name from the combined Cosby-Moe names. COSMO. Cute! The business was given to them, as a wedding gift, from a very grateful father.

Moe was rich, but not attractive. Lewis was poor and very handsome. The first impression is that handsome Lewis wanted Cosmo as his own personal playground. Not so. It was Moe's idea all the way. Lewis would be very happy doing nothing. Moe is the brains and the drive behind it. Her success came from her own fantasies of being beautiful. She had an eye for the beautiful and created within each beautiful woman an attitude. Lewis was the PR person. It was very clear he had to earn his keep.

She assigned Phil the task of bringing in younger models, which, although in their teens, could be made up to pass for early to midtwenties. Fresher faces . . . longer staying power.

"Johnny, that's a lot of information for one session. So you think it's legit?"

"Absolutely, Tony."

I paused. Johnny's breathing on the other end of the phone line was the only audible sound.

"Johnny do you think you could arrange a meeting between me and Moe? You know the nervous father wants to meet the lady in charge."

Johnny hesitated. "I-I guess so."

"Is there a problem with my request?"

He gathered his thoughts. "No, Tony. No problem. I'm a little surprised you want to meet with her. Phil is running things on a day-to-day basis and I believe what he told me to be true. In fact, I called my old Waspy law firm and asked a friend if he could get some information on the Philips-Cosby clans. He had it right there at his fingertips. It turns out the old man uses the law firm for some of his legal activities. I got their whole background from them not Phil. Phil just gave me the business stuff."

"Did Phil come off like he was running things?"

"Well, yes, kind of. But he did say he reported to the owners of the agency and his recommendations had to be approved by them. I think that was honest."

"Johnny, it's not a matter of honesty, it's a matter of control. If Amy is going to be part of the agency I want to make sure the person in control is directly involved in her development."

"Tony, with all due respect, Amy has not even been in to see them, taken pictures or whatever it is they do. She has not been accepted."

"True. But if she does go in, I want things to be right. Because once she goes in, they'll want her. Johnny Three, if you're having a problem with my meeting Moe Cosby, just tell me. I'll set it up myself."

Using *Johnny Three* he knew I was losing patience with this conversation.

"No problem, Tony, I'll set it up."

"Johnny, business deals are one thing. My daughter is something else. Someday, if you're lucky enough, you'll understand."

"Tony, I don't have to wait, I understand now."

"Good. Book it and we'll be there."

"'We'll'?" he questioned.

"Of course 'we'll.' Think I'd go see that shark without my lawyer? Call me." I hung up.

***

It was nearly six o'clock. The phone rang.

"Tony. Johnny. Tomorrow. Two fifteen. I'll meet you at seventy-seventh and Madison at two ten."

"No problem setting it up?"

"None. In fact it was a lot easier than I expected."

"How easy?"

"She knew who you were and who you worked for."

"Really?" I was flattered but curious.

"I'll fill you in, Tony, when we meet."

"Two-ten. Seventy-seventh and Madison. Thanks."

I hung up, picked up my private line and dialed.

"Hello, Connie. I'm on my way home. Is Amy there?"

There was a slight pause and then an excited voice.

"Dad?"

"You'll be able to call him around four tomorrow afternoon."

She knew there was finality in my voice that was impenetrable. "Thanks, Dad. Hurry home."

I disconnected the call by pushing down on the telephone cradle. Releasing it triggered a dial tone. I dialed another number.

"Hello." It was her.

"Chris. I love you."

"Me too."

"He's there?"

"We're having an early family dinner."

"Think of me during dessert."

"I think I'm going to make bananas dipped in milk chocolate."

"I'll call you in the morning."

"That will be perfect."

22

THE MEETING AT COSMO'S went incredibly well. Moe Cosby was a little wisp of a woman who, as if using it for protection, stayed behind her desk. Her nearly chinless, ruddy face, framed by mousy brown thin hair, made it difficult to believe she was in the beauty business. Sitting very elegantly in silence was Lewis. He had the look of a forties movie star. I envisioned him hanging out poolside with Tyrone Power or Charles Boyer. The only nervous person in the meeting was Phil Bolton. I'm sure his other discoveries never demanded such a meeting. Johnny melded into the background.

"Mr. Manfredi, it's a pleasure meeting you. This is quite a coincidence. Just last Saturday I was the dinner companion of Richard Armstrong." With each sentence her high society accent became more pronounced. "When we broached the subject of our businesses he raved about his media division and of you. I have a feeling you know this, but he's a big fan of yours."

"Well thank you, Mrs. Cosby."

"*Moe* is more than appropriate. Now, about Amy, Mr. Manfredi. Or may I call you Anthony."

"*Anthony* is inappropriate, *Tony* is fine."

So that's why the meeting was so easily set. *Richard Q. nice going.* She smiled a broad smile. It highlighted the only thing about her that was physically attractive: her teeth. They were absolutely perfect. Healthy, white, and beautifully shaped. Just the right spacing. Too bad they were surrounded by a wire thin upper lip and a sagging lower one. Her unattractiveness continued to contradict her position.

Amy's situation was handled very quickly. She convinced me all was legitimate, and that Amy would be treated properly.

"Moe, I just want to make sure she's treated professionally. No that's not what I want to say. If she's got it, let her know. If she hasn't, let her know that as well. No delays. No strokes."

She stood and walked from behind her barricade. No wonder she remained seated in back of it. She was only five two and so frail for what I guessed to be an early thirtyish lady. I have never seen such a bustless, assless, hipless, thin-ankled, thin-wristed woman in my life!

"Tony, we never stroke. We don't have the time. I'll decide if Amy has it, and if she has, as with any minor, I'll need your permission to sign her." She looked over to Phil, who looked relieved, and instructed him to get Amy to her within the next forty-eight hours. The meeting was over.

Amy went in to meet Moe on Friday. Phil was told to arrange a weekend shoot. Monday I received a call from Moe.

"Tony, I'm looking at Amy's proofs. Your daughter is gorgeous in person and twice as beautiful when photographed."

"Moe, thank you very much. I respect your opinion and it makes an already proud father prouder."

"Tony, is there any chance we could have lunch one of

these days?"

Other than Karen, I was not use to dealing with women in power business situations. I came back defensively. "Only if I buy."

"Well, to tell you the truth, I'm such a fanatic when it comes to food, I seldom go out. I have my meals prepared here and prefer eating in."

I wanted to tell her she could use a good meal. An eggplant sandwich from Peggy. Or some Lasagna from Connie. And to wash it down some of Joe Sweets' espresso with Francine's wine or pepper biscuits on the side.

"Moe I'd like that. When?"

"Tuesday?"

"Tomorrow?"

She was pushy and I didn't like that! Whether she read it in my voice or she really meant next Tuesday, she answered. "No, next Tuesday."

I flipped through my daily calendar. Tuesday had a penciled in, therefore tentative, Johnny Three-LA TV meeting around eleven. There was a vertical line through *2PM* indicating the possibility of our having lunch. Easy decision.

"Tuesday it is." Out went the penciled *Johnny Three* and in went the penned-in *Moe*. I started the vertical line toward *2PM* when Moe laid down the ground rules.

"I eat at twelve noon sharp and finish by one o'clock."

I stopped my vertical decent at *1PM*.

"I'll be there at five of. Sharp! You can throw me out whenever you wish. Can I at least bring something to drink?"

"No, I drink only bottled water."

"And I only drink Doctor Brown's Cream Soda. Cold, no ice cubes."

The fencing was over. "It'll be waiting for you."

"Good. Tuesday."

We both raced to hang up first. I hoped she smiled as I did once we were off the phone. *This is fun.*

Johnny had arranged for a copy of the proofs to be sent to the house. There were some that contained an *M* inked in the corner. I was told they were the ones Moe had picked. I had expected something entirely different. Most of them were facial shots from all angles with various expressions.

Additional shots showed Amy modeling clothing. Slacks. Fur coats. Gowns. Skirt and blouses. Not one bathing suit or lingerie shot. I was surprised but relieved. Our house was a gallery all week long. Family and friends stopped by to view, eat, drink, and give their opinion.

Uncle Joe stopped by on Sunday. After dinner, I walked him to his car.

"Do you think it's okay, Uncle?"

"Of course. 'Cause you're gonna keep your eyes open. Right?"

"Right." We hugged each other.

"Uncle, I have a feeling there might be a business here."

"For the company or for us?"

"Both, Uncle, always both."

"That's good." He patted the right side of my chest. Then he started shaking his index finger at me. "Remember keep your eyes open." He got into his Oldsmobile, slammed the door, and drove off quickly. Just like his phone calls.

I walked back into the house. Connie was looking at the pictures. She placed them down and looked up at me. It was a different look for her. She had something to say.

"Tony, Amy is beautiful and so are all the other models. Make sure it's only for her that you are doing this."

I couldn't believe my ears. Connie never questioned me about my faithfulness. Was the accepted notion of women's intuition taking hold? I didn't want an exhange fearing my tone would betray me. How stupid. How selfish. I betrayed her! I walked over to her and kissed her on the forehead.

"It's only Amy."

As I walked away I could feel her eyes following me. If she knew, she would take the Italian high road and life would go on.

***

At twelve-noon sharp, two floor-to-ceiling, high-gloss white doors swung open. Moe's entrance was preceded by the jingle jangle of bracelets. With a posed smile and an extended hand she chirped, "Welcome back to Cosmo."

Standing near her secretary's desk, I put down a magazine I was pretending to be interested in and grabbed her hand. I couldn't resist.

"How can a delicate person like you wear so many bracelets and not hurt yourself?"

She was totally disarmed by my greeting. Her smile disappeared. She brought her other hand up next to the one I was holding and looked down at both wrists. They were indeed covered with charm bracelets, wrap around chain things, and bangles one after another in different widths with assorted carvings. All gold. All clanging in different keys. She was speechless. She was taking me seriously.

I immediately sensed she took every criticism seriously

even those meant to be kidding.

"Moe, they're great." I took hold of her other hand. "There's just a lot of them!"

Wanting to make her feel better I bent down and kissed the back of each hand. Her smile reappeared. This time it was an honest smile. One of acceptance and pleasure. Beneath the physical unattractiveness, below the no-nonsense businesswoman, was a fragile female. She held both of my hands and with me in tow backed through the doors from whence she came.

I didn't remember her office being so frilly. Every pastel color created was represented. The chairs and sofas were done in matching flowered printed chintz. The tables were Queen Anne loaded with picture frames and knickknacks. The bastion of a desk was a white and gold Louis-the-something-or-other. The soft blue walls were covered with photographs of all the current and past Cosmo models. The carpet was a wall-to-wall sea of peach.

She let go of my hands and gestured to the right side of the office. The doors mysteriously closed behind us and we walked to a beautifully set table for two. Real flowers in the center, real lace napkins, real silverware, real crystal; too bad the food was unreal. Cold soup. Vegetables that were practically raw, and one tiny piece of very plain fish. I think it was salmon. I hate salmon! The best part of the meal was the mixed berry desert and the Doctor Brown's Cream Soda. She had three bottles of it placed in a champagne cooler. She was delighted with her own attention to detail.

By her lead and my encouragement, the luncheon conversation focused on her. She was schooled abroad. She spoke four languages not including Italian. She married late in life. *No kidding!* Twenty-nine. She was an only child, and had none. Met

Lewis in New York at the ballet. Short courtship. Big Newport wedding. He's very helpful in the continued success of the business. Bought the agency from Phil who had a couple of models and was barely making it.

I looked down at my watch. "I have five minutes."

"Or until I throw you out."

She reached behind her and from a tiny table brought a pale pink eight by eleven envelope. "It's Amy's contract. I'll need your signature as well."

I took it from her, and I believe she expected me to pull it out and sign on the dotted line without question. "Moe, I'd like to have Johnny Three--"

"Johnny what?" She smiled disapprovingly.

"Well he's our attorney. You met him. John Caprio the Third. We grew up together and I can't stop calling him by his neighborhood name. I'd like him to take a look."

"It's mostly boilerplate legaleze." She was developing an attitude of a spoiled brat who was not about to get her way. "Only the names and dates change. That's all."

"That's all? That's what I'm concerned about. Amy is not just a name or a date."

She started to say something I was not interested in hearing, so I talked over her. "If Johnny and I think it's right, she'll sign and so will I. If not, maybe the boilerplate has to be changed."

She slumped back into her chair as though she had just been slapped. "Are you always so protective?"

"Only about people I care about."

"What about non-people. What about things, businesses?"

"Most of my 'things,' as you call them, and the successes

I've enjoyed in business, are associated with people. I do protect them."

"Tony, you are really a no-nonsense kind of guy."

"And you mighty Moe are a no-bullshit kind of gal. So beyond Amy's contract, how can we do something together?"

She carefully dabbed each corner of her month with her napkin. Why do society types do that? There's nothing there to wipe. She reached for a white, gold-trimmed telephone. She clicked the cradle once, unconsciously wiped the mouthpiece with the same napkin, and spoke into it. "Sharon no calls, no interruptions."

She paused listening to the response.

"That's right, no interruptions! No exceptions!"

"There goes your one o'clock schedule." I quipped.

She shot back, "Somehow I think it's going to be worth it."

We both sat back in our chairs waiting for the other to begin. Being a polite guest, and anxious to see what she had in mind, I allowed her to start.

"Tony, since my taking over, the Cosmo Agency has grown substantially. Mind you it can remain a very successful number three, but that notion is distasteful to me. It's bogged down and I can't budge it."

She looked down at her lap. A smear of white scalp peeked through her hair. Like a little girl in distress she talked into her lap.

"I haven't shared these thoughts with anyone, and I'm a little embarrassed about sharing them with you."

"Don't be."

She looked up trustingly. "I like to think of myself as a person who reads other people accurately. I know a lot of people wonder about Lewis and me. He was my first important people-test."

"Did he pass?"

"So far. And it's been a long test. He expects nothing from me other than a comfortable life. He also understands he must earn his keep. He actually does so incredibly well in the P.R. area."

"What do you expect from him?"

"In order of priorities. Good P.R. Good date."

I wanted desperately to ask her about her non Cosmo life with him. Sex, kids, vacations together, holding hands, home cooked meals, but I knew the answer to all of them. Zero. I stuck my toe in just a little.

"Good P.R. is easy, 'good date' is complicated."

She had changed from vulnerable to frigid. "Discrete philandering is acceptable."

Now I looked down at my lap.

"That is why I believe we can work together. I have made my evaluation of you. You are a person whom I can trust. One who will protect our partnership. One who has a power base. One who can place Cosmo ahead of the pack."

Does she know more about me other than the company's man side?

"How do you see this 'partnership' evolving?" I asked.

"Magazines."

"Magazines?"

"Yes. The beauty business is not just having a stable of models. It is selling them to various editors of beauty magazines. Their clients. Their advertising agencies. This leads to model endorsements and enormous commissions."

She leaned forward and continued, "There are only

two major beauty magazines that do eighty-five percent of the business. Several insignificant minor publications fight over the remaining fifteen percent. Cosmo has to sell its product, our beautiful ladies, to the top two. We have not been able to break through."

"Why?"

"It's like a monopoly. They prefer doing business with the same old agencies for the same old fees. Everything remains constant, therefore comfortable. Actually the only item that changes is the models. The editors give us the professional courtesy of perusal, but never the delight of a hiring."

"Moe, it's tough to change people's habits. They have to have a strong reason to change. They have to be made *un*-comfortable before they change. I don't think that's the course you should be taking, primarily because I wouldn't be able to help you out. I'm not interested in convincing some editor that a Cosmo model is better than a 'whatever' model. It's short-term. Some other agency will come along and re-convince them, that their model is better."

"Tony"--she was amusing herself--"there's no such word as *re-convince*." It was harmless.

"Hey, Moe, what is this, an English class or Model Hiring 101?"

We enjoyed the joust.

"I think you're aiming too low," I said.

She was no longer amused but puzzled.

"You mentioned there are several other beauty magazines that fight over the remaining fifteen percent of the business. Of that group, which magazine do you think has the most potential?"

Without hesitation she answered. "*The American Wom-an.*"

"So let's buy it, and use it for Cosmo."

She covered her mouth with her napkin in time to muffle a feminine choke. "Did you say buy *The American Woman?*"

"That's what I said. Now at the sake of backing off some, it would have to make some financial sense, with growth potential."

"But, Tony, you don't even know if it's for sale!"

"Moe, very cliché, but everything's for sale."

"Let's say it is, and the purchase price works. The growth potential is based on one thing and that's circulation."

"That's only one item. What about the current staff, and what does the magazine stand for?"

"I have a knack for creating an attitude with my models. I can do the same with that magazine. I know a lot of the editors there and their support people. They're a very bright group, but misdirected. Properly lead, style and content are not the problems; circulation is."

"I know about circulation. It sounds very similar to the record business. A label can have talented recording artists, but if the marketing, you call it circulation, is not right, the public will never know about them. So how do they get to know it? I mean how do the American people get to know *American Woman?*"

"It all happens at the newsstand. Just like product in the supermarket, shelf position is everything. The two most successful magazines are always up front. The others are practically under the counter. The American people are conditioned to grab that which is most prominent. Once they do, they subscribe, and off you go!"

"Got it! So here's what we do. You get me in touch with the decision makers at *The American Woman*. I'll run it by Richard Q. You and I will meet with the magazine people and structure a deal--"

I braked my enthusiasm.

"What's wrong, Tony?"

"Before any of us do anything you and I should have an understanding. No a deal."

"Like what?"

"If this whole project flies, M. R. Tedes, will automatically become a partner in *The American Woman*. I think it's only fair that the company become a partner in the Cosmo Agency as well."

"On what basis do you think the company should be entitled to a Cosmo partnership?" Her frigidity returned in full force.

"I would like to structure it in such a way, that the company funds one hundred percent of the purchase price for the magazine, you are installed as its editor-in-chief, with an equity position and an appropriate salary. In return for our financing and positioning, you transfer a percentage of Cosmo to the company."

"What percentages are we talking about?"

"Moe, it's premature, but if the company funds it all, it should own a large majority of the equity. Say eighty-five fifteen."

"Sounds like you're repeating the magazine market share to me."

"It's a number."

"What about sixty-five, you, thirty five, me."

"Not even close."

"Seventy thirty."

"You like this. That's closer to it. We'll expect the same split on the Cosmo side."

"One problem, Tony, I don't own it one hundred percent. Bolton owns a third."

"So then Bolton will have to give up some points as well. Is he worth keeping?"

"I think so."

"Time will tell. Let the seventy-thirty stand."

It was time to go.

"Moe I love spending the time with you. I had a feeling we would be doing business other than Amy's. I'm glad."

As I walked through the hot white double doors accompanied by the bangles band, my mind raced through the process. *I'll handle Richard Q. and the* American Woman *people, Johnny Three can do the legal paperwork, and Dom can handle the circulation.* I had a feeling the Media Division was about to get into the magazine business.

23

THE WORKDAY was coming to an end. I always believed
in reasonable hours. When you must stay and put in the time, you
do it. And when you can leave it behind that was equally acceptable. This could have waited, but I was too excited. As soon as I
stepped out of the elevator, I called Mann Management. I asked
the receptionist to put Dom and Johnny on the line together.

"Hey, Tony, I got this pain in the ass lawyer in my office
with a shit eatin' grin on his face. What's goin' on?"

"Some good stuff. Guys, I know it's late in the afternoon,
but I really need to see the both of you. Can we meet in my office
in a half hour?"

"Tony, I'm married 'n Johnny hasn't had a date since
high school. Where we goin'? See ya in a half."

"Tony, me too!" Johnny's enthusiasm was comically intrusive.

"Johnny, quit bein' a fuckin' brownnoser," Dom said.

"Okay, Dean and Jerry see you in a half hour."

I hung up the pay phone to the sounds of Elvis Presley's
"Let Me Be Your Teddy Bear." That bubblegum song drew me

toward the newsstand and into thoughts of Johnny Diamond. If it weren't for his bad habits, he too could have been equal to the superstar Elvis.

"Do you have *The American Woman?*" I asked the guy at the stand.

"No, but I got a coupla Orientals behind the *Boston Globe* pile!" *Rim shot!* He loved his own humor and started laughing uncontrollably. You couldn't help but get caught up in his own enjoyment. He finally got a hold of himself and looked around behind him. Just as Moe had described, the magazine was on a lower back shelf along with several other women's publications.

Heading out the door, I fanned through *The American Woman* and knew the shelf space was going to change for this baby.

***

I could hear Dom and Johnny coming a mile away. Their ballbusting was laced with laughter and idle threats. Dom's salutation was a request for a quick game of high-low-jack. "Why high-low-jack?"

"Well, Tony, Mr. Lawyer claims he was the best player in the neighborhood. I wanna piece of his wallet!"

"High-low can wait, this is more important." I felt like a killjoy, but I wanted to get on with the meeting.

"This is a two-pronged meeting. One. The purchase of the television station in Los Angeles is on track. Johnny you and I will be flying there sometime next week. By the way I mentioned the possibility of the trip to my Uncle Joe, and he expressed an interest in going with us. He's never been and he would like to 'see the Pacific and a few movie stars before he dies.' He'll probably out live us all.

"Two"--I walked around from behind my desk and sat on its corner--"I just came out of a meeting with Moe Cosby and I think there is a business there for us. She is going to put us in touch with the owners of *The American Woman*."

They looked puzzled. I reached back on my desk and taking the issue I tossed it on the coffee-table in front of them.

"It's a magazine for women. I think we can buy it and use it to increase her modeling business, which we will have a piece of, while at the same time delivering profits from the magazine itself. Provided . . ." After a perfectly placed company pause I continued, "Provided we can solve the distribution problem. Dom, that's your responsibility."

Johnny acted a little surprised. He looked at me then Dom.

"Johnny. I demonstrated to Moe how magazine distribution is very much like record distribution. Dom knows how to do that. So instead of 45s, it's magazines. Same approach."

Johnny was comforted. Dom understood.

"Yeah, Tony, that fuckin' distributin' can be a pain in the azz. But ya right! Records or books, same shit. I'll start lookin' around."

"Good, Dom, but don't do anything until I finish the buyout.

"Johnny you'll handle all the paperwork on the magazine buy and the modeling agency partnership.

"Last but not least"--I reached back once again on my desk and handed Johnny the pale pink envelope--"these are the contracts for Amy. There's a lot of boilerplate stuff there. Read it all, recommend, and let's talk before I send it back to Moe."

I walked back behind my desk and opened the top middle draw. Dom was leafing through the magazine and Johnny was stuffing the envelope into his briefcase. The leafing and stuffing stopped suddenly as I shuffled a new deck of cards. "Okay, suckers, anyone for high-low-jack!"

24

NOT ONE MOVIE STAR greeted us at the Los Angeles airport, but Uncle Joe loved the plane ride. He kidded with the stewardesses, won about twenty bucks playing gin with Johnny, and never talked business.

When we arrived at the baggage claim area, a large brown leathery-faced man dressed in light gray slacks, royal blue short-sleeve sports shirt, and shiny white loafers came up to Uncle Joe. Johnny and I were too far away to hear the exchange, but there were smiles and a handshake that took Uncle's skinny hand deep into the chest of the stranger. Uncle Joe walked the man over to us and introduced him.

"Joe Fat I want you to meet my favorite nephew, Tony Manfredi, 'n his favorite lawyer Johnny Caprio."

My extended hand was greeted with a bone-crushing grasp and a guttural welcoming grunt. Ditto for Johnny.

"Joe Fat came out here right after the war 'n loves it. He came to give us a ride to the hotel."

Johnny innocently accepted Uncle's explanation. I knew there was more to it. Uncle's jumping at my invitation to fly to the Coast was taking on new meaning.

In our years together I never over-thought Uncle's situation. I knew he was "connected," but to what extent seemed unimportant. I found out in sunny Southern California.

***

Driving down Sunset Boulevard was a first timer's treat. Wide streets, palm trees, green lawns, perfectly shaped shrubs of all varieties, mansions with only one architectural similarity . . . *huge*!

An abrupt left turn spoiled the tour. As if it had disappeared, the white Cadillac swung off Sunset into a covered garage. Joe Fat brought the sedan to a halt, and two bellboys came running out of a dingy office.

"Mr. Trillo we were waiting. Just like you told us to."

So Joe Fat has a last name.

He didn't say a word. He just handed them some bills, and as if hitchhiking, pointed his thumb over his shoulder to the trunk. We walked to an alcove and got into a small elevator, which creaked nonstop to the fourth floor. As we got out Johnny offered, "I'll go back downstairs and register for all of us."

The first complete statement Joe Fat uttered was, "It's done. Everything's handled. Don't tip nobody."

Uncle Joe put his arm on Joe Fat's huge shoulder. This time I heard.

"So Joe Sweets, how's my crazy cousins the Vespias?"

"They're fine. Takin' care of business."

Three other bellboys opened three doors. Joe Fat pointed to the first one and announced, "Joe Sweets welcome to Hollywood. I got the one next to you for Tony. They connect. Counselor you're cross the hall."

The rooms were furnished in heavy Mediterranean. Dresser, full bed, a couple of chairs, bedside tables, and lamps. I walked out on to the balcony that overlooked a quietly busy Sunset Boulevard. Looking east, the famous strip snaked though the Hollywood Hills. Dotted with predominately white and terra-cotta cottages, they gave way to a bald spot that held high the *HOLLYWOOD* sign.

I felt very much alive in this very unreal town. The sun, though low in the western sky, was warm. Uncle had walked onto his balcony. Separating us was a rectangular wooden planter filled with waist high scrubs.

"Hey, Tony, just like the piazza's in the old neighborhood."

"Yeah Uncle I miss the clotheslines."

Our exchange was interrupted by a very businesslike but fey-sounding man.

"Good afternoon, gentlemen. Welcome to the Château Marmont. I am Ernest the day manager." He waved his arms as if accepting some applause from his audience. He continued, "My staff and I are here to serve you. If there is anything, be it so small, so seemingly unimportant, we shall accommodate you."

With that dramatic reading he clapped his hands and in walked bellboys carrying wine, cheeses, fruit, flowers, and our luggage. Johnny followed the last bearer in, just as Ernest did his big closing.

"The Château Marmont is yours to command." He bowed, clapped his hands again, and shushed the staff out.

Joe Fat closed the door behind them. "Whatta queer!"

He actually laughed.

"Fellahs, Mince would like you to join him for dinner at his place. He eats around six thirty. If it's okay, I'll pick youse up in the garage around six."

Joe Sweets answered for all of us. "How is Mince? I haven't seen him for a few years."

Joe Fat nodded affirmatively. "He's good." He turned and left the room.

Johnny who had not said anything in awhile commented. "Joe Fat speaks very little."

Uncle Joe countered with, "Yeah, but his deeds are very big."

Six on the dot we exited the hotel's garage. Joe Fat drove giving us a lackluster Hollywood house tour.

"There's Bogie's old joint. There's where Gable and Lombard lived when she died. Jack Benny's place. People say that mooh-len-yam Rochester lives in the back." He laughed at his own colored joke. We slowed down and entered through a large opened gate. On the white square trusses was scrolled *BEL AIR*.

A private uniformed patrolman saluted Joe Fat as we passed. As we wound up the hillside mansion after mansion marked our way. Near the top we approached another gate, and although it was closed, it jumped out at you. It was black wrought-iron and in the middle of each grille, at least twelve feet high, were curlicue *Z*s. Joe Fat honked the horn once and from a small tree grove came two men. Each grabbed a gate and pulled it open. We drove through. No waves; no thanks. I looked back and they were silently pushing them closed.

The driveway had to be a half a mile long. There were gardeners everywhere. We pulled around a huge fountain bursting with waterspouts and stopped in front of a gigantic stone Moorish mansion. We were greeted on the wide staircase by a portly man. His hair had a natural reddish tint to it that complimented his fair complexion. His casual attire was all black. He smiled and his blue eyes filled up as he and Uncle Joe embraced. They remained in each other's arms, exchanging inaudible Italian. Joe Fat's smile was as broad as the staircase he was standing on. He was obviously pleased with the greeting. Finally the two separated, but still holding hands, Uncle Joe introduced me.

"Mince, my favorite nephew 'n the light of my life, Tony Manfredi. Tony, this is my childhood friend 'n partner Mince Zito."

It's always a little awkward meeting some of Uncle Joe's cronies. They all have these unusual nicknames, and it's difficult to know how to greet them. I remembered that playground story about Joe Newport and how 'he's not Joe, or Newport, he's Joe Newport! One name just like Joe Sweets.' I couldn't do the 'Hello Mince,' so I went for the "respect the elderly" approach.

"Mr. Zito, it's a pleasure to meet you."

"Mr. Zito!" He turned to Uncle Joe. "Is that who lives here?"

Uncle smiled.

Mince bellowed, "Tony, it's Mince. I don't know how to answer to anything else." He came down a couple of steps and embraced me, not in the same way as he did my uncle, but an embrace nonetheless.

"Mince, I'd like you to meet Johnny Three Caprio." I was now in my element and the names came easy.

"Johnny you look just like your ole man. How's he doin?"

Mince looked up at Uncle Joe. "Joe Sweets, could we tell Johnny a few stories about his ole man or what?"

Joe Sweets laughed agreeing, but shook his index finger no.

"Joe Fat go tell the people were gonna have a drink by the pool."

Obeying he leapt up the stairs taking two and three at a crack. We took our time as Mince talked to Uncle Joe in Italian, occasionally pointing to various parts of the estate. I understood that he had spent a bundle fixing up the place from the main building to the guesthouse to the gardens, and the biggest problem was redoing the pool area. "They tried to steal me blind those Jap rat bastards," Mince growled as he led Uncle Joe to the patio.

The entire evening was spent out on the patio poolside. We drank and ate. The conversation was harmless. Hollywood stories. Who is queer, who is fucking who, how much money is wasted, what a big business it is. I was getting a little weary, and still functioning on East Coast time, I asked, "Uncle, do you mind if I go back to the hotel? Johnny and I have a big meeting tomorrow morning regarding the purchase of the television station, and there are a few points we would like to go over."

"Tony, not at all. In fact I'm comin' with you. I'm too old for these late hours."

We all stood up.

"Tony," Mince spoke up, "I'd like to visit with you when you get a break. Joe Sweets tells me you're doin' great stuff."

I looked over to Uncle Joe. He was smiling.

"Sure Mince, I think things should be reasonably under control by tomorrow night. Should we have dinner?"

"Tony, this is the best restaurant in L.A. Let's do it here so we can talk."

We all exchanged handshakes and started to leave.

"Hey, Tony!" Mince was lingering behind. He waved his arm beckoning to me, "Come over here I wanna show ya something."

I excused myself from the threesome. As soon as I was by his side he put his arm around my neck and turned me away from the group. "You see those statues?" He pointed to a line of Romanesque statuary. "They was brought in from the old country. Cost me a fuckin' bundle. Those custom agent rat bastards."

I didn't know how to respond. He stopped talking but continued to point and wave his arm making sure his back remained to the group. He whispered toward the statues, "No Johnny tomorrow. It's our business."

With exaggerated vibrato he continued, "'N that one, that fuckin' goddess cost me a quarter. Do you believe it? Those art rat bastards." Having delivered his important message, we turned toward the group and all of us exited with *Thank yous* and *Good lucks*.

＊＊＊

Johnny did an excellent job of setting up the parameters for the television station meeting. Documentation of ownership, financial reports, FCC opinion letters supporting the purchase, a firm offer subject only to FCC approval: all had been prepared, exchanged, reviewed, and ready for acceptance. It's easier when twelve million dollars, a little over the market value of the station, can be guaranteed quickly without a hitch. It's also easier when the sellers know the buyers are in the broadcasting business and intend on establishing themselves in the Los Angeles market.

The company was buying the lowest-rated independent

station in town, but was outwardly showing interest in a higher ranked Indie for more money. All the pre-meeting due-diligence work paid off. Johnny and their attorneys drafted an agreement letter that only needed the signatures of their president and our Richard Q.

Literally in one working day the deal was done except for one tiny incident. Around five o'clock, after we had all agreed on the sale, we were touring the lot. There were three huge hanger-type buildings used as soundstages for the various locally produced programs. We were told that they were originally built for the silent movies and how, back then, two or three one-reelers were produced on the lot each week. It was rumored, but never verified, that Charlie Chaplin made a few movies here. But then he was rumored to have made movies on virtually every lot in Hollywood.

A tall, extremely handsome man, wearing too much television pancake makeup, approached the group. With great flair he asked, "Is there a Mr. Manfredi among you?"

I stepped out of the cluster and extended my hand.

"I'm Tony Manfredi."

His theatrics continued, "Ah, Mr. Manfredi. It is my pleasure to meet my new leader. I am Grant Tanner." He actually took a half-step backward and bowed.

I had no idea who this guy was. He was dressed like one of those comical directors. Jodhpurs tucked inside high brown boots, sports jacket with a suede shooting patch on its shoulder and silk cravat outlandishly pouffed around his neck.

"I am the host of the *Afternoon Cinema*, but for years I have worked on this very lot as a movie actor."

Trying not to show my disbelief toward this buffoon, I

acknowledged, "Mr. Tanner it is my pleasure to meet you."

He did not reciprocate. "That my dear Mr. Manfredi remains to be seen."

What drama!

"Well, Mr. Tanner, you got my attention. Now what?"

Tanner continued, "I have been on this lot since . . ." He paused, obviously stopping himself before he revealed his age. "Since the old days. I have been a star here and these"--pointing with disdain to the sellers--"these incompetents have not agreed to my new contract."

I tried my best to be understanding, but Tanner was not buying it. As if reciting Shakespeare he continued, "I have studied the ways of the Federal Communications Commission, and I know what I must do if my contract is not honorably renewed."

"Mr. Tanner that doesn't sound so honorable to me; it sounds more like blackmail. Be that as it may, the new management team will review all the talent, and all the programs, and they will decide who and what will be renewed or dropped. I give you my word it will be fair and objective. In the meantime, I am sure both parties will agree to keep you on until that review takes place."

He raised his arm pointing to the sky. Rolling each *r* he proclaimed, "Review! I, Grant Tanner, reviewed! I have been savagely reviewed my entire career and I refuse to be reviewed by some upstart. I shall proceed with my F.C.C. petition to deny."

He turned to leave and not a person in our entourage moved.

I went after him. "Mr. Tanner, I appreciate talent." Having just dealt with a group of Seventh Avenue Jews, I remembered one of their favorite words. "And talent with chutzpah is a rare commodity. May I buy you breakfast tomorrow so we may discuss your future with us."

He was pleased with his victory. "Indeed you may, Mr. Manfredi, indeed you may. Say the Polo Lounge at eight thirty. I must be on the lot by ten for rehearsal and makeup."

"Eight thirty then."

I offered my hand. He refused it with an abrupt about-face. With the group still frozen in place I broke the ice, "Showbiz I love it! Whether it's a rock 'n roll idol or a has-been movie star they're all the same."

One of the group spoke up, "Has-been movie star? He only wishes. He's never made it. His star is hooked to those B movies we run in the afternoon."

"How are his ratings?" I asked.

"Nothing great."

"Well let's see what I can accomplish at breakfast." It was clear the use of the singular *I* excluded them.

***

Driving back to the hotel, Johnny saved me from dis-inviting him to dinner. He decided he had some paperwork to tighten up and he would eat at the hotel. Joe Fat and Uncle Joe were waiting in the garage. I jumped out of one car and into another.

Once we arrived at Mince's place, Joe Fat took us directly to the pool area. There was Mince, dressed in his black on black outfit, drinking red wine. He stood and greeted us by putting an arm around each of our shoulders. Like bookends, he pulled us in closer to him.

"This is what it's all about. Friends who are partners,

who are close."

Once the three of us sat down, Joe Fat backed away and disappeared into the mansion. Mince was not wasting any time. "Tony, I'm glad you're here with your Uncle. There are things that have to be said that he can't say."

I looked at Uncle remembering our conversations on sharing. *What has he not told me?*

"I know what you're thinking. What big secret is there between your uncle 'n you? To some of us it's no big secret. It's fact. The other fact is he's too shy a guy to tell ya. So when ya told him you was coming to the Coast he jumped at the chance just so we could have this talk."

He turned to Uncle Joe. "Joe Sweets, how my doin'?"

"I'll let you know when ya through."

"It started durin' those Prohibitin' years. We was all from the neighborhood and starvin'. We started to get into businesses. A little bootleggin' here--"

I interrupted, "With Joe Newport?"

They got hysterical. Mince through his hearty laughter picked up where I left off. "That fuckin' Joe Newport what a coo-gootz. We had more laughs on that fuckin' boat. To this day I ain't laughed as hard."

He stopped to wipe some happy tears from his eyes. "Ah shit. How is that crazy bastard?"

"He's the same. Just no more boats."

"Anyways, Tony, we was bootleggin', some gamblin' joints, prostitutes, numbers, and to keep everything in order, protection. It was great! We was makin' a few bucks 'n havin' a good time."

I always loved these yarns, hanging on to every word like some kid listing to a ghost story, but because I felt Uncle Joe had held back, I developed an instant shoulder chip.

I interrupted. "Where was all this fun taking place?"

They looked at each other then me. An amazing thing happened.

"Tony, what's this I see?" Mince reached across the table and brushed my right shoulder.

"Joe Sweets, looks like a fuckin' chip!" They laughed. I didn't. They knew. I didn't.

"Tony, don't worry," quipped Uncle Joe.

Mince continued, "There's reasons for everything. Let me answer your question. We started in Providence. With Providence you have the state. Then we tried Bridgeport, then we was feelin' good 'n we went to Hartford. We owned the fuckin' state. People, cops, politicians, everything.

"Now it's expanding time! We know New York is too big to handle, 'n we got no stomach for that kinda fight, so we go north. Mass, New Hampshire, Vermont. We was like da fuckin'--what do you call that Nazi tank thing they did in Poland?" He looked to me for the answer.

"The blitzkrieg."

"Yeah, da fuckin' blitzkrieg. We owned those states in two shakes. Things was great. It was around Christmas. Your uncle 'n me's walkin' through the neighborhood when this fuckin' car, a mile long, pulls up 'longside of us. The back window rolls down, 'n I gotta tell ya, Tony, I almost shit my pants, cause I thought we was gonna get hit.

"Joe Sweets, am I fuckin' lying or what?"

Uncle Joe smiled and nodded his head, which I'm sure was full of instant recollection.

"So this window comes down 'n this guy sticks his head

out 'n yells 'Mince! Joe Sweets!' I turn 'n put my hand in my jacket pretending I got a gun. I never carried a fuckin' gun in my life! Where was the Vespia brothers 'n Emilio when ya really needed em."

The names screamed out at me. *Vespia! Emilio!* I wanted him to stop. I needed some explanations, but Mince plowed right over my thoughts.

"Your uncle, with more balls than brains, steps in front of me like a protector--"

Uncle Joe interrupts. "Protect your ass! You with that bullshit gun routine probably would have gotten us both killed."

Mince laughed and continued. "So Joe Sweets says something like 'What's it to ya.' The car just passes us and stops. Joe Sweets gives me an elbow to the ribs 'n points at the number plate. It was a New York plate. The backdoor opens 'n this big fuck gets out. 'Mister Tedesco wants to see ya.' It was one of those limo sedan things, so when we get in we're sittin' with our backs to the driver. They're facin' us, all alone in the backseat"-- he then extended his arms toward me--"as close as we are, was the man. Mister Tedesco."

My impatience won out over the excitement of the story. "So who was the man? This Mister Tedesco."

He dropped his arms and leaned back in his chair. In disbelief he answered my question with a question. "Who was?" He pointed his arm and index finger skyward. "Who *is* the man Mario Tedesco."

Uncle Joe interceded. "Tony, you may know him as Mr. Ted."

It took me a moment to lock into what Uncle had just said. I was stunned. Within seconds I relived my event. Pittsburgh! I remembered how Mr. Ted's name was casually dropped by Uncle Joe and how it would be the last name I would utter on this earth. I uttered it again. "Mr. Ted?"

They were silent. They just stared at me. An air of reverence came over the table. Led by them, yielding to it by me, I repeated his name softly, "Mr. Ted." The reverence turned to a reflective pause for all of us. It's one of those moments when no one knows exactly what to do, not awkward, not embarrassing, just there. I ran my hand across my wordless mouth, Uncle Joe looked down into his empty lap, and Mince fondled the long stem of his wineglass. I broke the benediction by lifting my glass of wine.

"To Mr. Ted. He saved my life. Long may he live."

They transferred their quiet reverence to hearty toasts. "He saved yours, Tony, 'n made ours," exalted Mince.

"He will always be a part of my life. Even after it's over," lamented Uncle Joe.

Our three wineglasses touched and the high-pitched tingle of the crystal echoed and ricocheted throughout the estate. It seemed to grow louder as it rose above the lighted palm trees into the star strewn sky.

Subdued, Mince continued, "From that day till this we was part of the company. Sure we had to prove ourselves, show our smarts 'n loyalty, but we was in. That's what ya uncle wants to tell ya."

From the moment I got into Joe Fat's car I knew, I just knew, this night would be filled with major revelations. I would be totally taken into their confidence. Totally accepted. Totally involved.

"What this meetin' is all about is to let ya know how involved ya uncle is and what he's plannin'." He turned to Uncle

Joe and asked, "Joe Sweets, are you sure about this?"

Even in the candlelight, Uncle's eyes turned that special color blue, twinkling as he responded, "Mince he's the one. I know. That's why we're here. Tell him."

Mince reached over and held Uncle's wrist. "This man is first, my best friend. Second, my partner for life. Third, when we proved ourselves to Mr. Ted he was given all of New England." The content of his last sentence hit me like a ton of bricks. As a cover, I looked down at a spoon I was fiddling with and shook my head in disbelief.

"All of New England! Does it mean exactly what it sounds like?"

Mince jumped on my question. "Fuckin' A. Mr. Ted gave Joe Sweets New England, and it's bigger than it sounds. It's from the New York border into Canada. Includin' Toronto, Ottawa, Montreal, and Quebec. New York City was Mr. Ted's, but upstate New York was your uncle's. By the way, in case you're wonderin', your uncle's still got it!"

"And what about you Mince?"

Uncle answered for him. "He's got the West Coast. From Mexico to Canada. From the Pacific to the Colorado River.

"Mince what about Alaska?"

They laughed.

"Too fuckin' cold, too much snow 'n ice. Like New England! Hey that gives me an idea. I'm fuckin' givin' ya Alaska. Those Eskimos must play the numbers like those mooh-len-yams, right? Right! Ya got it!"

They clicked their glasses, mocking their new deal. They were having fun again, while I was still trying to comprehend this carving up of the country. I spoke my thoughts.

"I'm having a hard time understanding this. What does it mean?"

They both started to answer together. Uncle Joe acquiesced to Mince.

"Go head Mince you're older."

"Yeah, by a minute! Tony, it means, cause we did good, we was given those territories to run with Mr. Ted's blessing. We in return do the right thing, 'n give a nice piece of the action back to Mr. Ted. He was then, 'n is now, the number one man in the country. 'N for that matter"--Mince rotated his arms symbolizing the world--"the whole fuckin' world. He runs it all!"

He was pleased with his dissertation and sat back anticipating my adulation.

"Mince I'll never be able to thank you enough. I was curious after my Pittsburgh episode, but Uncle masterfully threw me off course. Then Pearlie and the Vespia brothers made me more suspicious. It really wasn't until our playground meeting that his connection was confirmed. Never could I have imagined he was the New England boss."

Mince smiled, accepting my gratitude with, "*Is* the New England boss!"

"Just as you *are* the West Coast boss," I paid homage. He folded his hands on his belly and nodded. I turned to Uncle.

"There are so many questions--no, no--details, I want to know about. I don't know where to begin."

Uncle Joe answered the only way he could. "You'll learn as you go. Just like you graduated College with a degree, you'll graduate this college with a degree. It'll be step by step."

Trying to make a joke I continued, "I hope I don't flunk out!"

They didn't think it was funny. They stared me down. Uncle Joe started, "If I didn't think you could pass I wouldn't have asked ya."

Mince finished, "'N there's no flunkin' out. If you flunk along the line, you're out!"

There was a hardness to his statement that forced me to look to Uncle Joe like some kid who just got in trouble and was hoping to be bailed out by an older brother. Uncle didn't give an inch. He verified Mince's statement. "There's no flunkin' out, there's no 'I don't want to do this anymore,' there's no retirement, there's only commitment. Forever!"

It was the first time Uncle Joe frightened me. It was very clear without saying the words that once you're in, you're in for life, or it is your life! I swallowed hard and forced a question. "Uncle, I know you're grooming me, does that mean you're retiring? If so, doesn't that fly in face of what you just said? And, if not, why the grooming?"

"Tony, just like in your company things have to be orderly. People are groomed to take over 'n keep things goin'. I'm not retiring, not by a long shot. I just want to take it easy 'n sit in the background, helpin', watchin', until I can't sit anymore."

His seriousness turned to playfulness. "Then I lay down 'n die, then it's all yours. Simple!"

He made it sound so natural. The progression was simple. He worked for his company all his life. Was faithful. Made a living. He's probably worth a fortune! He picks a successor and sits back to make sure all goes well. Then he dies. Next generation.

"Uncle, you weren't groomed or picked?"

Where was I going with that question? Uncle saved me.

"Tony, Mince 'n me was picked by Mr. Ted. We was successful on our own, 'n we was merged." He looked to Mince for some appreciative acknowledgment of his merger notion.

"Hey, Joe Sweets, you been hangin' around your nephew to long with that merger shit. But it's true. We was merged."

Uncle continued, "Like I told you in the playground, things change. We need to stay in business but change our old ways. Everyone's after us. The Government, the locals, the competition." He thought for a moment and waved his hand in a circular motion. "Well we always had competition, but it's different now. It's from all over the world. They're out to bury us. We gotta be smarter, tougher, 'n richer. Richer!" He emphasized, "Richer that's our strongest weapon. It buys us whatever we need from people to things. That's why it's you. You got our company's blood runnin' through your heart, 'n your legit company's brains runnin' through your head. The two's merged, 'n like you've already done, you got us richer, 'n stronger, 'n legit."

There was silence at the table. I thought of them and their lives. They seem to be content. I don't have chapter and verse of how they arrived at this place or how they are able to maintain it. It doesn't seem important. They obviously live the way they want. Comfortably and in apparent peace. Peace, that I'm sure is maintained by street-smart diligence.

Certainly Mince flaunts it more. This hilltop estate, on God knows how many acres, in the most exclusive area in Los Angeles. Complete with mansion, guesthouse, six-car garage, tennis court, swimming pool, and bocce court. He can't go unnoticed. Maybe it's the flashy Hollywood environment. Whatever it is, it's a major contrast to Uncle Joe's tenement, bakery, no-frills existence.

There are so many questions. I never wanted to leave this spot until all of them were answered. Why Mince's mansion and

Joe Sweets tenement? Do they earn the same? Where is Uncle Joe's loot? Is it in the vault in New Haven? If, after all my deposits, I don't know how much I really have there, imagine Uncle's stash. How big are their groups? I have enough of an imagination to figure out the Vespias', but what about Emilio? That toothless, stogy-chewing baker! And the new man in my life, Joe Fat! I wanted to ease into some questioning.

"Is it possible to tell me who runs the other parts of the country?"

Uncle Joe stroked his chin.

Mince wanted to change the subject. "Tony, let me show you a car I bought. It's a thirty-nine LaSalle sedan. It was a pile of rusted shit, 'n I had it rebuilt, so it's better than new."

He started to get up. Uncle Joe nodded for him to sit down. He did, and Uncle Joe spoke.

"Tony, college begins. Don't ask too many questions too fast. It'll all come out. But to answer your question, there ain't too many of us. Mr. Ted runs it all. Day to day he runs New York City, New Jersey, Pennsylvania, Ohio 'n Delaware, 'n not so important for money, but for influence in our nation's capital, D.C. You know Chink Ciancola."

I smiled and in a stream of remembrance, the excitement of the hijacking hillbillies, the Colonel, the money made on cigarettes, came running back.

"Yeah, Uncle, he helped me out down South. I never really meet him but we talked."

"Well, Tony, that's his territory. The whole South. He still got Cuba 'n those islands, but things ain't too good in Cuba. It's good business down there. But it's got political problems."

Mince jumped in. "Yeah, that rebel rat bastard Castro's

given Chink some real 'ah-geh-da.'" He faked pounding his chest with his fist, which is the visual that always accompanies the Italian word *agita*, or indigestion. Mince went on, "I'd like to give that rebel fuck real ahgedda with a bullet. He could fuck up our whole Cuban deal. Gamblin', broads, real estate, 'n most important, Cuban cigars!'"

He looked me right in the eye waiting for some response. Someday I'll learn not to take everything these guys say so seriously. I should act more like I do with Dom, but that's easier because with Dom I call the shots. It must be that old parochial upbringing playing tricks on me. Respect your elders. I guess that's part of it, but their accomplishments and position is really what I'm in awe of. I gave it try anyway.

"Cuban cigars? Mince, you don't even smoke!"

"Ya right, Tony, but Mr. Ted does 'n that's really gonna piss him off!"

"If that's the case Chink should convert one of his warehouses into a huge humidor in case there is a revolution. Then Mr. Ted need not worry."

"Joe Sweets you're right. He's a fuckin' genius! I can't wait to get Chink on the phone."

Oh shit he's taking me seriously. Maybe it's that important not to piss off Mr. Ted.

"By the way," I asked, "why is Chink Ciancola called Chink?" They looked at each other like I had just asked them to give up their firstborn.

Mince, using an index finger from each hand, pulled back the corners of his eyes. "Cause he looks like a fuckin' Chink! Slanty eyes!"

I lost it and started to laugh uncontrollably. Hysterical,

I tried to utter, "What else could it be!" They joined in the moment and like the tinkle of crystal that earlier licked the air, our laugher boomed across the hills, undoubtedly all the way to Cuba.

Two other pieces of information were offered up that evening. One. The Midwest is run out of Chicago by a guy named Puppy Dog DiBiase. Two. The day-to-day business is attended to by the four regional heads. But throughout our evening, time and time again, it was made very clear, that any major consideration had to be cleared with Mr. Ted. The "meets" as they are called, are attended by Mince, Joe Sweets, Chink Ciancola, Puppy Dog DiBiase and hosted by Mr. Ted. They don't happen often and never at the same location. On occasion a foreign representative may be invited, but that's highly unusual. Each regional member brings his first in command, if he has one.

I found it interesting that Mince and Joe Sweets had no first in command. Without Uncle Joe saying it, that's what I am being groomed for. In New England anyway.

As we were saying our good-byes, bringing the evening to a comfortable close, I mentioned my breakfast meeting along with a brief explanation.

"Tony," Mince said, "maybe I should send Joe Fat with you in case this jerk-off doesn't get da message."

I liked the idea of muscle and accepted gratefully.

***

At eight fifteen the next day I went down to the garage and there waiting for me was faithful Joe Fat, reading of all things, the Hollywood Reporter. I was greeted with a "Mornin'."

I stepped around a small puddle of water created from

droplets from under the car. He noticed me looking at the puddle. "I wash the car every mornin'. It's white 'n ya gotta keep it
clean."

As we drove out of the garage the sun hit the windshield
like one of those atom bomb flashes you see in the newsreels. I
turned on the radio and Chuck Berry sang out, "Up in the mornin
out to school, the teachers teaching the golden rule . . ." What a
coincidence. I started some advance classes last night in geogra-
phy, math, and advanced management technique.

I love the mornings in LA. The gentle warmth engulfs
you. Unlike some Eastern mornings that can stifle you, these just
embrace you. Driving along Sunset, I thought of Chris and how
I would like to wake up next to her on one of these West Coast
mornings. Maybe that could be arranged. My fantasy was interrupted by a Joe Fat question.
He was referring to the jodhpur-wearing TV guy from the day
before.

"Tony, what do ya want to do with this guy?" *He's away
from Mince and I'm in control*, I thought. *I like that.*

"Well, Joe Fat, he's threatening to go to the FCC to contest our application for the station's license."

I could tell by Joe Fat's silence he didn't have a clue as to
what I was talking about.

"He's trying to screw up the deal by ratting to the government."

Joe Fat understood. "That little prick."

"I don't know that he's got one."

Joe Fat looked at me, and for the first time I earned his
broad smile. The sun bounced off several gold caps. It gave him a
cartoon hero look. Like, "Don't worry, I'll save the day!"

"Joe Fat we'll seat him in the middle of us and if I need your help you'll know it. Nothing harsh though." Joe Fat seemed disappointed. "Well just harsh enough to give him a message."

Joe Fat smiled again and his gold teeth sparkled.

***

The Polo Lounge at eight thirty in the morning is like no other hotel coffee shop in the world! It's like walking into a banana grove, without the bananas. There were huge tropical plants, with lush, wide, green leaves everywhere. The foliage was duplicated on the wall in white and green wallpaper. Every booth was taken. Everyone dressed from suits to Levis, were busy whispering face-to-face. Deals are made, then broken, then remade.

As soon as we sat down it was obvious we were out of place. We were the only table not making a phone call, or being paged to receive one.

It was nearly eight forty five and although I loved the people watching, I was getting a little upset with our superstar Grant Tanner's tardiness. I did the only thing one can do in the Polo Lounge, I asked for a phone! It was quickly brought to me by a handsome Mexican waiter.

I picked up the headset and a sultry voice on the other end asked, "May I have your number please?"

I gave it to her.

She continued, "Shall we put this on your room bill or breakfast bill?" They got you covered!

"Breakfast please."

"Thank you. Here's your party; enjoy your breakfast."

I bet that phone operator has the best script in Hollywood. The phone rang twice.

"Mrs. Cosby's office."

"Sharon, this is Tony Manfredi. Is Moe there?"

"She's just about to have lunch. May she call you later?"

"It's only ten to twelve. Put her on."

There was a slight pause then, "Tony Manfredi, don't tell me your handsome face has already been discovered by some Hollywood talent agent and we're not going into the magazine business together."

She's great! Too skinny, homely, but great!

"Hey Moe one discovery in the family is enough. That's why I called, to see if we are going into the magazine business together. Did you get a chance to see the people at *The American Woman*?"

"I actually didn't see them, but set a meeting the day after you return."

"Oh, so there was no fishing expedition on your part."

"I thought about it but opted to wait for you and your excellent salesmanship to help out. Do you mind?"

"Not at all. Anything new on Amy?"

"Your Johnny sent over a few notes and all is acceptable. I'm hoping to use her next quarter. Maybe around the holidays."

"We Manfredis love Christmas! It would be a great present to Amy."

"In addition to running the agency I have a direct line to Santa. Consider it done."

"Moe, thanks. I'll see you within a week unless some craziness takes place."

"Okay and stay away from those Hollywood vamps!"

"Bye." I hung up pleased that she was going to wait for

me, and proud that Amy would be seen around the holidays in a prestigious women's magazine. I was looking down at the telephone, meandering through my thoughts.

"Mr. Manfredi."

I didn't have to look up; it was Willie Shakespeare's voice, doing his opening soliloquy.

"Grant Tanner. Thanks for coming."

He was dressed in a gray version of his slapstick director's outfit. He bowed from the waist up then looked at Joe Fat. It's the same look the Joe Fats and Doms get from other people who think they're better, or is it they instinctively know this person is trouble.

"Grant I'd like you to meet my associate Mr. Angelo Trillo. "Everybody calls me Angelo." Added Joe Fat.

No smile, no handshake.

I got up and ushered Grant into the booth. He was annoyed at the thought of sliding in between us. It was perfect staging. I didn't want to spend a lot of time chitchatting with this guy, so under the pretense of Grant being a busy person, I called the waiter over and we gave him our breakfast orders.

"So, Grant, tell me about yourself. I like to get to know our employees."

He didn't like being called an employee, but I couldn't care less. He told us that he has been in this town since he was ten. Born in Davenport, Iowa, he came to LA with "my widowed mother." She was the first to discover his talent.

"From that discovery, to this day I have been a thespian, plying my talents in the movies and now television." He was auditioning.

"Tell me about your movie career."

By now our coffee cups were being filled from a sterling silver coffee pot. He waived off the cream and sugar and rambled on. How he started in the silents. Worked with some of the greats. Chaplin, Arbuckle, Nora, Chaney. Then the early talkies. Barrymores, Duke, Cagney.

I thought, *How Hollywood to use one name.*

"Married?" I asked. The one-word question threw him.

"What?"

"Are you or have you ever been married?"

With an impertinent air he responded, "Acting has been my bride. My spouse." He liked what he just said.

"Mr. Manfredi we are to talk of my contract with Channel 13, not of my talent as a movie actor."

I took a sip of coffee.

"Grant isn't it unusual that talent represents itself? I thought, particularly in Hollywood, talent would be represented by agents or managers or both."

His ego well in hand he responded, "I have been most successful representing myself."

"Then it's safe to presume you do not have an agent or manager, and our dealings will be handled one-on-one."

Now he sipped his coffee. "Correct."

"Tell me about your contract and the FCC."

Before he got the chance to answer our food was delivered. It was timed perfectly, because our star was getting a little cranky.

Joe Fat ordered steak and eggs. I ordered scrambled eggs with lox and onions. We were both happy with what we saw on our plates.

Grant was served last. The plate no sooner hit the table

and Grant hit the ceiling.

"You call this swill eggs Benedict! They are unacceptable. Take them back to your swine cook with the following instructions. Grant Tanner likes his eggs firm, the English muffin
lightly toasted, minimum fat on the bacon, and the hollandaise
fresh! He waved the waiter and the eggs Benedict away.

"Grant I can see our negotiations are going to be tough."
My attempt at humor went the way of Grant's eggs.

Arrogantly he said, "There will be no negotiating. I will
present a package to you, or to whomever is running Channel 13,
and it will be accepted. Point for point."

I slashed into my eggs trying to maintain my cool.

"Or?" I questioned.

He drummed all his fingers on the edge of the table. He
kept drumming until I asked again.

"Or?"

His drumming didn't stop but it lightened. "Or I will go
to the FCC with a group that has already vowed to support me
with a request to deny the license."

"On what grounds?" I asked.

He unloaded with his rehearsed knowledge of the process. "Lack of service to the community. Mr. Manfredi, in case
you are not aware, all television stations are licensed with that
as a major stipulation. A station must be aware of the community's needs, and service those needs through its broadcasting of
programs and announcements. The needs are assembled through
a series of meetings between station management and various
community groups and individual leaders. These meetings are
entitled station ascertainment.

"Your station Mr. Manfredi, not only has never been

faithful to those ascertainment meetings, but has falsified its public records. All the so-called community programming is buried on Sunday mornings. Your license will no doubt be rebuked."

"So, Mr. Tanner," I went formal as he did, "it sounds like we either agree or lose our license. That's assuming of course you can prove all this and the FCC agrees with you. That will take time and money."

"Is this a poker game, Mr. Manfredi? I have time. And my supporters have money. They are well aware of the profitability of owning a television station, and are salivating at the opportunity to get in without a huge investment."

"Angelo?" I looked past Grant.

Joe Fat stopped eating and looked back at me.

"Angelo, it sounds pretty pat to me."

Grant didn't turn to look at Joe Fat for any possible response.

"Tony, excuse me for buttin' in, but time 'n money's one thing. What about the battle itself? It takes balls to fight that one."

"Good point, Angelo. Mr. Tanner, do you and your supporters have balls?"

He winced. "How crass!"

Just then the waiter appeared bowing like an Oriental servant. He started to apologize and tell Grant how a fresh order was being prepared.

I stopped him. "Please we are at a very vital point in our negotiations and the eggs can get here when they get here."

The waiter looked at me, then Grant, then Joe Fat, who's slight head jerk screamed *Get lost!* The waiter left.

"Mr. Tanner, we were talking about crass balls. Your

balls."

He started to get up, but being wedged between us, in a slippery leather booth, his escape was impossible.

"Angelo, Mr. Tanner doesn't like your balls connotation."

This was great. We were just like all the other movie moguls in the room. Whispering, negotiating face-to-face. I was getting back to the edge I loved so much.

Joe Fat shifted his fork from his right hand to his left. I never noticed his hands before, but they were huge, with hair on every finger. In the crotch of his thumb and index finger was a small tattoo. It could have been some secret symbol of some secret order. Being a good Catholic kid, I recognized it immediately as the Sacred Heart of Jesus Christ!

I knew he wasn't about to stab Grant with his fork. That's not the way it's done in public. It's reserved for some back room in some plant. But what did he have in mind? His right hand slipped unnoticed under the table.

"Tony, I don't think Mr. Tanner here's got the balls."

Grant was just about to answer with what was certainly going to be some snide remark, when his mouth opened so wide we could have shoveled all the eggs Benedict in the restaurant down it. His face turned white, then pinkish, then red. His purple hue was my cue.

"Mr. Tanner we will negotiate your contract in good faith once we have the license. If we don't get the license because of you and your group, my associate Mr. Trillo will complete the castration. We Italians, for generations, loved the sounds of the castrati. You are familiar with them?"

He didn't move his head or answer. There was an under-the-table jerk, and he nodded affirmatively.

"Good. There will be no license opposition from you or your group. Right?"

Without further prompting from Joe Fat, he nodded acceptingly.

"Good." I looked over at Joe Fat and when he released Grant's balls he nearly fainted. I lifted his glass of juice and offered it to him. He took it into his two shaking hands. I looked around the room and not a person was aware of what had just happened.

"Grant, first, you should never try to threaten people unless you're equipped. We're equipped. Second, you should never try to pass yourself off as something you're not. Your ratings as a movie host stink. But I am willing to give it some thought and work with you on improving your rating situation. And while we're on the subject of 'nots,' you were never in any way, shape, or form a silent or talkie movie star. My research reveals you were a bit player. You never even had the acceptance as a character actor. You're lucky to be working at all. Television has saved your star-studded ass. Don't fuck with it."

Just then the eggs Benedict were brought to our table. Grant used his napkin to cover his mouth while he continued to catch his breath.

"Grant, sorry we have to run. You'd better shovel those down, because makeup's waiting. See you on the lot."

Joe Fat and I slid out of the booth together and as we started to leave he reached back and handed the waiter two one-hundred-dollar bills. "Pay the bill 'n keep the rest with this one. 'N give this one to the cook. Tell him my eggs was great!"

***

I didn't want to leave Los Angeles, Hollywood in particular. I felt good being there. It was jam-packed week, and I loved it. At the airport I excused myself from the group and headed for the pay phone. Chris and I had prearranged a time for me to call her.

It rang once.

"Tony?" She said with excited hesitation.

"'Tis I straight from Hollywood."

She repeated my name, but with a softer, relieved tone. She was missing me terribly. I knew that deep emptiness. Caused by missing someone so much, it emotionally overtakes you.

"Chris, what would it take for us to be together out here for a few days? It's warm and inviting, and exciting, and no one knows us. We could be a couple. I thought about how we could rent a motorboat for a day and go to Catalina."

"Tony, a sailboat would be so much more romantic."

Like my vision of ocean swells, we drift so easily into our sexual fantasies. I broke the two-way silence.

"I don't know how to sail. In fact, I don't know how to run a motorboat, but how tough can it be. I could ask Joe Newport!"

"Who?"

"That's a family inside joke."

"Oh, Tony, if only we could."

"Think about it, Chris."

"We can. I want us to be together here. I'll call you from New York. I love you, Chris."

"I love you, Tony."

My California trip ended, but it was the beginning of a most powerful association.

25

CHRISTMASES ARE LIKE FLAGSTONES on
my life's lawn. I accept their support and although I know each
step brings me closer to the end, I step further on.

The Christmas of '57 was no exception. Amy made the
December cover of *The American Woman*. The issue contained
a short biography on her, which concluded with the magazine's
editor-in-chief predicting Amy's success as the "Sensation of the
Sixties!" Moe assured me our interest in purchasing the magazine
had no bearing on the prediction. As far as Amy was concerned,
she got the cover because of her beauty, along with Moe's normal
selling job to the editor-in chief, who had no idea we were pursuing the magazine directly with the family that owned it.

The Adam family only owned it. They haven't been involved in its operation since the late thirties. The three remaining
Adams are inseparable brothers, grandsons of the founder. They
were extremely wealthy, influential and boasted how for generations an Adam headed the Adam American Publishing House.

It sounded great, but the heading was more figurehead
then operational head. In our case they moved slower in the de-

cision-making area. What kept them from agreeing to sell wasn't the dollars offered, but their reluctance to admit *The American Woman* was the only family failure. With this one exception all their magazines were successful. They catered to the typical male or female American. Their ability to touch the right American chord was remarkable. They had "Red, White and Blue" running through their printer's ink. If a theme song were to play, each time you opened one of their magazines, it would most definitely be *The Star Spangled Banner.*

For the hunters and fishermen, it was *The American Outdoors Man,* the number one selling magazine in its specialty field, as was *The American Seamstress, The American Handyman, The American Kitchen, The American Sport.* Only *The American Woman* fell flat. The publishing world claimed they were unable to move from blue collar to white collar, from woods to worldly, and that's why *The American Woman* was failing.

With our negotiations, in spite of their indecision we were closer now than ever before, but nothing would happen until after the holidays, or worse, not until the Adams returned from their Palm Beach winter stay. *April!*

***

Connie felt about the spring as I do about the Christmas season. Spring is her beginning. With an adult's appreciation and childlike amazement, her examination of the earth for sprouts from the previous fall's planting was only surpassed by her scouring of the area's nurseries for additional plants. On a few weekend outings, I watched in disbelief at the patience of the growers. With each tiny seedling she picked up came questions on shade, sun, water, feeding, heartiness. Innocently, I commented on the grower's easiness, and as if representing the entire group she proclaimed, "They love the life cycle as I do." Connie would place the flats of plants in the ground with great care. Year after year, she welcomed their return, while others though blooming only once, would always be remembered by her.

We were on a walking tour of her garden one day in April when the phone rang. I left Connie bent over talking to a young group of crocus. It was Moe Cosby.

"Tony, they're back from Florida and ready to talk."

"Moe we've been here before, and quite frankly I don't want to waste another word on them if they're not serious."

"They're serious."

"How do you know?"

"Something I learned from you. I just know!"

I never liked my own philosophies biting me in the ass.

"Okay, Moe, when?"

"Tomorrow. Sunday brunch at the Field Club in Greenwich. Do you know the place?"

"Yes, but I thought last names ending in vowels were not welcomed there. Not to mention -stein, -berg, -sky!"

"Tony, no one knows this, but the Adams used to be the Abrams. They're German Jews for Christ sake! The worst kind. Arrogant to the core, but with a little twist they became the Adams and now they can go anywhere."

"What time?"

"Twelve thirty. Sports jackets are okay, but a tie is required."

"Oh, Moe, this sounds like a very quiet, conservative club, so leave your bracelets home!"

There was a pause that I let lay there, knowing she immediately took to heart what I had just said and was probably looking down at her wrists.

"Tony, you're the only man I allow to get away with that."

"Moe, you're the best! See you at twelve thirty."

When I returned outside Connie she was close to the door. "Who was that?" I was surprised at the question.

"It was Moe."

"You love being surrounded by beautiful women."

Trying to make light of a peculiar Connie comment I said,

"I certainly do. I have you, our daughters and..." Before I could continue, she said, "any others?"

The painful doubt in her voice over rode any accusation. She quietly returned to her crocuses.

A mutual uneasiness nearly wilted the newly planted flowers.

***

The Field Club was exactly what the name conjures up. Acres of wide-open fields of manicured lawns for tennis, badminton, croquet, and skeet shooting. Not one bocce court in sight! The interior was stale. It smelled of turn of the century Wasps. Everything had a gray to pale green cast to it.

Moe and I met in the entry area, and once we announced ourselves were led to a small private room off the main dining area by the original silent butler. There, sitting around a fully set table were the three Adam aka Abram brothers. I had never seen all three of them together, but there was no question they were brothers. As they stood to greet us they were all about five ten, the same thin build, the same blue eyes and blond thinning hair. They practically looked like triplets. Right down to their mannerisms.

The fourth person was introduced as Dudley Robinson, the family and business attorney. The five of us stood there like a Harris Tweed Jacket ad, while Moe's wrists went jingle-less through the handshaking ritual. The silent butler bowed and closed the door as he left.

I liked the Adam boys immediately. They got right down to business.

"We discussed in great length your offer to buy *The American Woman*. In fact it was the subject of many a day down South."

Down South must be their way of keeping their Palm Beach, Florida, mansion, and lifestyle a secret. Too bad it was spilled practically on a weekly basis, in the society section of the Sunday *New York Times*. My "down South" was making another cigarette run with the help of Chink Ciancola!

"Hopefully, Mr. Adam, it didn't interfere with your relaxation."

They ignored my comment. "Quite frankly, Mr. Manfredi, we would like to eliminate the magazine from our roster gracefully."

I interrupted, "And profitably."

That they didn't ignore. "Without question, Mr. Manfredi."

It was Moe's turn. "The last time we discussed the matter you felt the offer was acceptable. So the financial issues have been handled. It appears the gracefulness is the issue here."

"Quiet true, Mrs. Cosby."

There was finally a difference in the Adam brothers. Only one was doing all the talking. The one sitting in the middle. Stefan. He wasn't the middle child, but the youngest of the three. Connie read a lot about the middle child, squeezed in between the eldest and the baby. And when the kids were all the same sex it compounded the problem. It could create real hang-ups. That was not the case here. I had turned Dom and Johnny loose on gathering information on this group and found out a few unimportant items. Oscar is the oldest. Otis the middle kid. Stefan the baby. As a trio they would take turns leading the pact. For this deal, it's brother Stefan.

All were married with many kids, but Oscar has been a widower for about two years. His wife died of a heart attack, in Palm Beach, on the tennis court. His dead wife would turn out to be the key to the deal. I knew Oscar missed his wife terribly even though he found time to bury his sorrow in the crotches of twenty-year old bimbos flown in to soothe his grief.

"Gentlemen, unfortunately in the business world gracefulness is nonexistent."

I could feel Moe stiffen with my comment.

I continued, "Having said that, I have a proposal that in my opinion is as close to graceful as it comes.

"Oscar our research indicates that your wife Edith died quite unexpectedly a couple of years ago."

I gave the table a few seconds to remember her. Oscar reacted with a bowed head and a fake sniffle.

"I obviously didn't know her personally," I continued, "but was so touched by the information I had received about her, that I had decided, regardless of the outcome of our negotiations, to share my thoughts with you."

Simultaneously the three Adams leaned forward. Moe cleared her throat as if to signal me to watch out. She had no idea where I was going. Dudley the lawyer didn't budge. Not that he was such a sharp poker-faced player, he was just a stiff!

"Oscar your wife was a firm believer in the American way. She felt the past accomplishments, and the future growth of our country was based on the continued freedom of the press."

There was only polite acceptance of my opening remarks. But not one person at the table challenged it.

"I don't know for certain if her views were discussed with you privately Oscar, or with anyone from The Adam American Publishing House, but she strongly believed in the press. Particularly the printed word."

I paused for some response and only got a noncommittal grunt from Oscar and shoulder shrugs from the other Adams. My confidence grew so I continued to shovel it their way. I needed a prologue to my pitch. These guys needed to be handled, and I needed to be put on the edge. It was working just fine. My remarks were too ingratiating, too personal, too American to be disputed. It was obvious old Oscar didn't know anything about his dearly departed wife.

"Unfortunately her beliefs were relegated to a few people as her energies were directed to family and friends. But nonetheless she believed and believed strongly. I would like to bring her beliefs public, certainly with style and grace.

"Oscar, wasn't Edith a graduate of Smith College?"

"Yes, Mr. Manfredi. At the top of her class. As you may know Smith is one of the most prestigious all women's colleges."

He was hooked, now I had to reel him in very carefully. I began slowly, "It is hard to believe in this day and age, Smith College is without any formal journalism school. I would like to propose a building be built in her honor and a journalism school be established to enhance the printed word."

I guess I have been hanging around to many showbiz types, but I couldn't resist the theatrics of it all. I stood up and slowly circled the table to let the thought sink in. I stopped in front of the bay window overlooking a gently rolling knoll. It was sunny outside and crystal clear. I opened my hand wide and swept my arm across the breathtaking landscape. Nearly whispering I continued, "The Edith Adam Journalism Building for the American Woman."

Oscar quickly reached in his rear pants pocket for a handkerchief. Now he was genuinely choked up. The two Adam boys sat there looking at me in stunned silence. Even the stiff, his mouth wide open, stared out the window looking for the name to appear in the treetops. Moe, as if praying, covered her nose job, missing chin, and thin lips with both hands.

I walked over to Oscar and placed a hand on each of his shoulders. "Adam Publishing and the M. R. Tedes Company would build it together. We would share the costs equally, with our construction division doing it at cost plus ten percent. We will purchase *The American Woman* magazine at the last figures quoted and from that point donate a percentage of its earnings to Smith College under Edith's name. That's the economics.

"Now for the gracefulness. Because Adam Publishing is a family owned enterprise, it would be unfair to ask the family to share in this tribute to Edith. Therefore the family, understanding Oscar's loss and his desire to remember his wife, has decided to remove the magazine from the publishing house, freeing it and Oscar to dedicate the magazine, and a portion of its income, to her alma mater Smith College, on behalf of Edith who so believed in the freedom of the press."

I removed my hands from Oscar's shoulders and gently patted his upper arms. As I slowly walked to my seat I took a studied look outside the bay window. It was enough time for them to digest what I had just proposed.

Stefan spoke up. "The last offer remains in place."

I countered, "With a couple of minor exceptions."

The stiff leaned forward.

I continued, "The sharing of the building cost will naturally increase your outlay. Of course we'll agree on a budget before the ground is broken. The proposal for the building and the journalism school will be left with Oscar to accomplish. Any associated expenditures in that area, which I'm sure will be minimal, will be borne by your group. Once the board at Smith agrees we'll conclude our arrangement. Please understand Adam Publishing must hire our construction company to build it. Our bid will be very competitive even with the additional ten percent.

"It's the middle of April. Gentlemen, let's agree to conclude the sale on or before the Fourth of July. That's a very American date. It's also my daughter Amy's birthday. Any questions or thoughts?"

I looked at each of the Adam brothers, then the stiff. I accepted their silence as a confirmation. I glanced over to Moe.

She smiled a full smile and asked, "What's for brunch?"

***

Three weeks after the Field Club brunch, I was ready to present the entire magazine proposal to Richard Q. Knowing he was pleased with all that I had accomplished with the media division, and by his own admission flabbergasted by the financial returns, the meeting would be perfunctory, but one should never underestimate Richard Q. I had a financial pro-forma schedule ready to go. The strategy for the purchase buttoned up, which included Smith College, the folding in of the Cosmo Agency, the financing of the entire purchase through CUF, the need for marketing strength, and lastly distribution.

I was a little surprised to find only Richard Q. and Karen attended the meeting. His staffers were not there earning their keep--by asking unimportant questions, taking negative views on positive issues, while always looking to Richard Q. for a "weather report." I had a few problems with them in the past, but because of Richard Q's support they were no longer a threat.

It was a non-meeting. Karen smoked more than usual during my pitch and wrote less. It's a dead giveaway that something's up! I had finished the presentation in record time. Usually, upon completion of such a session, I would take a deep breath and feel good. Accomplished. But now there was uneasiness in the room. I didn't feel good or accomplished. Richard Q. slowly pushed himself away from the conference table. First with his arms and then, with a Chief Operating Officer's arrogant privilege, continued with his feet. The thump of his heels coming to rest on the mahogany table ended the journey. The strained, squeaking sounds of his chair's wheels stopped. The entire move gave his six feet five frame a large berth.

Karen fumbled for another cigarette, even though one, just started, was smoking away in the ashtray. Something was up! I began an instant mental review of my presentation and stopped, realizing that whatever the problem was, it preceded this meeting. *No staffers!*

I moved first, gathering my flip cards, pretending to put them in the proper sequence. Richard Q. countered stretching his arms straight up, followed by a robust yawn, concluding with a violent head shaking. Karen just puffed away. It was not my move and everyone knew it.

"Tony, this buy came out exactly as you said it would. I appreciate your giving me and Karen updates as they develop. It makes the decision making process a lot easier."

He removed his feet from the table, slamming the front two legs of the chair down hard on the floor. He folded his arms and looking directly at me. "It's a deal, but it has strings."

I responded to what I heard the loudest. "Strings?"

Karen came up with a new one. She crushed the cigarette she was smoking out, and unconsciously picked up the one smoldering away in the ashtray. She was particularly uncomfortable with what was happening.

"I have a personal problem which this deal can solve. Tony, I never had to beat around the bush with you so I'll tell you straight out. It's Maggie."

I had no idea who he was talking about. I looked to Karen for some help, but she was buried in her empty legal tablet.

"Strings? Maggie? I'm sorry Richard Q. but I'm lost."

"In this case, I'm glad you're memory failed you. You first became aware of her down South with the help of the Colonel. By the way how is that crazy old coot?" He didn't expect an answer. "Then you talked to her when Johnny Diamond did himself in."

My mind was trying to lock in. *Strings. Maggie. Strings. Colonel. Strings. Johnny.*

Richard Q. was letting me fry. Karen reached over and put her hand on mine.

"Tony, it's Richard Q's lady."

"Karen, not my lady," Richard Q. snapped, "my fiancée God damn it! I'm going to marry her one day!" There was an irrational tone in his voice. He wasn't in control of that statement.

Karen pouted. This seldom seen femininity slammed her into the back of her chair. The subject was obviously taboo. I suddenly remembered Alan Morris telling me how Richard Q. was in love with that long-legged hooker.

"Well, Tony, I want her in on this deal. I want her to have an important position on the magazine. Maybe publisher."

I had no response. Again I looked to Karen.

Her answer was not to help me out, but get in a cheap shot herself. "Yes, Tony, Maggie needs another way to earn her keep." Karen slid he index finger in and out of the square hole on the top of her Camel cigarette package. Subconsciously or not, the gesture screamed of sex. Her next line eliminated any subconscious possibilities. "Get what I mean, Tony." She was seething.

"Tony, Karen is out of line. Maggie needs to earn some money so she can continue to live in the style she's accustomed to."

"What's some money?" I questioned.

He didn't hesitate. "Forty, fifty thousand."

It was showtime! I wasn't going to roll over.

"Richard Q., that's an awful lot of money. Even for a qualified publisher. Please understand that as part of the overall deal, that position was promised to Maureen Cosby and--"

Richard Q. interrupted me. "That skinny bitch. I'll deal

with her."

I leaned my elbows on the conference room table. "Richard Q. 'that bitch' has already been dealt with. I made a deal. A promise. As far as I'm concerned your proposal is a deal breaker. I can't and won't go back and try to change it."

Richard Q. spun out of his chair and turned his back to me blocking anything else I might say. He placed his hands on his hips. He was getting ready to unload.

"Richard Q., before you kick me out the door let me say I'm totally surprised by your willingness to compromise a terrific opportunity for the company. There has to be another way she, I mean Maggie, can earn a salary legitimately."

He turned around slowly. "You and your ethics. I'm not going to kick you out the door because you're too valuable to the company. But be on notice, just like all of us, if you screw up, and the company doesn't like it, you're out!"

I calmly responded, "Richard Q. I know this issue is very important to you and maybe I'm being particularly insensitive. But I do know the success of the magazine rests, by in large, on Maureen's shoulders. She can't be pushed aside by an inexperienced person. It would be doing a disservice to the company and undoubtedly we would both be out the door."

In a gesture of compassion that I will never see again from Richard Q., he moved behind Karen and placed his huge hands on her shoulders and squeezed.

"This is the most difficult for Karen. We have been together from the beginning. Me, an aggressive Wall Streeter and she my trustworthy secretary. We became successful together. You know I could not make it though the day without her. She has been in love with me since the beginning and I have not responded." He spoke as if Karen wasn't there.

"Instead I have fallen in love with Maggie a former prostitute, who, I will, by God, marry one day. The problem is I can no longer afford her. I have children in college, non-college kids in equally expensive private schools, three residences to maintain, and a wife who out of disdain for me, spends twice my earnings. I live paycheck to paycheck. It takes about forty thousand a year to support Maggie. Apartment, clothes, entertainment, travel."

Karen reached up and patted his hand. "Don't forget the jewelry." He squeezed her shoulder again. "Right, jewels." They had already made up!

Sympathetically I offered, "Richard Q., I understand. I can't put Maggie in as publisher, but I will make sure she is on staff and paid. Maybe not the entire amount, but I'll work something out. She goes on payroll as soon as the deal closes."

Richard Q. walked back to his seat. "Thanks, Tony." He smiled. "But let's close it fast I'm bleeding pretty badly." He smiled. I smiled back. Karen didn't. The meeting was over.

***

I was in my office starring out the window at a shapeless skyline, mentally rehearsing my approach to Moe, while simultaneously trying to find other sources of income for Maggie. I didn't hear my door open. A thin, metal clicking sound interrupted my thoughts. I swiveled around in my chair, in time to see Karen, who had just lit a cigarette, nervously clicking a Zippo lighter top.

"He threw you an un-hit-table ball, Tony." The tone surrounding her remark wasn't sarcastic or mean. It was soft, but filled with a foreboding message. With an open hand I gestured to a chair in front of my desk. She sat, uncharacteristically casual, legs crossed at the knee, skirt hiked high exposing her previously unnoticed legs. They were thin but perfectly shaped.

"Is that a warning Karen?"

"No. I have learned, when it comes to warnings, you're deaf." She smiled and blew smoke in my direction.

"So what is it?"

"It's going to be tough. I'm sure you can convince Moe to give Maggie some kind of job, but it won't be important enough or pay enough for Maggie. She thinks she's entitled to . . ." Karen paused looking for the right word to say while thinking other thoughts.

"Entitled to own Richard Q.?"

She was surprised I got into her head so easily.

"He's just another jewel to her. In fact"--she turned one hand upward as if clutching something in her five-fingered claw--"she's got him firmly by the family jewels!"

There was a painful look on her face then she laughed her whiskey laugh. We both appreciated the moment.

"Okay Karen what do I . . . I mean, what do we do about it?"

Her mood changed. With deliverance, she crushed out her cigarette.

"Tony, he's been putting off telling his wife good-bye and Maggie hello for a long time. Richard Q. is uncontrollably in love with that whore!"

"As much as you're in love with him?"

She reached for another cigarette and decided not to light up. She tossed the pack of Camels and the Zippo on my desk.

"No one knows how much I love him."

"I think I do." I was grateful she didn't pursue my response. It was one of those tender, weak moments when I could have spilled my guts out about my own deepest, secret love.

She continued, "He was right. From when we first met I was in love with him. And to this day I don't know if it's the man or the position of power."

"Power can be intoxicating."

She only nodded in agreement. I needed help with my Maggie challenge and she needed help with her feelings for Richard Q.

"Tell me about the two of you."

"Why?"

"Because it might help . . . help us both."

She opened up, telling me how they met at a small brokerage house down on Wall Street a few years before World War II. He hired her straight out of college as a secretary with a promise to help her get established in the brokerage business. They worked together for about eighteen months. He was the brightest, most aggressive man she knew. One night they worked late and had their first dinner together. He got a little loaded and she took him to her apartment to sleep it off. Her roommate was out of town. Richard Q., then known as Rick, passed out on the sofa. She went to bed and fell asleep.

She thought she was dreaming when he came into her room. He was confused and wanted a drink. She got up to get him a glass of juice. He thanked her, put his arms around her, kissed her, and took away her virginity.

Her voice grew softer with each remembrance. It was their only sexual encounter. Her last one and the beginning of many for him. He was married. Had kids. She didn't care. She was in love and wanted only to be as close to him as he would allow.

I was mesmerized, but needed to hear more about my hooker problem. "What about Maggie?"

"That cunt came into his life several years ago." From mellow to callous she continued. "A corpie friend had suggested this hooker to Richard Q. When I called to get the particulars, the hooker was no longer there, but a new girl was in the harem and the Madame thought Richard Q. might approve."

I threw my hands up begging for her to stop.

"You're surprised, Tony? Richard Q. can't do anything himself including hiring hookers. I do it all. He fucks them and I'm sure if I had a dick, he'd ask me to do it, with a follow-up report."

I felt sorry for her. "Karen, I wish it was different for you. I wish there was something I could do."

Hopelessly she advised, "Tony, do what you have to do. I normally have Richard Q's ear, but on this issue he's not listening." As she got up to leave she reached across my desk and scooped up her cigarettes. As she passed me, she lit up, blew a thin stream of smoke out of the side of her mouth, and clicked the Zippo closed. Hardcore Karen was back.

***

Moe being the pro she is understood the Maggie situation entirely. She volunteered to bring Maggie on as her executive assistant. Keeping her close would keep her out of everyone's way. She agreed to the twenty-five thousand dollar salary only if it could be spread. She would go on payroll at twelve-five. The balance would go through the Cosmo Agency above the signature of either Moe or her husband Lewis.

I asked Dom to pick up the financial slack. He loved the notion of having a long-legged "broad" as his executive assistant. "Hey, Tony," he said, "it's a steal at fifteen gees! Maybe I could put her out to, as you company guys say, offset the costs."

During the next couple of weeks I introduced Maggie to Moe. They greeted each other like old professional friends. Maggie was genuinely excited about working for *The American Woman*. When I introduced Maggie to Dom they greeted each other with fake smiles. Nothing genuine there. I believe that was the only time she set her long legs in Dom's office. When she was in a financial panic, her paycheck from Mann Management was hand delivered, seldom mailed.

There was just one more issue to address before we could launch our version of *The American Woman*.

***

I called Uncle Joe. We met at the playground. This time it was just the two of us. No kids screaming, no wind blowing, and not one surprising revelation. Dom waited in the car while Uncle Joe and I walked around the empty swimming pool. I explained how I needed to launch *The American Woman* in New York City. How distribution is key and shelf prominence critical.

"The distribution ain't a problem, Tony, because we control the unions 'n most of the truckin'. It's this, how do ya say, prom . . . prom-nence."

"Dom and I can handle that. It's like the record business. You just go out and talk to people. Dom knows how to do that real good."

Uncle Joe looked over my shoulder toward the car. "He's a good man that Dom. Ya know, Tony, New York City that's out of my league. I'm just thinkin', maybe now's the time to meet Mr. Ted and you can tell him your plan. Yeah, it's about time!" His blue eyes glistened over the notion.

"Uncle, will you be there with me?" I felt like a little kid going to school for the first time.

"Do you want me to be there?" The look on my face must have said it all. He was pleased that I was nervous about the meeting and would feel better with him by my side. "Done I'll set it. Let's go get some coffee an', I'm starvin'.'"

***

I told Dom our need for newsstand prominence was extremely important, and asked him to have a plan ready to go. I was assuming all would go well with my New York City launch meeting with Mr. Ted. Dom never once questioned the relationships between Uncle Joe, Mr. Ted, and me. I tried to bring him in as comfortably as possible by explaining how we would have free reign in New England, but for the first time we would be working directly with Mr. Ted's people in New York City.

"Hey, Tony, they never bothered us before, so why now? Besides I don't give a shit about them. I work for you!"

They never bothered us before because of Uncle Joe and his friends. That's how we were able to move around New York, Philly, LA, Cleveland, and dozens of other cities so easily.

The two-week "busy-ness" that started with my meeting with Richard Q. and Karen ended with one of Uncle's brief but jam-packed phone calls.

"Go to the Waldorf Thursday Noon. Vespias will be there. They'll take you." *Click.*

26

PUSHING THROUGH the buffed stainless steel revolving door, I left the Park Avenue noise behind gasping for one more horn toot, one last taxi yell. The lobby of the Waldorf Astoria hotel is like walking onto the most glamorous movie set. You could imagine your favorite actress gracefully waltzing down the red carpeted staircase or your favorite movie hero leaping up them, taking two or three steps at a time. There is a civilized buzz that is held captive in that lobby and resonates throughout its many interconnected corridors. It all ceases when the elevator's doors slide closed and you're asked "Floor please?"

I hadn't a clue. Vespia, a man of few words, saved me from total embarrassment. He asked for "T'irty-t'ree, Waldorf Towers."

The elevator operator hesitated. His ear was not attuned to the missing *th*'s as mine was, so I repeated the direction. "Thirty-three, Waldorf Towers, please."

I looked across the elevator, and seeing Vespia there in profile, leaning against the wall, I thought of the last hotel we visited. Johnny Diamond did himself in. Well sort of. I remembered the smiling Buick with the missing tooth. I wanted to ask him two questions. What did you do for my Uncle Joe over the years and which Vespia are you anyway?

I never knew their first names. My mind was having some fun with its thoughts. I smiled.

"Hey, Vespia," I started to ask. His square head swiveled under his black Borsellino. He put his huge forefinger over his fat lips then pointed his sausage-like thumb to the back of the elevator operator. My smile melted into the elevator's cables upward whir.

The elevator doors slid open. We were met by a tall thin man dressed in a black silk suit. He led us down a short hallway. Our six leather-heeled shoes echoed unevenly on the black and white marble floor. We stopped in front of an ornate white door. He rang the bell. It opened quietly. He looked at me then the open door. As I walked in another black silk suited man closed it behind me, leaving the thin man and Vespia starring at each other in the hallway. I was lead into a massive sunken living room.

Taste! That was my first impression. Although I was not an art buff, I knew the paintings hanging on all the walls, highlighted with special lighting, had to be important. The view of Manhattan was breathtaking. A huge white Steinway, strategically placed, prevented the skyscrapers from jumping into the room.

I walked across the plush carpeting toward it and while looking down at the keyboard, a gentle voice scaled over my thoughts.

"It's a beautiful instrument."

I turned to meet the voice.

"I'm Mario Tedesco."

There, standing in the shadows of the room, was the legend. Mario Tedesco. In person there is no way he could be called Mr. Ted. His presence demanded Mister Tedesco. But I wanted to blurt out, "Mr. Ted you saved my life in Pittsburgh!" Instead I extended my hand.

"I'm Tony Manfredi, Mister Tedesco."

He moved forward and engulfed my hand in both of his. "Tony, it's my pleasure. I have heard wonderful things about you."

Standing there, holding each other's hands, I was taken by his presence. After having met some of Uncle's cronies and hearing endless stories of others, Mr. Ted was a surprise. There was a guarded elegance about him. He was shorter than me. About five ten. Medium build. Straight black hair with streaks of gray. All gray temples. Dark, nearly black, eyes. A perfect Roman nose. Olive-skinned or suntanned, it was difficult to tell. But it was his carriage that won out.

Dressed in an exquisitely tailored charcoal gray, pinstripe suit, silken white on white shirt, black silk tie, black alligator wingtips, he moved toward the piano like a tango dancer. He took the white linen handkerchief out of his jacket pocket and wiped a smudge off of the mirrored backboard.

"This is a special instrument. I had it made for my neighbor across the hall, Cole Porter. We were close friends. We'd visit. One day I surprised him with this piano." He gently dusted the spotless ivory keys with his hankie. His brief story, told with such melancholy, his fondling of the piano, left me longing to hear more.

"Do you play Mister Tedesco?"

"No. Only Cole has played this instrument. What a talent!"

"He certainly is," I responded with equaled reverence and continued, "I believe he has written more great standards than any other American composer."

As if ignoring my observation he continued.

"One day he came back from a rehearsal. When he opened his apartment door, there I was with this piano. Through all his pain he was genuinely surprised. I asked him if he minded. He laughed and--I'll never forget this--he said, 'No problem, it's all right with me.' He paused and sat down at the piano and right there before my eyes he wrote, "It's Alright with Me" for his new show *Can Can*."

"Are you still friends?"

He took a short breath and returned his hankie to his breast pocket. "I think we'll always be friends in spirit. He had the piano moved out of his apartment into mine, but we don't visit anymore."

Here was a man who I knew had a huge power base and could have anything he desired but was hurting for his friend.

"Why Mister Tedesco? Friendships are so important in a person's life."

He looked at me for a moment. "Tony, I have never discussed this with anyone. Maybe because no one ever asked. Maybe because no one cares."

"I asked and I care."

He paused then continued, "Yes I think you do. It was a little while after *Can Can* opened. His legs were getting worse from his riding accident. He was not a happy man. There was a problem with the musicians union at the theater. In fact all the Broadway theaters were having union problems. They threatened to close Cole's show. Cole told me about it. He didn't know my background so he never asked me to do anything about it. But foolishly I offered to help. I had the problem attended to. Somewhere along the line a young piano player got his hands all busted up. It turned out that he was a very close friend of Cole's. If you know what I mean.

He turned his back to me and the piano and continued. "I went over to Cole's, like we did most nights for coffee. He confronted me with the story. Cole was my friend and I couldn't lie to him. I told him I had some influence and I was trying to do him a favor. It was the only time I ever saw Cole angry. He told me of this piano player and how he cared for him. He started to cry. He slammed the top down on the keys of the piano breaking the mirror and hobbled out of the room. I haven't seen or talked to him since."

Sympathetically I said, "I'm sorry. He should have understood you were only trying to do him a good turn."

"True, Tony. True. But I have some wonderful memories of our friendship. My good turn, my favor, though not accepted by Cole, was repaid a hundred times over."

What mystery. *One favor deserves another.*

"How did he repay you?"

"He taught me how to dress."

I was floored. "He what?"

Mister Tedesco turned around with a big smile on his face.

"Yeah, Tony, he taught me how to dress. I was a real *cavone.* Greenhorn. He taught me how to dress, talk, manners, wines"--stretching his arms to their limits--"art appreciation." Then slowly and quietly he revolved in place, and for three hundred and sixty degrees, we reviewed his art collection. It concluded with him whispering, "Thank you Cole. Thank you."

Mister Tedesco, holding my forearm, led me into a small sunlight breakfast nook. "You can tell me of your plan over a small lunch." With Uncle Joe's absence, I didn't want to get right into the business at hand. But what else could we talk about.

There was a muffled buzz. He looked down at his wrist watch. "Twelve ten. You're Uncle's right on time."

Uncle Joe entered and went over to Mister Tedesco. They embraced and spoke soft Italian words of welcome. Uncle Joe turned toward me and we exchanged smiles. His was full of pleasure that we were all there, mine was of relief that he had arrived. As soon as we sat down three men, all in black silk suits, entered. Each carried a bowl of minestrone soup, followed by a basket of warm Italian bread, olive oil, and a carafe of red wine.

The conversation flowed easily. Mister Tedesco asked me questions about my past, my immediate family, my opinion on big business. Uncle Joe was relatively quiet. But even in his brief participation there was one thing that was very apparent. Uncle Joe clearly worked for Mister Tedesco. Although there was openness in our conversation, Uncle Joe appeared to edit as he spoke. It was also very clear why Mister Tedesco ran it all. When he spoke, his choice of words, his presence, controlled the luncheon topics. One could only imagine what the power of his actions might be like. He was strong and forthright, augmented with style and grace. Uncle was still from the neighborhood. Mister Tedesco was from the Waldorf Towers.

I briefed him on merging the Cosmo Agency into the purchase of *The American Woman* and the individuals involved. I emphasized the importance of counter presence, which I said I would take care of, but I needed an edge on the distribution.

"I don't understand this edge you're talking about."

It's such a pleasure to be able to talk straight concepts rather than the "keep everyone happy" crap I go through at the company. If that question were asked by Richard Q., or worse yet, by one of his "staffees", I would dig down into my presentation case and retrieve a thoroughly prepared, pass-around-the-table presentation supported by my old standby, flip cards!

"Mister Tedesco, we need a day or two lead time. If one or two of the leading women's oriented magazines were delivered a day or two later than *The American Woman*, it would expose our magazine to buyers who may have already read the older issues of the competition. Our early deliveries would give us counter presence which would entice them to try us. I know, just like in the record or TV program business, that if the product is right, they'll continue to buy. I believe we have a terrific product."

"Why?" he asked.

"Because, unlike the competition, it will address those important issues that will bring the younger woman into and through the sixties." I talked without taking a spoonful of soup. They finished theirs.

"Tony, why New York? You and your uncle could do this in New England. If it catches on there, then everyone will join in."

Uncle Joe answered. "New England's ready to go. But Tony thinks New York's more important right now."

"That's right, Uncle, because New York is the media control center. Virtually all the advertising is placed through New York based advertising agencies, for New York–based clients. The fashion world is in New York, therefore all the columnists, photographers, models are here. If the word gets out in New York that *The American Woman* is the new woman's magazine to be associated with, the rest of the country and the world will follow."

"How long do you need this delayed delivery system to be in place?"

"Six months."

Uncle Joe stopped sipping his wine and Mister Tedesco tapped his lips with his napkin. They were uncomfortable with my answer.

"Gentlemen, six months may seem like a long time. Don't think of it as a half a year. Because the magazines are issued monthly, look at it as only six delayed deliveries."

Uncle Joe and Mister Tedesco looked at each other in relief. They lifted their wineglasses to toast.

"That's a different story. We're not used to six months lead time on anything. Your uncle will receive a contact name from me. Then you can put one of your people in touch."

"Mister Tedesco, I would like to offer the services of Dom Triano."

Mister Tedesco put his glass down on the table hard. "If I wanted a name I would have asked for one." He was unhappy with my offer. "Knowing too many names can be problematical. It's better not to know too many particulars. All I care about is that it gets done profitably. All you should care about is that you have approval."

A black-silk-suited man appeared with a huge tureen. "More soup, Mister Tedesco?"

"No, John, maybe my guests would like seconds." It was clear the luncheon was over, so Uncle Joe and I gave our respective "No, t'anks" and "No, thank you."

***

Throughout the magazine's planning stages, visions of Mister Tedesco holding court in his Waldorf Towers lair stayed with me. The background music for my thoughts came from every recorded Cole Porter song I could buy. Dom thought I had totally lost my commercial ear for top-forty rock and roll, while Moe complimented me on my exquisite taste.

***

July Fourth was the target date we established to complete the sale of the magazine. Moe pointed out the most advantageous time for a new magazine to hit the stands was in the fall. She was shocked when I told her to go ahead and prepare the first issue. Shoot for October, but for sure be on the newsstands in November. She didn't say a word but *How?* was written all over her face.

I ordered, "I want you to hire people who will help you put it together for that October-November date. If the Adam's sale falls apart, the company will have spent a small bundle, but I think it's worth the risk. We can make the short time frame work in our favor. No time for industry gossip. The competition won't know what hit them."

The prototype of Moe's first issue was on the boards and ready to go. She had all the elements in place. In-depth interviews with known personalities. High fashion. Women's subject matter: sex, divorce, sex, financial independence, sex, parenting, sex, horoscope, sex. *The American Woman* was indeed quickly moving into the sixties.

On June 15, 1958, the sale closed. A press conference was held where Oscar Adam, with pomp and circumstance, pledged that the Edith Adam School of Journalism at Smith College would be dedicated by the fall semester of 1960.

It was time for Dom and me to arrange for the distribution and newsstand prominence. November was to be the first issue, so it would be delivered within the last ten days of October. I phoned Uncle Joe for the New York contact. "His name's DeeDee Dipiro, and he only knows Dom's name. He's in the Bronx yellow pages under Triple Dee Trucking." *Click.*

The road near my Byram home, like Uncle Joe's playground, became Dom's and my outside meeting place. It was on this lane that Dom told me how he did Johnny Diamond. We could walk and openly talk of our business, our families, our friends.

"Dom, your contact is DeeDee Depiro at Triple Dee Trucking in the Bronx." I gave him the ad I tore out of a pay phone booth's yellow pages. "He only has your name. You two guys work out who's going to do what. We want to be in position the last ten days of October for the November issue."

Dom looked down at the ad. "When do we start?"

"Well, as I see it, you're going to have to convince the various newsstand operators, the chain stores, to place the magazine up front, and that shouldn't be too hard, because the competition is going to be delayed. So it's a personnel problem."

"Tony, personnel fuckin' problems are a labor of love for me."

I stared straight ahead and savored my response. "Good Dom, then let's start on Labor Day."

My whimsy didn't get by Dom. "Tony, you're fuckin' butee-ful."

***

On October first we again strolled the Byram lane. Fall in New England brings the freshest air of the year. The clarity of the days, the high, cool sun, for the moment it puts to rest the dread of winter, which lurks behind the next gold leaf tree.

"Dom, remember when we were kids how much fun we use to have in the fall?"

We exchanged memories.

"Goin' back to school."

"Smell of leaves burning in the park."

"Makin' sure the oil drums were filled up in the basement."

"Football."

"Cheerleaders."

"And now, Dom, it's newsstands. How we doing?"

"Tony, as always, there are some easy ones and not so easy ones. But you got it all. All the chain stores fell in line right away. They understood our delivery plan or no deliveries for them anyhow. A few independent newsstands gave us a problem, but it was handled. They really got nothing to lose, because if the magazine takes off, they'll be sellin' the shit out of it and everything else."

"Dom, do we have a majority of New York City in line for distribution?"

"Yeah."

We took a few steps and I knew Dom was busting at the seams to tell me a story.

"So where did you have a problem?" I asked.

As if about to pray, he put his hands together and shook them toward the sky. "God this guy knows me like a fuckin' book."

Dropping them on my shoulders he turned me to face him.

"Tony, there was this one stand. A big one, on the corner of Madison and Fifty-fifth."

His excitement in the telling grew. "Now, I remembered how important Madison Avenue was to you because of the advertising, so I thought I'd handle this one myself. Well this guy wouldn't budge. Even when I offered him two hundred bucks to try it he turned me down.

"Tony, I bought some other stands for twenty bucks!

"Anyways, he gets pissed off and said when he was a cop he had the chance to take some scratch from lowlifes but never did, so why start now."

"Hold it, Dom, are you going to tell me a story about doing a cop?"

"Nah, we didn't do him, besides he was retired. He got a bullet in the knee or something like that. But this cop was like a physical nut."

"What?"

"You know a workout nut. Used to go to the gym every day, barbells, weights, sweat, all that shit. Anyways he loved showin' his strength by catchin' bundles of newspapers and magazines. People actually stopped and watched him. What a fuckin' show off."

We started walking.

"Dom, you got to be kidding."

"On my mother's soul." He pressed one hand against his chest and raised his other to the sky. "Honest. A truck would come down the street, toot its horn, he'd run to the corner, and catch the bundle with his arms and chest as the truck drove by. Anyways this cop wouldn't give us the right time of day, so I take a ride on the back of a truck with a couple of my people."

I grabbed his forearm and looked at him mischievously.

"Nah, Tony, I told you we didn't do him."

I was mildly relieved.

"But close!"

I kiddingly made a fist, pretending I would hit him if I didn't like the answer.

"We came down the street, the truck toots, he runs to the corner ready to catch my forward pass. There's about ten of his fans looking on. Me and two other guys heave this package of newspapers at him and boom he catches it and goes flyin' into his fuckin' stand."

Dom stopped talking and threw himself, back-first, against a tree. "This fuckin' cop caught a stack of newspapers wrapped around two cinderblocks."

I was stunned. "So what happened?"

"He broke both of his arms. and if he had a ship tattooed on his chest, we sunk that fucker."

I shook my head in disbelief.

"I put a little note on the package SPECIAL FUCKIN' DE-LIVERY. When I visited him at the hospital, he told me his cop's pension didn't cover this kind of thing, so I picked up the tab. He's with us."

I put my arm around his shoulder. "Dom, you're bu-tee-ful."

Bashfully, he dipped his head in appreciation.

"Now go long!" I yelled. Like a quarterback I faded back and passed an invisible football to Dom, who caught it over his shoulder, sidestepped one tackler, straight-armed another and threw both his arms up as he scored a touchdown.

***

Good planning is essential for success, but luck, as fickle as it may be, is the ingredient that pushes concepts over the top. *The American Woman* hit New York like Dom's cinderblocks. It blew the competition off the newsstands. By the summer of '59 it became a national phenomenon. It was a must read by contemporary women and a must buy by advertisers. Because of its glamorous content, its sexuality, its approach to feminism, the magazine became a news item. The television networks covered the story of this aggressive, breakthrough publication. Newspapers had two-page spreads on it. It became material for many standup comedians around the country. It was even mentioned in a country and western heartbreaker song. Cowboy meets cowgirl they fall in love and she leaves with her suitcase in one hand and *The American Woman* in the other.

As all this attention grew, Moe, to her credit, knew she wasn't the correct image, so lady luck steps in, in the form of Maggie, Richard Q's long-legged mistress. Moe tutored Maggie for the role. She was finally earning her keep. Her wardrobe was changed from 42nd Street cheap, to Fifth Avenue chic. Her natural beauty was enhanced by the slightest application of makeup. She handled herself perfectly as the Executive Assistant to the Publisher. Using one name, *Maggie*, she portrayed the worldly woman of the sixties that was high lighted between the pages of *The American Woman*. Independent enough to be able to choose her man and lovers. Support herself. Marriage and family was part of the plan, but in due time. Content with her beauty and proud of her body, she became *the* icon of the feminine self.

During the magazine's sprint for success a nineteen-year-old model was making a name for herself. She was the first teen model ever to be photographed. Moe's earlier instincts about Amy were correct. With two covers to her credit, our adopted daughter was on her way. I softly suggested using our last name would smack of nepotism. She immediately decided to use her deceased family's name. I took the success of Amy Carpenter, supermodel, in silent disappointment.

***

The fifties were coming to a fast close. I was sorry to see the decade end. It was an upward ten years for me. I had grown into a successful company executive, a responsible father, attentive husband, passionate lover, skillful organization member, and privately cash rich. I stopped counting the money in the Haven Vault and just took what I needed, but the stash never seemed to shrink.

The largest withdrawal came each Christmas, when I would give thousands to Dom. We would argue. He didn't want it, but I wanted him to have it. The disagreement was always settled by our playing *mo-dair*. It's an Italian street game played with fingers. Together each player would thrust out one hand with a calculated number of extended fingers. Simultaneously, in Italian, the players would yell a number from two to ten. If one player yelled a number that equaled the sum total of the two hands, and the other player yelled a number that did not, the player who yelled the correct sum would win the point. Two out of three points won the game. Obviously yelling was very much a part of the game, as was psyching out the competitor before the thrust, which was followed by vengeful wins, passive ties and angry losses.

Dom and I would walk our Byram lane, stop, have our cursory argument as I presented him with an envelope full of money, and play modair. The lane was never so noisy, the fun so full. Dom won only once and the money was returned to the vault only to be added to following year's Christmas bonus.

27

NOVEMBER 22, 1963, JFK was assassinated. It shocked us all. Everyone who lived it could tell you exactly what they were doing at that moment. I was with Mister Tedesco. We had just finished our meeting, when John, his number one, walked over to him, knelt down on one knee and started to whisper in his ear.

"John." Mister Tedesco was slightly annoyed. "You never have to whisper when Tony is here." He gestured for John to stand.

"Sorry, Mister Tedesco." He was very tense. "I just received a telephone call and was asked to give you a message. The caller said you would understand."

"Yes John. I'm listening." A little annoyed he asked, "What's the message?"

"A call from Chicago, Sir. The Texas Rangers just rode out of town. You can see the rest of the movie on TV."

"Thank you John." John quickly left.

"Come, Tony, let's see what the fuss is all about."

We walked into a paneled library and he turned on the

set. "I Love Lucy" was on and he flipped to Channel 4. Chet Huntley and Frank McGee sat side by side. McGee was repeating, partially pausing between each word, what was being told to him on the telephone. "The President died approximately twenty five minutes after the shooting . . ." His report trailed on as Mister Tedesco lowered the volume and turned off the set.

I wanted to hear more, but I was not allowed. I looked into Mister Tedesco's eyes.

"Tony, debts have to paid. Order maintained."

That statement, accurate but cold inforced how we survive. Mr. Tedesco had the same mental boxes that I do. None the less, I was so angry with him. How could he so passively brush away the death of my hero? A hero to the entire country. I wanted to say so much to him, ask him a thousand questions, but I knew, you don't say or ask Mister Tedesco those kinds of questions or make certain statements, no matter how much he knows you.

***

The decade was only three years old, and things were changing. I hated the sixties, couldn't wait for them to pass. All that make love, not war bullshit was tearing the country apart.

Amy was doing great as a model. She was flying all over the world for shoots. She too was changing. She distanced herself from the family. Sure she was busy, making good money, living an exciting life, but she was different. She seldom visited us, her telephone conversations were edgy.

One day she said she was off to Bermuda for a photo shoot and could not come over to the office for lunch. Dom told me the very next day, he saw her get into a rented sedan and head not toward one of the airports, but uptown. I asked Dom to check her out. About a week later Dom reported that Amy has been seen around 96th Street. It was the border between civilized downtown and the underbelly world of uptown.

"What the hell was she doing there?"

Dom knew I was pissed. He didn't answer, just shrugged his shoulders in that I don't know manner.

"Dom, don't give me that shit. Find out what the hell is going on." Dom spun around and couldn't get out of my office fast enough.

I slumped down into my desk chair. *What's going on?* She lives in the village. Loves the village. I wanted her to live more in midtown, but no, she loved the village. So I know she wasn't apartment hunting. *Is it a guy? So what!* She can date.

One thing I do know, Amy has always told Connie about her dating and boyfriends. From high school on, like a couple of school kids, they would talk of it. I doubted that Amy would go as far as to tell Connie about her sex life, but I know she told her who she was seeing, even if it was a onetime thing. Connie in return would edit and tell me.

I knew of no fellow uptown. My paranoia jumped into high gear. I called Connie. My instincts were correct. No uptown guy.

I couldn't wait anymore. I called her.

"Hello," a sleepy voice answered.

"Amy, it's Dad."

"Who?" I wanted to believe she was kidding, but I knew she wasn't.

"Amy, it's Dad. Are you Okay?" My voice was stronger and more deliberate.

"Dad? Oh, Dad!" She was trying to regroup. A slight cough and a clearing of the throat followed.

"Dad. Yes, Dad."

"Hi, Amy. Amy, one second, my hotline just lit up." I lied. I put her on hold and buzzed my secretary. "Get my car and find Dom. Tell him to wait for me at Amy's apartment now!

I went back to Amy. She had those few seconds to gather herself.

"Hi, Dad, I hope that was good news on the line." She was doing her best to act normal.

"Just business, Amy. How you doing? How was Bermuda?"

"Oh"--a huge pause--"great!" She was lying. I knew it. She always gave us a blow-by-blow of her shoots. She was still in awe of it all. Like a kid.

"That's good, Amy. I just thought of you and wanted to check in. Let's try to have lunch one of these days."

"Okay, Dad." She hung up.

It was nearly three o'clock in the afternoon. She sounded like I just woke her from a deep sleep.

***

I got to her place in no time. Dom was not around. I didn't wait. Putting privacy and courtesy aside, I didn't knock. I used my backup key to get in. It had been some time since I was there. It was a bright apartment, with the correct mixture of yard sale and new furnishings. Like her mother, Amy was always so neat. Today the joint was a mess. I gently knocked on the bathroom door.

"Amy." No answer. Fear crept into my body. From head to toe, I felt this weakness, this cold. I flung open her bedroom door. She was lying on her stomach across her bed. Both arms hung over the side inches away from the telephone. She was wearing panties and bra. Her long hair matted over her face. I rushed and rolled her over on to her side. Her face was covered with her own vomit which had dried in spots locking strands of hair in place over her cheek and mouth. She was breathing.

"Tony," I heard Dom call from the living room. It's amazing what fathers do to protect their daughters. Here she was, unconscious, and all I wanted to do was cover her up, so no other man would see her in her underwear. I gently put her back on her stomach and threw the sheet over her body. Dom entered. "Tony, what the fu-u-u--," he caught himself, "happened?"

"I don't know. Shut the door."

Dom had smartly closed the door to the apartment and then quietly closed the bedroom door.

"Dom, she's sick from something. Maybe she got some kind of bug on one of her island shoots. Help me get her in bed the right way and then I'll call Dr. Rossignoli. Dom, get her feet and let's turn her on her back and then under the covers."

I put my hands under her armpits, determined not to have the sheets expose her body, while Dom grabbed her calves. We rolled her onto her back.

"Jesus Christ!"

I looked across the bed to Dom who was starring down at her feet. I ran to his side. Her feet were right side up, toenails freshly painted, with most of the cotton between her toes still in place.

Dom pointed down to her big toe. Between it and the

long one next to it were measles-like scabs. Festering with dried blood and God knows what else. I held her other foot in my hand and removed the cotton from between the same toes on her other foot. The cotton came away reluctantly. Strands of cotton stuck to another mound of sores.

"Dom, what the hell . . ."

"Tony, this is bad shit."

"What the hell is going on?"

Dom reached down under her feet and retrieved a small syringe. "Tony, she's usin' some kinda dope."

"What the fuck are you talking about!" I started to reach for the needle and Dom pulled his arm away.

"Tony, let me check this out. You better call Doc Rossignoli right away and tell him to get an ambulance. I think Amy's oh-deed."

"What?"

"Oh-deed, Tony. Too much drugs or bad drugs."

"She's a junkie?"

"Tony, this is some kind of dope. Maybe she just started who knows."

"Dom, you know who knows. It's part of our wonderful fuckin' business. We know; now it's biting me in the ass. Find out what the hell is going on here and fast."

***

Amy was quietly removed from the apartment and brought to a very private sanitarium in Connecticut. She was shooting heroin between her toes so as to not damage her model's arms. Later I found out she had also injected herself under her tongue but found that to be too painful. Dom had reported that she was going uptown to make her buys.

She was released after three months and went to our home. She was putting on some weight, talking openly about a lot of things except her habit. Her intuitive mother suggested she see a psychiatrist. She did. I wanted her cured forever, so I demanded she go more than once a week. He had offices in midtown, and she obediently went three times a week with the proviso that she could move back into her apartment. She did.

When she did, I called Dom.

"Dom, you know the score. Amy is okay. She is seeing a doctor three times a week and has moved back into her old apartment. I want an insurance policy. Get the word out on the street that no one, under any conditions sell or give her any kind of dope. They probably know her as this hotshot model, but don't know of our connection. If they sell, they die."

Dom did his job. The word spread like wildfire: Holding an American Woman cover, Dom warned, "See this model? She's the mistress of some heavy mafia guy. She is not to be sold any kind of shit."

Amy was doing fine. She was working less, but claiming she enjoyed her downtime. She remained distant, I believed out of embarrassment. We never discussed her addiction. The silence helped me place this undesirable issue in one of my convenient mental boxes. Connie would on occasion say something that indicated she and Amy talked of it, but I choose not to hear.

***

Nearly one year passed. Then an instant replay: I call

her; she is incoherent; I rush over. Mingled with silent prayers, I thought of how could this happen again. How this time I would make sure she was completely cured. *Oh God, how could I have not seen this coming again!* My heart was pounding out of my chest. My mouth was dry yet my hands slid on the steering wheel from the wetness of my anguish. *Jesus, how could I have fucked this up?*

She died in my arms, telling me she was sorry, thanking me for saving her life. What a fucking joke!

The funeral was quiet. Close family and friends. A few of Amy's model buddies came by to pay their respects. Not knowing what to say or do, or how to pray, they stood awkwardly over the closed casket. I made sure the world would never see Amy's emaciated body and that she would only be remembered as the magazine cover beauty. Connie ebbed from the stalwart of the family to an uncontrollable sobbing broken woman. I put my arm around her in hopes of comforting her, knowing she would do the same for me to ease my guilt. I should never have allowed Amy in the anything-goes modeling business. I had ignored Uncle Joe's advice to keep my eyes open. I should have been aware because maybe, just maybe, she never got over the slaughtering of her parents. What the hell kind of a father was I to her, anyway? Was it all a sham? Did I adopt her to ease my guilt over the horror I caused?

Hoping to find some solace, I stood up to make another pilrimage to the casket. As I turned, I saw Chris standing in the back. Her tears visible. Was she there for Amy or me? I nodded ever so slightly. She responded in the same manner then turned and left. I watched her walk away and then looked to Connie who stared at me, exhausted. My mind was blank except for the constant repeating of Amy's last words, "Goodnight, Mr. Mann."

The next day I sat at my desk thinking of Amy in the ground. Cold, alone, but at peace. Thankfully Dom walked in, the hopeless reverie lost.

"Dom, go uptown and find the person who sold her the stuff."

Dom was caught off guard.

"Tony, Amy may have gotten it somewhere else."

I stood up and reached over the desk and grabbed him by the lapels.

"Dom, two things. One: don't use her name in connection with this crap, and two: find the person; I don't care how or where."

Dom grabed my wrists. He nodded. His acceptance of my order was unconditional.

Such pain demands a soother. Mine was not drugs, booze, gambling, eating or whatever. I was addicted to lust, to love. Chris McKay was my drug of choice. After nearly a decade of meeting wherever, whenever, she gave me an ultimatum. Not in anger, but in desperation: "Marry me, or forget me."

Her love for me and her misery at home was destroying her. But I could not do either. I knew her life as mother and wife was empty. Her true family love, her father, died calmly one night while reading the newspaper. She was alone in her own family. Except for me there wasn't anyone in the world who she could love and be loved in return.

I, on the other hand, was content with both lives. I had a wife and family that I loved and whose love was returned a hundredfold. My business family was filled with a different kind of love. But I knew I could not survive without my drug. I needed her nearly as much as she needed me. So I created a separate special box. I told her I couldn't leave everything behind including her. I wanted her to be a bigger part of my life, but it had to exclude my leaving my family. Ah, those convenient boxes. There is no question I took advantage of her loss, her unhappiness.

I have never been close to a family split. We Italian-Catholics just hung in there. Good or bad we hung in. So I was surprised by the way Chris's separation from the Good Doctor went. I had expected all kinds of problems, wailing, gnashing of teeth and property disputes, children's custody. I guess it's the Wasp way of dealing with things. She told her husband she could no longer stay with him and their sons. That her life was loveless, empty. She grimaced when she told me he actually stopped reading his journals and said, "Fine when will all this occur?"

He was shocked at her answer.

"Immediately! I have an apartment in New York City that I will be moving into."

"Wait, we haven't settled any of our finances yet," was his response.

"No need."

Sarcastically he said, "Oh, I see it's money from your dear old dad's estate."

That pissed her off. "My dear old dad didn't have an estate. It all belongs to my dear old mother."

Arrogantly he fired back, "If you think I'm going to pay for your big city girl lifestyle you're crazy."

"No need, it's already paid for."

His put down got him angrier, "Just one minute Mrs. McKay! What are you saying? You have some sugar daddy paying your bills? How absurd. Do you take me for a fool?" He forced a sarcastic laugh.

"John you are a fool. A fool as a husband, father, professional, and lover. Did you think I was visiting museums and going to concerts on all those New York trips? I have a lover. He is mine and I belong to him. We have been together for years. Yes, John, you are a fool."

It is difficult to fathom, but when a person is alone in life there is nothing they would not do to ease the pain and cure the loneliness. Even walking out on a husband and two sons who were, for all intense and purposes, not there. She walked out that night and never looked back. One evening while we were together the telephone rang.

Chris answered it. "Yes" A very long pause. She was obviously listening and finally said, "John that's impossible."

I knew immediately it was Doctor John calling. After a few minutes she hung up. No good-bye, no good night.

I quipped, "What does he want to do make a house call?"

She smiled, "He was practically in tears, begging me to return. He missed me so. He would make up whatever needed to be made up to me."

I listened.

"Tony, the man hasn't a clue as to what I am all about."

I added, "I do and if I ever forget, I have a feeling you'll remind me." She came over to me and knelt down in front of me. I bent over and kissed her deeply. We made love on the carpet in front of the fireplace just like in the movies.

The next day I called Dom and told him about the telephone call from Chris's husband and how I didn't want him calling the apartment anymore."

"Tony, maybe we should change your telephone number." He was kidding and I knew where he was going.

Together we said, "Maybe we should change *his* number!" We laughed. Kids, always kids.

"Yeah, Tony, consider the line disconnected."

Dr. John never called again. Once in a while I wondered what Dom did or said to convince him it was not a good idea.

Chris was safe, in a beautiful apartment right off Park Avenue in the fifties, always close. She fit the New York lifestyle perfectly. She made new friends who would occassionally question her about her past but mostly her present. She attributed her present to her loving father who left her very well off. As for her past, she would discuss her loneliness in the marriage. She shared with her friends how she tried to reach out and contact her sons only to be notified via a legal letter that she has no right to her children. She knew her resentful ex had contaminated her sons to a point of disinterest. Her friends felt the heartache and understood. They complimented her on her courage to leave and to live. It was survival: them or her. She choose her. And me.

***

"Tony, it's Dom."

"No shit!"

Dom was all business. "Tony, remember that guy we was lookin' for? I think I found him."

An uncontrollable anger welded up inside of me.

"Where?"

"I'll fill you in tomorrow at Michael's baptism. He hung up.

"Dom," I yelled into the buzzing telephone. "Dom . . .

son of a bitch!'" I wanted to get to that guy now, not later.

***

Christ, I remembered I'm the kid's godfather. It took several heart-to-heart talks with Peggy to convince her they could not have children and adopting was a wonderful way for them to become a real family. Connie, with her wisdom and compassion really made it possible, but I willingly took the credit and praise.

"Connie, did you get the Triano's baby anything for his baptism?"

"Tony, you said you would handle it."

"Right."

Next stop the vault. I reached and grabbed a package of bills. One thousand dollars in hundreds. I began to finger through them intending to pick out a few, when I realized it was found money. Dom helped me earn it; his kid deserves it. I put the entire bundle in my pocket and left.

***

Michael's baptismal Sunday will go down as one of the classics. Only immediate family and close friends attended the church ceremony. The lack of people was more than made up for at the reception. Dom decided to have it in the old neighborhood so his family and friends could attend. They would never think of going to New York, while the New York group was happy to make the trip.

Penn Street Hall never looked so good. It was a basement hall, where people with little means held various wedding, baptism, confirmation receptions. The entire hall was decorated in powder blue and white. Papier-mâché streamers crisscrossed the ceiling, coming together in the center where a huge blue and white corrugated ball hung. The tables were decorated with white tablecloths. Over the cloth was a cross hair effect of blue papier-mâché bands. Napkins blue, plates white, cobalt blue glasses. A bouquet of white and dyed-blue carnations was the center piece.

Like all halls there was a tiny stage. A trio of piano, bass, and drums was off to the right. Every seat was taken. No one dare RSVP negatively. The background music gave way to a drumroll.

The crowd looked to the door, and in walked Dom. There was pride written all over his face. Peggy was by his side carrying the newly sainted Michael. His handmade baptismal gown was so lacy and ornate Michael could have been a Michelle. Peggy, like most Italian wives, knew what to do to make her husband king. She stopped the procession and gave Michael to Dom. He smiled, kissed her rewardingly on the forehead, and in one masculine gesture lifted the baby horizontally above his head. It was a very Romanesque march down the center of the room. The conqueror has entered Rome carrying the treasures of his conquests.

The crowd loved it and went wild with applause, whistles, and yelled bravos. As Dom approached the stage, I flared off to my table where Connie, Uncle Joe, Aunt Ella, Ann, and Roberta sat. Connie was all smiles while she gently applauded. As I approached she pointed her applauding hands toward me as if to say well done, Godfather. I, in return pointed to her, knowing she would understand that she was the one who made this whole event happen.

Dom reached the stage and in the most gentle manner placed little Michael in the white, wicker bassinet with one huge blue bow on top of the canopy. In gold letters, scrolled along the side read *Michael Anthony Triano*. He wanted to name the baby either Dominic Anthony or vice versa, but Peggy insisted on Michael named after her brother, who died in infancy. I loved this stuff; even though I could not wait to hear from Dom, I was into the joy of it all.

***

The entire afternoon was a party. Food, champagne, wine, dancing, laughs, and many toasts to the newest Triano. As the afternoon wore on, the little bassinet began to disappear. Envelopes of all shapes and sizes where stuffed into it or hung between the basket-weaving of the wicker. Little Michael was virtually covered in *ah boost*, Italian for envelopes stuffed with money to give the kid a boost in life.

I started for the stage with my offering. Dom intercepted me. Knowing he was going to try to wave me off, I clenched my fist and pretended I was going to give him a knockout punch that started from my knee.

Now he was in full performance. He leaped up on the stage and, in front of the envelope-riddled bassinet, knelt down on one knee and extended his arms in a vaudevillian act of protection.

I played my part. Using the envelope as a fencing sword I made some Errol Flynn moves. The audience loved it. Dom knew he was beaten so, with a grand gesture, rose and bowed, allowing me to place the envelope on the bow. We laughed and embraced. The crowd gave us a standing ovation. Such antics for two grown men.

As I began to retreat from the stage, he pulled me back for another embrace. With his back to the audience he whispered, "Eggplant sandwiches for life." To the other cheek I anticipated another kiss but got another whisper. "I will visit our man tomorrow morning."

We parted. With a fake smile I said, "Not without me. Pick me up at ten."

Like nothing happened, I applauded the applauding audience.

28

TEN A.M. Dom was alone. As I got into the car the radio blared, "Love, love me do." I reached over and lowered the volume.

"Tony, I don't blame you, that British stuff has no soul. Give me R 'n B any day. And what a stupid name for a group. *The Beatles!*"

I was not interested. "Dom, what's the deal?"

"He's some "moohl" uptown known as Tiny Dark."

"How do you know for sure it's the guy who sold Amy the stuff?"

"Tony, there are certain things I do and therefore know for sure. This is one of them. No one had the balls to sell after the word went out for two reasons. Their supply would be cut off as would their heads. No one fucks with us that way."

"Okay let's go."

"Tony, go where? I'll deal with this moohl. You stay out of it."

"Dom, drive. This is not street business it's personal. I want to see this punk and I want to see him go down."

"You know I don't want you near any of this stuff. It's not like we was riding in a truck with some hillbillies to deal with. This is the big time and we have to be removed from the action, protected."

"Dom, are you telling me someone else is going to take care of this?"

"Not on your fucking life. I know what it means to you and I was going to take care of it personally."

"Fine then, I want to watch."

"You was never that close to this kind of thing, but you're the boss. I just want you to know I get nervous with you so close. Not for me, but for you."

"Dom, I know, but I got to go with you."

We drove uptown on First Avenue. Around Ninetieth Street he slowed down and eased over to the right lane. He wove in and out of the double parked cars and trucks, always looking to the curb.

"Dom, how do you know he is going to be here?"

"Because he was told he is to collect a new batch of shit and to watch for a black Lincoln sedan."

"Where."

"Ninety-sixth and First."

"Then why are you crawling? Go right to Ninety-sixth."

"Tony, you have been in an office to long. These punks are Nervous Norvices. They just don't hang out waiting for you to pull up. They are always casing the joint. It's for their own protection. Cops, junkies, other pushers."

"Why would he be afraid of other pushers? Doesn't he know he is safe with us?"

"Tony, it's big money out there. There are some renegade

groups that have taken a few bold steps."

"Like who?"

"Some Latinos and, more scary, the Chinks from downtown."

"Is it a problem?"

"Not yet."

"What does that mean?"

"We have handled it so far, but it happens now and again. They knock off one of our pushers, steal the shit and sell it on their own."

"Dom, I have enough competition in my legitimate world, I don't want it where we can do something more dramatic than, alternative marketing or acquisitions."

"We do. We have our own marketing plan. You fuck with us we kill you and dump you at your own doorstep. They get it for awhile. Then they come back. They're fucking gnats!"

"Well, keep swatting and don't let them get a foothold.

"Jesus, I had no idea."

"Tony, don't worry. When it's on the street, it's mine."

For the first time in our lives together, I didn't feel confident with his response. It was bothering Dom more than he wanted me to know.

"There!" pointed Dom. We were around 94th and he spotted Tiny Dark.

"How do you know it's him?"

"One of my guys showed me. There's no mistake, Tony."

Tiny Dark was just that. Like a jockey, he was slightly built with shiny black skin. He was dressed in jeans and a leather jacket with lots of pockets. He walked with tiny steps. Each hand tucked in his jean pockets. His shoulders slightly hunched as if he were heading into the wind. He never looked straight ahead. His head moved from side to side. He would practically turn around, almost walking backwards, checking where he had just been. His eyes never landed in one place. Darting. Always darting.

This was a very nervous guy and rightfully so. When I saw him, I saw Amy lying on that bed. Dead. That scumbag sold her, her last high. That hunched over weasel killed my beautiful Amy. I was crazed. I began to breathe heavily. Dom pulled the car over behind a Coca Cola truck that was making a delivery.

"Tony, it's getting close. Are you sure you don't want to wait here? Take a cab back?"

"Not on your life," I snapped.

"Okay, then drive. I'll work from your side."

I knew the plan, pull alongside, call him over and do the deed. One more pusher bites the dust.

"Dom, you drive. I want to do this myself."

That old excitement came roaring back. I wanted to do it, for Amy and my own rush.

Dom looked at me in disbelief. "Tony, enough with the vendetta. This is serious business. Leave it to the pros."

"Dom, this *is* my business. It *is* my vendetta. Now drive."

Before he pulled out, he reached into the glove compartment. He handed me a gun. As he did he clicked a tiny lever.

"The safety is off. It's a silencer so no one will hear gunshots, only Tiny Dark will feel them."

Dom continued with his instructions. "I'll pull up alongside. You roll down the window, and shoot from inside the car. Pull the trigger as many times as you want, but make sure the bullets are hitting him, not anything or anyone else."

The gun lay in my lap. When I touched it, I expected

cold steel, but it was warm. I grabbed it; my finger automatically locked on the trigger. My other hand grabbed the silencer.

Tiny Dark was just crossing 96th. Dom beeped the horn. Tiny Dark spotted us and smiled. He pointed to the corner. We pulled over just as he stepped on the curb.

"Now, Tony, now!" Dom whispered not wanting to frighten off the prey. I rolled down the window. We were nearly side by side.

"Tiny Dark," I yelled out the window. I gestured for him to come over to the car.

"Dom. Stop!"

Without hesitation Dom stopped.

"Hey man, what's happenin'?" Tiny said as he shucked and jived toward the car. Waving past me he continued, "Hey, Dom! I'm honored to see you on the street."

He looked at me. "You're a new face. What kinda gifts do you bring old Tiny Dark?" He moved toward the open window.

"Special stuff. It's a high class blend for only your best customers."

"All my people are high class. Doctors, lawyers, show people."

"Show people?" I was playing this game. "Like anyone I would know?"

He named a few TV stars and then said, "And lots of model types."

"Models?" My heart was racing even faster.

"Yeah, sometime I would give them a discount for some head. But Dom you always got your share." He was a little nervous at making that revelation.

"Models, huh."

"Yeah, the only problem is no tits on these broads. All legs, lips, and great asses."

I had enough. Rage replaced excitement and query. I pretended to reach down on the floor of the car.

His curiosity brought him closer to the window. I reached up and grabbed the front of his shirt at the collar. He was surprised.

"Ever hear of Amy the model?"

His eyes widened. He knew. He tried to pull away, but I held tight. I raised the gun up to his face and with two pulls of the trigger it was over. His head jerked back as the bullets went into his face. I braced for a blood splatter, but it never happened. With a little shove he hit the sidewalk.

Dom did not squeal away like in the movies, but slowly entered traffic. I adjusted my outside rearview mirror to see. He was on his back. People just walked around him. Another junkie-wino passed out on the streets of New York City.

Dom was silent. No panic. I was without any emotion. The thrill preceded the act and now I was empty. I just took another person's life and I was void of any feelings. Dom started to say something but I pre-empted him.

"Dom, how should I feel?"

Not the Dom who was always animated, he looked at me, stone faced.

"It depends."

"On what?"

"Tony, there are things that have to be taken care of. It's a decision that must be made and depending on the circumstances you may feel differently each time."

I couldn't believe Dom was giving this slice of philosophy about killing another person.

"Dom, I feel empty but at the same time relieved. Like I paid a debt. This sounds nuts, but like when I was a kid and went to confession. I was scared to death, before, during, and waiting for my penance. Once I got absolution, I felt great! Is that fucked up?"

"Do you feel great?"

I looked down at the gun still in my lap. I engaged the safety switch and tossed it on the floor between my feet.

"Dom, all I feel is relieved. I had this angry thing stuck in my throat and now I feel it's gone. I couldn't care less about the creep."

"Bingo, done deal!"

"That's it?"

"That's fuckin' it!"

"How come I'm not worried about being caught? I could get caught, but I'm not worried. What's with the emptiness?"

"Tony, you won't get caught. It's broad daylight; a junkie-pusher was killed. The cops won't be bustin' their humps to find out who did it. It's one less pain in the azz to them. But if you did get caught, it wouldn't be you."

"What!"

"Tony, you're as clean as a whistle. I would take the fall."

"Dom, that's bullshit."

"No Tony, that's friendship. Besides you wouldn't last two minutes in the joint!"

"Yeah, Dom, like you're a three time loser or something. You've never been arrested even for a traffic ticket."

"You are right, sir! But I've been up there to visit some of my fellow workers. They tell me shit. It's a fuckin' sewer."

"Dom, you're the best."

"Tony, because you made me the best, you are.

***

I was like that confessional kid again. I felt compelled to tell someone. Connie, she would be horrified. Chris, she wouldn't get it. Uncle Joe.

"Hello, Uncle Joe, I need to talk to you about something important."

"If it's that important, then come up to the bakery."

"I'll see you tomorrow."

***

I was there bright and early. Uncle was somewhat surprised by my arrival.

"Tony, how are ya? The family? Good?"

I just nodded affirmatively.

"Tony, sit we'll have some coffee an'."

I interrupted, "Uncle, let's go to the playground for a walk and talk."

"Tony, the neighborhood is changin'; it's not the best place to go these days. You are safe here. Say what you got to say."

"Uncle, have you ever killed anyone? I mean because of business not without motive." He looked at me coldly. He sipped his espresso. He didn't respond. I couldn't wait for the answer.

"Uncle, I did. Yesterday. The pusher who sold Amy the drugs." I was spewing out the story.

"Whoa, wait. No more. I told you once I'm not your priest. I don't want to hear this."

"But, Uncle."

"Tony, I don't want to hear this shit! You did what you did. Whether it was for business or personal reasons. It's done. But watch the personal reasons. It can get you in big trouble."

He wasn't going any further.

"Uncle, that lowlife had it coming!"

"Tony, our family is from the Naples area, Isolleta, Arché; you're acting like a *ca-ba-dost* from Calibrase."

Legend has it the people from that region had thick heads from falling on the rocks so often. He was telling me I was a thickhead and to shut up. I did. And so did the rest of the world. Not a single reference to the killing anywhere. No calls from the authorities. Nothing. It was like the bastard never existed.

29

I RECEIVED A SECRETIVE telephone call from Karen.

"Tony, Richard Q. wants you to attend a board meeting next Thursday at one thirty."

"Karen, what's this all about?"

"You'll find out when you get there. Make sure you have all your division's year-to-date figures and a copy of your action plan."

"Is this a pop quiz or something?"

"Tony, I told you all I can. Be there. Be ready. Thursday, one thirty."

I didn't once sense she was taking a drag on a cigarette. Could she have quit smoking! Shit, could Richard Q. be quitting! I felt this was big doings. Within minutes I had assembled my staff, sans Dom, and ordered them to get me prepared. They knew the drill. I had never presented anything to the board. The highest I got was Richard Q. I wondered if he, like Flanagan, took all the credit for my successes at the board meetings. I always felt he was straight with me. He had a flock of flunkies to push around, and

I was not a member of that club. Yeah, he could be ruthless, but seldom if ever with me.

Thursday at one thirty I walked into the boardroom. I guess those rooms of power are all alike.

Long mahogany table, real black leather chairs, silver trays with crystal water decanters and glasses, a few ashtrays. At each position a legal tablet, two sharp pencils and leather-bound agenda book.

The walls were void of any art. I remembered Richard Q. demanding that when you make an important pitch there should be nothing to distract them from you. He was practicing what he preached! I was a little embarrassed to be the last one in. I guess my face showed it.

"Tony, welcome", a standing Richard Q. said smiling. "No you're not late. We got together about fifteen minutes ago. Let me introduce you around."

There were six people there; however, I was only facing three of them across the table. Two of which I knew.

"Moe Cosby you know as well as Oscar Adam."

"Mrs. Cosby" I nodded. She, the devil, reached across the table to shake my hand and at the same time wiggled her wrist. No clang! I could barely reach her skinny hand. The shake was strong, welcomed and we both enjoyed the secret humor.

"Mr. Adam." He just bowed his head in acknowledgment. Arrogant German Jew.

"This is Arthur Taylor, the president and C.E.O. of N.Y.N.E.B. His bank over the years has been an integral component to our success."

"Tony, nice to meet you." His smile was returned by mine.

Richard Q. stretched out his arm beckoning me to come around to the other side of the table. I passed behind Karen who sat there smokeless. As I turned to face the other three members my knees almost buckled. I felt that groin tingle again. There facing me were two strange faces and one I knew.

"Here are the money boys," boasted Richard Q. "Our investors. Myron Wick III."

Prematurely gray, he sat tall in his seat. He was lean, the preppie athletic type. Drop dead handsome, he smiled a full smile and the contrast of his white teeth and Florida tan screamed *I'm rich and a health fanatic!*

Next was the familiar face.

"And Mario Tedesco."

There were about a thousand emotions going through me at once. *I know this guy. It's Mr. Ted, he runs the entire United States! He's a friend of my Uncle Joe's! Did you have the President assassinated? How about a Cole Porter tune!*

I greeted him repeating his name very carefully.

"Last but not least, Paul Paulson. We call him Coach because he owns a couple of professional sport franchises."

I had a difficult time comprehending Mr. Ted's attendance. *What the hell was he doing here?*

"Tony, please take that seat." Richard Q's booming voice jarred me out of my thoughts. He was pointing to an empty seat next to Moe Cosby.

"Gentlemen and lady"--he gave Moe a courtesy yank--"there are two items of importance on this quarter's agenda. First, as you know, and can clearly see in the attached report, our company has enjoyed more profits than ever before and nearly forty percent higher than our projections, which unto themselves were bullish. This profit is due to Tony's division. The Media Division. Created, developed and managed by Tony, it has brought us these incredible riches. It is with great pleasure that I would like to recommend to the board a change in management."

Where the hell is he going with this.

"I have been your president and C.O.O. for a long time and I need a break!"

Some laughed openly, sincerely, while others gave him phony chuckles. My eyes glanced over to Mister Tedesco, for he was the only one in the room that really counted. His smile was sincere and he seemed to know what was next.

"So my esteemed board members, I would like to propose that I kick myself upstairs to Chairman and C.E.O. and appoint Tony Manfredi in my place as President and C.O.O."

I never know what to expect in situations like this, but I'm always pleasantly surprised. I like to think it was a spontaneous announcement, when in fact I know it was pre-arranged, hashed out and approved. Richard Q. continued his presentation.

"With a show of hands, all in favor?"

Everyone raised their hands. I noticed Mr. Adam was a little slow on the upbeat.

"Passed," Richard Q. shouted slamming his hand on the table. Karen scribbled something in her pad and everyone applauded.

Richard Q. looked at me. "Tony, you and I will discuss the particulars later."

I nodded, outwardly showing my surprise and comfort for the promotion. Inwardly I thought, *What's the big deal? I know the value the Media Division has brought to the company. I've been running it like a President. So now I have the rest of the com-*

pany to manage. I hope it doesn't slow me up. I didn't want to get entangled with all the corporate crap.

"Tony, before we move onto the second item, would you like to say something?" Richard Q. was all smiles. I cleared my throat in an attempt to gain a few seconds of thought.

"Richard, I am very surprised and very grateful. I want to thank you for all your support and guidance over the years. The Media Division, would never have existed if you didn't believe in me and share the vision." I bowed my head in humble thanks.

"Thank you, Tony. Now I would like to discuss the second issue on today's agenda. It is time we reopen the notion of taking the company public."

This was a bulletin to me. It was interesting to see the reaction of the board members. Without uttering a word, sides on the issue were clearly taken. Adam and the Coach wanted it. Moe couldn't care less. Wick and Richard Q. wanted it badly. Taylor was interestingly silent on the issue. It was Mister Tedesco that broke the awkward silence.

"Richard, we have been down this road before. Under no conditions can I agree to our going public."

I was the only person at that table who fully understood that statement.

"Mario"--Richard Q's use of his first name struck me as disrespectful--"it is so important for our future growth. We give up no more than twenty percent of the company to the public, raise a huge amount of capital for expansion and debt relief, and individually become wealthier. Arthur can certainly arrange for the underwriting and public offering."

Arthur appreciated the acknowledgement of his power,

but was noncommittal.

Why not? He would make money on both ends. A commission for his work and huge return on his personal investment. Isn't that a conflict of interest? Don't go there, Tony, your whole life is a conflict of interests!

"Richard, I appreciate your interest in the company and our personal pocketbooks, but as I have stated in the past, I am totally opposed to this concept." Mister Tedesco began to straighten his pocket square. A sure sign this meeting was coming to a close.

"Mario, as in all matters I would like to bring this to a vote. A show of hands. Please."

"Richard, you can show all the hands you wish, I will not support its passage."

Mister Tedesco was trying very hard to keep Mr. Ted under control. Richard looked around the table while Mario stared at him.

Richard Q. demanded, "It's on the agenda and protocol demands we vote."

"In favor?" He raised his hand. It was quickly followed by Adam's and Wick's. Mister Tedesco folded his arms in defiance. It was quiet, very quiet.

"Well?" Richard was visually polling the room.

Mister Tedesco breaking the deadlock asked, "Those opposed?"

Moe, Paulson shot their arms up in unison. Mister Tedesco looked to Taylor, who was not moving until he was trapped in Tedesco's stare. He raised his hand.

"Well Richard it's all tied up, but you know where my vote is going." Raising his arm was beneath him. "Your proposal has been rejected."

Richard Q. practically begging said, "Mario, I can't tell you how disappointed I am. We have such an opportunity--"

"Richard it will not ever happen while I'm involved. Give it up."

"Never!" Richard Q. fumed.

With the same coldness as the JFK incident, Mister Tedesco said, "Never is forever, not a good plan."

Richard's face changed a lighter huge of red.

Ignoring Richard's obvious anger, Mister Tedesco suggested, "I propose this meeting be concluded and the minutes entered."

"I second" agreed Moe.

It was over. Within seconds everyone left. I was the last to enter and among the last to leave. I approached Richard Q. who was stewing in his defeat. "Richard Q. I want to--"

"Tony, get the hell out of here. I'll deal with you later."

Karen reached for her first cigarette and looked at me as if to say "You heard what he said."

"Thanks anyway." I left.

***

A couple of days later I was called into Richard Q's office. "Tony, I'm sorry I snapped at you the other day. That fucking Dago got me crazy."

"Richard it's okay. You were disappointed and I can understand you're being pissed."

"Pissed?" He started moving around in his chair like he had a sudden hemorrhoid attack. "That Mario thinks he has all the answers. I have been trying to get this company public for years and for years he has held it up. I tried to buy him out, but couldn't. I can't understand why he doesn't want to go public."

I knew. *Public* is the operative word.

"Richard, maybe the best thing to do is let it be. He may come around on his own or agree to leave the board somehow."

"Tony, that's pie in the sky bullshit. He's not going anywhere." There was a pause. Richard Q. was thinking. He stopped squirming. "Tony, I don't want to offend you, but I have to say you people stick real close together. Jesus, why didn't I think of this sooner? Tony, you're Italian. He's Italian. You get him to see my way."

I started to say something. He put up his hand. "Tony, I'm not taking no or any other excuse from you as to why you can't. You're my trump card. I'm playing it and you are in the game."

"Richard, I don't even know the man. How the hell do I get to meet with him let alone enter into discussions about your wanting to go public?"

"Tony, you're a resourceful guy, you figure it out, but get to him before next quarter's board meeting. Karen will give you his telephone numbers."

The meeting was over. I wanted to yell you *dumb fuck, I have his private number. If you fuck with him he'll have you killed!* Instead I said, "I'll do my Italian best." I couldn't resist a little zinger.

Richard Q. didn't react. Karen ripped off a piece of yellow legal tablet and handed me Mario's telephone number.

***

As always I called Uncle Joe first. Explained the situation and with Uncle's blessing called Mr. Ted. It was a brief meeting. I explained how Richard Q. played the Italian card. Mister Tedesco preached to me about the loyalty in our heritage. How we did business with Jews, Germans, Irish as long as it was in our best interest and we controlled the situation. I told him about the strong Latino presence forming, and behind that an Asian influence. How these two groups are trying to move in on various businesses of ours.

"So, Tony, do something about it. That's what you get paid for. It's not wise to let upstarts get into our businesses. Control is key.

"Now, what about Richard?"

I didn't mince words. "No yes vote from you, he'll fire me."

"You're the C.O.O. He can't fire you without the board's approval, which will never happen."

"So what do you suggest I do?"

"Nothing!"

I waited for further guidance, but instead I got a "Nice seeing you again. Say hi to your uncle for me."

John appeared out of nowhere and escorted me to the door.

Going down in the elevator I tried to justify to Richard Q. my failure in convincing Mr. Ted, I mean Mister Tedesco to agree. By the time the doors opened I accepted my fate gracefully. My severance package would be substantial for a couple of years of survival. Oh, yeah not to mention the hundreds of thousands in the Haven vault!

***

"Mr. Manfredi, Mrs. Cosby is on the telephone."

"Moe give me a jingle for old time's sake." Without missing a beat I heard her shake her bracelets into the phone.

"Tony, I'd give you more than a jingle if you only asked." I liked her for many reasons. Sex was definitely not one of them.

"What's going on, Moe?"

"Tony, I'm having a little get-together at our summer cottage in the Hamptons Labor Day weekend. Can you come?" She ran down the guest list the last being, "Richard Q." and my executive assistant Maggie aka..."

I interrupted. "How's she doing anyway?"

"Actually she's turned out to be quite a talented lady."

"I'll say."

She didn't bite. She went on about the weekend saying how people will begin showing up starting at noon on Saturday and stay through noon on Monday.

"Most of them will sleep in the house, except Richard Q. He requested Maggie and he sleep on the boat."

"The what?" I asked.

"The boat! He knows my husband has a sailboat tied to the end of our backyard dock. I don't know why Lewis even needs the boat, he never uses it."

"Moe, sounds great. I'll check with Connie and let you know."

I like to wrap things up as quickly as possible. I called Connie, asked her about the weekend, she agreed. I told my secretary to call Moe's and accept. I was very curious about the Hampton's and the lifestyle it offered the very rich.

***

Uncle Joe called to lament the end of summer.

"Ya know, Tony, each summer is more important that the one before."

"Uncle, you sound a little mossy today."

Mossy is word that is a derivative of an Italian expression, *Quan da moss*, which completely describes how one feels when they are down and feeling sorry for themselves.

"Hey, Tony, at my age I'm entitled. Anyways, I just called to say hello. So enjoy the long weekend. Don't work; it's Labor Day remembah!"

"Thanks, Uncle. Hey, by the way, I'm going to Moe Cosby's fancy-schmansy place over the weekend with Connie." I told him I was a little uncomfortable because Richard Q. is going to be there and I didn't want to get into what happened with Mr. Ted.

"Tony, no is no and that's it!"

I didn't need to go further so I told him how Richard Q. and his girlfriend were sleeping in the sailboat and everyone else in the main house.

"Tony, the guy wants some privacy. Ya can't blame him for that. I hope he doesn't get seasick." He liked his joke. So did I. We chuckled and said our good-byes.

***

We arrived around two o'clock. The directions were perfect. I wasn't ready for such a "summer cottage." The driveway seemed like it was a mile long. It slowly curved through weathered spruce trees until a manicured lawn broke the scene and exposed a huge three story brick mansion. The white trim gleamed in the afternoon sun. The plantings were exquisite. We were greeted at the door by a butler who requested we leave the car and luggage where it is and pointed us to an open set of French doors. As we wandered through it appeared that the front lawn we just left went right through the house and continued down a gentle slope to the water's edge.

There at the dock was Richard Q's whore house. A two-masted ketch, royal blue hull, the most exotic wooden deck that looked like it was covered it plastic it was so shinny. Chrome fittings that could blind a person.

"Tony, Connie!" A genuine, enthusiastic greeting accompanied by the jingle, jangle of Moe's own background music.

She grabbed my hand as if not to let me get away, then she went directly toward Connie. She kissed her on both cheeks.

"Welcome, really welcome. I never get to see you."

Connie accepted her exuberance with a warm smile.

Moe turned to me. "Him I see and talk to a lot."

Connie in awe said, "Moe, what a beautiful place."

"Thank you. This is a beautiful place. My father built it in the thirties as our summer cottage."

She liked that fact that we were impressed. "Come meet some people and have some lunch."

As we crossed the lawn the new bossa nova sounds played through hidden speakers. Thank God it wasn't any of that English invasion stuff that we missed the boat on. Even in the middle of a Saturday afternoon, the Stan Getz and Astrud Gilberto music was filled with sensuality. I glanced over to the boat expecting it to be bobbing up and down to the rhythm of the music or the humping of the twosome.

The food was primarily from the sea. Crab, lobster, oysters, little neck clams. Moe proudly told us that all the vegetables were grown right on the property. I wondered where!

Champagne flowed as did the conversation. I felt very relaxed, mostly because I didn't bump into Richard Q.

Fuck him, I'll figure something out!

***

Around six o'clock we were all told where our rooms were and how we should plan to meet in the living room at eight. Dress was casual, but Moe in her own way hinted the men should wear jackets. She disappeared through the French doors, leaving her guests to fend for themselves.

Her husband Lewis, acting as the assistant cruise director announced, "The time is yours until eight."

He followed Moe. I looked at my watch in an uncomfortable gesture, like, what do we do now folks? Connie suggested we go to our room relax and get ready for dinner.

Just as we turned toward the doors, Richard Q. burst threw them. He was obviously already on his way to a long drinking weekend.

"Hello party lovers!"

He was a symphony in linen. His lime green blazer, pale blue shirt, and white slacks looked like one wrinkled clump of laundry resting on his canvas shoes.

She on the other hand was impeccable, in a cheesy sort of way. Her hair up. Her tight top, down off the shoulders. Her shorts, very short. As she turned to help Richard Q. adjust to the slope of the lawn the cheeks of her ass hung out.

Not one guy, including me, said a word or gestured in any way to give away our inner fillings. Like, *what an ass! What legs! What a fuck!*

"Tony, my C.O.O., my man."

Shit, here it comes.

"You look great!"

I doubted he could even see me. "Thanks Richard Q."

"Just call me Dick. Here you can call me Dick; right Maggie, Dick. That's me, big Dick."

We all became immediately uncomfortable.

"Richard let's get you onboard." I put my arm around his waist.

Maggie's arm and mine interlocked. She felt soft and warm. The kind of warmth one has after just stepping out of the sun. I could not remember ever touching her before this.

I became excited as we walked down to the dock. He didn't say a word. I looked past Richard Q's face and into Maggie's beautiful face and whispered, "If all is well, dinner is to be served at eight."

"Thanks, Tony. Thanks for everything."

She looked at me as if the same excitement was moving from our arms to other parts of her body. I had to focus on the thanks not on the everything.

"You're welcome."

Somehow Richard Q. gained his composure just before he boarded. He stepped on board and walked the deck without any assistance heading straight for the cabin below.

He turned and looked at the two of us. "See you later, Tony. Maggie, you coming?" It's like he read our libidos and severed them.

***

By eight fifteen all the guests had gathered. Except for Moe and Lewis, we didn't know anyone there. As it turned out the guests were part-time friends and full-time clients of Moe's. She worked the room with the grace and charm that her breeding brought.

Connie and I stayed close to each other and when approached were most congenial. This is not my favorite kind of party. Connie loved it. She was able to observe, mingle, and later, comment on the characters involved.

Moe with a champagne flute in one hand and a crystal bell in the other announced dinner was being served. For once it was the pure ring of crystal and not the clang of her bracelets. We followed her into the dining room. The long Queen Anne table was beautifully set with crystal glasses, exquisite china, gold wear and only candelabra for light. Stan and Astrud once again joined the party. We found our names written on scallop shells and took our seats.

Moe, seated at the head of the table, just completed a gracious welcoming toast when Maggie strolled in and headed straight to Moe's side. She appeared a little uncomfortable, but it was hard to tell, for everyone watched her cross the dining room in a flowing Pucci print Mu Mu. Even with all those bright colors, it was clear she was braless. Her breasts, preceding every long stride, pointed firmly forward. The outline of very skimpy panties acted as a beacon, leading every male's eye to her incredible ass!

She whispered a short message in Moe's ear. Moe nodded affirmatively and with a hand gesture encouraged Maggie to speak.

"I would like to apologize to Moe and Lewis and her guests on behalf of Richard. He is a little under the weather." She smiled for a second and we all got the message. "The Moet in the cabin got him a little sea sick!"

We all laughed, supporting her humorous attempt at handling an embarrassing situation.

"See you tomorrow on the croquet court!" She kissed Moe gently on the cheek. As she left, mine was the only shoulder she touched. Moments. The edge. Fantasy. Thank God I love shrimp cocktail!

***

Dinner conversation varied. An occasional burst of laughter from one part of the table or another. Tingling of glasses. Courses coming and going. A standard high end dinner party. It was about nine forty five.

Before the next delight was served up, there was an explosion that light up the windows behind Moe.

There was that split-second of confusion, followed by another split-second of silence.

Guests yelled, "What the hell!" Oh my God! What's that?" Multiple gasps.

Everyone was up and running toward the floor to ceiling windows. I headed for a little anteroom that was just off the dining room. To my disbelief the sailboat, what was left of it, was ablaze.

Someone yelled to call the fire department, another to call 911. One idiot wanted to call the Coast Guard. I wanted to call Mr. Ted or Uncle Joe. All I could think of was the assassination of JFK.

Lewis ran past me through the French doors and I followed. He stopped about midway to the dock. The flame was hot and high.

"My beautiful boat." I wanted to punch him out. He never used the thing and more than likely two people just went up in flames.

There was nothing that could be done. The fire department arrived, but by the time they got water to the boat only the hull was barely floating. The entire top of the cabin was gone, the two masts, one was blacken like a used wooden match, the other floating in the water, its metal rigging, still attached kept it by the hull's side. There was no sign of Richard Q. or Maggie.

Did they get off the boat? If they didn't they are now two charred chunks of nothingness.

The local police arrived followed by the State Police. Moe was in shock. She sat on a lawn chair staring at the heap in total disbelief.

The officer in charge asked us to all go into the living room. We did. Names were taken. A few questions asked. They would be working throughout the evening into the morning. So we should be available for further questioning tomorrow. He wished us a good night.

Good night? Are you shitting me!

Not one of us is ready to go to our rooms to sleep. We all wandered away heading for our little comfort zones. Connie and I entered our bedroom. She was visibly upset.

"Tony, do you think they were on board?"

"I don't know for sure, but I would guess they were."

We put on our pajamas and sat, overlooking the scene.

Connie was thinking deeply about what had happened:

"They were wrong doing what they were doing. They were doubly wrong to flaunt it. It's only right that they go together. That kind of unfaithfulness has to burn here or elsewhere."

Laced with bitterness, Connie's Catholicism and intuition were having a field day.

We moved to the bed and just lay there. Our breathing became syncopated and we dozed lightly. At one point I was awakened by a feeling, a dream, I don't know, but my shoulder was touched in the same way Maggie last touched it. It wasn't Connie, for she had turned on her side and was sound asleep. It was Maggie's farewell. What a waste.

***

I met daybreak head on. Connie was still sleeping. I lay there for about an hour itching to get up and find out what happened. I heard some footsteps in the hallway. If they're up so am I.

Connie stirred and joined me. We wandered downstairs and about a quarter of the guests were there. No Moe, no Lewis. Coffee, juices and pastries were on the dining room table. I looked out the window and only a few official types remained.

I excused myself and walked out to one of them. "I don't want to interfere, but can you tell me anything?"

"Who are you?"

"I'm one of the guests, Tony Manfredi."

He pulled out a pad and wrote my name down. "Well, as far as we can tell, it was a fume type accident. It happens a lot on these boats. Most of the time no one is on board though."

"Were they on board?"

"Who?"

"Two of the guests."

"Who?"

"Richard Q. Armstrong and Maggie--" *What the hell is her last name?*

Even though he wrote something in his pad he really didn't care. I never gave her last name and he didn't ask. "Yeah, there were two bodies. A male and female. We got them out just before daybreak."

"Burned?"

"Charred."

"Jesus. Thanks for the information."

"No problem."

I walked away convinced Richard Q. was drunk out of his mind and didn't know what hit him. I hoped the blast killed Maggie quickly. When I entered the house more guests had wandered down. A detective was in the midst of them, telling us it was okay to leave. Like a fast forwarded movie everyone seemed to head for their rooms, gathered their belongings and bolted. So did we. We never saw Moe and I didn't care to see Lewis.

30

THE TUESDAY AFTER LABOR DAY Monday couldn't come fast enough. I went downstairs and jumped in the parked car. Dom had two paper cups of perfectly mixed coffee. One of his newfound female groups was singing on a cassette.

"Nice sound, huh, Tony."

"Nice, Dom. It's almost like the old days of R & B."

"I hated to see that music go, Tony. This is close. Thank God it's not that British shit."

"Dom, you keep saying that. We missed that fad. It's a good thing you found this other sound or the record company and all its ancillary pieces would be in deep shit and I don't mean that British shit. Do me a favor and don't knock that music. We missed, so let's get on with it." I sipped my coffee.

"Tony, what's up? You really pissed about the British music miss or is there something else?"

"Well, Dom, I'm not thrilled that we missed. It's millions and millions of dollars. I guess I get pissed when you knock it, like it doesn't exist and are so grateful we weren't involved." I took another sip to calm me down. "Fuck that Dom, I need some information."

"Name it."

"Richard Q. and Maggie were killed in a boat accident over the weekend."

"Holy fuck!"

"You know nothing about it?"

"Nothing, Tony! What kind of accident?"

"The boat blew up. It was docked at Moe's summer place."

"Tony, on my mother's soul, I don't know shit."

"Can you find out what the deal was?"

"Tony, this is too big. It's not down here on the street. You better talk to Uncle Joe."

"You're right. Don't do any sniffing around, but keep your ears opened."

There was that pause that both of us knew there is a punch line coming, but who's going to throw it! I did.

"And maybe it will have an English scent!"

He lifted his coffee cup in a farewell gesture and with his best Cockney said, "Quite right, pip-pip, and fuck thee!"

We laughed. I got out and poured the remainder of the coffee into the gutter. "See ya, Dom."

***

When I walked into my office Karen was there waiting.

"Karen I can't believe what happened."

She was silent. No cigarette.

"I wanted to call you immediately but I didn't think it was appropriate. When I called this morning Mrs. Armstrong told me she is glad the bastard is gone."

I moved around toward my desk chair. "Karen I know this is not the time, but I do believe in his own crazy way he loved you."

"What crazy way might that be?" she snapped.

"He loved you. I know he did. He just was infatuated with Maggie. I don't believe there was any true love there."

She snapped again, "I bet there was every time he fucked her." She started to get up and fell back into her chair and sobbed. I reached across the desk and handed her my hankie.

"Karen, for as long as I'm here, you're here."

She looked at me through red eyes and said, "I think you'll be here a long time. I got a call from Mike Wick who has called for a board meeting tomorrow morning. He wanted to make sure you will be in town."

"What time?"

"Ten."

"Karen it could be they want me out."

"Tony, you're the reason this company is a success. They'll kiss your ass and offer you something to guarantee you're staying."

"Karen, they know I was Richard Q's guy and he did piss off some of the board members. Maybe they feel now's the time to make a major change. Richard Q. is gone and now we can dump his Dago sidekick."

"Tony, you're dreaming. No way. I know those guys and they wouldn't dare touch the golden goose."

"Karen when it comes to all the inside political bullshit you always know best, so I'll go with what you think. Tomorrow at ten will tell the story."

I walked Karen to the door. Her little bit of corporate business brushed away the tears. Outwardly she was okay, but inwardly who knew. I had my own diagnosis. She was hurting big time.

I thought about calling Uncle Joe, but if Mr. Ted were at the board meeting maybe I could have a private conversation with him and get the information I was seeking. *What are you nuts! Like he would open up to me. If I did that, I could be on the next yacht to oblivion.*

"Uncle, it's Tony. I just wanted to let you know my boss Richard Armstrong was killed over the weekend in a freakish boat accident."

Silence.

"Yeah, Uncle, there was a weekend party at Moe's summer house and the boat that Richard Q. was sleeping in blew up."

"What a nightmare."

"What?" I was incredulous.

"He blew up; that's what happened. How's the family?"

"Good, Uncle, good."

He must have known I was not happy with his dodging the subject. "Hey, Tony, even the worst things happen for good reasons. He's gone and there's nothing anyone can do about it. The good stuff is you'll probably get some big job out of this. That's it, bad for good."

"Well, Uncle, there is a meeting tomorrow and it could be as you described or they'll kick my ass out of here."

"Tony, you go, you listen, you see."

"You're right. Say hi to Aunt Ella for me." We hung up.

***

The meeting was quick. I was re-confirmed as the COO reporting to the board. I demanded that this structure remain intact and that if a CEO were to be appointed I would be it and my replacement must meet my approval. Like Richard Q, I didn't want someone between me and the board.

There was no resistance. I was congratulated with handshakes, nods, and a kiss on the cheek from Moe. The last person to leave was Mister Tedesco.

"Nice work. Let's meet for lunch and discuss business."

"It would be my pleasure, Mister Tedesco." Why do I always choke up with his name? I so want to call him Mr. Ted.

"Good. I have some traveling to do and I won't be back until the first part of October. I'll call you when I return and we can set a date." He turned and walked away.

I had no time to reply, merely accept. We parted.

***

It was the strangest period of time. Every day I would check my desk calendar, not for the mundane workaday stuff, but to count each October day waiting for Mr. Ted to call. I tried calling my uncle a few times and Aunt Ella said he was not around. Strange again. *Not around, what kind of answer is that!*

I tried again. "Aunt Ella, it's Tony."

"Hey, Tony, how are you? Jesus, we haven't seen you or family in months. How's everything?"

"Great, Auntie. Look I need to talk to Uncle Joe. I hate to be a pest, but you keep saying he's not around. What does that mean? Is he okay?" "Sure he's okay; you're uncle is always okay. He's not around cause he's not around, Tony."

I wanted to jump through the telephone and ring her neck.

"Auntie."

"Tony, listen, he's okay, but he's not around, period."

Now she wanted to reverse the charges and ring my neck.

"Okay, Aunt Ella, when he does come around tell him I called and I'd love to talk to him."

"Sure, Tony, say hello to everyone." She was gone. Where the hell is "around"? She has been with him forever. She knows the ropes. She is no doubt protecting him and won't speak of anything connected to him over the telephone.

***

"Dom, get Johnny and let's have some coffee an'. We'll meet at Tutalo's around two."

Like wombs, there are places, that we can go to and feel safe and warm. Tutalo's Café is such a place. On the edge of Harlem, it's an Italian oasis in a neighborhood known as the Black Sea. In its day, protected by an invisible shield from everyone and everything that could harm the clientele, Tutalo's was the hang out for the mob as it was known during Prohibition through the end of the war.

It still remained a safe haven for whites in black New York. The remnant from those wild days was its owner. His name is Frank, but everyone who is anyone, knows him respectfully as Whas Wha Tutalo. A bootlegger, bookie, bon vivant, made man. When my uncle talked of Whas Wha, his eyes lit up. It was the first time, and the only time, I got a direct inkling of the mob when he referred to him as being a "made" man. It's that point in a man's life when he takes another's for the cause. Whatever the cause may be, it was so directed and blessed from on high.

Whas Wha met us with open arms and kisses. His energy, smile and twinkling eyes denounced his seventy-plus year.

"Tony, so long since I see you. How's Uncle Joe?"

He looked over to Dom. "Hey, Dom, those mooh-lenyam singers you brought in last week tried to get in on their own yesterday. I told them I was booked and sent them to Sylvia's."

Dom reached over and patted him gently on his cheek. That's the "Don't worry about it" sign.

Whas Wha looked at Johnny then me.

"Whas Wha, he's with us. Johnny Caprio, meet the best restaurateur in New York City, Frank Tutalo."

"Johnny, if you're with him, call me Whas Wha."

Johnny actually breathed a sigh of relief. They shook hands. Whas Wha guided us to a booth. I don't think the joint had changed since it opened in the twenties. Maybe a couple of paint jobs, but the same color. About three feet of beige plaster barely visible because of the slew of celebrity pictures. Mostly black and white pictures were autographed to Frank, but there were the important, connected ones. They were addressed to Whas Wha. Sinatra, Martin, Yogi, Marciano, DiMaggio, LaGuardia. They all ate at Tutalo's, and who knows what other services he provided. You don't ask, you just know.

"Tony, what's your pleasure?"

"Whas Wha we only came for some coffee an'." He was surprised that's all we wanted.

"We needed to meet."

"So meet, have some coffee an', but first a little something."

Within minutes dishes of fried calamari with slivers of hot peppers, *scungli* salad, and *baccala* strips were served up. Warm Italian bread for sponging up all the various juices wrapped up the "little something."

"Fellas, we're on the verge of bigger and better things. I don't quite know what they are but I feel it. With Richard Q. gone, I am totally in charge of the company and we can do anything we want as long as it's profitable and outwardly has the appearance of legitimacy."

"Tony," whispered Johnny, "so much of our revenue is generated in the entertainment business."

Dom, with a mouth full of bread and *scungli* salad responded, "That's why they call it show business! Tony, I'm sure we can do other things, but we got records, singers, TV and radio, management and agents, newspapers and magazines, some movie stuff. What are we missing?"

"Dom, you're right, we have that covered, but we must expand. We need more of the same, certainly, but we need more of something new."

Dom looked at me sheepishly and darted his eyes toward Johnny. "Johnny Three, you are about to be brought into a very small circle. A circle that has no beginning, no ending, no way out." Dom stopped chewing. "Johnny, you're being brought in because I know it will be okay."

Johnny stared directly at me. "I'm ready."

"Dom, tell him." I didn't want certain words to pass my lips. How hypocritical, but that's that side of me in conflict with the other.

"Sure, Tony.

"We do some other stuff that is not all showbiz. We

oversee"--he gave me a nod acknowledging that I prefer the word 'oversee'--"very expensive prostitutes, narcotic distribution, equity loans, union negotiations, and when necessary, motivational therapy."

Dom was very pleased with himself. Johnny missed the humor of it all.

"Equity loans?"

"Yeah, Johnny. It use to be called loan-sharking, but we prefer 'equity loans.'"

Johnny was silent waiting for more.

"We take an equity position in your life!" Dom broke himself up.

"Actually Johnny, Whas Wha was the innovator of the street loan. He learned it in the army and brought it home with him to great success."

Johnny glanced over, trying to spot Whas Wha. He wasn't there.

"Tony, you control a lot of businesses and I see a lot of other . . ." he was stuck for a word.

"Johnny, as an attorney you should never be stuck for words; the word you're looking for is *businesses*. Businesses and businesses."

Dom jumped in, "Yeah, and both are doing well thank you."

"Dom has been by my side from the very beginning and together we built this Media Division along with other businesses. He is an excellent motivational therapist!"

We both laughed and for the first time Johnny got it and joined in the fun of it all.

"Johnny, it is the most exciting position to be in. Walking--no--running on the line between legitimate and illegitimate."

"That's real living on the edge, Tony." Johnny said the magic word.

"Edge is where I live and must always live. I'm dead without it."

There was silence at the table. Both Dom and Johnny looked down at their dishes. Maybe the edge business frightened them. Maybe they felt it was the wrong reason to be doing what we were doing. I didn't care. They had their reasons; I had mine. Edge, power, money. In that order.

"So, guys, maybe that edge business hit you wrong, but that's what drives me, along with other stuff."

Johnny responded, "Tony, not at all. Whatever it is that motivates you, it's working. So who am I to contest it?"

"Hey, Tony, who gives a fuck. I get off on other shit, so I guess in my own way I walk on the edge. Like the Johnny Diamond thing. I fuckin' loved the whole bit."

"Dom" Johnny three asked, "you did Johnny?"

Dom looked at me for confirmation. I nodded.

"Yeah, 'cause he was singing off fuckin' key."

Johnny, now feeling inside the circle, burst into uninhibited laughter. As the laughter faded I ordered,

"Let us go away and think of how we expand all, and I mean all, our businesses. Right?" We brought our glasses up to a toast of confirmation.

"Johnny, along those lines, I read where New Hampshire has started some kind of state lottery. They are calling it lotto. As I understand it, the people buy tickets with numbers. The numbers are pulled and whoever has the right numbers wins."

"Hey, Tony, it's like the 'nigger pool'!"

"You're right, Dom, only bigger. Imagine all the people in a state putting money down in hopes of picking five or six numbers and winning. There is a future in this lotto business and I want us to be involved in it.

"Johnny, your first official order is find out what it's all about and how can we participate."

Johnny nodded, and little did I know that the next twenty years the lotto would bring us millions upon millions.

"On another subject, I have tried to contact my Uncle Joe. He's not available. I think he's out of town. My Aunt Ella is doing the perfect 'I don't know' routine. God love her. I feel something is going on with his people. Keep your ears opened."

I looked around for Whas Wha to get the check. I caught his eye and he walked over.

"Tony, if you take one nickel out of your pocket I will be pissed off and squeal to your uncle."

"Come on, Whas Wha, it was supposed to be coffee an', and you gave us a banquet."

"Tony, my pleasure. I'll make you a deal. Tell Dom to send his moohls somewhere else." There was no humor in his request, but I loved the acknowledgment of the pecking order.

"Dom, you heard the man."

"Done deal. For the record, they came with me once and I would never send them here without me." Whas Wha reached down and patted Dom on the cheek reciprocating Dom's earlier act of forgiveness. "Good boy. Love you guys. Tony, say hello to your Uncle. I really miss him and the boys."

***

It was too late to go back to the office and too early to go home. Like a quick cut in a movie, Chris and I were in each other's arms. As we lay side by side on the sofa, she told me of her goings on. With each department store mentioned she removed an article of my clothing. The simple garments first. Tie, belt, loafers. She described her luncheon with her girlfriend Sara. They talked about sex. What they liked. What they wondered about. My shirt was unbuttoned. Her tongue licked my nipples, her lips suckled on my neck.

"Sara said she made it with two guys at once."

Down the center of my chest to my belly button. Her long fingers unzipped my fly. My erection bolted through the slit in my boxer shorts. I started to remove her blouse.

She stopped me and never looking up whispered. "No it's my treat."

I so wanted to ask, why don't the three of us get together. But, I knew it would dilute that drug, that addiction which carries me away to another place of peace and contentment. I held Chris's face in my hands, kissed her gently on the forehead. "The two Tonys need you now."

31

PART OF BEING in the entertainment business is to read the "trades" on a daily basis. *Variety* and *The Hollywood Reporter*, the bibles of the biz! Most of the time one of them would do, but it's not being in touch if you don't read both. I usually read them with my second cup of coffee, before the day really begins.

I can't believe I'm saying this, but I actually miss that pain in the ass Francine and her homemade pastry. I now have a secretary who wishes to be called Zowie. Why Zowie? Who the hell knows! She's proud of being part of the free generation. Her real name is Mafalda DeFilippo. Maybe Zowie is not so bad. She reluctantly brings me my coffee and never any *wandie*.

On this morning, October sixteenth, I opened the trades and read about the death of Cole Porter: *PORTER WRITES HIS LAST LYRIC. TUNESMITH SUCCUMBS TO STONES.* Fortunately, once I got passed the "baffo" headlines, the story was kind to this incredible talent. There was one segment of his life missing. Mr. Ted. I reached for the telephone to call Uncle Joe.

"Bakery."

"Emilio, is my Uncle Joe around?"

"Tony, for you he's always around."

A few seconds later Uncle was on the phone. "Tony, what's up?"

"Uncle, glad you finally surfaced."

"What am I a submarine?" he joked.

"Well I tried--"

He interrupted, "Yeah, Tony, Aunt Ella told me. So what's up?" *Sooner or later I'll learn not to have any meaningful conversations with him on the telephone.*

"Uncle, I just read where Cole Porter died and I remember Mr. Ted knew him."

"Yeah, so?"

"Well, I would like to call him and tell him I'm sorry he's gone."

"Tony, that's a nice thing to do. He'll like it."

"Thanks, Uncle. When am I going to see your face?"

"When you come down to Providence. You're the busy one, I'm just hangin' out with Emilio." He laughed.

"See you, Uncle."

"You will." We hung up.

***

"John, this is Tony Manfredi. May I speak to Mister Tedesco?"

"One minute." I heard some muffled voices then, "Tony, Mister Tedesco would like to see you. Can you come by Friday around ten?"

"I'll be there."

***

I'm glad certain things don't change. The Waldorf Towers should always remain the Towers, John, Mister Tedesco's man, should never change either. I was openly welcomed by him. Mister Tedesco was a little on the quiet side.

"Tony, a little coffee?"

"Only if some an' comes with it."

He turned to John, "It's so wonderful to see some neighborhood traditions still remain. Do we have any an'?"

"I think we can arrange it." John smiled and headed for the kitchen.

My little bit of humor picked Mister Tedesco up.

"Come, Tony, let's sit."

We sat and looked out as the sun shined on a perfect New York City fall day.

"So, Tony, why did you call?"

"Well actually, Mister Tedesco, I called just to pass along my condolences on the death of your old friend Cole Porter. I really didn't expect to meet with you, but it's a pleasure."

He slipped back in his chair and carefully adjusted the white linen pocket-handkerchief in his muted maroon, striped silk robe. Even in his bathrobe he could have walked up Fifth Avenue and been the best-dressed man in town.

"Tony, I am touched that you remembered. Some other people knew of our relationship, but not one person contacted me."

"Well, Mister Tedesco, the first time we met you told me of your friendship, the piano, your favor, and because of it, the loss of that friendship. It was a very touching, heartbreaking story."

"Sometimes we do things that we perceive as being correct. With all the right intentions and it is misinterpreted. That was the case with Cole and me. I did what I did with an open heart, for our friendship, for his talent, for the love of this man."

His last comment seemed strange. It was too telling. Maybe that was his edge. Running the entire country from his tower. Brilliant, brutal, alone, and in love with a man.

I never heard of a Mrs. Tedesco I was always aware of his polished speech, his gracefulness as he moved about. His admission that Cole dressed him. Maybe undressing him would more in order. *Tony are you nuts!*

Carrying a tray filled with lots of cream-filled, powdered sugar homemade pastries, John entered just in time to save me from an edge that I could never recover from.

John asked, "Do you prefer coffee or tea?"

I opted for coffee. Naturally Mister Tedesco went for the tea. Unimportant chatter bridged the pastry and drink deliveries.

"Tony, I was out of town for some time. There was a meeting."

I took a fork full of a Napoleon.

"We met, and your Uncle Joe represented you very well." So that's where he was.

"All of us were there. It was a long time between gatherings. Not that we meet that often. Years ago, that Kefauver thing smartened us up. We continued to conduct business as usual, with the use of special couriers."

"I would have loved to been part of the meeting."

"Well you were sort of. On the agenda was a conversation about you. That's what I meant by your uncle representing you. We all looked at the numbers. We knew what the skim was from Vegas, from the street businesses; even though your numbers were not as big, they were cunningly earned. They appeared legitimate.

That's where we must be heading. Doing what we do, but doing it your way. Legitimate, of course with the necessary support. All the guys, Chink from Atlanta, Mince from LA, Puppy Dog from Chicago, and Joe Sweets from the East all felt very comfortable and safe with you. Joe Sweets territory is very profitable, thanks to you. Because of Vegas only the West Coast does better.

"Tony, we decided to pass along the East Coast to you once your uncle is through with it."

"I don't get 'through with it.'"

"It's his until he decides he doesn't want it anymore."

"I thought nobody retires?"

"Tony, true. We work until we die. Other guys, way down the line, who have no real connection can, as you put it, retire."

He took a sip of his tea, but no pastry. Looking out the window he continued, "Up here we don't retire." There was a disconnect in his voice that made me fear the day when I get my gold watch and head for the chaise. "Tony, it's a natural progression."

I must have had the face of a confused kid, which forced him to go further. "Your uncle has not been feeling well. In fact he's in bad shape."

I had started to take a bite and stopped as if frozen in place.

Mister Tedesco continued, "He has cancer and his time is running short. He wanted me to tell you."

Astonished I asked. "My God why didn't he say something? I don't get it. We're so close you would think he would say something to me."

"Only Ella knew and us."

Now I was pissed. "Who's us? Why not me?"

He calmly answered, "That's the way he wanted it until the meet."

I didn't want to hear it. "Jesus he's in Providence right near New Haven where they have some of the best medical facilities in the world. Better yet, I'm in New York. He can stay with us while he's being treated. We just can't let it go." I not so gently put my dish on the tray.

"Tony, we don't have anything to say about it. He wants it to be over. He knows he hasn't got a chance and he wants it to pass. That's why we met. He's the first of us to go."

"Goddamn it, he's not gone yet! I won't let him just dry up and blow away."

"Tony, it's not your call. It's his and we agreed with it. It's done."

I wanted to scream out "Fuck you and your *cavone* friends." How could I let the one person in the world, who reached out and gave me life, just *be done!* I loved this man with all my heart and wanted to always make him proud that he chose me.

"I was about to call you so we could have this conversation. From here on it's up to you and Joe Sweets."

I needed to leave and get on the road to Providence. Mister Tedesco, always one step ahead, knew it.

"Tony, you have things to do, so please feel free to leave." I don't know what possessed me, but I reached over and held his hand.

"Thank you, Mister Tedesco." I reached down, and like the kid who kissed the bishop's ring when I made my confirmation, I kissed his hand.

Like the bishop, he patted me on the head. "You're good for us, Tony. Go see your uncle. He's waiting."

***

During my drive I rehearsed over and over again what I would say to Uncle Joe to convince him to do something about this illness. By the time I arrived I had positioned it in my mind that he knew what he wanted to do and why. He made it clear he didn't want to do anything about it, because he knew the cancer would kill him anyway. He was such a fatalist. I could have handled the entire issue on one of his short telephone calls for Christ's sake!

When I walked into the bakery, Emilio's head guided me to the backroom. No greeting. Unlike him. He too knew why I was there and had already written the final chapter.

When I walked in Uncle Joe was sitting behind the same table that he sat behind when we first meet a thousand years ago. This time the room didn't seem so sanitary white and his eyes not so blue.

"Tony, just in time." His sentence didn't seem to end. *In time for what?*

"Uncle, let's not screw around. Mr. Ted told me about your illness, and I'm here to make sure you do something about it."

"Tony, I'm going to do something about it and that's nothin'." Haven't I heard those words before?

"Uncle, you are a stone's throw away from one of the best medical facilities in the world. They can help you."

"Tony, what can they help? I went to my doctor and he said I got cancer and I'm loaded."

Desperately I said, "What the hell does one doctor mean? Maybe he made a mistake. Get a second opinion, please?"

"Tony, the truth of the matter is I ain't feelin' so good. I feel slow, I get tired. I am tired. I ain't interested in dragging this thing out. It's like when a tough decision is needed in the business and I made it."

I dropped my head and talking to my lap I asked, "How long?"

"He said six, seven months at the most."

Fuck!

"What can I do, Uncle?"

"Two things, Tony. One, watch the business, and two, pray for my soul."

As if high jumping over the first, all my Catholicism came rushing into my consciousness with the second part of his request. My God is this guy going to burn in hell for all eternity? How could that happen? He's my Uncle Joe! As if I were talking to every priest, brother and nun in my life, I thought, *I'll tell you, you sanctimonious son of a bitch, he did a lot of terrible things. He stole, he contributed to the demise of his fellow human beings, by drugging them, selling their women, and God help us, killing them. So what! In his world he was loyal, honest and generous. Heaven or hell, the ultimate edge.*

32

THOSE CHRISTMAS STEPPINGSTONES

bit me in the ass. On Christmas Eve Uncle Joe was taken to the hospital. He never came out. It went quicker than expected. He wanted it that way. I swear he willed it. The cancer ate him alive. He was slight and wiry in life, but in death he was a mere strand of gray hair. Unlike the so-called mob funerals one sees in the movies, his funeral was unattended by miles of flower cars, mobsters galore and press. There was no notoriety. Attended by blood family members only, he was laid out in his home for two days. Mass and the grave.

Aunt Ella would remain in black until the day she died. I offered to take care of her. Get her someplace else to live. Money. She refused all of it. She lived on, in the same manner as she did while Uncle Joe was alive. I never saw her cry at the wake. Did she not love him? Did she not care that she was alone? No tears. It was strange.

I remembered as a kid when my grandmother died, there were friends and relatives crying hysterically. There would be moments of quite in the tenement and then out of the silence came loud uncontrollable sobs accompanied by "Oh my God, Jesus take me, why her."

Italian phrases of disbelief and sorrow mixed with the smell of two many flowers in one small room must have been too much for one of my grandmother's *comare*. This friend threw herself on the opened casket screaming her name "Anna, Anna" and asking, "*Perché?*" Why?

I asked the same question. Why? Why did he have to leave my life? It left such a hole in my being. I missed him terribly. I felt vulnerable. My protector, my adviser, my link to tradition was gone. Even as the distance between his death and my continued life grew, I missed him. There were times where I never thought I could go on doing the double life thing. It was like his leaving cancelled half of me. I needed to put his passing away. I did. I created a special gold plated mental box and stored him and our life together away. I needed to in order to continue. To survive. Every time I went to Mass and the priest asked for a prayer for the dead of the parish, I bowed my head and said a silent pray that he would be forgiven and saved. I said it sincerely and found some comfort in that he had received the last rights. That's six out of seven sacraments, not bad! But in my Catholic gut I had serious doubts if he made it. I hoped at worst, he's doing lots of time in purgatory.

***

It seems tragedies come in triplicate. First someone of note dies, usually a movie star, and then in quick succession two more buy the farm. The year 1965 was a few months old and like a plague running through the organization; Mince from LA died of a heart attack.

I received a phone call from Joe Fat who sobbed as he told me of Mince's passing.

"Tony, he was having such a good time. He had lunch at the pool, went for a little dip, and about five minutes after some starlet gave him a blow job, he grabbed his chest a yelled, 'That rat bastard broad' and died."

"Joe Fat, I know how close he was to you. I'm sorry. It's scary to think first my Uncle Joe Sweets, then Mince. Who's next? Keep things together. I'll have a talk with Mr. Ted and get things straight."

"Thanks, Tony. K'n I stay here until things get worked out?"

"You can stay there forever. Consider it your retirement home."

His tone changed to frightened concern. "Tony, I don't, I mean, you know, we can't, I mean are you retiring me?"

I remembered Mr. Ted's cold retirement one-liner.

"Joe Fat I used the wrong word. It's your place for as long as you want. None of us retire."

"*Ma-dawn*"--he used the Italian for my God--"Tony, you scared the shit out of me!"

"Take care of things there and yourself."

Joe Fat was reliable in certain areas, but under no conditions could he be in charge for any length of time. I needed to get someone in there I could trust, quickly, and with Mr. Ted's blessing.

In back of Mister Tedesco's Caddy, while John drove us around and around in Manhattan, I made my pitch to send Dom to the West Coast. He was a showbiz guy and could handle the

LA-Vegas scene and be loyal. Dom would need more supervision, but that was okay with the both of us.

It always appeared that Mister Tedesco was light on keeping tabs on his people like Mince, Chink and even Joe Sweets. I guess it was because things went well and they wouldn't make any major moves without his blessing. I wrote it off as different management styles.

In the back of the car he approved of Dom Triano's promotion.

"Tony, he's yours and as he goes so do you."

Within a month I found myself once again in the backseat. This time it was Chink Ciancola from Atlanta. He too left us via a major heart attack. I didn't have a replacement in mind, which led me to conclude I have to do a better job at recruiting people.

Johnny Three was not ready yet, but in training. I needed him by my side for business issues that required his expertise, but all the while he was learning how things were done. He became the street conduit.

Fortunately, that man of few words, Chink, had done his recruiting well. His nephew, Denny Almonte was offered up as his replacement. Mr. Ted told me to go to Atlanta and interview him for the job. It's so amazing to me how we use so many legitimate phrases.

"Interview?" What I heard about Denny was, like his Uncle Chink, a man of few words and lots of action.

I asked Johnny to go with me. Denny met us at the airport and, as arranged, drove to a small cabin by a lake.

Denny, surprisingly was our age. I expected an older guy based on what was said of his accomplishments. From childhood to adulthood, he was athletic. His trim, just-under-six-feet physique was a testament to his athletics. His only loss was his thinning hair. His nose, which looked like it was broken a few times, was too big for his face. His complexion was light compared to his dark-skinned uncle. There was a no-nonsense stare in his blue gray eyes. He observed everything that was said.

Blessed by his Uncle Chink, an okay from Puppy Dog in the Midwest, with a final nod from Mr. Ted, he organized the milk industry. Laugh as you may, it was an incredibly profitable operation. He received from the dairy farmers exclusive contracts to sell milk only to his organization. There were a few barn burnings, lots of dead cows, and one poor bastard was found chewed up by his own harvester. But, as Denny put it in the genre of the business "We should not cry over spilt milk!"

He smartly contracted M & R Trucking who hauled the milk to wherever it was suppose to go. With the milk came all the ancillary businesses. Milk and its by-products, hauling, wholesale, milking machines, feed, and finally slaughterhouses. His milk was shipped to our hotels in Vegas at a cost-effective price.

Whenever there was a dairy farmers strike, Denny was there orchestrating it. All for profit. His grasp of numbers was astonishing. He knew, percentages of gallons shipped, costs, and pre-tax profits.

"Tony, when I think of it, our uncles started back in the bootlegging days. All illegal but very profitable. I was doing the regular stuff until Uncle Chink said I should learn some legit schemes like you was doing. So I came up with what I call the milk-run project."

"Well, Denny, it sure is working. But I am not so sure we should be contributing so much tax to the Feds. I think we should look into a way of using the profits with minimum taxes paid. There is quite a spread there."

Johnny made a note on his legal tablet. I got the distinct impression that Denny didn't like my suggestion and surely didn't like Johnny making a note of it.

"Yeah, maybe" was his response.

I was not use to maybes. I wanted to tell him *do it you fuckin' farmer!*

"Let's keep in touch and work together on what we can do."

"Sure." The meeting was over.

Back in the plane I had mentally rehearsed my conversation with Mr. Ted. *Smart guy, good mind, a little thick, shouldn't be left on his own.* I knew Mr. Ted accepted my thoughts when I received a telephone call from Denny.

"Tony, this is the milkman. I talked to our best customer from the Towers and he said he was sorry about my Uncle Chink and that I should continue business as usual, but talk to you first on all matters."

I was silent. *What does this really mean?*

"So, Tony, I guess you're it. Do me a favor. Don't squeeze my teats to hard cause the cows don't like it and they could stop giving milk or worse yet kick the milker."

"Denny, no squeezing intended. It's business as usual, but if the cow kicks too much, they could end up in the slaughterhouse."

"Really?"

"Denny, really. I have been given the responsibility and I intend to act on it."

"You're the boss." He hung up. He is not going to be easy.

I called Dom.

"Tony, it's early here, what's going on?"

"Dom, Denny the milkman is reporting directly to me."

"So am I. So what's the big deal?"

"Dom, you I know and trust, him I don't know. I think he's a little pissed at the arrangement."

"Fuck him and his heifers."

"Keep your ears opened. Go back to sleep you lazy fuck!"

"Tony, you're right, I need my beauty rest. I could get discovered any minute."

"I hope not!"

"Love you, Tony. Say hi to everyone."

***

My next call was to the Midwest and Puppy Dog. As all the phone calls to these guys, it was brief and to the point. I was flying to LA and would stop in Chicago to meet him. Rather than a long meet, I suggested he meet me in his car at the airport, we could do our business and I would catch the next plane heading west in about two hours.

He was insulted. I am always amazed on what offended the old-timers. They could kill without a blink of remorse, but be crushed by the idea of a quick car meeting. I know it's the old school versus the new, but get over it!

***

My next call was to Chris. "Hooray for Hollywood" I

sang in my best Sinatra style. When I told her where we were going she acted like a schoolgirl who just got invited to the prom by the dreamboat of the campus.

"We'll travel separately," I said. "I have to stop in Chicago on the way out."

She was to take a taxi to the Hotel Château Marmont where they'll be expecting her. I arranged for Joe Fat to drive her around for the one day that she'd be in LA alone.

"By the way we leave the day after tomorrow. So pack up your steamer trunk."

33

CHICAGO AIRPORT is like every other big city one. Busy!

I wandered outside and within seconds a big black Caddy pulled up to the curb. A round-faced man introduced himself through the back window. "Tony. Puppy Dog."

When I got in his round face was attached to a round body. It was like sitting next to a snowman dressed in a cardigan sweater.

"Puppy Dog, thanks for meeting me. I'm sorry it's under these conditions, but I do have to get to L.A. and I thought I'd kill two birds with one stone."

"Tony, bad choice of words. I might be gettin' the wrong idea." He told his driver Lou-Lou, who never acknowledged my presence, to drive around.

"We have never met, but my uncle spoke highly of you."

"Joe Sweets was special. I miss him."

"Me, too." There was a pregnant pause.

"Cigarette, Tony." I nodded no.

"Puppy Dog, I want to let you know we're happy with

what's going on in your territory--"

I was interrupted. "We're happy? Whose 'we're'? I only know 'him,' Mr. Ted."

This may be a once around the airport and out.

"Mr. Ted blessed this meeting and has given me some latitude on what we can discuss." *Does this guy know what the hell I'm talking about?*

He was silent.

"Basically, we're happy, but we think you should be looking closer at trying to funnel money through legitimate businesses. We--"

Fuck this.

"Puppy Dog, I want you to get a plan together showing how you intend to use your position and put the revenues to better use in legitimate enterprises."

"Hey, Tony, it's been working great for longer than you've been around and I think it will continue to be great, so leave it alone."

"Can't do that. Times have changed and we have to change with them."

"Suppose I say I don't wanna?"

"I don't think that makes sense. Mr. Ted has a master plan and I am here to execute it."

"*Execute*, that's another bad word."

"Puppy Dog, you're taking this all the wrong way. We need to change. I am here to help you out. Show me what you have in mind and I'll try to help you make it work if it makes sense.

"Look at Chink's nephew; he's doing incredible things down there."

"Hey, Tony, fuck him and his milk. I'm doing good and that's okay with me."

"I think you're taking a very short view of this, but it's your territory and I'll discuss it with Mr. Ted."

"By the time you get to L.A., he and I will have talked and I'll have a plan for *you!*"

There was no misunderstanding. He's pissed and is threatening because he is being threatened.

"You do what you must, but I'll be coming through here again in a few days, and unless I have different orders from Mr. Ted, I expect to see your plan. Open up, Puppy Dog. Get creative! I'm not here to do anything but make you and all of us richer and more powerful. We need to appear like legit businessmen doing legit things. It's worked everywhere else."

"Lou-Lou, take him back. We'll see you maybe in a few days, maybe not."

I was dropped off where I was picked up. No good-byes, just a drive away.

For some reason I wasn't angry with him. I know it's hard for some people to change, but I also knew he was a problem and had to be dealt with.

When I entered the airport lobby, I did get angry. What the hell was I going to do for the next two hours!

***

I'm a very organized human being, but there is something that when I examine it I am amazed on how I get anything done. I'm a scrap-paper, note-maker kind of guy. I scribble notes on torn pieces of paper. All colors, from all kinds of places, neatly kept together in a zipped up plastic bag in my briefcase. Now I had a couple of hours. I took out the bag like a kid taking out his bag of crayons, for review.

The first piece contained a scribbled note: *LOTTO. NH. J-III.*

I went to the pay phone and called him.

"Tony, as always, you are on to something. People buy tickets based on numbers they pick. Each week five or six numbers are picked and if there is a winner with all the numbers he wins. If not the pot continues to grow until someone wins."

"So how do we participate in this lotto business?"

"I don't know yet, but we'll figure it out."

"Do that, Johnny; we should all put on our thinking caps."

When I hung up, I was hung up. If it's such a good idea why is he taking so long to come up with something? More importantly, in my gut, I know, there is something there for us, big time!

***

L.A. gets me so excited. I've only been here twice, but there is a definite buzz that I get. I love the whole showbiz thing.

Joe Fat was waiting for me. We greeted each other with a genuine embrace.

"How you doing, Joe?"

"Tony, I'm good, but it's not the same. Don't get me wrong Dom is great, but I gotta tell ya I miss Mince."

"We all do Joe. He was one of kind and I don't think that kind can be duplicated. What else is going on?"

"Well, there is a very pretty lady waiting to see you. I drove her around and showed her the sights."

"Is she okay?"

"Tony, better than okay; she's bu-tee-ful!"

I could hardly control myself. The car barely stopped and I was out, grabbing my luggage and dashing into the lobby.

"Mr. Manfredi, so nice to--"

I interrupted, "Thanks, what room number?"

"Five seventeen."

I was off to the elevator and within seconds gently tapping on the door. When she opened it, my heart took a leap for I knew what was in store. As if she were waiting for me forever, she backed away clutching her see through negligee.

I closed the door behind me and let the two bags slip from my hands.

"I thought I would never get here."

"I thought you would never come."

I walked toward her and welcoming my advance, she released her negligee. It gently flowed open. My eyes devoured the sight. It was a montage of whiteness. Her soft shoulders melded into the top of her full breasts, down to her flat tummy, and lower to her beckoning upper thighs. All of this succulence was wrapped in a white virginal bra, lacey panties and the ultimate sexual touch, a garter belt attached to thigh-high stockings.

"While I was touring, I went by Fredrick's of Hollywood. Joe nearly passed out when I asked him to stop!"

"Glad you did." I moved toward her and brought her body close to mine. The mixture of lace and flesh was beyond stimulation. We kissed deeply and, still in each other's arms, made our way to the bedroom.

***

The telephone ring seemed to be extra loud.

"Good morning, Tony. Welcome to Tinsel Town."

"Morning, Dom. What time is it."

"Time to get your azz in gear!"

"Right. I was still very tired. Groggy. I looked over the scene. Chris was laying on her stomach sound asleep. Her virginal wardrobe was scattered on the bed and floor next to it. In my bleary state I struggled to put on the white terry cloth bathrobe, but clearly remembered last night. Kissing each piece of lingerie off her and delighting in the deliciousness of what was released.

I quietly showered, dressed and left a note with a wad of money. THANKS FOR A FUN EVENING. LOVED YOUR OUTFIT. HOW ABOUT LUNCH? YOUR LAST NIGHT'S TRICK.

The LA sunshine is special. There is a glow which seems to be beamed at the Hollywood sign high in the hills, warming the bare front and back of each and every movie star.

Joe Fat was behind the wheel Dom next to him. "Morning, guys." I got in the backseat.

"Is there someplace we can have coffee an'?"

"How about the Polo Lounge?"

I just nodded. "I was thinking more along the lines of behind Uncle Joe's bakery."

Even at ten thirty in the morning when most business types should be at their desks, the Lounge was humming. I have to admit it is stimulating. I love the whole scene.

As soon as Dom was spotted, we were ushered to a table. I always felt a little uncomfortable when we would leave someone like Joe Fat behind while we dined in style. But he knew his place and easily accepted it. Why can't I?

We ordered breakfasts without looking at a menu.

"Tony, you look tired."

"Yeah, it must be the time change." It never occurred to me if Dom knew about Chris. *So what if he does.*

It is a standard practice in our group, that there is life outside of our marriages. One has nothing to do with the other. Little mental boxes for all of us. I flashed on last night's lovemaking and for a second I wish I had wakened Chris for another taste.

"So, Dom, how are things?"

He, without reservation, told me how the business was under control. He had done in movies and television what he did in the music business. The talent agency was managing the biggest stars, directors, writers, and some producers. He was able to "package" our people to projects that we in return would own a percentage of.

"Any problems with getting them to sign on?"

"Not really, Tony. One guy gave me some shit, but sadly his pool house burned down with his favorite Filipino houseboy in it. He came around the next day and was happy with the arrangement. Word gets around real fast in this town. It ain't so big!"

"I wish I could say the same for the Midwest."

"What happened on your way out?"

"I don't think Puppy Dog gets it."

"Should I take a trip?"

"Thanks, Dom, but this has to go to Mr. Ted. It's his call. I was supposed to stop by on my way back, but I know him and he is not going to change so I'll go directly to New York and speak with Mr. Ted."

"You know I'm here if you need me."

I smiled and grabbed his wrist. "I know."

"Hey, Tony, watch the touchy stuff around here, they will assume we're faggots."

"Well we're not, but I do love you, Dom."

"Me, too." He motioned for the check. "What are you going to do while you're here?"

"I think I want to charter a boat and sail to Catalina."

"That's very romantic." He knew.

***

I don't know a ketch from a sloop, but I rented a graceful yacht with two masts and two crewmembers. The requirement was simple. Sail to Catalina and back. Good food and wine and the crew stays on the island for the night.

We arrived at the dock early the next morning. Chris was appropriately dressed in navy pedal pushers, a wraparound white top of some sort that outlined her breasts and nipples. It reminded me of our chance meeting on the train.

She kicked off her shoes as we stepped onboard. As I followed her, that horrific scene at Moe Cosby's place where two lovers were blown to smithereens flashed by.

Could the same be in store for me? After all, Puppy Dog's not thrilled with me and he is the last of Mr. Ted's people.

For the first time I showed some fear of losing my life and almost didn't go. But then again, what's life without the edge. I boarded.

We motored out of the harbor and as we drank our coffee, the sails where hoisted and with a gust of wind we were leaning to one side and sailing quietly toward our island in the sun.

"Twenty-six miles across the sea, Santa Catalina is a calling to me." The Four Preps tune stuck in my head while we glided quietly over the swells.

As we approached the tiny harbor, the skipper and his one crewman were busy getting ready to anchor. The sails went down, the boat secure. They boarded a small dingy that we were dragging behind and with a wave shoved off yelling, "See you tomorrow. Enjoy!"

Chris finished her glass of lemonade. It cooled her insides while her body was warmed by the sun. The suntan lotion melded softly with her perspiration. A small, but beckoning drop slid between her breasts. I watched it and so wanted to lick it dry.

Chris turned her head toward the disappearing dingy to acknowledge their good-byes. Her breasts pressed together trapping another delicate drop. I bent over and with the tip of my tongue licked it. It was deliciously salty.

She responded, "Let's go below."

We made love in the cabin and during the night we went topside and mixed our passion with the warm breeze of the Pacific. The bobbing of the boat created a rhythm that enhanced our own.

***

A thump alongside the boat woke me. Daylight, coming through the oval window above our bunk, bathed Chris's nude body in its morning light. I wanted to begin all over again but Voices from the returning crew prevented me from diving in. "Ahoy, Mr. Manfredi."

Ahoy, I thought. *I got you're 'ahoy.'*

"Fresh coffee and the best donuts in California."

"We'll be right up."

I nudged Chris to wake up; she did and started to slip down the bunk for her own special breakfast. I stopped her.

"The crew is back."

She pretended to be annoyed and made some kind of childlike sound. We dressed and before we were topside the yacht had come about and we were heading for the mainland.

***

The love cruise was over and time to get back to business as usual. I drove Chris to the airport and during the return trip made the decision not to stop in and see Puppy Dog. I was in no mood to try to convince him to change his ways so that his and our lives can continue successfully.

I called him and lied, saying I had to fly straight to New York; Mr. Ted wanted to see me.

He was relieved but gave a phony reply. "Geez, Tony, I thought we could spend some good time together. Maybe next trip. So long."

34

PULLING UP in front of The Towers made Catalina seem like twenty-six million miles away.

John took me immediately into the living room where Mister Tedesco sat reading the *New York Times*.

"Tony, good to see you. How was Los Angeles?"

Before I could answer, he continued, "More importantly, how was the Midwest."

"Mister Tedesco, that's why I'm here."

Still glancing through his newspaper he said, "I'm not surprised. Sounds like Puppy Dog is out of sorts. I thought he would beat you here, but he felt it wasn't necessary. Is it?"

What did Puppy Dog say to him? I really didn't care, but he is the last connection to the old gang.

"Mister Tedesco, we had a very brief conversation, and I don't think he was receptive to the new way of our doing business. It's not business as usual. It's business that has to change in order to survive and I don't know if he's up for it."

"I can tell you he's not, but it's not his call. He put the newspaper down. "We have to make an adjustment."

I thought I knew where he was going, but it's hard to interpret where the connection to the past is long and loyal.

"I believe major adjustments are in order."

"Tony, it's difficult to make those adjustments with people who have been with you for most of your life. Who would give up theirs for you?" He went silent.

Does this mean *No!*? Like a bluffing game of poker I remained silent. He looked up at me.

"You're right, Tony, the business is changing and we must change or become obsolete. Our businesses have always been inflation-proof, impenetrable but that no longer exists. We must move on."

"Shall I make arrangements for the adjustment? Dom has stepped up and volunteered. I know him and he can be trusted."

"Tony, Puppy Dog maybe old-fashioned in the new way of doing business, but he is no fool. Dom could not get in Chicago let alone get close enough to him to make the adjustment."

"I am not in favor of hiring outside talent."

"Nor am I. Which reminds me, some time ago you took it upon yourself to make an adjustment on some uptown colored guy. I understand why you wanted to do it personally. You should know, key people don't do such things and they certainly don't do it without the proper approval. If it wasn't for your Uncle Joe pleading your case there would have been some consequences to pay. Even you, Tony, have to follow the rules."

I was shocked that he knew about Tiny Dark. I would have killed that fuck no matter who said what.

"In any case, John shall take care of the Puppy Dog details."

"John?" Mister Tedesco did not acknowledge my questioning his call.

"Just because he hangs around the apartment, taking care of me does not mean he cannot take care of what needs to be done. In his day, he was the best."

I thought, *Is it still his day?*

As if reading my mind, Mr. Ted went on. "When you have certain talents, they're never lost."

"Like riding a bike?" Rightfully so, he ignored my cliché.

"I will instruct John once you leave. There is no need for more ears to hear of this adjustment."

You know when the meeting is over.

"Tony, your responsibility is to find a replacement that we both approve of. Keep in mind--*both*. I have always had great confidence in your judgment, but in this case I need to feel good about who will replace him.

"It certainly won't be one of my people, they sadly are all gone. One day I too will be replaced. That will be an interesting decision and one I hope I am a party to.

"Go now. There is business to attend to. I shall keep you posted."

There was a melancholy pause. "I miss your uncle and the rest of the guys. I will miss Puppy Dog as well."

He was truly moved by the loss of his team. I started to wonder how he can go from the sadness of the loss to the coldness of eliminating one of his own. I stopped myself smack in the middle of this analysis. Boxes. We all got boxes.

Would I take out Dom? With each step, as I headed toward the door I determined I would. For the sake of the business I would. The hell of it, Dom would understand.

***

One phone call to Mr. Ted and he approved Johnny Three Caprio as the Midwest replacement and added that John will be traveling to Chicago soon.

A deadly quiet overtook my being. I knew I was the bellwether for events to come. Like the leader of sheep, but not Judas, I had put into motion a human play that would have the most unusual closing act.

***

Remembering Mr. Ted's observation, Johnny Three and I flew to South Bend, rented a car, and drove to Chicago. We were there to step in when the adjustment took place. Dom let me know he was not supportive of my going, because it put me directly on the street in the mid-west, and he was concerned about that. I appreciated his concern, but I looked to the possible excitement of it all.

Not knowing when the adjustment would happen or where, we had to be ready. A few days passed when plastered all over the *Chicago Tribune* was the lead story: Mafia leader and bodyguard killed by unknown assassin in downtown Chicago. Don't they know there is no such thing as the Mafia!
A picture taken through the windshield showed two obviously dead guys. Not a lot of blood and guts, but none the less very dead guys. Clean and very efficient. Very John-like. The picture was accompanied by a brief bio with the names of the deceased in bold letters. It was a bodyguard Lou something or other and Joseph DiBiase, but no mention of *Puppy Dog*. Why would it? That nickname belonged to the old gang. *And then there was one.*

35

IN QUICK SUCCESSION a "meet" was called. The
mantle was handed over. I gave them a brief outline of the new
direction and everyone went home happy and content. Johnny
was in place and it would not be business as usual in Chicago.
Before I left the hotel I called Mr. Ted.

"Tony, when are you coming back?" His voice sounded
different. Meek, not in control.

"I get in late tonight."

"Good; come by around noon tomorrow." He was gone.

***

It was one of those strange Eastern weather days. One
minute a winter sun was shining only to be replaced by a snow
shower. I looked at my watch. A snowflake smeared the dial. I
wiped it clean. It was eleven forty-five. I walked through the revolving doors of the Towers and headed straight to the elevators.

I rang Mr. Ted's doorbell and waited for John to open up.

I had toyed with the idea of congratulating him on his

Chicago adjustment trip, and confirming that he's still got it, but that would not be what Mr. Ted would deem humorous or necessary.

No answer. I rang again. Then knocked.

Nothing.

Maybe I got the time or day confused. I went back downstairs to the lobby and headed for the main desk. Before I could say anything the man in charge recognized me as a regular visitor.

"Mr. Manfredi, good day."

I didn't acknowledge his pleasantries.

"Is Mister Tedesco on holiday?"

He cleared his throat and went to a log. He ran his finger down the page. "No, sir. He left a do not disturb message."

"Do not disturb message?"

"Yes, sir. As of last night after dinner. No room service, no telephone calls."

"Did he leave the suite?"

"I can't say, sir."

"This is highly unusual for Mister Tedesco."

"True. He seldom leaves the premises."

"You know I am a close associate of Mister Tedesco's so you'll understand why I am concerned. May I have a key to enter his apartment?"

He balked.

Accepting his hesitancy, I said, "I understand. Then would you send someone up there with me to let me in?"

"Certainly, sir." He beckoned a man in street clothes. "This is Henry our security chief. He will take you upstairs and help you in this matter."

The manager went into the backroom and returned with

a key. He gave it to Henry. "Our regular passkey does not apply to Mister Tedesco's suite."

I was not surprised. We silently rode the elevator. I lead the way, so I'm sure it gave Henry some peace of mind knowing I had been there before. He placed the special key in the door. As soon as it clicked he opened it. I stepped in front of him.

"Henry, I need to go in alone."

Now Henry balked. "I can't allow that, sir."

I took out a roll of bills. Hundreds. I'm guessing a grand or two and said, "Who's going to say anything?"

He knew there was more in my hand then he made monthly. He looked over his shoulder like he was already guilty of something took my bribe and whispered, "Not too long, sir."

***

I lifted the key out of the lock and entered closing the door behind me. It was quiet except for some soft music. I stepped into the living room. Looking around I noticed a large reel-to-reel audiotape slowly revolving. Round and round it poured out a simple piano rendition of the mournful Cole Porter tune "Love for Sale."

"Hello," I called out softly. "Mister Tedesco. John. It's Tony Manfredi. Hello."

Nothing.

I moved toward the kitchen. I poked my head through the swinging door and found everything immaculately in place. I had never been in any of the bedrooms so I was wandering around blindly. The first door I opened, to the right of the fireplace, looked like a guest bedroom or maybe John's. I moved across the living room to the other side of the fireplace and pushed open a matching door.

It was a large bedroom. The gray and maroon colors were somberly soothing. There, lying on his back, dressed in a stylish charcoal gray suit, white on white silk shirt, purple silk tie, blue suede, wing-tip shoes, was Mister Tedesco. His hands rested on his midsection clutching an envelope.

It didn't immediately register that he was dead. I didn't know what was going on. Napping in a suit? Music? It all came rushing home as I approached him and saw a tiny drizzle of blood making a pathway down his neck onto the satin pillowcase.

I was numb. I slowly moved around the bed. Across the room, sitting upright in a boudoir chair was John. He startled me.

I started to ask him what was going on, when his stare, frozen in place, stopped me cold. His arms hung straight down on either side of the chair. It was not until I saw a small pistol lying on the floor did I realize not only was he dead too, but I was sure he did Mr. Ted and then himself. Trying to confirm my theory my eyes flowed, as if in slow motion, between the two corpses.

I knew the security guy was outside and getting antsy. I reached down a pulled the envelope out of Mr. Ted's gray hands. I half expected my action would release the stench of death. I started to open the envelope when the doorbell rang. I stuffed it in my inside pocket. I went to the door and a very nervous Henry was waiting.

"Henry, something terrible has happened here." He looked past me and couldn't grasp what I was saying. He checked it out for himself. When he came back he was a shade whiter than when he left.

"Call the police. I'll wait here." All I wanted to do was

read the goddamned letter, but I knew better.

It felt like Henry just went down in the elevator when it bounced back up empting cops into the hallway. "Who are you?" Before I could answer, Henry interceded. "He's Mr. Manfredi an associate of Mister Tedesco. He found the bodies."

The cop--or excuse me the captain--took off his gold filigree hat and walked past me into the suite. Like I wasn't there, several cops filed past me all mumbling something or another.

In no time the captain came back out. "This is a crime scene. Did you touch anything?"

"No."

A skinny cop next to him started writing things down in a tiny notepad. "How do you know the deceased?"

"As Henry said, I am a business associate of Mister Tedesco. He is a board member of a company that I am the COO of."

"What about the stiff in the chair?"

"That is John; he is Mister Tedesco's butler."

"Why were you coming to see him?"

"I just returned to New York from a business trip and I wanted to fill Mister Tedesco in on the details." It's so hard not to call him Mr. Ted.

"Okay, for now. Give the sergeant your name and telephone number."

So I could get the hell out of there and read the note, I did what he told me to do.

As we walked down the corridor, Henry said, "Mr. Manfredi, I am truly sorry about your loss."

"Thanks, Henry," I replied. I felt he meant it. Why not? He was a few grand richer. *Not so cynical, Tony.*

36

I WANTED TO CRAWL into a very safe place so I could read the note. I never take the subways, but today it felt right.

I came out the revolving doors and headed for Lexington Avenue. I went down the first stairway. Bought a token and went through the turnstile. Within seconds a train approached and I got on. Not knowing where I was going didn't matter. Near the door I found a seat that holds only two people. I took it and made sure I sprawled out enough so anyone thinking about sitting next to me would get the message.

As soon as the subway lunged forward I reached into my pocket and retrieved the letter. It wasn't even licked closed but had wrinkles which I was sure were created by Mr. Ted in that last second of his life. It was one page and written in penmanship that belonged in the Renaissance, not on a rattling subway in New York City.

Dear Tony,

    This is most unusual, but necessary. I had confidence that

*you would arrive as planned and that my last words would be safe
with you. Things have changed so in this world of ours. The final
loss of those friends near and dear to me, along with the change necessary to survive, have brought me to this decision. As you are well
aware, no one with any stature in our business retires. I didn't want
you to be obligated with the arduous task of dealing with my retirement. I have asked John for one last favor, which I am sure he will
fulfill. I ask that you take care of him as he has taken care of me
over these many years. With no one to leave my meaningless worldly
possessions to, I leave to you alone the most important asset, the business. It is yours to do with as you please. Know your people, trust
them alone and do what you must. I now join those who have gone
before me, somewhere I don't know. I hope and pray Cole is there to
play for me with a full, forgiving heart.*

With respect and fondness, Mario Tedesco.

***

"Hundred and twenty-fifth Street!" The porter's yell
tore me away from what could have been a blank sheet of paper
in front of me, not this good-bye letter. His name jumped out at
me. *He's gone!*

As I got up I was immediately swept down the aisle by
the black herd of people wanting to get out of this tin can. Un-
ceremoniously I was deposited on the platform. The afternoon air
was chilling as the delicate snow shower continued.

I thought of faithful John doing his duty and not wanting to leave his master, joined him. I didn't know whether to yell
in anger at the top of my lungs or cry in sorrow to the depth
of my soul. Then, like at the Pittsburgh plant, I seemed to have

floated out of my body. A single white dot above the black mass.

I drifted toward the Manhattan skyline. Not far from the Empire State stood a monolith of a building that, with all the success I brought to the company, I helped design and build.

I drifted further into this mental haze and stared at the letters revolving around my building like a cobalt blue ticker tape: M. R. Tedes Co. . . . M. R. Tedes Co. . . .

M. R. Tedes Co. . . . M. R. Tedes Co. Around and around, the company name went.

Blurred by snowflakes the letters seem to melt together.

M. R. Tedes Co. melded into Mr. Tedesco.

As his name faded and I floated back to the platform, it became crystal clear that everything was one and one was everything. My two lives, though separate, were one.

Thoughts of the Holy Trinity flashed through my brain. Mr. Ted—God the Father—was there from the very beginning. God the Son—Uncle Joe—watched over me. The Holy Ghost? I didn't have the answer.

I could hear all my boxes coming undone, slamming into each other, metal on metal, screeching for release, only to be drowned out by by the high-pitched whistle and squeeking brakes of the the city-bound commuter train. I looked down; my shoes overlapped the platform threshold. Should I continue living this life on the edge or step back?

THE END

ABOUT THE AUTHOR

THOMAS M. BATTISTA was born and raised on Federal Hill, the Italian neighborhood in Providence, Rhode Island.

In the fifties, Tom was a member of a Doo Wopp band whose regional hit record enabled the group to tour and perform on various "Bandstand"-like programs. It was there that Tom was smitten by the production of television shows. He worked at numerous positions at a local TV station, and in his early twenties headed west to pursue "the big time."

The first stop was San Diego. Tom was a stage manager and then a director. While directing the local news, the number one anchor man in San Diego approached him, asking whether Tom would direct a live Saturday night talk show. The answer—"yes!"— launched a fifty year friendship as well as Regis Philbin's journey in television talk shows.

Then to CBS in Los Angeles. Departing ten years later as Executive Vice President, Tom created his own production and distribution company.

In the late nineties, Tom became the President of StoryFirst Communications and spent the better part of the next four years in Russia and Ukraine, building the first commercial television networks in the respective countries.

Tom is semi-retired, still married to his teenage sweetheart with four children and five grandchildren, and lives on two beaches: one on the Atlantic in Rhode Island and the other on the Pacific in San Diego.

CPSIA information can be obtained at www.ICGtesting.com
Printed in the USA
268019BV00001B/3/P